THE JADE
CRUCIBLE

THE JADE CRUCIBLE

JANICE MILLER

THOMAS NELSON PUBLISHERS
Nashville • Atlanta • London • Vancouver

DISCLAIMER

My apologies for taking liberties with the date of Chinese New Year during this, the Year of the Boar. The holiday fell on January 31; I moved it to January 5 to compact the action into a shorter time frame. Other than that, all cultural aspects of this book are rigorously factual.

All characters and names are fictional, however, and are in no way intended to depict anyone real, either living or dead, except with regard to certain historical figures such as Dr. Sun Yat-sen.

Published in Nashville, Tennessee, by Jan Dennis Books, an imprint of Thomas Nelson, Inc., Publishers, and distributed in Canada by Word Communications, Ltd., Richmond, British Columbia.

Scripture quotations are from the NEW KING JAMES VERSION of the Bible, Copyright © 1979, 1980, 1982, 1990, Thomas Nelson, Inc., Publishers.

Library of Congress Cataloging-in-Publication Data

Miller, J. M. T. (Janice M. T.), 1944–
    The jade crucible : Alexis Albright, private investigator / Janice Miller.
    "A Jan Dennis book."
        p.   cm.
    ISBN 0-7852-7706-4
    I. Title.
PS3563.I4117J33 1995
813'.54—dc20
                                            95-21674
                                                CIP

Printed in the United States of America

1 2 3 4 5 6 — 00 99 98 97 96 95

The scaly arms of the dragon reached out to embrace me at midnight, twelve short days before Christmas.

The first shrill jangle of the phone disturbed my sleep. Groggy, drowned in darkness, I didn't know I was awakening to a living, breathing nightmare. Fumbling, I captured the receiver from the bedside table and said, "Yes?"

There was dead silence, as if the line stretched to the flat blackness beyond the stars.

I coaxed a note of confidence into my voice: "This is Albright Investigations. Can I help you?"

The silence grew.

I was silent too. I felt a sudden rush of dread then wondered if I was having a bad dream. But I was awake. I could feel my heart beating slowly, steadily. I'd fallen asleep with the drapes open. My narrowed eyes ticked across sinister shadows then fixed on the muted, glittering light framed in my sliding-glass balcony doors.

The higher floors of Waikiki's condos and hotels shined coldly. A few other balconies sparkled with red, blue, green, and golden Christmas lights, even at this late hour. Here and there a window framed a glowing tree. I smothered my rising anxiety and continued to wait.

Suddenly I heard someone breathing, as if a hand cupped over the speaker had been removed. A sense of menace made me shiver. I started to hang up.

At that moment, a rough male voice whispered, "You Alex?"

My throat closed; I had to swallow before I could say, "Alexis Albright, yes." I glanced at the luminous green dial on my clock radio as it ticked over to 12:02.

"You going out in the morning?"

That snapped me wide awake. "Why?"

"Stick to your path along the canal," the raspy voice said. "Watch out for the water."

"What?"

"They come across the sea," the voice intoned. "They come without letting even the sky know. Watch out, they're invisible like ghosts." The line clicked and went dead.

I stared at the receiver then gently replaced it in the cradle, sat up, turned on the bedside lamp, and contemplated the peculiar warning.

Who came across the sea without letting the sky know? What was this eerie mumbo jumbo about being invisible like ghosts? And why should I watch out for the water in the Ala Wai Canal?

The man-made canal separated the mile-and-a-half length of Waikiki from the rest of Honolulu then ran into the sea. The water was eternally placid, if a bit polluted. To be sure, the sealife that lived in the brackish water wasn't always pleasant. But during my morning run, I had no intention of getting close enough even to touch the surface, much less disturb all that lived beneath it.

I shook my head and tried to shrug off the odd message. My name was in Honolulu's Yellow Pages under Private Investigators.

That drew the nuts and fruitcakes into my life at any season of the year.

Come on, Alex. Your midnight caller is just another twisted prankster trying to find a way to amuse himself. Forget about it.

But the warning wasn't so easy to shrug off.

I *was* going out. I did almost every morning. The man on the phone seemed to know that, which added an extra note of dissonance to an already discordant season. This would be the first Christmas I'd spent in Hawaii since my husband David died after taking two 9-mm slugs in his head during a drug bust three years before. I wasn't exactly decking the halls, and I certainly wasn't ready for any prank caller's tidings of comfort and joy.

Unfortunately, even at Christmastime, evil exists. So far this week, in just Waikiki, a young Japanese tourist was raped and robbed in a shopping mall three blocks from my condo; a knife fight among youths of various ethnic backgrounds erupted several blocks east of me; and I'd heard police sirens responding to numerous calls, day and night, that I assumed were domestic fights or robberies or other negative symptoms of the season.

In that moment, my three-bedroom condo/office seemed forlornly empty. My live-in nephew, Troubles, had gone back to Colorado to spend the holidays with family. I had to stay here and handle an upcoming job that would run through the holidays. I'd taken so many pro bono cases during the past year that I was facing a serious cash crunch that further dented my holiday spirit.

I started to get up then had a sudden, uneasy feeling. An invisible presence had entered the room, bringing a chill with it.

I turned—and froze as I glimpsed my own misshapen reflection in the seaward window: my short blonde hair was a tangled mess, my blue eyes seemed to have hollows under them, my usually healthy complexion was ghoulish and pale, and my white cotton nightgown looked like a shroud over my slender frame. I blinked and realized that the effect came from the glittering blue lights on the balcony to my left, which reflected at a slant in my window. I blinked again and my reflection came into better focus. I looked sleepy, but not so bad after all.

Sliding open the glass door, I stepped onto my balcony. It was about sixty-eight degrees, a typically balmy Christmas season. The sky was black. The trade winds were warm and gentle, and the smell of the sea was a salty, ancient perfume. The sounds of late-night traffic and other noises drifted up from the streets. I looked over the edge to see the seasonal glitter of Kalakaua Avenue, eight stories below me. Christmas is the peak tourist season in Waikiki. Any number of people were out looking for holiday cheer, even in this hour after midnight.

Along the avenue and the side streets, the trunks of the palms and other trees were strung with tiny golden-white lights that spiraled from the base to the high green fronds or treetop leaves; more white and bejeweled lights were captured like fallen stars, some nested in treetops or among newly blooming plumeria flowers and coconuts. The stately old Moana Hotel was visible at an angle, in all its refurbished colonial elegance. Sparkling strands of ruby lights wrapped in dark pine curled up the thick, snow-white pillars at the front of the porte cochere; a huge red-bowed wreath hung above the circular driveway, where gleaming-white, gold-trimmed Mercedes stretch limos were parked near the palms. Apparently there was a very exclusive shindig in process. I could see the miniature doormen in their tropical whites, strolling here and there and talking with the toy liveried chauffeurs.

A lonesome feeling washed through me; David and I had wandered past Tiffany's in the Moana Hotel a few days before our last Christmas together. The window display in the small shop had featured a miniature Ferris wheel with a pewter finish, rotating and glittering with tiny internal Christmas lights. A gorgeous snow-jade ring with a wide pavé of ruby and diamonds surrounding the cabochet was displayed in front of the Ferris wheel, on fake snow that looked like shredded coconut.

I'd stopped, enchanted. "David, look at this!"

He'd stopped and looked too, then turned to tease me. "Since when did you develop a passion for jewelry?"

I'd frequently told him I thought expensive jewelry was wasteful and pretentious. Which was true—there was always a better way to spend money. But I loved jewelry, and he knew it. It was my one materialistic weakness. I loved to gaze at the way the facets captured light, at the many beautiful hues in the variously colored stones, at the wonderful and creative ways in which different stones were set into precious metals. David had bought a Tahitian gray pearl necklace and earrings and several other smaller things during our first year together. Each gift pleased me immensely, but we couldn't afford to pay for them. Period.

"This isn't jewelry," I said, still gazing at the ring in the window. "It's a work of art. Look. The white jade is flawless!"

He narrowed his brown eyes to examine it.

"See the color," I said. "It's pure satin white. What they usually call white jade has hints of gray or brown. This is a truly remarkable stone."

"How much do you think a piece like that is worth, anyway?" I could see him calculating our budget.

"Too much," I said. I grabbed his hand and dragged him away.

That Christmas morning, I opened a large silver-wrapped gift under the tree and found myself looking at a black velvet jewelry box from Tiffany's. I'd opened it to find the white jade ring.

David had put it on our MasterCard. It was the finest piece of jewelry I'd ever owned. I told him I was going to return it. We had just put a huge down payment on the condo that year, and the budget was tight. He demanded that I keep it.

"I'll pull some extra hours," he said. "Don't worry about it. I'll pay for it."

He had worked long hours all right, though not just to earn overtime. A sudden flood of the smokable form of crystal methamphetamine called "Ice" had hit the islands. Several teenagers had overdosed, and the violence that comes hand in hand with the drug skyrocketed. David and his partner had worked day and night for a couple of months, trying to break up the trafficking network. He'd been shot to death while busting one of the key dealers.

I paid off all the bills with the insurance money. My Christmas present was ultimately paid for with David's blood. I tried to wear the ring, but couldn't. I tried to give it to my mother. She wouldn't accept it. I wanted to sell it, but couldn't bring myself to completely part with it. I finally put the ring away and never wore it again.

I shook off the pain that came with the memory.

A sudden gust of wind whipped my white cotton nightgown against my ankles. I inhaled the sea air, breathing deeply, letting it relax me. The greasy-spoon smell of coffee and frying burgers wafted up from the fast-food joints along the side street. I turned my head to look out over the black-glass sea. I could see people strolling in the suffusive light that leaked from the hotels onto the inky beach. A sliver of moon glinted on an occasional breaker. I felt an immense loneliness. I slid the door shut and pulled the drapes, closing out that other part of the night.

Walking through the empty condo, I turned on lights, checked every room, avoided the unlit Christmas tree that stood in my living room and the fresh pine wreath with red cranberries and plaid velvet ribbons that hung on my wall. Troubles had insisted on decorating for me before he left. The fragrant smell of fresh pine was everywhere.

The phone call still worried me. It's a creepy feeling, knowing that your movements are being tracked by a sinister stranger. On the other hand, if you're a seasoned operative like I am, it's not exactly going to terrorize you into immobility. I combed through my recently closed cases and wondered if any outstanding business might complicate my life. Nothing threatening loomed into my memory. Finally, I decided to take my little pearl-handled .22 derringer along on my morning jog. It was palm-sized, and its small, white doeskin shoulder holster would fit snugly under my T-shirt. If there was going to be trouble I'd be ready for it. If not? Merry Christmas, Alex. Here's a gift of a little fear.

I checked the locks on both the front door and the office door, and looked through the peephole to the empty, lens-distorted hallway. Finally, reassured that all was well, I turned the lights off, went back to bed, sent up a silent prayer, then drifted back to sleep.

2

Four and a half hours after the spooky phone call, my clock radio split the silence with a howling version of "Jingle Bell Rock." I slapped the off button and rolled out of bed. I did my toilette, threw on my black jogging pants and a T-shirt, drank a quick glass of orange juice, and was out my condo door, the elevator whisking me down to street level, by four-forty-five.

In the lobby I motioned for Marty, the pint-sized security guard, to come over and talk. Marty had come from California by way of the navy and he'd stayed. He was about sixty years old, still strong and fit. His blue eyes were kind; his disposition generally belied his wrinkled, sour appearance.

"Mornin', Miz Albright, Merry Christmas. What can I do you for?" He managed a tired yet cheerful smile.

"I was wondering—" Suddenly I felt foolish. "Um . . . have you noticed anybody unusual hanging around this time of morning?"

He raised a grizzled eyebrow. "Just the usual riffraff. A few street people wanderin' around, and I have to run off a late-workin' hooker now and again. Why?"

"I'd appreciate it if you'd keep your eyes open for anyone unusual."

His eyes narrowed with interest. "Something I can help you with?" He did an odd job for me from time to time, and he managed to turn even the most mundane tasks into high intrigue.

"I've been told someone is watching me. It's probably nothing. But if anything unusual turns up—"

"What might I be looking for?"

"I don't know, Marty. Maybe nothing. But just in case, I'd appreciate your help."

He frowned ferociously. "I'll be happy to keep my eyeballs peeled."

The condo where I live has tight security, especially at night. The bottom two floors are shops and restaurants, accessible until 2 A.M. when the lounges close. A mesh gate comes down to close off the wide escalator then. The next three floors are offices. The rest of the building is all private condos, some with office space attached. At night you have to be buzzed in. To do that, you enter a code then talk through the intercom—which works fine for me; I don't like unexpected visitors.

But I did like the idea of twenty-four-hour security guards. If someone was hanging around outside the building in the wee morning hours, Marty would surely notice. And if the watcher was somewhere else along my route? I had my double-barreled .22 derringer strapped to my chest.

I smiled at Marty and waved. Then I went out into the dying night.

自由

I like to hit Waikiki's jogging paths just before the crack of dawn, while the tourists are still soundly in bed.

That morning, I jogged all the way down to the library at the Diamond Head end of the Ala Wai Canal then back again, halfway home. I kept an eye on the deep water beside me: it shined like black isinglass rippled by a gathering sea wind, strewn here and there with tiny pinpoint reflections of city lights. Nothing leaped from its black depths to assault me. No one approached me, friend or foe, no one was lurking behind trees or buildings. The derringer stayed in its holster, and the midnight phone call began to seem like part of the night's restless dreams. Gradually, I relaxed.

I reined in at a water fountain and gulped down the sweet cold water, then stood straight and breathed deeply as I rocked back and forth to loosen the tendons in my legs. I leaned into a tree trunk and did a few more stretches then glanced at my watch. Five-thirty.

The sky showed false dawn. Behind the black mountains, a faint luminescence tinted the sky. The street lights still cut their soft, circular glows into the liquid blue of the dying night. An occasional brilliance of Christmas lights still glittered from the balcony of a high-rise or the grounds of a hotel, though most of the seasonal glitter had been extinguished hours ago. The city's holiday lights would blaze again at nightfall, in all their resplendent glory.

In an hour or so, the denizens of Waikiki would begin to pop out of their hotels and condos, to fill the jogging paths, restaurants, parks, and beaches. Not long thereafter, people in casual finery would also appear, on their way to church or synagogue or temple, and I would join them. But for now I had the entire world to myself. The silence was broken only by the tentative songs of birds, by the dark water lapping at the sides of the canal, by an occasional car rolling past on the boulevard.

A dusting of house and streetlights spread up into the heights, beyond which loomed the lush, jagged, volcanic Koolau Mountains. Daybreak was just beginning to sculpt out the machete-thick foliage that carpeted the mountains like filigreed green rubber. I squatted down on my heels, to savor the light as it broke the serrated rims, flushing small shafts of blues, greens, and golds into the approaching day.

In the canal, the water shimmered with a sudden brush-stroke of sunlight. A large fish leaped up, celebrating daylight, then splashed back in. The ripples fanned outward, wider and wider, coming toward me till they met the stone-lined ledge of the canal and broke in a sudden glint of light.

I leaned out over the edge and looked, to see what had caused the glint. It was low tide. The canal waters had receded, revealing a sodden pile of old clothing deposited on the usually submerged rocks. Something was caught in the clothing, something that gleamed golden and inviting.

I'm not fond of the rock-walled inner banks of the Ala Wai Canal. Nasty things live there. Blue-black crabs. Rats. Huge, black water bugs. I picked up a long tree branch, and staying well distant, I poked at the pile of clothing, trying to see what had glittered. The pile felt mushy at first, then was suddenly resistant— and then it gave, revealing a glittering watch attached to a lifeless wrist.

I dropped the stick. Shocked, I bent forward and gawked at my grisly discovery.

Death comes in many shapes. This time, the hands and bare arms were the smooth, puffy consistency and color of dirty bread dough. The body was twisted, the legs and arms akilter. The light defined the clothing: tattered blue denim pants and a thin, soggy white T-shirt. The upper arms were skinny, the small feet bare and discolored.

It was a small, thin boy in his teens. The water had already begun to deform his features, but my best guess was that he was Chinese.

An acidic lump filled my throat. I felt a leaden rush of grief so intense it made me dizzy. I forced myself to turn, to breathe deeply several times to hold back the adrenaline that was trying to flood my body. The panic broke through. I ran, full-out, to the nearest payphone, halfway up the block, and punched in 911. My voice was ragged as I told Police Emergency what I'd found.

After I'd finished talking, a brusque female voice said, "Your name, please?"

I gave her my name, phone number, and address.

"Please wait." The voice was robotic, but it sharpened as she began to relay my message to the dispatcher, who would in turn notify the Waikiki substation. She suddenly thanked me and asked me to please stay at the scene so the police could take my statement, then she hung up. The tiny Waikiki substation was only a few blocks away, and I could already hear the sirens coming toward me as I headed back to the canal.

I paced back and forth on the sidewalk, working out the adrenaline while I resisted an unpleasant impulse to stop and stare in horror at the body. After a long two minutes, a blue-and-white cruiser screamed in, lights flashing.

I didn't know either of the two uniformed officers who jumped out of the cruisers, but I pointed them toward the body. I stepped back out of the way as several three-wheeled Cushman electric cars also screeched up, gears grinding, dome-lights slashing the newborn morning with electric blue. An ambulance siren wailed in from the direction of Queen's Hospital. A young patrol cop began asking me questions. I explained how I'd made my grisly discovery as she wrote on a clipboard braced against her hip. As I talked, an unmarked black Plymouth sedan wheeled up and skidded to a stop.

Jess Seitaki stepped out of the passenger side, frowning intently. He was chief detective with the Hawaii State Police's homicide division. His medium height made him a bit taller than many Japanese-Americans, and his short black hair was gray at the temples, showing his forty-some years. He wore a red-and-gray aloha shirt above razor-creased dark gray slacks and taupe loafers. Jess was always fastidious in everything he did.

Jess looked surprised when he saw me. He had been my husband's partner in police work for eight years, before transferring to Homicide. We attended the same church; his family and I were close friends. He gave me a curt nod of greeting and strode up to me.

"Alex."

I said, "*You* got here fast."

His eyes narrowed and turned hard. His shoulders slumped.

"Seems we have a floater, someone said a kid." He gave me a second look. "What are *you* doing here?"

"I found the body," I said.

We both looked toward the canal where police officers were already crouched over, looking at the grisly mess. I sketched in the details for Jess, without mentioning the strange midnight phone call. *Stick to your regular path along the Ala Wai*, the voice had said. *Watch out for the water . . . they're invisible like ghosts.*

The mysterious caller had set me up to find this body. That much I knew. But I wasn't going to tell Jess about the eerie phone call until I knew exactly what this death had to do with me.

Jess peered intently at me. "You're pale. Are you okay?"

"I'll manage."

He hesitated then said, "Yes. I expect you will. Why don't you go on home, have Troubles make you a pot of hot tea or something."

"Troubles is on the Mainland, for Christmas."

"Then go over to Denny's, go sit down. Do something to put some color back in your face. I'll be in touch later, after I check this out." He turned toward the canal.

I watched him walk up to the group of uniformed cops, who stepped aside as he began to examine the situation. The crime-lab van pulled up, and two men climbed out, then opened the rear door. I turned back to the young cop holding a clipboard.

I filled out one of the brief statement sheets for her, signed the form, then stepped back out of the way, to watch again. Crisp blue-black uniforms were everywhere now as cops partitioned off the boulevard with orange-pink flares and unreeled yellow plastic tape to cordon off the crime scene. A reporter from HGTV arrived, with cameraman in tow. As usual, they'd beat the competition to the scene. The police photographer had also arrived. Flash bulbs popped.

Jess and his colleagues began their investigation. I watched till I saw the medical examiner arrive, and the ambulance attendants start climbing down the wall to retrieve the body. The criminalists were already down there, wading through the murky, rocky water at the side of the canal.

I finally turned away, sickened by the abrupt brutality of death, by the waste of yet another human life.

Sadly, I headed for home.

CHAPTER

3

The rest of Sunday turned out to be bright, golden, and crystal blue. Jess phoned about 8 A.M. to check on me. After I'd assured him I was okay, I said, "What about you?"

"Tired, but that goes with the territory."

"Any idea yet what happened?"

"Not much," he said. "Though we may have a quick ID."

"How so?"

"The kid apparently matches the description of a missing illegal alien who came in on the smuggler's ship *Dragon Venture* last week," he said. "Immigration has been looking for him for several days."

"He escaped from their holding pens?"

"The pens are full. They put this kid and his cousin in a private residence in Makiki, a youth home. They got away."

"What youth home?"

"Can't say till I've checked it out."

"Any lead into the other kid's whereabouts?"

"No. And that's all I can say."

"One more question, Jess. Please. Any lead into the cause of death?"

"He'd been beaten, but we won't know what happened until he's been autopsied."

I tried to force away the afterimage of the young, slightly bloated body.

Jess said, "Look, I've got to run and check out a lead. I'll talk to you later."

"Thanks, Jess, for letting me know. I really will be okay."

I made it to the nine o'clock church service in spite of my morning's misadventure. But my emotions were in such turmoil that I couldn't connect to the sermon or even the songs. After church, I went home and wandered through the condo, doing small chores while I tried to sort things out.

I had been too keyed up to eat breakfast. Now I opened the fridge and took out half an avocado, a tomato, some lettuce and sprouts, and wholegrain bread, planning to fix a veggie sandwich. As I rinsed the vegetables and began to slice the avocado I kept looking at the cherry-red phone on my kitchen wall, hoping it would ring.

I wanted the mysterious midnight caller to explain one thing. No matter who'd killed the boy, someone would have discovered the body soon after daylight. I wanted to know why he'd brought *me* into it.

I couldn't quit thinking about the young boy, sprawled across the submerged rocks. Sudden anger roiled up in me like hot, red lava. I set down my sandwich and stormed onto the balcony, blinking back tears. I stood with my hands gripping the railing, looking toward the canal. I prayed. The pain solidified into a small, cold stone in my chest. I went back into the kitchen, retrieved the sandwich, then sat at my counter skimming the Sunday paper and nibbling on what tasted like week-old cardboard.

The Sunday paper is printed early. There was nothing in it

about the Chinese boy's death. I thumbed past stories of blood, mayhem, and corruption in the world, then did the crossword. When I'd finished the paper, I took a short nap. I didn't want to leave the house in case the mystery man called. He *was* going to call again, I absolutely knew it.

I'd set my watch alarm for two o'clock so I could catch the top of the Sunday afternoon news. I woke up with a headache, slouched back on my plum-colored sofa, and hit the TV remote.

Lenni Apana was HGTV's anchorperson. I knew her, though not well. She was a willowy, Hawaiian-born Chinese about my age (thirty-three), with flawless skin, sleek chestnut hair clipped in a short rice-bowl haircut, and huge almond eyes set in a pixy face. Today, she wore a forest-green, high-collared suit and small pearl earrings. She looked like an elegant model for an Asian airline commercial, but I knew she was a breezy, no-nonsense newshound with the ability to hit the jugular on the first strike. Recently, her investigative reporting had helped put a bribe-taking senator behind bars, she'd exposed a rapist who was preying on office workers downtown, and she'd helped bust up a car-theft ring with some pretty crusty players. She had a reputation for taking the tough jobs, and she'd never been known to flinch.

Apana and her news team had been busy. After the glitzy scenic lead-in, the camera zoomed in on her. A professional snowy smile of greeting melted into a stern frown.

She said, "Good afternoon. At the top of the news: Honolulu-based private investigator Alexis Albright discovered the body of a young Chinese illegal alien early this morning, where it had come to rest on the rocks in the Ala Wai Canal."

I cringed at the sound of my name. Just the kind of publicity I didn't need. But the words "illegal alien" made me skim past that problem and pay close attention.

She said, "U.S. Immigration and Naturalization Service authorities identified the victim as an undocumented fifteen-year-old boy named Dru Chun Yuen. He was allegedly a political refugee from the People's Republic of China."

All illegals claimed to be political refugees. The smugglers tutored them, telling them it was the only way they could stay in the United States if they were caught.

The camera cut to old news footage I'd seen late last week. At the weathered pier beside the Coast Guard station, a dozen or so bedraggled Chinese aliens were being herded off a spiffy white Coast Guard cutter and into a waiting multiethnic circle of Customs and INS agents, who stood with scowling faces, handcuffs, and several handy nightsticks. The agents' guns were holstered, which meant they weren't expecting much trouble from the would-be immigrants.

In a voice-over to the footage, Apana said: "The young murder victim arrived in Hawaii aboard the Chinese fishing trawler *Dragon Venture* last week. On the basis of an anonymous tip, the Coast Guard stopped the *Dragon Venture* as it was entering Honolulu Harbor. Authorities found the hold full of undocumented Chinese attempting to enter the Mainland via Hawaii."

The scene cut back to the studio. Lenni looked grim. "The illegal aliens are recruited in remote Chinese villages, and the journeys are coordinated by modern-day slave traders known as Snakeheads."

The Chinese illegals came on the screen again. Now they were plodding toward a line of waiting gray INS vans with steel-meshed windows: they seemed frightened, their eyes lowered, their frail backs bowed, though occasionally one would look up at the authorities with a black flash of hatred that startled me with its intensity. They were mostly men, about half of them under thirty, I guessed. They were dressed in ragged Western attire that had probably been purchased where it had been made—in China. I tried to pick Dru Chun Yuen out of the crowd, but the features in my memory resembled nothing living, and I quickly sealed off the image.

The camera cut back to Apana. She said: "There is an exploding horror behind China's Bamboo Curtain. In a recent two-year period, an estimated sixty-five thousand people were arrested for trafficking in bought or kidnapped women and children who are sold into factories, restaurants, and farms as virtual slaves. This inhumanity is spilling out from China's shores. The illegals found aboard the *Dragon Venture* may have been kidnapped and sold into literal slavery to purchasers in the United States. However, other would-be illegal immigrants pay up to $50,000 each in order to make the dangerous trip from China to the U.S. Often, they and their entire families sell everything they have in China as a down payment on the trip, then sign contracts to work off the balance. These enormous debts are usually structured so they cannot be repaid. Either way, the immigrants become virtual slaves."

The camera cut to a different angle. Lenni explained that Dru Chun Yuen and his younger cousin, Mock Sing Druan, had walked away from a local youth home. "There has been a three-day, island-wide search for them," she said.

I'd heard nothing of the search. Probably because I hadn't tuned into the news for several days.

The scene cut to an early morning image of the Ala Wai Canal; the sun was up. HGTV's videotape must have been taken a short time after I left. The cluster of police and others who'd been at the death scene this morning were watching as paramedics carried a black-bagged figure strapped to a stretcher up the steep, rocky bank of the canal. I looked away.

Apana's voice-over said, "Authorities think the victim may have been recruited by local drug traffickers, who use teenage boys as couriers."

An ice cube found its way to the pit of my stomach and settled there. The age of the most violent offenders kept getting younger and younger.

The camera cut to a man that Lenni Apana introduced as Alan Liu, Hawaii's coordinator for the U.S. Immigration and Naturalization Service's task force on Chinese alien smuggling. He was a stern, thickset Hawaiian-Chinese with a blunt face, wire-rimmed glasses, and a brush of gray hair. He wore a white aloha shirt with dark blue flowers, and dark trousers—the general uniform of Hawaii's civil servants.

Angrily, he said, "The problem is the Chinese Mafia, or Triads.

They're scrambling for every last cent of profit before Britain returns the Crown Colony to China when the lease runs out in 1997. They're looking for a new place where they can ply their criminal enterprises of heroin trafficking, illegal gambling, protection rackets, and trafficking in human contraband. The slave business is one of their most lucrative ventures. They are reaping hundreds of millions of dollars at the expense of the pitiful, frightened Chinese people who are lured into slavery on the pretext of finding a better life."

The camera cut back to Lenni. "Almost one hundred thousand illegal Chinese have entered the United States in the past few years, and many of them will remain indentured to the Triads for the rest of their often-short lives."

The camera cut back to Liu. He said, "These illegals are usually forced to join violent crime gangs or to otherwise sell themselves in order to survive. They arrive penniless and don't speak English. After a lifetime in China they're terrified of authorities. They're terrified of being deported so there's no chance they'll solicit help from the police. A new twist on an already ugly business is that an increasing number of them arrive addicted to heroin, which further increases the Triads' hold on them. We believe the illegals are deliberately and methodically addicted while en route in the holds of renovated fishing vessels, such as the *Dragon Venture*."

I felt a blow of anguish to my midriff that made me short of breath. It made my heart ache. There was so much evil in this world, so much that needed to be stopped . . .

The camera cut back to Lenni in the studio. She thanked Liu again then said, "Now for the rest of the news." She smiled warmly and began to explain how the Hawaii Visitor's Bureau was pleased with the growing number of Asian tourists who were currently flooding to the Islands. There had been a three-year drought of visitors, and the local economy had suffered . . .

I grabbed the TV remote and clicked it off. I felt sick.

This evil of slavery was something new to me, something new to the West. It was back, coiling up out of the graves of history.

And the evil was growing, all over the world. The enormity of it made most ordinary people go numb with disbelief.

I could hear their denial: *Here, now, today? Slavery? That went out with the Emancipation Proclamation, Alex. You must be imagining things.*

I sat there contemplating all that Lenni had said. What would it feel like to literally be sold like a slab of meat? The very thought of it filled me with an emptiness that I had never known before.

My thoughts returned to the dead Chinese boy, and suddenly I could imagine him in the filthy hold of a slave ship. What had his journey been like?

In a word, brutal. One ship recently boarded outside of San Francisco Harbor had been on the high seas for a very long time before arriving. Customs officials had opened the hold to find people literally stacked atop one another, half of them sick with infections and even one dead body pushed up against the wall. In another incident, a whole shipload of illegals had gone down just last month, in high seas near Guam.

I thought about a bright-eyed, hopeful young Chinese boy enduring the agony of the journey, believing that once he reached the United States—what Chinese people still called the Golden Mountain—he would be free from poverty and could begin a new life. He hadn't known he was being sold into slavery. None of them did. No wonder I'd seen such black, poisonous hatred flash in some of their eyes. Maybe they'd begun to realize what was happening to them.

I looked at the phone again. The mysterious caller had known that the boy was dead, and where I would find him. Once again, I wondered if he had killed the boy—and if so, why he had involved me. I sighed with frustration. Apparently, he wasn't going to phone me and clear this up. I checked the time, saw that Lenni Apana would be off the air by now, then picked up the phone and dialed the HGTV newsroom. Lenni had covered the shooting death of my husband. She had handled the news coverage of the incident and all the aftermath with much genuine compassion, and we'd been casual friends ever since.

A man with a stressed-out voice answered then passed me along to Lenni. There was a guarded quality in her voice, as she said, "Hello, Alex. I guess you already know you made the news."

"Hi, Lenni. Nice story, but it would have been better if you'd left me out of it."

"If you didn't *make* news, you wouldn't be *in* the news," she said with impeccable reason. "But I know you, Alex. If you called, that means you're going to let me make it up to you."

I laughed. "I admit I am curious about a few things."

Government offices were closed on Sunday, or I could have phoned Immigration and probably gotten the same information without creating a professional debt. But I didn't want to wait till tomorrow.

"First of all," I said, "what's the deal with the kid being put in a youth home?" I'd heard Jess's version of this, now I wanted to hear hers.

"The INS simply didn't have the space to hold them all. Two of the youngest boys and several others were released to Social Services and tucked away in various places until their cases could be heard and they could be granted political asylum—unlikely— or sent back to China."

"Or dissolved into the city's ethnic soup," I said cynically. "Where exactly did they put the victim?"

"He and his cousin were placed in the care of an older Chinese-Hawaiian woman named Elma Chang. She used to teach high school and speaks several Chinese dialects. I spoke with her. She says they were both good boys who just decided to take a stab at freedom. They climbed out a bedroom window—can you believe it? The social worker in charge filed reports immediately, which was why Dru Chun Yuen was identified so fast."

"What about the second boy? Any sign of him?"

"Not yet. We're all hoping he's still alive and hiding some-where. God alone knows what they got into."

"Did the police give you a cause of death?"

"Tentative. Drug overdose."

My heart skipped a beat. Jess told me the kid had been beaten. What was going on here?

I said, "Ice? Heroin?"

"They weren't sure yet."

"Was he an addict?"

"No tracks except one injection, they said."

"Suspicious," I said.

"Yes. Could have been a hot-shot."

"I heard he'd been knocked around some."

"So it seems. But the actual death was probably caused by an overdose, according to the pathologist. She won't confirm it until they've done the autopsy, of course."

"Is there a Hawaiian connection to the traffic in illegals, or were they just transshipping the people through here?"

There was a long silence, then she said, "What do you think?"

"I think that even if they were transshipping, they'd need some kind of local connection."

"A few of the illegals stay here, most go on to the Mainland," she said reluctantly.

"Who takes possession of them?"

"The short answer is, people who want to make a lot of money. The long answer is, an especially busy Snakehead is currently running Chinese slave laborers into Hawaii, Los Angeles, San Francisco, Vancouver, B.C., and New York City, so who knows what all he's doing? With Hong Kong set to change hands, the Triads have been accumulating more and more property in the United States, and the illegals are put to work in restaurants, factories, and other labor-intensive places. It's a dirty but lucrative business, Alex. As bad as anything that's happened in my lifetime."

An edgy quality had crept into her voice, and I realized I was somehow cutting close to the bone. I decided not to pursue that line of questioning lest I lose her. Instead, I said, "Do the police have any leads into who killed the kid?" I kept the tense edge out of my own voice.

"Not that they're telling me about. Look, Alex, I have to run. I'm working on a special—"

"Really!"

"—and we're filming down in Chinatown."

"Why Chinatown? Something to do with the illegals?"

She hesitated then said, "That's part of it. But I had this special planned before the *Dragon Venture* came in. Chinatown is changing. I want to document it. My grandfather used to have a grocery there. My mother was born in a tiny apartment upstairs from a small jewelry shop on Smith Street. My parents have several friends who are Chinatown merchants, for thirty years or more. Now, over the past few months, they've been talking about moving out."

"Really!"

I didn't get to Chinatown often, and when I did it was usually just to drive through. But now I remembered that the last time I'd been there, several stores had been newly vacated, windows boarded up or soaped over. There was a dissolute feeling to the usually bustling mauka, or mountainward, part of the district, though the waterfront end of the area was pretty much the same.

I said, "Because of the street crime?"

"Yes."

"I'd heard it was getting bad down there, but I had no idea—"

"You know how it used to be around three in the morning?"

I did. Certain parts of Chinatown were Honolulu's tenderloin. In the wee hours, on the street corners there would be people in various stages of intoxication and disrepair, homeless people, drug addicts and alcoholics, hard-core hookers. There were late hours' bars and all-night porno theaters and upstairs massage parlors featuring gutter-junkies. You had to watch your step, or you'd get the tip of a syringe through your shoe.

"Pretty raw," I said.

"Well, that whole scene has spilled over into the daytime," she said. "Three A.M. transplanted to three in the afternoon, or eight in the morning. Twenty-four hours a day. My mother's friend runs a small Asian grocery. She says a group of teenaged drug dealers work right outside her door now, hustling her customers as they come in. People don't want to fight them so they just don't shop there anymore."

"Can't she get help?"

"She tried to run them off herself. They pulled a gun on her and laughed. They're more and more brazen, more violent; most of them think a jail cell is a step up."

"There aren't enough jail cells to hold them all anyway," I said dryly.

"That's part of the problem. The police arrested two of them, and three days later they were back in front of her door, more aggressive than ever. It's a mess down there, Alex, and getting worse."

I thought about that. I'd recently read in the paper about a young man and his wife who'd confronted a burglar in their living room in one of the new city-sponsored Chinatown high-rises intended to help upgrade the area. The young man had wrestled the burglar to the ground and recovered his goods, but not before the burglar bit him. Now the victim almost certainly had hepatitis, and possibly AIDS. Chinatown had once been a fascinating place to me, but it didn't sound like much fun anymore.

"It's scary," Lenni said. "But that's not the worst of it." Her voice dropped a couple of octaves and fell to a near-whisper. "This is strictly confidential. I'm sworn not to even tell the police."

"You have my word," I said.

"The real trouble is coming from a new gang of Asian kids working the area. Not only are they dealing drugs, but they're jacking up the merchants for protection money and they've got people seriously scared."

I processed that. So far, Honolulu had escaped the serious gang violence that plagued most Mainland cities, including the increasingly violent Asian youth gangs. The local powers-that-be had managed to keep out the L.A. gangs when they'd tried to move in, and had otherwise kept a lid on youth gangs, with the exception of a few knots of troublemakers here and there. If what Lenni said was true—and I'd never had any reason to doubt her word—then this was something new in the history of Chinatown.

I said, "There are some pretty tough merchants down there, people you don't push around. Why won't they go to the police?"

"It's these kids, Alex. They're ruthless, and more violent than anything we've seen. My mother's friend was actually afraid to talk about them, even to me. She's been paying them off. I couldn't believe it. She said she'd rather give them money than be killed."

"That's serious."

"Yes. She wants to sell out, but nobody will buy down there right now. I don't know. Chinatown has always been Honolulu's high-crime area, but all of a sudden it's worse. It's like something evil is sweeping in."

"Sounds frightening," I said.

"Yes." She was silent for a long moment, as if thinking, then in a brighter voice, she said, "Well—that's more or less what I'm up to—on the Q.T. The city fathers are working on the crime problem, of course, but if you ask me they're moving too slow to do much good. I want to stir up the mayor's office, the judiciary, try to get more police assigned down there, get them to build more jails if they have to, anything to fix the problem."

"Sounds like you've turned into a full-time crime reporter."

"No. I'm still working the anchor desk, with an occasional special. Street crime is only one aspect of it. I'm also working on the illegal immigrant angle, tying all this into some early aspects of the Chinese immigration to Hawaii—you know, showing how Honolulu's Chinatown began when the plantation owners brought in so-called 'coolie' labor—how I hate that word—and how certain things never seem to change when it comes to the dark side of human nature."

"It's a one-hour special?" I wanted to keep her talking. Like most people who were doing what they truly loved, when you got her talking about her work, she became tireless and always said a lot more than she realized.

She indeed became more animated. "The production manager is letting me do three one-hour segments. I'll be doing hours and hours of actual filming. I'll examine how some of the early Chinese immigrants were literally shanghaied and pitched into the holds of ships, then brought to Hawaii and forced to work in the sugar and cane fields. Drawing a parallel to what the Snakeheads are doing now. I'll bring it up to the present, more on the *Dragon Venture* and the illegals and all that."

"Nice idea."

"I also want to research the early Chinese gang lords and the opium trade and other interesting parts of Chinatown's history, then talk about the current drug situation and how much worse it is."

"Fascinating."

"It is. And you'll love this part. I'll be doing a snort segment on the Charlie Chan era, the 1930s, when Chinatown had red-light palaces and dime-a-dance places, gambling halls—well, I guess the gambling is still there."

She was right. There were private games all over Chinatown, most small-time but a few high-stakes. A favorite game was the complicated cross between dominoes and gin rummy known as mahjong.

"I'm tying in a short history of the 1930s Chinatown areas they called Hell's Half Acre, Blood Town, and Mosquito Flats," she added. "There are some fascinating stories. Why don't you come watch us film? I'll tell security to let you on the set."

"When?"

"I'm finishing up some exteriors this afternoon. We'll be moving all over Chinatown, carrying cameras and cables and equipment, hard work. But tomorrow morning we'll have a fixed set at the Chinese Cultural Plaza. I'm going to interview some of the Chinese businesspeople and see whether or not they feel threatened by the possibility of a large influx of Hong Kong Chinese into Hawaii when the British lease on the Crown Colony runs out in 1997. Why don't you meet me there and I'll take you to Wo Fat's for lunch? Maybe I could even persuade you to give a statement about finding the young boy's body."

I tensed up. "Sorry, but I have an appointment." Which was

true, but I would have begged off anyway. The last thing I wanted to do was go on TV and talk about my grisly discovery.

"Break it," she said.

"I can't. I'm starting a new case."

"Something I should know about?" Her voice was suddenly keen with interest.

Truthfully, I was going into my new job more or less blind, so it wasn't hard to obscure the details. Insurance mogul Abe Reuben had hired me but refused to tell me anything about what I'd be doing until I was briefed by the client, who was an art collector and dealer. The pay was excellent, the client was a very reclusive big shot, the job would run through the holidays, and that's all I knew.

I said, "It's just an insurance job. But I'm meeting the client tomorrow for the first time and it's taken a while to put it together. I can't cancel out. Maybe we can have lunch another time."

"Well—" She refocused on her own work. "You can see some of the clips from my interviews on the evening news, if you're interested. I'm going to thread them in for a few weeks, to build up interest in the special. I'll be taking a two-day break starting Christmas Eve, but I'll be filming in Chinatown after that, all the way up to and including the festivities at Chinese New Year. The people in the newsroom always know where I'm filming. Call when you're ready to visit."

I thanked her and hung up.

I'd already thrown on light tan cotton slacks and a white ribbed T-shirt when I changed out of my church clothes. Now, I glared at the phone for another five minutes, daring my sinister midnight caller to phone in broad daylight when I was ready for him. He didn't. I ran a brush through my short blonde hair, put on my oversized sunglasses, grabbed my small leather purse and keys, then breezed out the front door, going anywhere just to get away from my growing bondage to the silent telephone.

I took the elevator down then went out through the revolving doors and onto Kalakaua Avenue. It had turned into a beautiful Sunday afternoon. Across the street, the surf was up and surfboards dotted the bright blue water. The carnival-canvased catamarans and sleek outriggers were moving in and out from shore, filled with tourists. Kuhio Beach was packed solid with sunbathers in a crazy quilt coloring of bathing suits against the golden sand.

Staying on my side of the street, I kept pace with the clusters of sightseers and Christmas shoppers. Before long, I found myself heading toward the International Marketplace. Once there, I veered in past the huge carved tikis and elbowed my way to the frozen yogurt stand. I bought a small low-fat chocolate cone then edged on past shoppers, past display carts and kiosks bearing everything from T-shirts to tikis to trinkets to Santas on surfboards. I strode past some tarnished tinsel decorations and out of the Kuhio side of the Marketplace, where I tossed most of the tasteless cone into a trash can, then veered toward the Ala Wai Canal.

I hadn't consciously chosen the destination, but before long I was walking beside the placid blue-gray water, retracing my morning's path, moving slowly toward the spot where I'd found the boy's body.

When I reached the exact place, I stopped and looked down at the water. It was deep blue here, opaquely innocent. The only sign of the morning's tragedy was a swath of trampled grass and some displaced stones at the water's edge. I thought about the senselessness of the boy's death. Fifteen years old. Little more than a child. Such an ignoble and unnecessary waste. Who knew what the hissing Snakehead might have said to this boy to make him risk so much in the pursuit of freedom?

Maybe the boy had parents back in China. Perhaps the entire extended family had banded together in order to come up with the $2,000 to $3,000 down payment for the trip, in the hopes that as soon as the young man made good in the Golden Mountain, some of them might follow.

Once the victim landed on U.S. soil, the rest of the $20,000 to $50,000 came due, and the illegal Chinese aliens would be locked in sweatshops, chained in restaurant kitchens, forced into brothels, manipulated into violent street gangs, and forced to deal drugs or act as drug and money couriers. They'd be stuck in the basement rooms of laundries or other labor-intensive businesses for years and years while attempting to pay back the debt.

Most never learned a word of English, which further enhanced their dependency on the evil slavemasters, especially since so few Americans understood the many Chinese dialects. No matter how hard the victims worked, the debt for food, lodgings, and other made-up costs always outpaced their wages. When people caught on and tried to flee their supposed obligation, they were often murdered outright as examples to others. As I thought about it, I could almost hear an evil hissing, as a wind suddenly rustled throughout the palm fronds and rippled the water.

The key was to catch the Snakehead and chop it off, to stop the lies that were hissed into the ears of gullible, desperate people. But that was the hard part. Because behind the Snakeheads were the Triads, and each Triad had one *Lung tao*, or Dragonhead, who created a new Snakehead each time the authorities managed to lop one off.

I shivered as I thought about what it would feel like to be locked in a basement, forced to work day and night; or to be locked in a brothel and forced to engage in beatings and degradation; or to be locked in the hold of a ship: one New York-bound ship called the *Golden Venture* had spewn forth some three hundred Chinese aliens, along with flies, rodents, filthy clothing and blankets, urine, and fecal matter.

How could anyone exist like that? It was too awful to even contemplate. I shook off the feeling of horror. No point in worrying about it, it would never happen to me. The people who fell prey to the Snakeheads were sad, miserable people who'd never known the concept of freedom. They weren't like me. I was an American. I'd been born free and knew what freedom meant; I was willing to fight to death for freedom. Besides, to get into that kind of situation, I believed you had to be gullible, let greed cloud your common sense. It was sad but true. A certain type of person fell into that snake pit, and I definitely wasn't the type.

I stood like that for a long time, thinking things over, brooding and staring down at the murky water. Finally, a small family of Vietnamese immigrants came along with fishing poles and buckets and straw sitting mats, and settled down beside the canal to catch their evening's meal of black Samoan crabs.

I went home.

I skipped the Sunday evening service at church. A mistake. I needed all the spiritual wisdom I could get just then, but at the same time I was too restless to sit through a service.

I had a quick dinner of spicy noodles and green papaya salad at the Thai restaurant downstairs, then I came back up and tried to read. All evening, I was hyper-aware of the telephone.

Finally, about nine o'clock, the phone rang. I swept it up: "Albright Investigations."

"Aunt Alex?"

My shoulders slumped as I heard the voice of my twenty-year-old nephew, Troubles. He was calling from the Mainland. Any other time I would have been delighted to get his phone call, but right now I was focused on just one thing.

I said, "Yes. Hi."

"You okay?"

"Fine, just preoccupied. What's up?"

"Would you check the cable on my Honda to make sure I remembered to close the padlock?"

The fire-engine red motorcycle was his treasure, and I assured him that I had already checked and it was fine. It was parked in our section of the garage, behind an alcove, and not likely to be bothered. All the same, I assured him I'd check it again, just to be double sure.

Though it was late in Colorado, I could hear cheerful voices and scraps of Christmas music in the background. It sounded like a Muzak rendition of "Winter Wonderland." Troubles said there was deep snow on the ground and the sky was ablaze with stars.

"Did you turn your Christmas tree lights on yet?" he asked.

"Not yet," I admitted.

"Are you going to?"

"Maybe tomorrow."

"It's almost Christmas, Alex." I could tell by the tone in his voice that he was going to insist that I develop a little holiday cheer. He said, "Why don't you go over right now and turn on the lights?"

"Pretty soon. I was reading."

"Do it, Alex. Come on, it took a lot of work to decorate that tree. I want you to see it lit up."

I sighed, stood, carried the portable phone over to the tree, and bent down and plugged in the lights. A blaze of colored brilliance filled the room: red, green, blue, and gold lights in perfect rows with perfect symmetry. It was a beautiful tree, an eight-foot blue spruce decorated in natural style with tiny carved birds in it, real cranberries, plaid bows and popcorn strands and balls and apples and all sorts of old-fashioned cheer. The lights were the big kind that I usually love. Although I appreciated his efforts, the tree didn't supply any instant joy beyond the momentary pleasure of seeing the warm lights blink on.

I said, "It's beautiful. Thank you for working so hard on it."

"You're welcome," he said. "Merry Christmas." I could tell it made him happy. That was good enough.

I talked to my mother for a minute, and to my older sister, Jennie. She was Troubles's mother, divorced from his father, and she also had one younger son, Georgie. My father—a retired rancher turned real estate broker—and my newly married younger brother and his wife made up the rest of the family group. They were wrapping presents, snacking on popcorn and homemade fudge. They'd driven to nearby Telluride yesterday to ski. I forced myself to sound cheerful, but I felt left out and alone.

"I don't suppose you've managed to find time to come home after all," my sister said accusingly.

"Even if I could get away, it's too late. The planes to the Mainland are booked solid." In fact, they were overbooked and people were waiting on standby.

"Well—how's the job coming?" my sister asked, conceding the argument. She'd tried her best to convince me to come home, even offering to pay for my ticket. She still thought I was crazy for trying to survive as a P.I. After her chaotic divorce from Troubles's father five years ago, she'd become a realtor in the Telluride area, just as land prices there started to skyrocket. She was getting better at it every day.

I explained that I hadn't really started the holiday job yet. I didn't tell them anything about finding the boy's body. There's more than one way to ruin someone else's Christmas, and I'd never talked much about my work to my oh-so-normal family anyway. All it did was make them worry.

When we signed off, I went back to my reading. I was trying to wade through a tome on forensic science, a subject that usually fascinated me but which failed to keep my interest tonight. I was waiting again for the phone to ring.

It didn't.

Finally, just after midnight, I gave up my vigil and went to bed.

The next morning at 8 A.M., my phone finally rang. It was Marty, the security guard.

"Miz Albright?"

"Yes?"

"You asked me to keep my eyeballs peeled."

"Right."

"There was somebody here early this morning, about the time you usually go out for your morning run."

I felt a tingling sensation on the back of my neck. "I skipped this morning," I explained. The image of the dead boy was still too raw for me to be comfortable resuming my morning workout. I said, "What happened?"

"Not much. Just a blonde man, looked like an older-type surf bum, if you ask me. He sort of hid over behind that big banyan tree and looked this way, then when I gave him a good once-over, he tried to act like he was waiting for the restaurant over there to open up, you know, but it seemed to me like he was watching this building."

"Describe him."

"It was just getting daylight, and he more or less stayed back in the shadows beyond the street lights. But I'd say he was six foot one or so, had shoulder-length, sun-streaked hair. Couldn't see his face much. Broad shoulders, like a surfer or weight lifter."

"What was he wearing?"

"Khakis, I'd say. And a light-colored T-shirt."

"Anything else you can think of?"

"No ma'am. After he seen me watching him, he more or less took off. I mean, he waited around just a minute to make it look good, but I could tell he wasn't interested in no breakfast, he was interested in this doorway. Besides, that place doesn't open till six-thirty, and it was barely 5 A.M."

"Good work, Marty. In fact, excellent. But why didn't you let me know earlier?"

"He was already gone. Besides, I kept figuring you'd be down any minute to go for your morning run. But now I'm about to get off shift, and haven't seen hide nor hair of you—"

"Thanks, Marty. You did the right thing."

I'd hand him a fifty-dollar bill when he came on shift tomorrow, even though I could barely afford it. But sometimes he was worth his weight in solid gold.

I felt a small rush of exhilaration as I hung up the phone. Unless I was mistaken, I finally had a small lead into the identity of my midnight caller. At last, I had a place to begin. With luck, I'd find him and flush him out, nail him, and make him tell me why he'd set me up to find the body of the young Chinese illegal. Maybe he'd even know who'd dropped the body in the canal.

CHAPTER 4

Abe Ruben was a sixtyish guy with a ruddy face, a receding hairline, weak blue eyes behind thick, dark-framed glasses, and a multimillion-dollar income as CEO of the Hawaiian Fidelity Property and Casualty Company. He'd hired me for several cases in the past two and a half years, mostly to dig up information on potential clients and examine insurable assets to make sure they really existed.

That Monday morning, he wore an open-throat silk shirt in navy blue, with matching pleated slacks in cavalry twill, cuffed, with polished Salvatore Ferragamo loafers in oxblood-red leather and a thin, matching leather belt. I knew from past experience that the understated yet elegant clothing was chosen by his wife, who was the late boss's daughter. He'd married his job, but he would have made it to the top one way or another, in spite of his mild-mannered appearance. He had an eye for money like nobody I'd ever seen, which was probably why Honolulu's rich and famous used his company to insure their ample assets.

Abe was leaning back in his chair, trying to look indifferent while he studied the polished tip of his right shoe. I was sitting across from him on his high-backed, green-leather, brass-studded armchair, trying to keep the heavily pressurized steam in my brain from escaping out of my ears.

I forced myself to remain sitting and said, "All you had to do was pick up the phone, dial my number, and tell me, Abe."

"The client just phoned *me*, Alex. You were already on your way here."

"What an inconsiderate jerk. I gave up my Christmas holiday to take this job and now, just like that, he's decided not to hire me?"

"Not exactly." He looked up at me cautiously, as if he expected me to hurl something at him the moment he made eye contact. He actually braced himself, craning his neck forward in expectation as he searched my face, then he visibly relaxed, foolishly reassured by my fixed expression.

He said, "The client just wants to hold off, that's all. He had to fly back to Hong Kong for a couple of days. Some problems came up. But frankly, he was also disturbed by the publicity you got when you found that—uh—dead body in the Ala Wai Canal yesterday morning. That will need to be straightened out."

"Fine," I said.

I picked up my mocha leather handbag from beside the chair and uncrossed my legs, ready to stand. I'd worn my tailored dusty-rose linen pantsuit for the occasion, with a mocha silk shell and matching shoes. I hadn't been able to fit comfortably into the slacks for a while, and I was pleased to be back down to my normal weight of 135, not bad for being 5'9" tall. My unruly blonde hair was combed back from my ears in a sleek style that brought out the finer features in my face, and I'd even applied pale rose lipstick and blusher. I thought about the trouble I'd gone to getting ready for this meeting and felt the steam boil up again.

"Alex," Abe said. "The client wants to check you out in person, that's all. Just go over there Thursday. For Pete's sake, he's inviting you to *lunch*!"

"What an honor," I said dryly. "A chance for him to waste more of my time."

"It is an honor," he said. "I've known Henry Li for three years, and he's become a personal friend. In those three years, he's invited me to dinner exactly twice, and never to his home. The Hong Kong Chinese are like that, Alex. Their social commitments aren't taken lightly."

"Hong Kong?"

"Yes. You know they're investing heavily in the Islands, hedging their bets against 1997."

"Henry Li is the name?"

"I thought I'd told you."

"You didn't. You told me every part of this deal was confidential."

"Yes, well—you must understand then why Henry got upset when suddenly you were making the TV news. He doesn't want to hire someone who is dragging news reporters around with them."

I gave him a scathing look. "If this inconsiderate jerk is from Hong Kong, why is he insured through you?" I knew there were any number of international banking and insurance houses in the Crown Colony, and usually Hong Kong natives were hesitant to do business outside their own circles.

"He opened a branch office here a couple of years ago, and he's bought a home and some other properties. He also has an office in New York and one in San Francisco." He directed a piercing gaze at me. "This account isn't small potatoes to us, Alex. Nor is Henry's invitation for you to come to lunch Thursday. It's a way to apologize for any inconvenience he may have caused you. I really think he's still going to hire you, but he had some bad luck with their last chief of security—in fact, he flew to Hong Kong to fire him. He wants to be sure they don't make another mistake in judgment just because they're under the gun on this."

"Who's 'they'?"

"Henry has an assistant who handles a good deal of the business these days. A woman named Mi-Lin Ming. She'll, of course, have a say in who they hire for this job. It's a very serious matter."

"So why all the mystery? You said you'd fill me in on the details today. Instead, you're helping them waste my time."

"I can't tell you what the problem is without Henry's say-so."

"Which means?"

He shook his head, as if to say I was impossible. "Okay. I'm going to go ahead and explain a couple of things before they see you, just to get you off your high horse. Then they can talk to you and make up their own minds about what they want to do."

I gave him an even more scathing look. "I should have known better than to accept a job blind, anyway. But I trusted you, Abe. When you said the job was reputable and they wanted me to start today, I took you at your word—"

"Alex, Alex. They just need a few days to work some things out, that's all."

I could see he was beginning to feel harassed. It pleased me.

"And by the way," he said. "Mi-Lin said they'll pay you full rate for whatever time you spend on their behalf, whether or not they use you long term. Which includes your trip down here today, as well as lunch Thursday."

I frowned. "They're *paying* me to come to lunch?"

"That's a rather indelicate way to put it. I'd prefer to say they're treating you with professional respect, and feeding you in the bargain."

I said, "Really. And all this just to check me out. What will they do, feed me then examine my hooves and teeth?"

"Be fair, Alex. Henry Li relies as much on his impeccable reputation as on his abilities. Scandal is something he just can't afford right now. If you'll calm down and listen, I'll try to explain."

"I thought you'd already told them everything they needed to know about me," I said, unmollified.

He sighed. "Would you like something to drink, Alex? Coffee? Tea?"

I felt my anger turn into a weary resignation. It wasn't Abe's fault that some of his clients were first-class jerks; he seemed to be doing his best to fix the situation. And I did need the money I'd earn from this job, even short term.

I said, "Coffee, Abe. Cream and sugar. And a Christmas cookie from that tin out on your reception counter, please. I slept late and missed breakfast."

A victorious glint flickered in his eye then vanished. He gave me one of his thin smiles, and said, "How about a bagel instead? We just got some poppy seed, fresh this morning."

I nodded, he touched the button on his intercom, ordered beverages and bagels from his secretary, then turned back to me.

I said, "So what's the bottom line?"

"Let me first of all say that I'm acting in a private capacity for Henry. A favor for a friend. He's insured through us, of course, but this theft is being kept purely confidential until it's sorted out."

I sat up straighter. "This is about a theft?"

He leaned back in his chair, made a steeple with his fingers, and gazed sadly at the ceiling, as if he might find a dramatic cue up there. Then he turned the gaze on me. He looked like a very sober owl.

"Henry is an antique jade collector, as well as a jade merchant. More than two million dollars worth of his jade collection was stolen from Honolulu International Airport last week. Henry and his chief of security shepherded the pieces from Hong Kong. They were part of a display that was going to the Museum of Manhattan for an exhibit next week, and Henry was bringing the artifacts here because he wanted to personally clean and polish them before shipping them on to New York."

"Why aren't you using your regular insurance investigator?"

"Henry doesn't want to file a formal claim, which is required before an official company investigator can be assigned. If that happens, the FBI will automatically be notified because the theft was committed at the airport. Then the Royal Hong Kong Police will get into the act, and so on. Henry wants the problem handled more discreetly than that, if possible."

Abe's secretary came in. She was one of the super-organized, immaculately attired, middle-aged local Japanese women whom so many Honolulu executives like to hire. She smiled neutrally at me as she served our snack then made a slight bow as she went out—a custom that had more to do with her heritage than with Abe's superior ways.

I swallowed a sip of hot coffee, felt instantly revived, and said, "Henry Li must like to do things the hard way."

"The jade business is highly risky, and in the financial stratosphere where he does business a lot of multimillion-dollar deals are done purely on word of mouth and a handshake. In other words, trust. Even the hint of a scandal might hurt him badly. Which is why he's uncomfortable about hiring you after your recent exposure to the press."

"I doubt if that's going to be a regular thing," I said dryly.

"All the same, it worries him."

I was already thinking about something else. "You said that Li doesn't want to file a claim. Can he afford to eat two million bucks worth of jade rather than stir up a scandal?"

A pause. Then, "I suppose you don't realize who Henry Li is."

"Not really." I rarely found myself moving in the high-glitz world of international jade collectors.

"Henry is a very wealthy man," Abe said. "Even by Hong Kong standards, which are stellar. He could 'eat'—as you put it—two million and more, easily. But he's sharp about money, and furthermore he's not crazy. He's not going to just walk away, Alex. That's why he asked me to find someone really good who might be able to discreetly help him."

"I see." I knew that Abe was deliberately flattering me, but hearing how valuable you are is never a bad way to spend time. I said, "What exactly would he want me to do?"

"Find out who took the jade, of course, recover it if you can. And keep your mouth shut; that was one of his strongest specifications and one reason why I suggested you. He and Mi-Lin wanted to know everything about you. When I told him about your background with the DEA, that seemed to clench things. I suppose he figured that if you could pass DEA security clearance and work for them, you were fairly close-lipped."

I thought again about my bank balance. "If I decide to go, do I phone him and accept his lunch invitation, or work through you?"

"I have Henry's phone number right here," he said as he opened a drawer.

He handed me an ivory-colored business card with both Honolulu and Hong Kong phone numbers embossed on it. He moved his phone toward me, and I dialed the number—Honolulu, of course—but there was no answer, not even an answering machine.

"Keep trying," he said. "In the meantime, I'll try to reach Mi-Lin and let her know you'll be there Thursday."

I nodded, and his secretary buzzed him, saying he had a phone call. I finished my bagel and swallowed half my coffee while Abe snarled into the phone about a false claim that they weren't going to pay. He'd just hung up when his secretary rang again and told him his next appointment had arrived. He looked at me helplessly. I had the sense he was floundering.

I excused myself, drove home, changed into a simple black one-piece bathing suit and went to the beach where I swam hard, venting what was left of my anger. While making butterfly strokes through the warm, blue water, I thought about Henry Li and the prospective job. Li already sounded like he was going to be impossibly difficult. On the other hand, I was used to handling difficult people. Even more important, I had all sorts of bills coming up the first of the year and not that many other options at the moment.

After a while I forgot about work and focused on the splendid day. I backstroked out to the area they call the Sandbar then floated while the heavy waves broke around me. A tour helicopter dipped into the sky, came low, and two people in striped shirts waved. I waved back. Farther out, people were parasailing, surfing, kayaking, and riding on the catamarans. It was too nice a day to stay mad.

After I'd totally exhausted myself, I went back to the condo, showered, and toweled dry with a fluffy lemon-colored bath towel. It was only Monday. I had time. If I decided I didn't like the way things felt after I'd met Henry Li for lunch on Thursday—well, I'd simply refuse the job and stay broke. There was always my MasterCard, with its multi-kazillion percent interest rate.

I stepped into sailcloth slacks and pulled on a matching shirt with yellow triangles on it. I went into the kitchen. The hard swim had kindled my appetite, so I rummaged in the fridge and found a half-empty package of blueberry muffins that Troubles had somehow missed. I really needed to go shopping. Extracting two, I noticed they were slightly stale. I bit into one. Hard, but not molded. I took out a quart of fresh-pressed orange juice and sat down for a semi-real breakfast.

After I'd eaten, I tried again to phone Henry Li. Abe had given me some pamphlets that Li presented to select patrons of his business. I thumbed through them as I let the telephone ring.

They were slick glossy foldouts showing his Hong Kong office. The first shot showed a ground floor segment of a colonial-style building, complete with a discreet brass plaque outside an adjacent high wall and a side entrance through a lush garden. Waist-high stone lions guarded the entryway: one with mouth curled up, one with mouth curled down, to simultaneously encourage the good spirits to enter the premises while discouraging the evil ones.

I studied the pamplets carefully, not wanting to miss a thing. Henry Li's showroom looked like a small museum, with dark polished teakwood everywhere. The back wall was a mural displaying a ceramic, coiling golden dragon against cream-colored tiles. The beast's face looked more like that of a pug-faced, whiskered pig than a dragon to me. The side walls displayed faded oils of China clippers and lacquered etchings of miniature ancient peasant villages. There was a large black-lacquered screen inlaid with abalone shell flowers, and paper scrolls depicting cranes and dwarf pine trees and other Chinese symbols of good joss—that is, good luck. In Chinese tradition, everything happens because of joss.

There were close-up shots of items inside highly secured display cases: jade, jade, and more jade, carvings and jewelry and polished loose stones, along with some gold and ivory pieces. The text informed me that Henry Li was born in Hong Kong, the son of an honored and ancient family originating in Shanghai. His father had been a general in Chiang Kai-shek's Nationalist Koumintang Army. The family had fled to the Crown Colony when Mao Tse-tung Communists moved into Shanghai in 1949. The father had then founded the jade brokerage.

I didn't know much about traditional Chinese culture. My Chinese-Hawaiian friends were as Americanized as I was, and most of the time I didn't even think about their ethnicity. But I did know that this brief allusion to ancestry would be vitally important to the Asian people who might do business with Henry Li. Next to joss—the good or bad luck which determined one's ancestry—the ancestry itself was everything.

The pamphlet explained that General Li's number one son, Li Fei Tsu—last name first in Chinese—had also been given the anglicized name of Henry Li in order to expedite his passage through European and American circles. He had received degrees from several universities. Then, at his father's death, Henry Fei Tsu Li—as he was now known—had inherited the business.

He was advertised as a patron of the arts, as an expert broker of both raw and finished jade, as well as a dealer and collector of the world's most exclusive ancient jade artifacts. Apparently, he was a darling of the Asian art world, for a list of the coming year's exhibits included the top art institutes in Manhattan, Singapore, and Tokyo. He even had one coming up in Beijing.

I was still listening to the phone ring at the Honolulu residence of this world-class jade merchant. Nobody was there. I hung up, turned to the back page of the final brochure, and there, in blazing banality, was a picture of the man who would determine my immediate financial fate.

Henry Li sat at a polished desk partly covered by an appliquéd cloth-of-gold. The desk itself had a carved design of inlaid dragons. There was a green ink blotter beside him and he was holding a pen. I also noticed that the small signature seal known as a chop was in an opened velvet case next to an inkpad. The small circular chop would, of course, have his signature carved into it in Chinese characters. Chops were used to seal all Asian business deals, while English and U.S. deals would be dismissed with the mere barbaric stroke of a pen. At one side of the desk was a flawless porcelain vase in green and gold, and behind him were display shelves holding small artifacts I couldn't quite make out.

He was a slight Chinese man of indeterminate age. He wore an expensive black chalk-striped suit. He had thinning dark hair, birdlike bones and small features, and he seemed frail at first—till I looked into his eyes. They were ancient and cold.

I immediately disliked him. I felt a pang of remorse as I realized that he was not someone I wanted to do business with. Part of my reaction was based on my residual anger at his failure to show up at our planned meeting at Abe's office this morning, and his implication that I didn't quite measure up. But there was more to it. Instinctively, I knew that this relationship was not going to work.

I sighed. Something else would come up.

I put aside my concerns and dialed Jess Seitaki's home number. Jess's wife Yoko answered, asked me how I was doing, then reminded me of a small pre-Christmas dinner party that night— which I had indeed forgotten about—starting at six-thirty.

"Can I bring anything?" I was feeling too guilty to bow out, though I really didn't want to go.

"Just yourself. It's all catered."

She told me that Jess was out shopping for Christmas gifts for their two college-aged children. Could she have him return my call?

I told her I'd try him later, that I was planning to go out for the afternoon. I promised to be on time for the party—I was notoriously late for social functions—then I signed off.

Restless, my day's plans having fallen through, I dialed the HGTV newsroom. The secretary told me that Lenni had finished her work at the Chinese Cultural Plaza that morning but would be filming in a small upstairs community room above a restaurant

THE JADE CRUCIBLE 45

owned by a longtime Honolulu Chinese family. She gave me the address on Pacific, just off River Street, dead center of Chinatown. I checked my watch. It was noon. If I hurried, I might still catch Lenni at Wo Fat's.

I wanted to know more about the young murder victim whose body I had found. Jess wasn't available. But maybe Lenni's homework had been brought up to date for the forthcoming evening news.

5

Downtown parking is always a nightmare, and more so during the holiday season. I got lucky enough to find one parking slot on the lowest level of a parking garage on Bethel, where I left my little gray Honda Accord. I climbed the fire stairs and came out the back way, just mauka of the waterfront. I turned inland and headed toward Hotel Street.

Chinatown.

The cultural shifts within Honolulu are subtle to outsiders. But to those of us who live here, social nuances occur all around and in a variety of ways. Often, it's as if you are stepping through an air curtain into a new climate. Sometimes it's a bath of warm welcome, but sometimes it's a wall of icy hostility, depending on your own ethnicity and that of the area you're visiting. Either way, it's an almost impalpable cultural divide that is nevertheless real. Even the air you breathe suddenly tastes different.

For me, the air curtain that separates Chinatown from the rest of downtown Honolulu hangs just past Nuuanu, when I hit Hotel

Street. There, the financial district's classic territorial architecture and glass-and-steel high-rises give way to a slapdash mishmash of all types of lower buildings, all old. Some are five- or eight-story brick or stone, where low-rent offices are located. Most are only two or three stories, a few with tiled dragons inlaid upon their facades and pagoda roofs with upsweeping corners, and dark doorways with the inevitable scowling/smiling lions standing guard. In certain areas, steep stairs lead up to secretive places.

The people are more casually dressed than the office workers in the financial district. There are more Asians, from various countries—though all of Honolulu has a large Asian-American population. Some people avoid eye contact with you; if they do look at you, the expression may be suspicious or speculative, depending on whether they're trying to make a buck or keep one. If they smile at you, they're probably going to try to sell you something. If they scowl, it's to keep you away so you don't try to take something from them.

I kept expecting to encounter one of the tough young Asian drug dealers Lenni had talked about, but the area seemed much the same as before. Chinatown has so many faces that no one person can ever get to know the whole truth about the area anyway.

The area's proximity to the waterfront still makes it a prime mustering-in place for Asian immigrants of every kind—that is, the kind who don't come with first-class educations and tons of money. The Asian upper crust buy high-rises and mansions and hotels and entire city blocks, and live in mandarin luxury here, as well as in their homelands. There is no wealth quite so immense and opulent as Asian wealth; no poverty quite so achingly desolate and complete as poverty in Asia.

Rent is low in Chinatown. People are more likely to look the other way if your documents aren't in order. You can buy the Asian food you're used to in the small grocery stores and cubbyhole restaurants, and you'll probably find people you can talk to, whether you're speaking one of the many Chinese dialects, or Filipino, Vietnamese, Laotian, or something else. There are herb and acupuncture shops, if you don't trust Western medicine; tailor shops where you can get cheaper clothing than in the bigger shopping centers. There are small Buddhist temples and other meeting places in the area.

I walked past a lei shop. There was a tiny, older Chinese woman sitting inside the open-air cubicle, threading white and yellow plumerias onto waxed string. Her hair was bound in a steel-gray bun, and she wore a black shirt with a mandarin collar, faded Levis, and cloth slippers. The leis hanging on pegs inside the refrigerated showcases were gorgeous: orchids and tuberoses, maile leaves and chrysanthemums.

She looked up and smiled toothily. "You like da kine flower? I make cheap."

Pidgin. She was local; her people had probably been here a hundred and fifty years. She probably owned a mansion in Makiki Heights and the building that rose up around the lei stand.

"No thanks," I said. "Another time."

I walked on past as her smile folded up. Business was apparently slow for her today.

I thought about the history of the Chinese people, about drug dealing in Chinatown and the boys who were extorting the merchants. The earliest opium poppies were found centuries ago in the Middle East, then India. British merchants deliberately introduced opium to China, to balance out the trade exchange for Chinese tea. The Chinese tried to get rid of the British opium trade. The conflict ended in a series of wars that lasted from 1839 to 1858. The Brits won. They continued trafficking opium and deliberately addicted huge segments of China's population in order to balance their Asia trade. That, by the way, is why Hong Kong and the Territories were leased to the British to begin with—as a settlement of the last opium war. Many of the great old merchant houses of Hong Kong began as opium financiers or shippers.

The Chinese Triads had taken over where the Brits left off. They'd fled China when the Communists took over, moving mostly to Hong Kong. Now, with China taking back the lease on the Crown Colonies, it looked like they were planning to come farther West.

The dragon had come full circle. It had seeded the earth with dragon's teeth, so that its evil spawn seemed to be springing up everywhere. Nobody was safe anymore.

Triads.

Symbolic of earth, wind, and fire, the three elemental parts of Chinese reality. The brutal Chinese Mafia.

The known Triads use colorful names: the 14K, the Wo Group, the Fuk Yee Hing, the Tang Yee. These people trafficked in countless tons of heroin, excelled in illegal gambling and the inevitable violence that went with it, and ran extortion rackets wherever they set up shop. Some of these Triads were even running slave ships such as the one that had brought the young murdered boy to Hawaii's shores. The Snakeheads oversaw the men who went into China and lured victims into the spider's web of slavery. But the Triad ruler—the Dragonhead—was the one who ultimately reaped the largest share of the profits.

Triad members had become ruthless in a way that was beyond cruelty. Sophisticated, intelligent, they preyed upon their own people first, so that Chinese communities in most major U.S. cities found themselves victimized by one or another branch of the Hong Kong Triads. The cities with the biggest Chinese communities— New York and San Francisco—had several Triads, serviced by sociopathic street gangs—mostly kids—who had taken over the jobs of the old hatchet men.

Honolulu had been more or less immune so far. The Triads preferred to prey on the weak and helpless. Most of Hawaii's Chinese citizens were far from that. Many were professional people, well integrated members of the community. But things happen, even here. Most outsiders never hear about them. The Triads flourish in a climate of silence and fear, and there are bound to be victims everywhere.

I walked past a darkened doorway and glanced inside at a flurry of activity. It was a tiny noodle and dumpling shop, with harried people scurrying about, frosted in flour, preparing the fare that would find its way into the store coolers and ethnic restaurants of the city.

I overheard some of the conversation among them. It was all in Chinese. Were these the latest immigrants, or simply Hawaiian Chinese who preferred their own language when among themselves? I had a sudden, insecure feeling. How much did I really know about this area, anyway? I only got down here once or twice a year. I hadn't even done that for the past three years since David's death. I actually couldn't remember the last time I'd had a reason to come to Chinatown.

My thoughts had carried me past small shops, bars, office doorways, and into the center of the few remaining blocks of true Chinatown. The signs on the front of the Chinese businesses have bold red, white, or black characters with English subtitles. The language on the street becomes interspersed with the singsong cacophony of old country Chinese, or Vietnamese, or even Filipino. This was the area where Chang Apana, the real-life model for the 1930s detective Charlie Chan, ruled the mean streets as a Honolulu police detective. But the secretive, closed society of Charlie Chan's Chinatown is no more. Thousands of Asian immigrants have arrived in Honolulu over the past two decades—most of them legally. Some have been assimilated, some have not. For years, the non-Chinese have surrounded the traditional Chinese core with encroaching establishments, and even the shrunken area of old Chinatown is now interspersed with Filipino and Vietnamese restaurants and other multiethnic shops and stores.

The successful Chinese merchants have moved on up to the heights in every possible way. After all, the Chinese have been in Hawaii for almost two centuries. Many of them have become the wealthiest people in the Islands—even in the United States. Scores of Hawaii's doctors, dentists, politicians, police officers, accountants, university professors, and other distinguished citizens have Chinese surnames, and the same or similar surnames might be found on the boards of Hawaii's most important corporations.

In other words, Hawaii teaches you not to stereotype people of any race, and especially not the Chinese.

At the same time, people of certain cultures do tend to hang together until they are fully assimilated into the wider culture. And so there is still a Chinatown, where the less fortunate Chinese newcomers often arrive, and where some old-timers prefer to remain.

自由

When you step past the air curtain, the smells change from that of city soot and car exhaust to the faint bloodied scent of freshly gutted fish and poultry, the aroma of overripe vegetables, and the faint pungent smell of sesame oil and sizzling stir-fry. Some of the odors originate in the open-air Chinese groceries along the street and in the adjacent food arcade; others come from the plethora of small restaurants and food stalls. There are broad Chinese characters written on most stores here, whether they're selling Chinese bric-a-brac or textiles or footwear or furniture. Certain restaurants add smaller English lettering, perhaps extolling the many virtues of the syrup-basted, crispy-skinned ducks dangling in grease-spattered windows, or the noodles, dim sum, manapua, preserved fruits, or other favorite dishes also on display.

The odors are not unpleasant, except for the bloody underbase from the butcher's tables and fish displays on crushed ice. Nor are the smells as different as those of "real" Chinese dishes, which feature such oddities as monkey head, bear's paw, baby mice, lizards, and of course, the ever-popular snake. No, the food in this American Chinatown is Americanized Chinese. The main ingredients are fish, poultry, and vegetables, though some of the vegetables—bamboo shoots, bean curd, black fungus, sea cucumber, and several varieties of mushrooms—are unusual to the American palate. But you can also find such American fare as chop suey, a dish that was invented in San Francisco. And of course all ingredients are prepared and served up with a distinctively Chinese-American flair.

Most of the food is pretty much the same, and generally too oily for me, whether it's labeled Mandarin, Pekingese, Cantonese, Szechwan, Chiu Chow, Hakka, or whatever. The menus are often larded with favorite local fare, such as potato-macaroni salad, Korean barbecue, and Spam musabi. But you don't go to Chinatown for gourmet dinners. There are dozens of better Chinese restaurants all over town, and especially in the upscale tourist areas such as Waikiki. You go to Chinatown for local flavor, for atmosphere, for the feeling of a trip abroad in the space of a few square blocks.

Wo Fat's is a historic landmark in Chinatown, one of the oldest, largest restaurants. I went in and immediately saw Lenni and her crew sitting in the far back, at a large round table with a black gondola in the center, which is used for rotating the family-style dishes so people can serve themselves. I waved. She saw me, waved back, and motioned for me to join them.

The hostess was a short, scowling, thick-waisted woman in a high-necked, skin-tight, green-and-red satin cheongsam that was side-slit to her knee. She was determined to sit me down and get me out of the way. I told her I was meeting friends, then I pressed through the lunch crowd and to the back, where I took a chair at Lenni's large table, beneath a strand of green tinsel that dangled from the Christmas decorations on the wall.

"Alex!" Lenni expressed surprise and delight that I had shown up after all. She gestured for me to sit down.

She wrote, produced, and directed her own specials, so her film crew was small. They were already eating, serving each other from the various bowls of dim sum and chow mein and chop suey and other varied dishes. Lenni introduced me, and they each stopped eating long enough to say hello.

To my left was a thin haole woman with large, luminous eyes and gray-streaked brown hair pulled back with a rubber band.

"This is Janine Reynolds, who handles my background and scripts," Lenni said.

She nodded.

I said the appropriate words.

Next I met two fresh-faced, muscular young men in their late twenties. These were Jake Waters and John Takawa, who operated the video camera. Barry Leong was a tall, lanky Chinese-Filipino about forty years old. He was her audio expert, and as Lenni introduced him he stood, made a slight bow, and reached across to shake my hand, making it necessary for me to remove my bright red napkin and partially stand too, so I could return his handshake. A fair-complexioned, middle-aged husband and wife team with the last name of Murphy made up the rest of the party. The Murphys handled security and kept the curious crowds away.

Everyone but Lenni was dressed in casual attire: T-shirts and denims, khakis, or slacks. Lenni, who would be on camera, was dressed in a tailored plum silk pantsuit with a snow-white silk blouse, and even now her makeup was meticulous, her gold earrings had a burnished sheen, and her black pumps looked like they were fresh out of the box.

We wished each other Merry Christmas and Happy New Year, then *Kung Hee Fat Choy*, a prosperity wish that had become the official greeting for the Chinese New Year.

"When does the Chinese New Year fall this year, anyway?" I asked. Everyone seemed to be looking at me, and I felt as if I should say something.

Lenni smiled. "January fifth."

"Early," I said.

"Yes."

The Chinese New Year was always celebrated on the evening of the three hundred sixty-fifth day of the lunar calendar, a system which I could never understand. I knew only that the holiday floated between January and February, that downtown streets were mostly shut off on one special night, while the citizens of Chinatown offered up their hospitality to all of Honolulu in a deafening frenzy of lion dances, gong-ringing, firecrackers, and other celebration. Red Chinese characters, flags, and facades appeared everywhere, and the holocaust of firecrackers came in red skins that overflowed the gutters after the first couple of hours, by morning you could barely wade through the debris.

I'd read somewhere that the traditional intention of all this chaos was to drive away the *Nien*, an evil gigantic monster that lived beneath the earth and liked to rampage through people's homes, crops, and lives, after the sun had shown itself three hundred sixty-five times. Someone had discovered that this monster was afraid of noise, light, and the color red, and ever since then the Chinese had been driving it away with the appropriate medicine—though of course the holiday had become similar to Western New Year celebrations now, that is, a way to celebrate the old and welcome the new.

Lenni signaled, and the waitress scurried up and set a clean white plate in front of me, so I could partake in the family-style fare. She presented a small round teacup and filled it with green tea from the white porcelain pot on the table. She then handed me a pair of black lacquered chopsticks. I thanked her, and she scurried away, small and efficient and totally overwhelmed by the rapidly growing lunch crowd.

"We could get your interview right after lunch, before we start filming," Lenni said. She pretended to be looking at the noodles she was twining around her chopsticks, but I could see she was looking from under her eyelids at me, wanting to catch my reaction.

"I've decided not to go on camera," I said easily. "Believe it or not, finding that kid was a difficult experience for me."

"Always hard to see anybody get hurt," the audio technician agreed.

"But it's important to find the persons who did it and put them behind bars," Lenni said with feeling. "I'd like to interview you, Alex. I'm trying to keep people focused on the death and help put some pressure on the police department."

"Sorry to be difficult, but no."

The female Murphy was offering me some food. I held my plate up beside the gondola, she handed me some tongs, and I used them to dip into an ample platterful of the deep-fried Chinese hors d'oeuvres called dim sum. I transferred a steamed shrimp dumpling to my plate, then a triangular rice dumpling filled with chopped vegetables, then allowed myself one deep-fried spring roll. Someone turned the gondola, and Lenni said, "Try some of the fried rice. It's good today."

"I'd really like to help you," I said. "But maybe in a different way." I spooned some of the rice onto my plate.

"Lenni tells me you're a private investigator," the female Murphy said.

"That's right."

Everyone was eating again, and I bit into my spring roll. The crust was predictably oily, but the interior was filled with chicken, mushrooms, bamboo shoots, and bean sprouts. Tasty indeed.

"I bet that's interesting work," Janine Reynolds said.

"When there's work to do," I said.

I was used to the curiosity. There weren't that many female P.I.s in Honolulu. Most investigative work was done by the big agencies, which were owned by men and which employed several key investigators and a small army of helpers.

"How'd you get into detective work?" the Japanese camera operator asked. I knew he was speculating about his own possibilities.

"After college, I worked for DEA intelligence for eight years," I said. "I quit when I got married. My husband was in law enforcement, and we talked about opening our own investigative agency someday. He was shot and killed three years ago during a drug bust. You may remember the incident, there was quite a media flap about it."

"I worked on the crew that covered the inquiry into his death," the audio expert said. "It was tough on you, I could tell."

"Yes." I looked down and straightened the napkin on my lap then looked up again and said, "After I managed to get back on my feet, I decided to go ahead and open an agency on my own."

"Is it hard to get licensed?" the Japanese kid asked.

I smiled. "That depends. You need a clean criminal record, and you need several years experience in investigative work, such as police work or insurance investigation. You have to pass a written test, and also be licensed if you carry a concealed weapon, which you need from time to time. And you have to be bonded. That's about it."

"Isn't it dangerous?" This from Janine Reynolds. I figured she wanted to hear a story. Everybody thinks a private investigator's life is one long, galloping adventure, just like on TV.

"It has its moments." I could hear the edge coming into my voice.

Others apparently heard it too. There was a short silence during which everyone got busy eating. Then the female Murphy politely changed the subject. "Are you going to be watching us work this afternoon?"

"If it's okay with Lenni." I took a sip of tea.

"I invited you." Lenni sounded a bit miffed that I'd even have to ask.

"Going to be a tough job this afternoon," the male Murphy said, around a mouthful of bean thread. "Lenni is taking on one of the tongs."

Lenni shot him a scowl.

I said, "I don't want to complicate anything—"

I knew that tong societies were mostly legitimate social organizations. But some served as cells of the Triads, or otherwise facilitated crime. The word still evoked the myth of oriental danger and intrigue.

Lenni smiled. "Don't worry about it, Alex. The tong we're going to is nothing more than a community organization, and it's semi-public anyway. It's where my mother plays mahjong. I'm sure it will be fine if you come along." She looked at her watch. "We're running late."

We quickly finished our meal. Walking back down Pacific Street, Lenni said, "I haven't seen much of you for a while. Are you doing okay?"

I glanced down at the pavement. She meant had I gotten over the trauma associated with losing David. "More or less," I said. "There are still some pretty bad days, but they're fading."

She nodded sagely. "I truly admired the way you stood up through all the turmoil. I never got a chance to tell you."

"Thanks. People seem to do what they have to."

"Not everybody," Lenni said, suddenly bitter. "Far too many

people stick their heads in the sand and pretend that nothing is wrong, even when the world is folding in on them."

"You have someone special in mind?"

"Just what's happening here in Chinatown. I never thought that the old-time merchants would bow their heads and look the other way if something like this started happening—"

"You mean the Asian kids and their extortion."

"That and other things. Look, let's have lunch soon and talk about it. I may be able to use your services."

I frowned. "Is something wrong?"

A tiny lick of fear passed through her eyes then vanished. "Not really. But I'm following some recent leads into the teenage thugs who are behind the trouble here. I've been uneasy lately." She grinned, embarrassed. "Guess I'm not exactly the fearless and intrepid reporter I'm supposed to be."

I smiled back. "I've always seen you as more the cerebral type."

"Thanks." Her voice dropped to a near whisper as she leaned in close to me. "I've been told the main Snakehead who runs the illegals is based right here in Chinatown."

That almost stopped me short, but a quick nudge from Lenni kept me going. I said, "Who?"

She shook her head and frowned deeply. "I can't say till I'm certain, Alex, but now and again when I'm down here I wish I had someone along for backup. I can't think of anyone I'd rather have backing me up than you."

I was touched, but didn't reply.

We walked in silence for about half a block, then I asked her about the boy whose body I'd found.

"The autopsy isn't finished," she said, "and there's still confusion about the cause of death. It seems there's a toss-up now between whether it was a hot-shot that killed the kid, or the beating that did it."

"That's strange," I said. A picture of the body flashed through my mind. It had been impossible to tell much about the kid, with his features already ruined by the water. I definitely needed to ask

Jess more about this. Perhaps tonight at the party. I said, "Anything else come up?"

She said, "Are you investigating this for someone, Alex? Was that why you were at the Ala Wai Canal yesterday morning?"

I gave her a startled look.

"You know I protect my sources," she said soothingly. "You can tell me what's really happening. I can help you clear it up."

"Lenni, I was just jogging. I do it every morning, you can ask my doorman."

The moment the words came out, I regretted them. I'd have to get to Marty first and tell him not to mention anything about someone possibly watching me if Lenni came calling, which she almost certainly would now that I'd shot off my mouth.

"We should work together on this," she said. "Pool our resources, you know."

We had reached the tong association's doorway. The aging wooden sign with both Chinese and English lettering was posted above a steep stairwell beside an herb/acupuncture shop. It said: HUNG LUHK BENEVOLENT ASSOCIATION.

Lenni said, "After this filming I have to get back to the studio to put together some clips for tonight's news. Why don't you phone me tomorrow? We'll get together and see what we can work out."

自由

I had never been in a tong society's headquarters before. I'd passed the various tongs' Chinatown doorways a hundred times, but even when the doors were open, someone was always lingering nearby. When you paused to peer up a rickety stairwell or stare back into the hostile depths, the unlikely guard would inevitably brace for action, then shoot you a ferocious scowl. This served to warn you that you were unwelcome. I'd always suspected some of the secrecy was because more than one illegal gambling game was going on. But I also knew that some of the secrecy was simply to guard against tourists who saw the Chinese people as curiosities on a par with the animals at the zoo.

All the same, even the good tongs had been founded centuries ago as secret organizations, and the bad ones were the nuclei of Chinese organized crime. And so, I suppose I was a bit disappointed when Lenni led me up one of the formerly forbidden stairwells and into a large, wooden-floored room with a small kitchenette in the back, and long formica-topped folding tables, numerous stacks of metal folding chairs, and a small dais to one side where someone could stand to speak to a crowd. It looked like a very small auditorium in an old schoolhouse, or the conference room at our church. Dr. Fu Manchu was nowhere to be found.

Lenni's crew had already set up their equipment before lunch. When we arrived, Lenni began chatting with the half dozen people in attendance, putting them at ease, explaining what she would be doing and how, while the others did their last minute equipment checks. I took the opportunity to step over and examine an aging notice posted beside the entrance.

It was titled "Excerpts from the By-Laws of the Hung Luhk Benevolent Association." The word *tong* was nowhere to be found. Apparently they didn't even *call* it a tong anymore, and in fact the word literally meant only "hall" or "gathering place" anyway. There were two columns on the poster, one written in English, the other in Chinese. The excerpted list of tenets and rules told me that the purpose of the organization was to benefit the members by helping them find honorable employment and otherwise seeing to their welfare; and by forming *huis*—that is, small financial groups—that would assist members with monetary emergencies and provide assistance with hospital stays, weddings, and funerals. The only tenet that could be construed as remotely nefarious was the last rule, which stated that all members would help one another protect their business territory from those who would encroach, but even that was appended "in accordance with the law." There was nothing about loyalty to the death, in lieu of being chopped to pieces with a thousand knives. Nothing about dying of electric shock, if one broke the eternal celestial society's vows; nothing about being burned to death by fire from the dragon's breath.

Beside the posted bylaws was a cork bulletin board, and I also examined that. There was a notice asking for volunteers to help decorate for the upcoming Chinese New Year, one inviting the members to a Christmas party, several notices for activities at local Buddhist temples, a travel agent's poster offering a discount to Chinese travelers who took the Beijing tour this coming summer, and even a notice for the Chinese Baptist Church, which was having a dinner for a long-standing deacon, to which all were invited.

Well. This was about as sinister as my mother's missions group, with the exception of the four well-groomed elderly ladies in dress blouses and slacks who sat at a card table to one side of the room clicking their bone-white mahjong tiles and making small talk. There had been money on the table when we'd first walked in. It had quickly vanished into several expensive handbags. Lenni had quickly looked the other way, and I assumed that was why she'd rushed straight into her work rather than introducing me to her mother, whom I spotted because she looked a great deal like Lenni except for the gray hair and a few wrinkles.

The ladies were on the *makai*, or seaward side of the room, the windows behind them were open, and the sky shined pure blue. We were one block mountainward, or *mauka*, of the ocean, and only a few short blocks from the newly renovated Aloha Tower with all its glitzy tourist shops and piers intended to lure ocean liners. But we were in a different world.

Lenni was ready to start filming, so I walked over and sat down in the folding chair she'd set up to one side and listened.

The assistant director counted down the shot. Cameras rolled. Lenni did an introductory lead-in, then turned to the small, white-haired Chinese man who had been positioned at an angle from her. His hair was cropped to the same short length all over his head. His face was round as the moon, with graying eyebrows that tilted up in the middle to give him a cheerful look. His faintly wrinkled skin was a burnished tan, as if he spent a lot of time beside a swimming pool, or deep sea fishing. His eyes looked almost shut, and a pensive smile floated on his face. He wore an expensive dark blue business suit—I guessed it was a Giorgio Armani—so new it must have been purchased for just this occasion. A gorgeous green jade and gold ring was displayed on his right, manicured hand, a wide gold wedding band showed on his left. His thick wristwatch looked like real gold.

Lenni introduced him as the CEO of one of the local banks.

She read off a list of his civic accomplishments, then asked him how he had come to belong to the association. He replied by talking about his grandfather, who had come to Hawaii six years before the Great Chinatown fire in 1900.

His grandfather had fulfilled his obligation to the plantation owners who had brought him to the Islands, then he'd borrowed money from a *hui* put together by friends to set up a noodle shop in June of 1899. The following January, the bubonic plague had broken out in Chinatown. The Honolulu Fire Department had set fire to the area where cases of the plague had been found, hoping to burn it out. They'd planned to contain the blaze, but strong devil winds suddenly blew in from the sea, and by the time the conflagration was put out, a full thirty-eight acres of Chinatown had been burned to the ground. Some seven thousand people were homeless, most of them Chinese.

"My grandfather and his friends started the association two months after the fire," he said, nodding agreeably at the memory. "He wanted to help people rebuild Chinatown, and the Benevolent Association has continued ever since."

The next interview was with a man who'd worked all his life as a blue-collar laborer at the Pearl Harbor Shipyard, but whose parents had gotten their start in Chinatown. The answers Lenni got were filled with local history and personality. But by the time she was ready to talk to the third person in the group, I was feeling restless. I excused myself and left.

On my way back to the parking garage, I inadvertently stepped smack into that parallel universe inhabited by the decaying ghosts we refuse to see, the world Lenni had talked about.

Curious, I'd poked my head into the ammonia-and-urine-scented cavern of a bar I was passing, to see what it looked like inside. It had a lit neon sign above the doorway: NEW SHATIN LOUNGE. Named for the famous Hong Kong Shatin Racetrack, no doubt. The barroom was seedy and depressing—a tomb for the walking, breathing, drug-and-alcohol addicted dead. I noticed that there was an already aging sign in the window that said, UNDER NEW MANAGEMENT, but the place looked like it had been around since they'd burnt Chinatown at the turn of the century.

A solitary man sat on the barstool nearest the door. His face was pale and wasted. The impression was of a strange decapitated head in a Hollywood horror film, preserved in invisible formaldehyde, his eyes unseeing. The flat, flaccid deadness of his features and lifeless blonde hair had a foretaste of death.

He blinked, startling me.

I looked farther down the bar, past the neon beer sign and behind the backbar. The dark, cavernous room was otherwise empty, not even a bartender in sight, just a couple of pool tables with faded green felt and nobody there to play.

I backed out, already blinking against the sunlight from just my brief gaze into that darkness. Moving on, I glanced to my left. I was approaching a thin, fiftyish-looking haole man, about five foot seven, who was leaning against the wall. He wore dirty denim slacks and a stained T-shirt. He looked like he might be homeless.

Two squat men—nut-brown, sunbaked, with veneers as tough as rhinoceros hide—were on the sidewalk opposite him, near the curb. I stepped closer, keeping to my natural stride. The man against the wall was trembling with excitement, lust flooding his eyes. His right hand jerked out in an involuntarily motion to grope the air, trying to fix on something just out of reach and much desired.

I glanced right again. The thickset, short man on the right was holding what appeared to be a glassine bag filled with white powder, holding it like a handler holds a treat for a dog in process of being trained. Come and get it, roll over, fetch. I could see that he was savoring the power the white powder gave him, relishing the other man's dependency and groveling need.

I was witnessing the absolute corruption of drugs, the ugly enslavement. The buyer's face collapsed into a plea, and I let my eyes tick back to the dealer, who was smiling with such evil glee that I felt my chest constrict from the cruelty in him.

I've seen dope deals. Believe me. When I was working as an intelligence analyst for the DEA, I not only listened to endless tape of deals going down, but I also went out into the field and saw deals of every size, shape, and color. So trust me when I say that this was as low as it got, this place where the addict had no pride, no self-respect, where everything that makes us uniquely human was sapped by both the drugs and the people who dealt them: because yes, the dealers have their own twisted needs, and not all of them are financial. The enslavement works both ways.

This one-on-one interaction was the inevitable source of the falsified *Miami Vice* glamour, this was the reason for the multimillion-dollar drug stings, the entire multinational bureaucracy trying—fruitlessly—to stop the traffic. This was where the drug dealers' Ferraris and Learjets came from, this was what fueled the economies of several countries around the globe. These pitiful people, right here, engaged in this demeaning ritual. If we're ever going to stop the drug traffic, this is where it has to be done.

The buyer was dangling from that razor-thin thread of the dealer's control. There was a black, oozing hatred emitting from the dealer, along with a satanic need to possess the buyer's very soul.

It was like looking at black earth over an open grave with a half-living corpse inside, seeing that drug dealer buried alive in his own black, oozing hatred. It was swallowing both him and the addict, destroying them both as absolutely as tar pitch swallows light.

All this was seen and assimilated in a split instant, the pressure of the interaction rolling in on me, and then I was part of it, through and past it, never breaking stride, wondering at the fact that their magnetic attraction was so intense that I had walked directly through their frozen, mutual worlds and neither one of them had even actually seen me.

Ah, life. How does God's noblest creation come to this slavish state of being? How can the same species that raised the great cathedrals in Europe, wrote great uplifting music, and learned to understand the stars also grovel in this fetid, stinking place where the soul is literally trapped and decaying?

This was far more than a physical addiction. It was spiritual warfare, a battle for mankind's soul, and it was all around me, all the time.

After I got home, I reflected on the incident again. There was something about it that kept troubling me.

There was an undercurrent of rot in Chinatown, bred by the historical poverty and social alienation of the area. This was where people of all races got started, true; but it was also where they were often finished, overdosed in a parking lot or a stairwell somewhere, shot or stabbed or infected with AIDS. Chinatown had become the area where the low-rent drug dealers and users plied their trade. There were people in alcoves with abscesses on their arms and legs from using dirty needles, people of all types turning tricks, people sitting in bars who had literally become pickled by the alcohol, and almost none of these peripheral people were Chinese.

I had to stop and look at it all again and again until I understood it. Because Lenni was right. Chinatown was changing. Something evil was sweeping in.

6

Reluctantly, I dressed for Jess and Yoko Seitaki's Christmas party that evening. The guests would include our pastor, his wife, and several of our closest friends from church. I wore a dark gray satin ensemble with palazzo pants and a tiny dusting of rhinestone chips across the bodice. I thought about wearing my good diamond earrings—the ones David had given me for our first anniversary. I decided to wear my glitzy rhinestone droplets instead.

I left Waikiki at six o'clock and drove to the Seitaki's stately home in the upper Nuuanu Valley, arriving at six-fifteen on the dot. Their wide, leafy yard was decorated with a huge lighted manger scene that contained dazzling golden-white angels, glittering wise men, and other assorted brilliance, all nestled beneath the lushly green banyan and plum trees, the koas, and Norfolk pines.

When I rang the bell, Yoko opened the front door. She was wearing a severe black dress that was just the ticket to show off her best gold-and-diamond necklace and her trim, tall figure.

She smiled warmly, gave me a quick hug, then stepped back, held me at arm's length inspecting me, and said, "You look lovely."

"Thank you. So do you. What's the new cologne?"

"Wind Essence."

"Really. I like it."

"Liberty House," she said. "It's one of Jess's early Christmas presents."

"You're a lucky woman." I felt a sudden twinge of envy that she still had Jess, and David was gone.

She gave me another smile, then a sudden somber blink. "And speaking of Jess, no business tonight, Alex. Not from you and not from Jess. I know what happened Sunday morning, and we aren't going to talk about death in this house tonight. We're celebrating Jesus' birthday, so absolutely no mention of work. Promise?"

I hesitated then said, "I do."

"Then *Mele Kalikimaka*. Let's have a wonderful time."

"Merry Christmas to you too," I said, laughing. Suddenly I didn't want to talk about work anyway.

I presented her with a small, silver-wrapped Christmas gift containing a bayleaf candle filled with holly and cranberries. She had already given me a gift. It and the small one Troubles had left for me were the only ones under my tree, and I hadn't felt like unwrapping them yet.

Inside, their house was decorated with an old-fashioned tree so much like my own that I wondered if Yoko and Troubles had put their heads together before he left. The guests were in a festive mood, and the buffet actually featured plum pudding and other English holiday fare, along with sushi, mochi, kalua pig, sliced pineapple, turkey and stuffing, poi, breadfruit, coconut cake, pumpkin pie, and other excellent pan-ethnic Island holiday food. The room was decorated with bird-of-paradise and anthuriums, with poinsettias in red, pink, and white. Yoko had decorated the flowerpots with huge glittering bows, and she'd sprayed the flowers with tiny bits of the same glitter, so that everything seemed to capture light.

I enjoyed the camaraderie. Yoko gave each guest a tiny yellow orchid plant from her garden, the simple pots wrapped with yellow-and-green plaid satin bows. Neither Jess nor I talked about the grisly discovery that had brought us together just yesterday morning. Aside from Yoko's request, it didn't feel like the right time anyway. In our respective lines of work you had to draw boundaries or you were working and worrying all the time and this was, after all, the Christmas season, only ten short days till Christ's birthday. I could phone Jess tomorrow. In the meantime, I would enjoy the night.

自由

I was home and soundly asleep by 11 P.M. At just past midnight, I sat up suddenly and rubbed my eyes. Something had awakened me.

It was a dark, moonless night. As always, I could see through my glass balcony doors. Beyond the city lights and holiday glitter, the sky was Prussian blue and pierced with stars.

The intercom buzzed, and I realized it had brought me awake. Apparently it had been buzzing for a while, or else the person ringing it was an impatient soul, for suddenly he leaned into the downstairs button and it buzzed persistently with a long grating *zzzzz*. Annoyed, I swung my legs over the side of the bed, dragged myself into the foyer, and pushed the talk button.

I said, "Stop, okay, I'm here. What?"

There was dead silence for a moment, as if I'd lost my caller, then an abrasive male voice said, "You Alex Albright?"

The demanding tone of voice on top of the annoying buzzer hit a nerve. "That depends on who *you* are," I said testily.

The next silence was even longer than the first one, but finally the voice said, "I need see you foah one job."

Local to "da max," this one. Heavy, heavy pidgin.

I listened carefully for any similarity to the voice that had awakened me two nights before and warned me to watch out for the water in the Ala Wai Canal. The intercom was tinny and there was some resemblance, but that other voice had been distinctive.

I decided this wasn't it. I rubbed my eyes again. I really wanted to go back to sleep, but I wanted to bury myself in work for the rest of the holiday season too, and my job through Abe wasn't going to work out due to my instant dislike of Henry Li. You can't bury yourself in work unless you have work to do, and I certainly needed to make some money somehow. Maybe—just maybe—this was the something that I'd hoped would come up in place of the job for Henry Li.

I said, "Who are you?"

"You don't know me. But I wan' talk."

One thing about being a private eye, you get used to meeting all kinds at all hours. I thought for a minute then said, "Okay, come on up. Eighth floor, my office is the fourth door on the left after you get off the elevator." I hit the buzzer to let him into the private elevator downstairs beside the intercom.

I went back into my dark bedroom and switched on the bedside lamp then stepped out of my blue pajamas, stepped into underwear, a pair of soft, stone-washed Levis, and dragged on a blue and yellow top. In the bathroom, I splashed water on my face. My eyes were bloodshot. I looked weary. But my cheekbones were visible again, too, and I was pleased once more about the twelve pounds I'd just lost. I dragged a brush through my hair and had just stepped back into my bedroom when I heard the buzzer on my office door ring.

I hurried into the office, shutting the bedroom door behind me and switching on more lights. As my visitor buzzed for the second time, I pulled open the door—

And stopped short, unable to hide my astonishment.

The man was tensile, coiled tight, and he examined me as I was inspecting him. There was a question in his eyes.

I wanted to say something polite, but it was too late. My reaction had already said it all. Awkwardly, I nodded hello, stepped back, and gestured for him to come in.

I knew who he was, of course. So did everyone else in the Islands. His name was Charlie Chang—no snickers, please, if you instantly think of Charlie Chan. There are only one hundred basic surnames in all the Chinese language, shared among over one billion Chinese people. There are over a hundred Chang families listed in the Honolulu telephone directory. Later, I looked, to see. Most of them are not even remotely related by blood.

In other words, both Charlie Chan and Charlie Chang are common Chinese names indeed, and I can assure you that any resemblance between Hawaii's most famous fictional detective and the man standing before me stopped with this similarity in name and race.

In fact, most of the time everyone—even people who didn't know him—called this man Paké Chang. That's pronounced "pah-kay," and it's the pidgin word meaning "Chinese," which some people say derived from the Cantonese word for father, *pai kei*. On the streets and in law enforcement circles, the man standing in front of me was often referred to as the Pakiké Paké, which translates roughly to "The Tough Chinaman." A lot of boys in the local crime syndicate have nicknames like that.

Paké Chang paused in the doorway and ingested every detail of my small office with two turns of his pit-bull head. Then he came all the way in, carefully shut and locked the door behind him, and lowered his compact bulk onto my butterscotch leather divan.

No slight-built Chinese, this man. He was about five-nine, stocky, solid, also part Hawaiian. I knew a bit about Paké, things picked up here and there from my friends in law enforcement. He'd worked his way up from the streets and had done time only once, for attempted manslaughter during a union beef. But you know how that goes. For mobsters, even the local variety, putting them in prison is like sending them away to finishing school.

Paké Chang ran the illegal side of Chinatown. His enterprises allegedly included such activities as high-stakes gambling, prostitution, drugs, extortion, contract murder, and all other forms of organized crime. A year before David's death, a federal and local law enforcement strike force had put away the crime boss who'd been running the illegal action in Waikiki. Recently, those who should know said that Paké had expanded to take over the

Waikiki action as well. Which meant he'd more or less hit top spot for a syndicate boss in Hawaii.

I hated drugs, and I hated every other enterprise controlled by Paké Chang. Yet we were allies in a way, if you can believe that. It worked something like this.

Hawaii is an economic crossroads between East and West, and it's also billed as the world's number one tourist destination. There's big, big money here, in both legal and illegal commerce. Which means that the local syndicate will at any given time find itself fending off rivals from places as diverse as California, Miami, New York, Hong Kong, Tokyo, Sydney, or other points on the globe. Every crook and his pit bull want to get in on the action in Hawaii, with the exception of the Italian/Sicilian Mafia. They've declared Hawaii a protected territory where all their crime families can invest money equally, and no one Cosa Nostra family gets to control the streets. This leaves the local syndicate more or less in control of the local action.

This brought me to the point at which Paké and I just might have something in common. Because the crime syndicate in Hawaii was as good a case as ever was made for the saying, "Better the devil you know than the devil you don't." As bad as the local syndicate was, they at least helped keep other crime cartels out, and some of those cartels were far, far worse in every way than our local-grown syndicate.

With the locals, a vestige of reason seemed to remain. Drive-by shootings and the all-out chaos that was taking over the inner cities on the Mainland was more or less discouraged as bad for business. Local street punks who worked solo and caused trouble were soon straightened out. The Los Angeles street gangs had tried to move into Hawaii for a while. They'd found themselves up against an immovable force in the form of a unified crime syndicate, police force, judiciary, and legislature, working in tandem against at least this one thing. Japanese organized crime—the yakuza—had also tried to move in, but seemed to have reached an understanding that left the locals in control.

I hope this explains why I could actually sit down and talk to

Paké Chang, now that I was finally meeting him. The Ice dealers who had been behind my husband's death had been part of an organization moving into the local syndicate's territory, and Paké and his people had lined up beside the police when it came to weeding the newcomers out and putting them behind bars. His motives weren't altruistic, to be sure, but there are layers of degree even in the world of organized crime. What it boiled down to was: in the worst tragedy that had ever happened to me, Paké Chang and his people had somehow been on my side.

I rested one hip on the corner of my desk, trying to act unintimidated, and said, "It's nice to meet you in person, Mr. Chang. What can I do for you?"

He shifted his weight and tugged at the corner of his faded blue T-shirt. No sleek, suited mobster, this one. In fact, here in the Islands the boys who put on airs are usually the ones next lower on the totem pole, while the bosses can usually pass for longshoremen or fishermen.

He said, "You found one dead boy in the Ala Wai Canal yesterday." It was a flat statement.

"I did," I admitted.

"One puka-headed Chinese," he said contemptuously. A puka, by the way, is a hole.

I didn't say anything.

Paké had been holding a rolled-up *Star Bulletin*, and I'd figured he'd just picked up the newspaper from the machine in the lobby as he passed by. Now he withdrew a manila envelope from the paper and held it out toward me. I leaned forward and took it, raising my eyebrows questioningly. He flicked his beefy hand impatiently, telling me to open it, and I did. I took out a sheaf of papers.

The top two papers were a photocopy of the statement I'd given to the female cop the previous morning. Not that he'd necessarily gotten the papers from her. The sleight-of-hand usually takes place a little farther up the ladder. I frowned in surprise as I saw the statement. A faint smile traced across his face, though it was nearly hidden by his short, wiry beard and didn't make it all the way to his eyes.

When I thought about it, I wasn't really surprised that a top syndicate boss could get a copy of a police report. There's a lot of overlap here between the underworld and the overworld. But what was the point?

"That boy you found," Chang said. His face was implacable now, a mahogany-colored tiki. "Da kine poho wan' make trouble for me."

I quickly translated the pidgin into English. "Da kine" can mean anything, a "poho" is a good-for-nothing. When it all soaked in, I did a double take.

I said, "That kid was causing trouble for *you?*"

He nodded his head ponderously, as if the concept perplexed him even more than it did me. He scratched thoughtfully at his short black beard, which was crosshatched through with springy silver.

"I go Hong Kong one week ago," he said. His black-coral eyes hooded over and his face became blank, as if he was determined that no facial expression would tell me more than his words intended.

Which told me he'd no doubt been in Hong Kong on syndicate business, probably brokering drugs.

"I come back Saturday morning early," he said, "I get into Honolulu International, I'm tired. But I hear my nephew, Kimo, he wen' hang out with da kine pohos, that one kid and another rascal. I think they wen' try to rip me off."

I frowned. An interesting concept, two teenage hoodlums from backwoods China joining forces with a mysterious third boy to rip off Honolulu's top syndicate boss. For what?

He eyed me darkly, and a little tic appeared at one jowly corner of his mouth. "Those rascals wen' bother my bartender at my bar in Chinatown, the Lucky Lion. They wen' tell him to pay them, or they wan' burn my place down."

"What on earth can I do?"

"I heah you one tittah. I pay you good, you find out what Kimo is doing, yeah?"

Being called a "tittah" isn't quite so seamy as it sounds. I've been told the word is originally Samoan for "sister," but wherever it started, now it means about the same as being called "one tough wahine," or "broad." Paké Chang, from his point of view, had just paid me a real compliment.

"You found one boy dead. Now you find out where that other boy and Kimo are," he said. "I goin' whack 'em."

I recoiled, creating more distance between us. "Uh-uh. Wrong. I'm not going to track anybody down so you can kill them."

Either a smile or a grimace pulled his lips ever-so-slightly upward. "I don' mean put one bullet in one's head. I jus' wan' talk to 'em, give 'em one lickin' and make da little buggahs straighten out."

Suddenly the ludicrousness of the situation hit me. "You have people all over these islands," I said. "Professionals. Why are you coming to me?"

He just stared at me.

"Or what about the cops? If you can get a police report on a homicide, surely you can call in a favor when it comes to having someone keep an eye on your nephew."

His face went tight and his eyes went as black as the bottom of the ocean on a moonless Hawaiian night. "No cops," he said.

Suddenly his pidgin was gone. Except for the lilt of his Hawaiian accent, his English was as good as mine. A lot of Hawaiians do that, change accents at will. Pidgin or quasi-pidgin for the tourists, and even heavier pidgin among themselves. But they can slip into the Queen's English whenever they're in the mood. And I do mean the Queen's English. After all, the Islanders originally learned their English from Captain Cook and other Brits who came to the islands in the late 1700s. Before they boiled Cook in a pot and ate him, over on the Big Island. Just kidding. Seriously, they just mutilated him then traded the parts around like baseball cards. And their English still has quite a hint of the Brit.

I picked up a pencil and drummed the eraser on the top of my desk. "You're going to have to fill in the blanks. I can't work blind, Mr. Chang."

Chang was silent for a long moment, studying me. Finally, he said, "Okay. This is about my nephew, Kimo Chang. My Auntie Elma runs the shelter where they took those boys from the *Dragon Venture*. Kimo likes to be a big shot, show off that he's tough. He hung around there some. I think he helped the two boys run away."

I considered that. It certainly wasn't impossible that Paké had a kindly, elderly aunt who liked to help others. The entire island of Oahu has less than 700,000 full-time residents. Asians and Hawaiians both tend to have big families, and after two centuries some extended families go through permutations that even a statistician couldn't comprehend. It's not unusual to find that an extremely honest cop comes from the same blood family as the blackest-hearted criminal—a fact that bothers the feds to no end, as they try to untangle Hawaii's criminal undergrowth.

I said, "What does that have to do with you hiring me?"

He gave me a dubious look, like I just wasn't catching on fast enough. He studied me for a long time. I had the good sense to remain silent and wait for him to decide just how much he wanted to reveal.

Finally, he said, "Kimo just turned seventeen, he thinks he's tough." He paused, looked harder at me. "He's so tough, he's going to end up like that paké kid who got whacked, if he doesn't get straightened out."

I hid the rush of grief that blindsided me as I remembered the young body in the canal. I picked up the batch of police papers and started to rifle through them.

"If you're going to work with me, you have to know what's up," Paké said. He paused, studying me as he scratched at his beard again. "I want you to understand that I have plenty of friends. I know people in the legislature, people in administration. I want this kept quiet from every one of them."

I felt an uncanny sense of disorientation. Was I being asked to join forces with the syndicate? Give me a break. But what else could he mean?

He paused and studied me again. I had the feeling he was making up his mind about something. Finally, he said, "That paké kid whose body you found?"

"Yes?"

"I want to know why Kimo helped him and his buddy leave Auntie Elma's. I want to know why they tried to get my bartender to pay them protection money, and I want to know why that one kid turns up right after, dead." A nerve jumped in his cheek, and his eyes suddenly hooded over again.

I said, "Why don't you just ask your nephew?"

He shook his head. "Kimo's stepping over the edge. I promised his mother I wouldn't let him get hurt."

"Let me get this straight. Do you want to hire me as a bodyguard for your nephew?" My mouth almost fell open at the concept.

"No." He said it flatly. Obviously the idea was as ridiculous to him as it was to me.

He shifted again, started to say something, stopped himself, and studied me through piercingly cold eyes. "You just find out what he's doing, that's all. Follow him around for a while, and report to me on where he goes, who he hangs out with. And keep your mouth shut. No matter what you see, you don't tell anybody but me. Nobody, no matter what. And you don't tell anybody you're working for me. I mean, you don't tell *anybody*, and especially not your cop friends."

I was insulted. "My services are always confidential."

"You tell them, it'll get back to me somehow. I mean, you *don't*."

"I never do." I looked him square in the eye and let him see my growing anger.

He returned my hot stare for a moment, then evidently decided I measured up, because he looked past me out the window, into the night sky, and sighed. "I wan' tell you this. Kimo, he comes to me about a month ago, says he wants me to turn him out." He stopped and squinted at me. "You know what my business is?"

"More or less. I watch TV and read the papers."

He nodded, apparently satisfied by my answer. "Kimo wants to be like me," he said. "He wants to whack out anybody who messes with him, that's what he says. He sees it all on TV, in the movies, thinks it's all a game. He don't see the scars, don't know about my bad heart or the nitro pills. He don't have to try to live with my bleeding ulcers."

I didn't say anything. The age of innocence for America's youth was long gone. It was nothing new to hear about a seventeen-year-old who wanted to grow up to be a killer. A lot of them already were.

Paké shook his head hopelessly. He said, "I try to talk to him, but he won't listen. I try to tell him he don't have any idea what kind of trouble he's getting into." He stopped, thought about it for a moment, then added, "You find out what he's up to. That's all. I'll handle the rest."

I thought about the dead boy. I even thought about my own nephew, nicknamed "Troubles" simply because he'd had so many of them throughout his life. He'd been dealing a little Mexican weed a year or so after his mother and father got divorced, when he was about sixteen. The divorce had messed him up pretty bad, and he'd started running around with a wild bunch of kids. My sister had caught him packing Mexican reefer into baggies and shipped him off to me for the rest of the summer. He'd straightened up immensely under my iron-fisted tutelage, if I didn't mind saying so myself. He'd come back here to go to college and had turned into the best friend I had. I trusted him now with my life.

Teenagers.

I guess what it added up to was that Chang had said the right words. That's the way it is sometimes. Reality shifts and you find yourself on the same side of the fence as someone you'd thought was your worst enemy.

He filled me in on a bit of background. His own younger brother, Peter, was a hardworking, honest, churchgoing man, and

Paké sounded proud of him for staying straight. Peter worked for the city and county, and he was Kimo's father. Kimo had rebelled against him a long time ago and Peter had lost control. Kimo had in fact been staying at Elma Chang's home off and on for a couple of months, moving back and forth as he pleased, which gave him even more access to the two Chinese illegals.

I said, "The other kid from the *Dragon Venture*, who is still missing. Do you have any idea what happened to him?"

"No."

"Can you find out anything?"

"I don't want to even talk about this to anyone. It's a family problem, not business. I keep my private life off the streets."

"Okay. The point is, are you hiring me to find this other missing kid too?"

He hesitated then said, "Only if it has something to do with what's happening with Kimo."

I thought about that. He'd given me the right answers. I said, "I have a reputation for being difficult, you should know that up front. I'd have to handle the investigation entirely my own way. It's not that I have an ego hang-up. It has more to do with the way I look at things. I mean, if I start trying to handle matters in someone else's way, I never get results."

His eyes slitted up and he looked at me for a moment, and I could see he wasn't used to handing over control of any situation. But finally he relaxed, and even shrugged. "No problem." He pulled out a wad of bills, probably drug or gambling money, and said, "How much collah you going to need?"

There you have it. "Collah" is another trickle-down British word, this one from collateral. Money. Cash.

"Three hundred a day plus expenses is my standard fee. A thousand dollar retainer for starters. I'll let you know how I spend it, and if I need less I'll refund the difference." I opened my desk drawer and pulled out one of my work contracts.

He gave me a contemptuous look of disbelief as I tried to hand it to him. He waved it away. "No paperwork," he said. He started peeling off hundred dollar bills. "I said I don't want a single soul to know about this." He was looking at me rigidly, the normal paranoia of the streets making his face tight and predatory and his eyes a hard glitter.

"I really do know how to keep my mouth shut."

"You better," he said, standing up in a menacing way. He didn't have to add "or else."

He handed me the wedge of money, searching my eyes, a threat in his own.

I took it, meeting his gaze, then laid it on my desk. He relaxed a bit. He gave me a number where I could reach him, told me it was his "wahine's" bar here in Waikiki, then I walked with him to the door and stood with it open as he walked down the hall to the elevator.

He touched the button.

The elevator car was still on my floor and the door opened immediately. As he stepped in, he turned to look at me. I felt suddenly uncomfortable under his hostile, slitted gaze.

The door started to slide shut, but he reached out one beefy hand and held it open. "It's the Jook Koks," he said. "You should know that much from the gate."

I tilted my ear toward him. "What?" I thought I'd misunderstood what he said.

A grim smile flitted across his face then was gone. "You're one smart wahine. You'll figure it out. I said they're Jook Koks." Suddenly he let his voice drop a few octaves, into a spooky, whispery rasp. "*Watch out for the water. They come across the sea. They come without letting even the sky know, and they're invisible like ghosts.*"

I felt the blood drain from my face.

Paké Chang was my midnight caller. As the full impact of that discovery hit me, I felt a naked panic but managed to keep from flying apart. I took a deep breath, then another one. *Control yourself, Alex. Whatever is happening here will make sense sooner or later, there's no reason to be afraid, get a grip, get through it, come on, breathe again.*

I finally said, "Did you kill him?"

He was standing there with a dark smirk on his face, still holding the elevator door open. I had the feeling he'd enjoyed my reaction to his dramatically timed revelation.

He said, "After you find out everything, maybe I'll let you talk to your cop friends. Maybe you can even tell it all to your friends in the DEA."

"What on earth does that mean?" I stepped out the door and turned toward him. I wanted to straighten out the rest of this puzzle. "Tell what to the DEA? And why did you set me up to find the dead kid?"

"You're one smart wahine. You'll see."

"*Did* you kill him, Paké?" I was moving closer to him. Anger began to set in and I felt my body stiffen.

"No. But I gon' whack out anyone who messes with Kimo."

"Wait a minute. I can't take this job. I need to know—"

But a broad grin swept his face and he let the door slide shut just before I could reach him. He was gone.

I felt my anger drain away; it was replaced by a gripping sense of curiosity and a sinking embarrassment at being manipulated. I fought an impulse to run down the stairwell after Paké and confront him in the lobby. But I knew it would be no use. If he'd wanted to tell me more, he would have. Maybe in due time he still would.

Maybe he'd phone some midnight and let his voice drop a few octaves and take on a tone of menace, and tell me where I could find the next dead body. Maybe he would again leave me wondering if he was the one who had killed the person, or if he'd just wanted to keep me current on all the death in the world.

I allowed myself a cynical grin and stepped back into my office. Don't tell me that God doesn't have a sense of humor. For a minute, I'd actually thought that Paké Chang was an unusual answer to my prayers, sent to solve my problems. Instead, he'd brought me a thousand more.

7

Oahu's Waianae coast is largely overlooked by the flood of tourists which inundates the rest of the island, though various Japanese developers have discovered the land. They've begun the process of turning the dusty, rugged coastline into wall-to-wall golf courses, Japanese style, which means "no locals allowed."

The Hawaiians and other ethnic groups who live there—working-class people, mostly—are protesting, of course. Frankly, things don't look too good for them.

But now—still—the H-1 freeway cuts through country all the way from Pearl City. The freeway meshes with Farrington Highway just before you reach the actual coastline, and you're in the country "foah real," as they say here. The thinner traffic becomes disproportionate with semis and dinged-up pickups and brightly painted VW bugs and customized vans and other metal manifestations of excessive testosterone. Most of these are driven by muscle-flexing local boys, a "boy" here being anybody male.

I'd pulled on a short black wig, changed into Levis and a khaki shirt, then stepped back into my tennis shoes. I'd inherited David's fishing vehicle: a clanky brown Chevy van I'd kept for sentimental reasons. When I got my P.I. license about six months after his death, I turned the van into a private-eye-mobile with an air mattress in the back for comfort, tinted one-way glass in the rear, and even a cellular phone in case I needed to phone out for a pizza.

I followed the coastline past Nanakuli, then through the small town of Waianae and toward the smaller town of Makaha, where Paké Chang's brother, Peter, lived. The word *makaha* means "fierce." The name describes the coastline, but some say the area is really named for an ancient tribe of cannibals who once lived here, preying on all who dared to invade their land. That bit of information comes from anthropologists by the way, so accept it judiciously.

Now, the scattered neighborhood that comprises most of Makaha is run-down, subtropical suburbia. Most of the houses are twenty or more years old, some are comfortable, some are shacks. The roads are clean, the sturdier houses are built up on cinder blocks so the winter storms won't drive the ocean into the living rooms. You can hear roosters crowing all day long—fighting cocks, mostly. But the area is hardly fierce any more.

Nor was Peter Chang fierce, at least not according to his fierce brother, Paké. Peter worked for the city and county doing road work. He wanted nothing to do with crime, little or nothing to do with his crime-hatching brother. But the son, Kimo, had other ideas. He'd watched his father work all his life and end up with nothing but a dilapidated house, five kids, a wife who hated being poor, and a mortgage that might be paid off right about the time he dropped over dead. I'd phoned Paké that morning at the number he'd given me. When he'd phoned back, he refused to even talk about the Jook Koks. When I said I couldn't do the job after all, he'd said in no uncertain terms that I'd taken his money and a deal was a deal.

I'd decided to at least take a shot at it and see where it went. I'd asked Paké a few questions about the Peter Chang family. I'd learned that Kimo had vowed that he wasn't going to end up like his father, so he'd adopted his uncle Paké as a role model instead.

Paké had refused to introduce the kid into his lifestyle, so Kimo had decided to do things his own way. Now, I was here to find out what way that was.

When I was almost through Makaha, headed toward the lava rock and scrub brush of Kaena Point—land's end, the place where the ancient Hawaiians' souls had allegedly departed from the earth—I spotted the street sign I'd been looking for and turned inland.

I did a drive-by of Kimo Chang's house. It was old and wooden, with a sagging front porch, definitely not one of the nicer dwellings. But there was a fresh green Christmas tree on the front porch, leaning up against the wall, ready to be taken inside and decorated. Someone was taking the time and trouble to care for the yard, and it looked clean. Paké had told me that Kimo owned a souped-up red Pontiac Firebird. One sat in the driveway, so the boy was probably home. I drove back to the two-lane highway, spotted a small swath of beach park, and pulled in beside a weathered gray cinder block building housing a public bathroom.

The sea was pale aquamarine here, falling away to turquoise, then deep sapphire. Pounders crashed into the jagged lava at the water's edge, no more than twenty feet from me, leaving a fresh, creamy froth on the sharp black rocks. The spray hit the side of my van from time to time. I rolled down the window on that side, to let in the cool salt air, then rolled down my own window and kicked back to wait.

The first half hour was relaxing, but after that I started getting restless. I turned on my radio, listened to Christmas music till I got tired of it, then I found a station playing Hawaiian cha-lang-a-lang, then tuned it out again. The Hawaiian language is pure poetry even if you don't understand a word that's being said. The Islands themselves are distilled beauty. But the tourist-targeted Hawaiian music doesn't do much for me. Ancient Hawaiian *mele*, or chants, are something else again. They conjure up the ghosts of the ancients, stir the blood and deepen the sky, open you up to eternity, even though their version of it might not be an exact match with mine. But I wasn't going to find any authentic Hawaiian chants on the radio, and besides, even better than that we have two excellent stations here, KAIN and K-LIGHT, which play mostly Christian music.

I listened to KAIN for a while. Then a talk program came on about marital problems and they lost me. This does not apply. I tuned out and finally found some decent jazz.

I'd arrived at three o'clock. At six, the sun just dissolving the darkness from the sea, the Firebird squealed rubber as it took the corner of the street, speeding onto Farrington Highway. I shook myself out of a torpor, hit the ignition then followed, careful to give Kimo Chang plenty of space.

It was easy to tail him. The highway is four-lane with a lot of stoplights as you go through the several small towns. There are very few major cutoffs till you hit the freeway. But when we hit the Waipahu exit, Kimo surprised me by slamming on his brakes and making a sharp right turn into the off-ramp. I was far enough behind him to manage to make the turn without squealing brakes, but just barely.

I followed him through the run-down section of the old town. The abandoned sugar mill sat slightly above the town. The heavy smoke from its towering smokestack had once melted into low, leaden evening clouds, but it had been closed down last year. A couple of rickety trucks passed me then turned left, cutting off my line of vision to the Firebird. By the time they were gone, I'd lost him.

But just as I passed a Quik-Chicken outlet (I'd eaten there once and learned what they did with the fighting cocks that got killed in the ring), I spotted him again, turning left.

I followed him into a residential district then stopped at the corner, well out of the streetlight, while he pulled up in front of a salmon-pink house with white filigreed wooden trim and a Spanish-style iron fence and gate. It looked like a homemade wedding cake that someone had dropped. But the pale green and lavender tree ferns and the deep green mango trees, illuminated by the streetlights, served to soften the effect, and there were Christmas lights in the window. Still, with or without a tree, I could visualize the inside: dark, carved, Spanish-style furniture, gilt-edged mirrors, clutter, bric-a-brac, plaster statues of the saints, and at least one large, gilded crucifix of Jesus, his face set in agony, the blood from the nails looking all too real. It was full-on dark now, and there were lights in a couple of windows, in addition to the Christmas decorations.

Kimo Chang honked his horn. One of the houselights blinked out, and a wiry Filipino-Chinese kid wearing a faded red tank-top and the long baggy shorts they call "Jams" slammed out of the house. He had a black baseball cap on his head with the bill turned backwards, and he was carrying a backpack that he tossed into the car. He jumped in behind it. Kimo revved up the engine, turned the tape deck up to ghetto-blaster range, then made a squealing U-turn and drove straight past me—his attention on his grinning passenger (thank You, Lord)—and sped back to the highway.

Once we hit the freeway, it was again easy going. I followed him all the way past the glittering lights of downtown Honolulu then southeast, till he took the Sixth Avenue exit into the Kaimuki area. In Hawaiian mythology, a kaimuki was the oven where the Hawaiian leprechauns—*menehunes*—toasted their ti leaves. Today, it's Honolulu's version of 1950s small-town America. Some of the storefronts might have been lifted from the set of "Happy Days," while others are low-slung, one-story relics from the plantation days. Kimo parked in front of one of the latter, a long building with a slatted wooden front and peeling green paint. There were three businesses in the building: a small grocery store with a lighted fly-specked window; a used clothing store next to that, the sign falling down, the windows painted over, a rusted padlock and chain on the front door; and beyond that, Hawaii's answer to the diner, a saimin shop, with a blinking orange neon light in the window that flashed SAIMIN-RAMEN, over and over again. The door to the saimin shop was open, and I could see two older Japanese men sitting at a counter, shoveling noodles into their mouths with chopsticks.

Kimo Chang and his friend talked earnestly as they climbed from the Firebird and strutted toward the small grocery. They pushed through the door and went inside.

I'd parked so I could see at a slant through the grimy windows. My low angle made it hard to see much, but I could detect rows of filmy-looking glass apothecary jars in the window holding what was probably crackseed: pickled mango, dried plum and lemon peel, seeds, nuts, and other Asian-Hawaiian snacks. A soft drink sign also blocked my view, and then there was a disintegrating cereal poster.

I was craning my neck, trying to see around all this, when Kimo Chang loomed into the window, opened a crackseed jar, and took a handful of something out of it. He stepped back out of my line of vision, and then a man's body came into view and the old-fashioned roll-up shade was yanked down to obscure whatever small view I'd had. A second later, the shade also came down over the oblong glass in the front door, leaving just the faintest hint of light leaking through.

Had they spotted me? Nah, not likely. Not because I'm such a good sleuth—though I am that—but because I would have seen at least some small reaction from Kimo, and I hadn't seen a thing. I waited a few more minutes, curious about what they were doing that required pulled shades.

And I waited.

It was almost eight-thirty when the shade suddenly flapped up, and seconds later the two boys swaggered out the door. The backpack had been fat when they'd gone in. Now it was deflated. They'd made a delivery of some kind.

Kimo peeled away from the curb, tires squealing, and I waited a moment then turned on my headlights, ground gears, and followed him. I wasn't worried at all now about being spotted. If they were going to, they'd have already spotted me, but neither of them had so much as glanced my way. In fact, being an adult is one way of being invisible to teenagers. Most adults are nonpersons to them: someone who couldn't possibly make any difference unless or until they're right in the way.

Down Kapahulu we went, then we turned right at the library and rolled down Ala Wai Boulevard, right along the canal and past the spot where I'd found the body of Dru Chun Yuen. The canal water was dark velvet now, fringed by black felt cutouts of coco palms. Pink-amber and ice-blue lights glittered in the high-rises beyond the golf course, their reflections spangling the water beside me. I wanted to go home now, take a long bath, eat a light dinner on my lanai so I could drink in this splendid night. But Kimo found a parking place beside the canal and eased into it. The traffic pressed me on past them.

I thought again about calling it a day. I was only a few blocks from home. But curiosity overcame the need for comfort and I drove around the block, came back by, spotted them heading makai—seaward—on Royal Hawaiian Avenue, toward the hotels and discos and carnival glitz of Kuhio and Kalakau Avenues. I was going to lose them.

I spotted a commercial parking lot and wheeled in. Three bucks an hour, but so what, it was Paké Chang's money. I parked the van, doubled back to where I'd last seen Kimo and friend, but they were long gone.

Waikiki's main strip was bustling with wall-to-wall tourists and hustlers, though it was after nine by then. Chances that I'd track the boys down were slender to nonexistent, but I decided to take a shot at it anyway. I walked past the movie theaters on Seaside, crossed Kalakaua, then walked past the Royal Hawaiian Shopping Plaza with its one-story Christmas tree made entirely from stacked pots of red poinsettias. A loudspeaker was playing "God Rest Ye Merry, Gentlemen," while on the lower level beside the fountain a hula show was in full force, complete with competitive ukulele. I felt a sudden rush of cultural dissonance.

I doubled back and walked through the mall. No need, now, to worry about them spotting me. The crowds were far too thick.

After about twenty-five minutes of aimless wandering, scanning the crowds for the two boys, I ducked into a sushi bar and bought some take-out. Then, grinding out on a thick California roll I'd purloined from the package, I started back toward my van, ready to head home.

I'd just started to turn mauka—mountainward—on Lewers Street when I heard a commotion behind me, heard someone shout an obscenity, and then someone cried, "Watch out!"

I wheeled around to look at the disturbance, just as a man yelled, "Fight! Fight!" and someone else yelled, "Call the cops!"

I threaded my way through the crowd that had already knotted itself around whatever was happening. Soon I could see that a slender Chinese kid about eighteen years old was struggling with a sunburned haole kid about the same age. From his dress and stance, I assumed he was one of the many Hawaiian-born Chinese who make up a large percentage of Hawaii's population. The haole kid had the surly look of a professional troublemaker. This time he'd apparently found all the trouble he could handle, because blood was streaming from gashes on his cheeks and lip and the Chinese kid was coming at him again.

"Knife!" The word cut through the night.

As a single body, the crowd surged back from the fight.

I could see the knife now. The haole kid held it, an eight-inch blade aimed at the gut of the Chinese kid, who either hadn't seen it or was too enraged to care, because he was still coming.

A split instant before the knife would have gutted the Chinese kid, a ball of fury I recognized as Kimo Chang dived out from the crowd and tackled the haole kid from behind, sending him crashing forward and through the huge front window of a camera shop. A guillotine of plate glass crashed around the kid, shattering on the pavement, shards and splinters flying everywhere. The kid reeled to one side and managed to catch himself on the metal window frame, but a shard of glass protruding from the frame ripped his hand and he cried out and fell forward to his knees, holding his wounded hand while blood gushed out.

That should have been enough. But Kimo Chang shot forward again and grabbed him, and I thought for a naive instant that he was going to help the kid to his feet. Instead he grabbed the kid by one arm, and made a fist as if to hit him again. The kid's scream was horrible. A gleeful, malevolent look was fixed in Kimo Chang's eyes.

The weight of the crowd had me blocked, but I managed to shove aside a bulky man who'd been in my way—nobody else doing anything, of course, except the few who were cheering them on. I hit the front row and hesitated, planning my best line of attack—blood all over the place now, both Kimo and friend still ready to fight, and I was just starting to step in and do something— maybe just get myself hurt, but at least do something—when the scream of a siren cut through the air and Kimo stopped in mid-motion. He cocked his head to one side and shook it slightly, as if bringing himself back to reality. He stood poised like that for just a split instant, and then he lunged through the crowd at the far side of the bloody arena, his buddy right behind him, the crowd milling more thickly now, agitated by the sirens, closing behind them. Two blue-and-whites screeched to a stop and the crowd surged forward again to surround them.

I looked around for the Chinese kid who'd been in the first part of the fray, but he was long gone. The only one left was the haole kid, who lay moaning in a mixture of broken glass and blood. A uniformed cop was already leaning over him. Ambulance sirens were screaming in from somewhere.

One cop went pale when he saw the kid. He asked no one in particular, "What happened?"

I was considering stepping in and naming some names when a tourist stepped forward and opened her eyes wide for the cop. "The Chinese guy hit him first," she said, pointing to the bloody kid. "The guy was yelling at him in Chinese, this one pulled a knife and went at him, and a couple of other kids jumped in."

The cop had whipped out his notebook and was furiously writing this all down. The ambulance screeched up and two attendants jumped out, turned white when they saw all the carnage, then started unloading their gurney while the driver, acting as a third attendant, went to work trying to help the kid.

I stepped backward, melting into the crowd. I wanted to absorb what I'd just seen and heard.

As I said, Paké Chang's syndicate has a strong grip on the drug action in Waikiki. If you deal, you pay your dues, and they especially dislike the outsiders who show up, thinking it's all up for grabs.

But Paké had told me that Kimo was in no way part of his organization. So why was Kimo enforcing syndicate territory? Was he just doing his uncle a favor? If so, I was pretty sure that Paké wasn't going to appreciate it, considering how it had turned out.

A dark thought spread through my mind. The boys had made a delivery up in Kaimuki. Had Paké lied to me? Were Kimo and friend transporting kilos of syndicate drugs to dealers all over the island, while I was following them around? That made no sense. If they were delivering Paké's merchandise, why would Paké want me to follow them and see what was going on? Was he worried they were ripping him off, since they'd tried to extort his bartender? And why would he even suggest that I might someday report it to the feds? Was he being sarcastic when he said that?

No, if they were moving drugs, it was far more likely they were violating Paké's territory. The thought made me shiver. If Kimo Chang was in serious competition with the syndicate for drug territory, he was looking at an open grave, uncle or no uncle. There were other people involved in the traffic, and they would be unlikely to cut Kimo any slack.

It was puzzling, and I played with a few more versions of the scenario before I decided I needed more information in order to crack the equation. But whichever way it went, there was a lot more going on here than Paké Chang had led me to believe. Because Kimo Chang was more than a mere errant youth. I'd seen that much already.

The kid was a full-blown sociopath, capable of creating man-sized mayhem. And he was going to kill someone someday, if he hadn't already. Furthermore, the more I thought about what I had just seen, the more certain I became that he was at cross-purposes with the syndicate, including his uncle. And by taking Paké's money, I had become the syndicate's eyes and ears, and I was watching him.

I had taken this job thinking I might intervene in the life of some poor, messed-up kid in time to make a difference. Now, it seemed I had stepped in over my head. As I walked back down Lewers toward my car, I felt like I was unraveling. I needed to seriously reconsider what I was doing. Because from where I stood, if something came down—and it was bound to—I was just as likely as not to end up square in the middle of the debris.

CHAPTER

8

I 'd been gone since early morning. When I got home that night, the green light was blinking on my answering machine. I stepped through the doorway and into my office, and hit the playback button as I tossed my bag onto a chair.

The first message was electronically logged in at ten that morning. Jess Seitaki. I'd been phoning to ask him about what was happening with the investigation into the death of the Yuen kid, but I couldn't catch him in. Now, he was sorry he'd missed me and would try again.

The second call, logged at 2 P.M., was a bit more interesting.

"This message is for Alexis Albright," a female voice said. It was very, very British, very cultivated. At the same time, it had the tinkling quality of wind chimes set in motion by a faint wind.

"My name is Mi-Lin Ming," the voice said.

Which meant the accent was British as filtered through the Crown Colony of Hong Kong.

"I wish to apologize for any inconvenience Henry and I may

have caused you," she said. There was a deep and humbling contrition in the voice. "We would still like very much to meet you, but something has come up for Thursday. We'd like to offer our hospitality at dinner tomorrow night. Please let us know if you can come." She gave me their phone number again, then hung up.

The call surprised me. After seeing Henry Li's photograph and deciding I didn't like his looks, I'd stopped trying to call him. Now, I again reconsidered my position.

I was still broke, unless I kept the money that Paké Chang had given me, which I couldn't do now. In fact, I was thinking in a dozen directions at once about how to get out of my commitment to him. Now here was an entirely pleasant person going an extra mile to try to give me a job that promised to be a good deal safer and saner and probably more lucrative than Paké's lunatic task.

I checked my watch. It was after eleven. I'd have to wait till morning to call her back, but suddenly the job with Henry Li looked very good indeed.

自由

I phoned Mi-Lin at nine o'clock the next morning and was again impressed with her charm. Her concern that they might have offended me made me totally revise my earlier opinion of Henry Li's operation. I accepted an invitation to dinner at seven-thirty that evening.

"Henry has to be at a meeting till after six," she explained. "And he wants very much to meet and personally brief you before you start work for us."

Well. That sounded a little better than being "checked out." Maybe I was back in business again.

I phoned Abe and asked him what was up. He said he'd explained to them that I'd been on my regular morning jog when I'd found the body, that I wasn't in the least involved in anything long-term or sinister, that the press interest in me had been temporary. He'd put in another good word for me and Li seemed to have gotten over his concerns about my abilities. I managed to hide the surprise I felt and thanked him.

That left me with two clients. Not unusual. On a good week I'll juggle several things at once and relish the challenge. But I still wasn't ready to juggle Paké or Kimo Chang's problems, especially when I was in the middle of what looked like a family-syndicate feud. As I dressed and ate a light breakfast, I kept thinking about Kimo and Paké, about the Chinese boy's body in the Ala Wai, about the brutality of Kimo's actions during the fight last night. The more I thought about the situation, the worse it seemed.

For lunch, I drove to Down to Earth and ordered a veggie burrito. I took it home, kicked off my shoes, then poured a cold frothy glass of lemonade, gave my beautiful, unlit Christmas tree an accusing glare as it reminded me of all the family camaraderie I was missing, and curled up my nose at my two measly gifts, still wrapped beneath the tree. I took my lunch out onto my lanai and sat facing the ocean.

I was depressed. Part of it came from being alone during the Christmas season. But it was more than that, it was a general and growing sense of discontent with my work—or rather, with what I was earning. I'd made many conscious decisions to forgo higher income in order to do what I wanted with my life, from the time I'd joined the DEA until now. But I was getting tired of the world's problems, and I was getting tired of being broke.

Usually, being a private investigator isn't all that bad. It allows me unbelievable personal freedom, unlimited adventure, and access to parts of life you'd never believe. After all, how else could you work for the syndicate and have them paying *you* dues? But I was definitely going to bail out, even at that. Just as soon as an opportunity presented itself. Because what had just happened with Paké made me realize that I was letting my financial problems get in the way of my good judgment.

I thought it over and decided that I'd become a slave to my business. There was never enough money coming in to buy me free time, and when I did get my hands on a few spare dollars, I always managed to run into someone who desperately needed help, and who needed the help pro bono. My charitable work was financed by any overlap from paid work, and that about summed up my money situation.

I didn't know how to say no. Especially when the person was really in trouble, and it seemed like most people I knew were these days. I didn't understand how people could indulge themselves in luxury while others were going without food. I didn't know how to build up a hard enough veneer to be able to put something back for a rainy day when a friend from church was about to be evicted from her apartment or her kids needed dental work, and I had money in the bank.

I wanted to go home for Christmas, like normal people did. I wanted to travel, do something exotic. A sense of restlessness wrapped me up and stirred me like a black, hungry wind, and I got up from my balcony chair, stood at the railing, and stared off at the bright blue sea.

Watch out for the water. What a piece of nonsense. What had Chang meant, when he said they came across the sea and even the sky doesn't see them? What utter drivel. Why was I associating with such people as Paké Chang, anyway? My mother asked me that all the time, and she was right. Maybe there was another life for me out there somewhere. Maybe I didn't need to hang out with all the predatory losers in the world. Maybe I should even become a bit more predatory myself when it came to my own welfare.

I went back inside, washed my plate and glass, then went into my bedroom. The discontent stayed with me. My Bible was on my bedside table and I considered reading a few verses, but at that moment it seemed like a tedious obligation. I'd missed church several times lately. It had gradually been turning into a responsibility instead of a joy. I had too much responsibility. I kept my nose too much to the grindstone solving everyone else's problems. What a lousy way to live.

I lay down on my bed and stared up at my cream-colored ceiling. Condo fees were going up after the first of the year. My car needed transmission work. My phone bill was going to be horrendous because of all Troubles's long-distance calls before I'd finally put him on a plane and sent him home. Furthermore, I'd paid for his ticket rather than admit to my sister that I was almost broke. And even though Henry Li's job would bring me a nice retainer, it wasn't going to carry me very far.

I needed a major change in my life.

I lay there in a sulk, feeling enslaved by my responsibilities and put upon by fate, until I finally fell asleep. When I woke up, it was still only 3 P.M.

I called home, talked to my family a bit, then hung up the phone, wondering what I'd accomplished. I felt worse than I had before. I remembered then that Jess had tried to return my call. I dialed the number for the Hawaii State Police headquarters. When the desk sergeant answered, I asked her to put me through to Jess's private office.

Jess was in a good mood. "Alex! What can I do for you?"

"I need some advice," I said. "We probably need to talk privately." I was aware that every word I said was being recorded. They'd put in recorders after the department was sued for not responding on time to a call that hadn't even been made.

"Meet me at the church in half an hour," he said.

"Done." I signed off.

I knew which church he meant. It was a bluestone relic from missionary days that rested in wide, parklike grounds not far from HSP headquarters. I rolled into the parking lot just twenty minutes after my phone call to Jess.

The church was quiet inside, cool, and private indeed. It smelled like centuries of furniture polish and elbow grease. The stained-glass windows were canted open, and birds were singing in the large banyan tree just outside. Jess showed up several minutes after I arrived, and we sat on a polished wooden pew where we could both see the double-wide doors.

"So how are things with you?" I asked.

Seitaki's eyebrows bent like hawk's wings, and his sculptured jaw set. "Busy."

I nodded. "'Tis the season," I said.

He smiled, then eyed me speculatively. "You want to know about the Yuen kid, don't you?"

"I'm still curious, yes."

"The coroner's final report came in," Jess said. "The best guess is that the kid died from an overdose of heroin, but he also had serious and possibly lethal cranial contusions. Actually, the pathologist is still having some trouble precisely establishing the cause of death."

"Meaning?"

"The kid had been beaten about the head with a blunt object. The blows were hard enough to be the cause of death. But the pathologist is still pretty sure the kid died from overdose, though just barely. In other words, if the drugs hadn't done it, the beating would have. It was that close."

"You're saying that whoever beat him was doing it while he was already dying of a drug overdose?" I cringed at the brutality.

Jess nodded. "That shouldn't be any surprise. If they'll kill you by pumping drugs into your system, they won't think twice about killing you any other way."

"Man. You're going to have your hands full trying *this* case— assuming you ever bust the perp."

"True. And the feds are interested too, which further complicates things."

I felt a little zip of anxiety. "Immigration?"

"Them, yes. But also your people."

"*My* people?"

"DEA. But—"

"Wait a minute. What does federal drug enforcement have to do with this?"

"They're not talking, just asking questions. Which I can't answer, either for them or for you. So . . . what's this about needing advice?"

I braced myself. "I may be in trouble, Jess."

He shot me a curious look. "That's the first time I've ever heard you admit it."

"Probably the last too," I said. "Look, just tell me this. What kind of person is Paké Chang?"

He eyed me speculatively, then said, "Tell me what you've done now."

I chewed on the inside of my cheek. I'd promised Paké not to say a word to anybody. But if I was no longer officially working for him—at least in my own mind—then my commitments to him were officially broken. I knew that was morally ambivalent, but I was willing to cut corners in order to get this off my chest.

I told Jess about Paké Chang coming to my office, and about my agreement with him. I told him about following the boys up to the small grocery in Kaimuki where they'd made some kind of delivery, and about the fight in Waikiki and my regrets that I'd gotten involved. When I'd finished talking, Jess's forehead was creased with worry lines.

He said, "Alex, Alex. I can't believe it. Why are you wasting your God-given talents working for that lowlife?"

I shrugged. "At the time it seemed like the thing to do."

"He gave you money?"

"My standard retainer."

He looked unhappy. "The only time Paké Chang hands over money is if he's planning to use somebody hard. Get out of it, Alex. It's a no-win situation."

"That's exactly what I intend to do. But I have all the enemies I need. I want to bow out gracefully. I can't very well do that unless I know enough of what's going on so I don't bungle things up."

Seitaki had a slightly sour look on his face now. "That sounds like a rationalization if I ever heard one."

"No, seriously, Jess. Think about it. I know he wants me to follow and report on his nephew. That's no problem. But there's something a lot bigger going on. His goal is something beyond Kimo's problems."

"What?"

"I don't know, but I can sense it. Other than that, I'm flying blind. If I understood what he really wanted accomplished, I'd know where to go to work convincing him that I'm not the person he needs for this job."

"So what do you want *me* to do?"

"I don't know. I guess I just want you to know what's going on, in case something happens. I don't mean to impose on our friendship, but I'm really worried."

"You should be. This could get heavy."

"Yes. Look, I really will ease out of it as fast as I can without leaving too many hard feelings."

"Good girl." He patted my shoulder, making me feel like a kid. Only Seitaki could get away with that kind of gesture. He stood and smiled. "In the meantime, let me provide you with some comic relief. The store in Kaimuki where Kimo Chang made his delivery? There's more going on than meets the eye, Alex. You really ought to check it out."

That totally threw me off base. "Why?"

His smile grew wider, but when I tried to get him to explain, he would only say, "Go see for yourself."

He walked me to my car and said good-bye, then climbed into his sedan. I let him drive away first. Then, as soon as he was out of sight I hung a left and drove past Queen's Hospital, then took the freeway on-ramp and drove straight toward the little grocery store in Kaimuki where I'd seen Kimo Chang and his sidekick make their delivery.

9

B ack in Kaimuki, I parked in front of the small grocery store and went in.

A tiny bell tinkled as I opened the door, but there was nobody behind the counter and nobody appeared. A musty smell filled the old store, with an underscent of rotted produce. I stood near the entrance and checked out the room.

An old glass-and-chrome flower cooler covered the entire left wall. The sliding glass doors opened onto pegs hung with leis: golden, white, and pink plumeria, yellow-white pikake, white tuberoses, pink and white carnations, all reflected in a mirror that made up the back wall. The knee-high base of the cooler had a motor thrumming inside and held large, fiery bursts of torch ginger and orange-red anthuriums. A couple of wilting blue hydrangea plants and a pot of pink daisies completed the palette. The cooler itself was immense and could have held ten times as many plants. The wide expanse of the mirrored back reflected the entirety of the small store.

The shelves were stocked, but most of the cans and bottles had dust on them, and the lettuce in the cooler looked seriously wilted even from where I stood. I was about to walk into the storeroom to see if anyone was there, when I heard a toilet flush from that direction, heard a door open, and then astonishment stopped me short.

The man who walked into the room was tall, bulky, his face poutishly handsome. I exclaimed, "Benny Frietas!"

He was also surprised. "What are you doing here?"

Last I'd heard, Frietas had been working theft and burglary for the state police. He'd worked with David a long time ago, when they were still in uniform. David had almost punched him out once because of some suggestive thing he'd said about me, and I'd strongly shared David's opinion of him. He had a beautiful wife and three delightful children, but he fooled around on her end-lessly—or at least, he had back then. That's a real sore point with me. I figure if you're disloyal to your spouse, nobody can trust you. Period.

One thing about Frietas, though. His motto was, one chance to a customer. Once you rejected his advances, a sort of sour grapes reaction kicked in. So far as I knew, my chance had long since come and gone. With luck I was already off the list of potential conquests. I hoped.

"Seriously, what are *you* doing here?" I asked, masking my thoughts. "Did you quit the state police?"

He grinned. "I'm working a hukilau."

"No kidding."

A hukilau is a seine net, used for fishing. Hence the use of the name for some of the police's sting operations. Suddenly the deflated backpack on Kimo Chang's arm made sense.

I said, "You mean I came in to buy some breath mints and walked right into a police sting?"

His grin turned wolfish, and he jerked his thumb in the direction of the flower cooler. "Mirrors everywhere," he bragged. "Lets us see everything that goes down in here. We got video cameras set up too. Everything goes on film."

THE JADE CRUCIBLE 101

"You mean we're being filmed right now?" I pasted a worried look on my face and felt ashamed of myself for catering to this jerk.

"Don't worry about it. We only keep the tapes of the actual buys. Come on, I'll show you around."

He pulled down the shades, stuck out the CLOSED FOR LUNCH sign, then turned a key in the lock and led me through a door behind the counter, into the one-time used clothing store next door. Now I could see why the windows had been painted over. Heavy paper had also been glued to the insides of the glass so that not so much as a glint of light would leak onto the streets at night.

I had to admit it was a good setup. Inside the room, there were a couple of overstuffed armchairs purloined from someone's attic, and a stack of tattered magazines. Two coffee-can lids overflowed with cigarette butts.

"It's incredible," I said.

It really was. Through a line of video camera monitors I could see the entire store from several different angles. There was audio monitoring equipment too, just in case the video missed something. At the back of this room were shelves with stacks and stacks of cardboard boxes, all of them dated with black magic marker, most of the contents inside little plastic evidence bags with tags attached. But some of the recent buys hadn't yet been tagged. I stepped over and looked at a small box of loose jewelry.

"Okay to touch this?" I asked.

"Sure, it's already been printed," Frietas said. He was enjoying my astonishment.

The top item was a gold and ruby ring, the setting carved like a dragon, with a dated paper tag attached by string, which said, "Purchased from Kimo Chang, 4-25, 8:30 P.M. by B. Frietas."

I swallowed hard, kept my face straight, then picked up the ring. "This is really beautiful. Where did you get it?"

Frietas chuckled. "Couple of local kids brought it in yesterday." He opened the top of a small box and pulled out a large plastic bag filled with smaller bags. "Here's some other stuff."

The bag held a breathtaking blue pearl necklace with a matching diamond-and-pearl ring. He tossed that aside and pulled out several ivory bracelets, intricately carved with fruit and foliage. I'd priced them at the jewelry store. About two grand apiece. Frietas tossed them aside as if they were whalebone.

He dipped into the box again, said, "Check this out," and handed me a small emerald-colored Buddha with rust-colored streaks. I could tell from its translucence that it was excellent jade. He took it back from me and dropped it back into the box as if it were made from cheap plastic.

I said, "Where'd the kids get this stuff?"

He shrugged. "Not from the International Marketplace."

The International Marketplace is a large, famous open-air shopping mall in Waikiki where you can buy every tourist bauble and gimcrack imaginable, most of it imported from Taiwan and other ports East and almost none of it valuable. To the unpracticed eye, though, certain of those objects can resemble the priceless oriental artifacts found in more discerning shops, but this was obviously grade-A stuff.

Frietas was an expert at pricing the goods he purchased. Only a handful of cops were.

I said, "What's it worth?"

"You and I could both retire if we had the nerve." He got a faraway, speculative look on his face, then refocused and abruptly gave me another wolfish grin. "Nah, I guess not. With my luck, I'd get caught."

Frietas pulled out another item, this one an apple jade snuff bottle. I took it from him before he could drop it back then peered over his shoulder, reached in, and helped myself to a black jade carving of a strange little beast: it was part unicorn, part deer, part dragon, and it was pure jadeite, the most valuable form of jade. It had the silken-rough texture and vitreous luster that only the highest quality of jade possesses.

I was looking at item after item carved from jadeite by master artists.

Stolen jade.

Stolen from Mr. Henry Li, collector and broker of rare jade artifacts, unless I was sorely missing my guess. Stolen by Kimo Chang and friend! I didn't know whether to be perplexed or elated.

"What will you do with all this stuff?" I asked Frietas.

"After it's cataloged and the reports are filed, it'll go to the police evidence room till the kids are busted and tried. That'll happen in about a week. We're about to wind this particular sting operation down."

"And then what happens to it?"

"If nobody claims it, I guess it'll be sold at auction." He leaned in close and winked. "Why? You want something?"

"Maybe. Is it for sale?"

"Only to the right person. We already have more than enough to put the thieves away."

"Sounds interesting. What kind of prices?"

"Negotiable," he said. Was he leering at me?

I forced myself to smile. "Look, I have somebody waiting. But I'll stop back by soon."

I turned, made a beeline for the front door, opened it, and let myself out into fresh air.

There was a 7-Eleven store not far from the grocery. I pulled into the parking lot, dropped a coin in the pay phone, then again dialed Jess Seitaki's number. I felt brilliant, ecstatic. Talk about solving a case fast, I hadn't even been officially hired yet.

I wanted to share the latest with Jess and see what he said.

Jess was out. I left a message: Thanks millions. Then I drove home, humming all the way, and started getting ready for my dinner engagement.

CHAPTER 10

A full hula moon was wrinkling silver breakers into the black sea. The water skirted the winding driveway, where royal palms and monkeypod trees were interspersed with eucalyptus and jacaranda, all of it woven into a thick, dark jungle by jade vines and tree ferns. Gaslit metal torches on both sides pressed back the black foliage. I turned a corner, and the light-blazed white house loomed up. A man-made lagoon graced the front; recessed lighting showed white lotus blossoms floating on the water. Maybe Henry Li really *could* afford to eat two million dollars worth of jade.

Not that he'd have to. Not with Alexis Albright, supersleuth on the job.

I already had it figured out. I was going to give it a day or two while I filled in the gaps, then I'd drop the solution square in Henry Li's lap.

He would be amazed.

The world would cheer.

I had never felt more smug. That is, that's the feeling I had till I pressed the door chimes and the door was opened by the woman with the lilting voice. Then I felt suddenly ugly and dowdy and completely outclassed—and totally stunned.

She was regal and completely self-possessed, like an ancient Chinese empress. And she was easily the most beautiful woman I had ever seen, even in movies, even in photographs.

She appraised me coolly, then held out a hand with effortless elegance. I took it and managed a decent handshake.

"I've been waiting for you. I'm Mi-Lin," she said, withdrawing her hand. "Please come in."

She gestured for me to precede her into the hallway. It was paneled in dark wood, so heavily polished that I could almost see my reflection as I walked by. A jade Buddha on a teakwood table sat at the far end, with a small jade jar of joss sticks beside it, and a filigreed gold match box. Those who entered the house could light a joss stick and place it in the small vessel at the Buddha's feet, then offer up a small prayer for luck, if they wished. On each side of the table that held the Buddha were sleek, four-foot-tall brass deer: the symbols of longevity. The recessed lighting gave them all a burnished quality.

"Henry is on the phone to Hong Kong," she said. She gave me a warm smile, and tilted her head in a charming manner, as if she knew the impression she had on people and had long since learned to woo them out of their stunned silence. Her profile was exquisite. She said, "Dinner won't be served till he's done. In the meantime, he's asked me to make you comfortable."

She led me into a huge, dimly lit room straight out of 1930s Shanghai. It felt opulent. Decadent. There were teakwood chests with red and gold inlay, heavy teakwood furniture upholstered in deep, rich green, and carefully arranged tables and shelves everywhere that displayed special pieces: brass pots and carvings, gold Buddhas, temple statues, and other Chinese treasures. There was even a light scent of jasmine incense in the air. A perfect setting for a dragon lady. Here, in this foreign setting, there was not a trace of Christmas.

I sat down on a gold brocade love seat and studied her while she walked over to a small teakwood bar and busied herself mixing something in a silver pitcher. She wore tinted silk stockings, the kind in style in Hong Kong and Tokyo. They were frosty plum, as were her high-heeled shoes. Her dress was snowy white linen with plum accents, tailored to make the most of her perfect figure. She'd enhanced the costume with a choker of flawless pale pink pearls that were obviously worth a fortune. A matching pearl ring adorned her right finger. Her long fingernails were painted a silvery plum color, and her pouting lips matched. Her deep brown eyes sloped into almonds, her lashes were long and sooty black. Her shiny black hair was swept up and held by ivory combs. In my beige cotton slacks and brown pullover, I felt like Colorado roadkill.

In her wind-chime voice, she said, "Would you like a cocktail?"

"I'd prefer iced tea."

She looked at me and tilted an eyebrow, as if I'd just committed an amusing social faux pas. She smiled and said, "Of course."

She pulled on a tasseled rope that I'd have sworn was stolen from the set of *The Maltese Falcon*. A thickset, scowling houseboy looked in, she ordered my iced tea, then he disappeared. As she tilted her head, I got a better look at the tiny ivory combs that held up her sleek black hair. They were carved in the same pattern as the bracelets I'd seen in Benny Frietas's grab bag. I felt a trace of my confidence return.

She finished stirring her martini then poured it into a thin crystal glass, added a cocktail onion, then came over to sit in the brocaded chair to my right. "I'm an art appraiser," she said. "I assist Henry in his business. I come to Hawaii frequently, to help him here."

I yanked myself out of my state of paralysis. I said, "You have offices here and in New York City and San Francisco. But Abe didn't tell me the name of the U.S. branch of Mr. Li's business." It was lame, but at least a place to start the conversation.

"H.J.K. Li's, Limited," she said. "We're just opening our Honolulu office down on Bishop Street. Henry brokers raw jade in Hong Kong and also deals in both antique and contemporary jade jewelry and artifacts. We also arrange shows for museums and set up art auctions."

"Have you been in the business long?"

"Years, darling. Very many years. But let's not talk about business. Let's get acquainted, so we can be friends."

Her sudden intimacy surprised me. But before I could respond, a door opened and Henry Li walked into the room.

I was looking at the same slightly built Chinese man with birdlike bones and small features that I'd seen in the photograph on his business brochure. He still seemed frail in build, though stiff of carriage. But looking into his cold, ancient eyes, I knew that my first impression of him had been correct. There was a foreboding intelligence there, but also a cold indifference that was chilling. He wore a green brocade smoking jacket that blended with the green, gold, and red of the room.

"Forgive me for making you wait," he said. His voice was richly cultured, also with a Hong Kong British accent.

Mi-Lin used one of her finely sculpted hands to gesture in my direction. "Alex and I have been getting acquainted," she purred.

As Li sat down, the houseboy returned with my iced tea. Li waited till the sullen young man was gone then said, "I deeply apologize for the delay. I believe Abe explained my reservations?"

"He did. I can understand why you might have been concerned."

He flicked the words away with a small, manicured hand. "I've decided to have full confidence in your abilities. I trust you will forgive my hesitation?"

I nodded and forced a smile. Maybe he wasn't so bad after all. Maybe . . .

He said, "As you may know, I'm a respected collector and dealer in rare jade. Pieces from my collection have been shown from Beijing to Paris to Moscow."

I forced myself to look impressed, since he so obviously expected it. I could see now that his left eye had a fading shiner. Curious.

"Mi-Lin is my most trusted advisor and appraiser," he added. He shot her a look that was supposed to be a beam, but it didn't quite come off. Her lower lip curled in a near-imperceptible expression of contempt.

"Did Abe fill you in on our problem?" Li asked.

"Not really. He just said there'd been a theft, and you wanted it handled outside the regular channels."

He nodded curtly. "Then you understand that we don't want the police involved," he said. "We can't afford so much as a breath of scandal right now. In my world, reputation is everything. Absolutely *no* mention of this must be made to either the police or the press."

"I understand."

"Now, as to your needs in the matter."

I was surprised. I'd thought Abe handled all that. I said, "I charge three hundred a day plus expenses, against a one thousand dollar retainer."

"Yes, of course." He looked at Mi-Lin. "See that a check is cut for her before she leaves," he said. "Triple her retainer, we'll be needing a lot of her time this month."

I felt a vast sense of relief. That much money would easily handle my immediate bills and allow me to return Paké's money and quit feeling sorry for myself about being broke.

I said, "I'd appreciate a brief rundown on what you need from me. What, exactly, was stolen?"

"Jade." He said the word with a dark grimace, as if he hated the very thought of it.

"Where did the theft occur?"

"Honolulu International. Didn't Mi-Lin tell you anything?"

"We were just about to get started when you came in, darling." There was a weary boredom in Mi-Lin's voice.

Henry looked back at me. "We had just returned from Hong Kong. That is, Mi-Lin and I, and our security chief. These pieces were particularly valuable so I didn't want to ship them. I had them packed in specially made velvet-lined trunks, then watched as they were loaded in the plane's cargo hold. I got off first and also watched the trunks unloaded here at Honolulu International. My chief of security was overseeing the shipment. But as he was loading the trunks into the boot of my limo, they were stolen."

"Would it be possible to talk to your chief of security?"

His face turned choleric. "I dismissed him. He's back in Hong Kong."

"I see. How were the trunks taken?"

He and Mi-Lin exchanged a dark look. Henry said, "I prefer not to go into the details. Suffice it to say that three boys took them. There was an altercation—a setup, I believe now—and the trunks simply vanished."

"Vanished from where exactly?"

"They had been placed inside the limo's boot, but it hadn't been shut and locked yet."

I frowned. "How large were these trunks, anyway?"

"Two feet wide, four long, and two deep."

"Small enough for one person to easily carry them both," Mi-Lin chimed in.

Henry Li shot her another dark look. She responded by tilting her head and looking at him scornfully.

"What, exactly, was in the trunks? I'll need an inventory." I was thinking again about the jade pieces in Benny Frietas's grab bag, and anticipating these two mandarins' grateful surprise when I swiftly cracked the case.

Li's face set hard for a second. I thought he was going to curse, but he stopped himself, and said frostily, "Mi-Lin?"

She went over to a teakwood desk and took out a thick manila envelope, brought it to me, then returned to her own chair.

I pulled out a thick sheaf of eight-by-ten colored photographs and a typewritten list. The photos were professionally done appraisal shots, with detailed insets in the corners to help identify the pieces. The photos were numbered to correlate to the list, which read:

- one 1-carat ruby ring in 24-carat gold setting, carved as a longevity dragon, value $120,650.

- four elephants' ivory bracelets, handcarved with fruit and foliage, value $1850.
- one pair diamond earrings, white, one carat each, pear-cut solitaires, value $26,250.

I scanned the rest of the page. There were jade bracelets, another ruby ring, a sapphire and diamond pendant, a matched set of lapis lazuli bracelets and earrings.

I looked up and said to Li, "You also deal in jewelry other than jade?"

Mi-Lin said, "I was foolish enough to put my jewelry case in Henry's trunk. He assured me it would be safer there than in my carry-on." She gave me a sour smile.

Li shot her a look of pure rancor. All was not well between these two. He said, "Yes, well, the jewelry can be replaced. The jade can't."

I picked up the second sheet of the list and began to read aloud. Li took the photos from me, and as I read each item, he held up the photo to show me.

I read: "Two cylindrical *lien,* or caskets, nineteenth century, value seventy thousand dollars. One jadeite carving of a leaping carp, value twenty-two-thousand, five-hundred. Six jadeite bowls, modern era, value twenty-five-thousand each. . . ."

I was looking up at the matching photos as Li held them up. The pieces were exquisite. There was the small emerald-green Buddha I'd seen in Frietas's larder. It was circa 420-550, Ch'ao Dynasty, valued at $25,000. There were snuff bottles, incense burners, and vases. Apple-green, mauve, emerald, Nile-green, shamrock, black—I'd never realized so many colors of jade existed! And there, in shiny black, was the odd little beast I'd seen on Frietas's shelf. The deer-dragon-unicorn.

I pointed at the photo Li was holding up. "What's that?" I asked.

"Ah," Li said, pleased. "You have an eye for art. That's circa Imperial Ch'ien Lung, about 1750. A very rare piece, a ch'i-lin, the symbol of a happy marriage. In Chinese mythology it was a noble beast which lived two thousand years. It left no footprint, no matter where it trod. This particular piece once stood in the Royal Palace in Beijing. Here's another piece you might appreciate."

He found the photo and held up the image of a grotesque little creature carved in gray and black jadeite. It had a long, curling beard.

"A bearded dog of Fo," he said. "A Chinese lion. Very rare."

I murmured my appreciation, and we went on to the vases, some carved with filigrees of flowers and butterflies, with trees and seahorses and mythological monsters. They were in various colors, but the most exquisite was snow-green jade: the color of the first budding twigs veiled behind a spring snowstorm, with the color of soft golden sunlight misting it all. Breathtaking!

When I'd seen all the pieces, I put the lists and photos back inside the envelope, and said, "So altogether these pieces are worth about two million?"

"More. Certainly more. I didn't want to get Abe overly upset. But the money's beside the point. It's the desecration I abhor. The impudence of the thieves. The very insolence! I want to know who took my treasures—"

I nodded. "I understand. And what day were the trunks stolen?"

"Last Saturday."

I had to keep myself from snapping up straight. The same day Paké Chang had come back from Hong Kong. Was there a connection?

I said, "I need a description of the boys, everything you can remember. And it really would be helpful if you could tell me how it happened."

Mi-Lin leaned back and smiled, sphinxlike. "Oh, go ahead, Henry, tell her what happened. Or would you rather I tell her?"

He shot her a dark look, then began to talk.

She'd stayed in the limo, to rest. He'd had a headache and had just climbed back in too, along with the chauffeur. They were waiting for the chief of security to finish loading the two trunks full of jewelry and priceless jade into the boot, and then they were ready to leave. But they'd heard a scuffling outside, had rolled down the window and seen three young boys—one local, two Chinese by the look of them—starting a free-for-all. The security chief had stopped work and turned to stop the ruckus. The boys had fought harder, had sailed right into him, knocking him to the ground in front of the limo. By the time things had straightened out, the boys were running away, the two trunks with them.

"Did you see where they went, or what they were driving?"

"There were thick banks of foliage nearby, and rows of trees along a fence. We believe now that the boys had a vehicle parked just behind the foliage." He explained that by the time the chauffeur went after them, all he saw was the tail end of a red sports car, screeching around the corner and toward the freeway.

I thought about Kimo Chang's souped-up Firebird. This story was getting good. "May I talk to the chauffeur?" I said.

"He's back in Hong Kong too," Li said too quickly.

"I see."

And I did. He was lying to me. I could tell by the tortured way the story came out, and I could also see it in the contemptuous look on Mi-Lin's face as she studied him.

For some reason, the lies made me even more interested. Why would Li hire me to solve a puzzle, then lie to me about what had happened? Talk about sabotaging himself. And what about Mi-Lin? Was she in on the lie? Why was she so contemptuous of Henry Li?

In some strange way it all fit together. Even the dead boy I'd found in the Ala Wai Canal was a part of this confusing pattern, but I couldn't make sense of it. I'd either stumbled or been dragged into something I couldn't begin to understand.

The servant came in and told Henry that dinner was ready, and as we moved into the dining room, I tried to sort things out in my mind by laying them into a time line.

I'd been approached by Abe to work for Henry Li several days before Paké's midnight phone call. Li's jade had been stolen the day before Abe called me, apparently. And then, Paké Chang had phoned me and brought me into the picture by making sure I was the one to find the young Chinese illegal's body.

Had Kimo and the two illegals robbed Henry Li? If so, I had to assume that Kimo Chang had deliberately targeted him. That was the only way the whole thing even began to make sense. But why would he do that? Did Paké know Henry? Had he helped Kimo set the theft up? And if so, had Kimo double-crossed him?

There were a lot of questions to be answered here. And I was interested enough now to want to answer them myself. I suddenly decided that I wasn't going to step out of Paké Chang's job after all, even though I was working for Li now. I wasn't going to relinquish any information I might learn in either camp. Not until I fully understood what both Henry Li and Paké Chang were up to, and why Paké had drawn me into the picture.

left Henry Li's Black Point mansion right after dinner, around nine o'clock. The undercurrents between Li and Mi-Lin were unpleasant, they'd started sniping at each other in earnest. I'd already learned as much as they were going to tell me anyway—at least for the moment. When I got home I turned on the living room lights, then checked my answering machine.

Two calls.

I hit the playback button, waited while the tape rewound, then listened as Paké Chang growled, "I'll call back later."

Okay. He'd told me up front that he didn't want me contacting him except in the most extreme emergency, and then I was to phone the Calabash Room, a bar here in Waikiki, and ask for Pua.

"She's my wahine," Paké had explained. "You can't reach me, you get in touch with her. She always knows where I am."

It had long been rumored that there was syndicate money behind the Calabash, so that added up. Now, I thought about phoning Pua, but I really didn't want to talk to Paké just then. I wanted to think things through so I could ask the right questions next time I saw him.

I played the second message. An unfamiliar man's voice snarled, "Alex Albright? Phone me. 555-8140. Pronto!"

Now what?

I mulled over the arrogance in the voice for a while, considering the possibilities. Then I dialed the number and the same hostile voice answered the phone. "Yeah?"

"This is Alex Albright," I said. "You left a message on my machine?"

"Right. I wanta talk to you. Do I ever."

"Do I know you?"

"Not yet, but you're about to. Look, I'm gonna lay it out for you. I'm working undercover six lousy months tryin' to make a case. I don't need *you* stepping in and screwing everything up."

"*Who is this?*"

A long pause, then, "Three guesses."

"You're a cop?"

"Close, but no coconut."

"A *fed?*"

"Bingo!"

Okay. Obviously I'd stirred something up. I bit the inside of my cheek, fought back my temper, and said sweetly, "I'm working on a case too. Maybe if you'd define your territory, I could—"

"Oh, yeah, right. I'll just run off some copies of all the official reports and have them delivered so you and your syndicate buddies will know exactly what the good guys are up to." His voice dripped with sarcasm. "Maybe you'd also like to see my informant list."

I was thinking fast now. What did he know about my sudden new involvement with Paké Chang? Working for Paké wasn't illegal—so long as I didn't cross the line. But were they watching him? And if so, were they going to be watching me too? I literally shivered at the thought of it. I'd had my condo bugged once before, and it was a living, breathing nightmare.

I said, "Maybe I have some information you could use."

He was silent so long that I began to wonder if I'd lost him. Then he snarled, "What's the catch?"

"No catch. I'm beginning to worry about what I've gotten into. If you can convince me that I'm on the wrong side, I'll bow out."

There was another long silence. Then he said, "Let's talk."

Great. I was going to flush him out. Furthermore, whatever investigation he was working couldn't be going very well if he was that quick to grab at a straw. He sounded like a frustrated cop who'd reached the end of his tether. I said, "You can come over now. I usually stay up late."

"Are you kidding me? I'm undercover six gruesome months and I'm supposed to drop by your office for *tea* or something? You're nuts. Meet me at eleven-thirty tonight, in the bamboo forest after the third switchback on top of Tantalus."

That was a good place for a clandestine meeting. Nothing up there but a bamboo-fern forest and spectacular views of the city, and an occasional discarded body or two.

I asked, "Why so late?"

"Because I don't want anybody to *see* me with you." His voice dripped with venom.

I wasn't looking forward to meeting this man. But I needed to know who he was and why he wanted me out of the picture. I also needed to know where my investigation was overlapping his own—and who he was working for. I swallowed my temper again, and said, "How do I know you're really a cop?"

"You don't. Pack some heat if you want to. If I try anything, shoot me. Shoot me anyway. I was already sick of this investigation, and now *you* come along."

"Okay, you're a cop. I'll try to be there."

"Don't try, do it! I'm driving a lime-green Mercedes 280-SL. I'll park back of the road."

A Mercedes? Lime-green?

"I'm driving a gray Honda," I said.

"Wonderful. Be there."

And the jerk hung up.

自由

Some handy items I'd inherited from David were his guns: a Colt .22 six-shooter (a collector's model) and a .357 Magnum Python with black-rubber composition grips. I also had the Savage 110-C rifle that he'd used to hunt pigs over on the Big Island, plus a couple of other handguns. But his favorite gun had been his service revolver, a Smith & Wesson Chief Special, a .38 with five rounds and a simple crosshatched walnut grip. That one I'd adopted for my own.

I'd been through the DEA's agent training course. I'd wanted to work in the field, but I changed my mind after learning about intelligence analysis. David had taught me more about guns, though. Since I'd gotten my P.I. license, I'd spent quite a bit of time at the Koko Head firing range. I was completely comfortable with my gun now, though I almost never carried it.

The late news came on at ten. I'd hoped to catch some new information about the human cargo from the *Dragon Venture*, but there was nothing. I clicked off the TV, loaded the .38, checked the safety, then went into the bathroom and took a shower. I toweled dry and put on a salmon-colored jersey blouse with a white collar and tiny stripes, white denims, then I climbed into my holster.

Though my .38-sized body holster is made from soft leather and fits snugly up against the left back of my waist, it's still a miniature prison. I wear it only when I have to, but tonight I wanted the peace of mind. Being armed is a strange thing. It gives you a psychological advantage, and after talking to the abrasive man on the telephone, I wanted an advantage.

I put on my white cotton jacket, shoved my .38 into the holster, and turned to look in the mirror. Good enough. I walked out the door at eleven on the dot. I'd be a little early, but I was antsy about the meeting and couldn't sit still any longer.

Tantalus is a steep knobby extension of the Koolaus that is also called Roundtop. The Manoa Valley lies to one side of the high hill, the city and shoreline roll off in front of it, and the dark mountains tower behind it. Tantalus Drive is a steep set of switchbacks that take you past ever more luxurious houses, all set back on the steep hillside and barely visible through the bamboo and fern forests and high fences and gates. The jungle-thick pothos vines with their foot-wide leaves wind around the tree trunks till all the foliage is laced together into an impenetrable thickness, even in some of the residential areas on the lower slopes of the hill.

The masked light of the houses with their occasional glitter made me nostalgic. Maybe it was the colored Christmas lights: warmth in a world filled with cold, predatory creatures. As I drove past an especially homey-looking house, I suddenly wondered again what I was doing with my life. I'd been invited to Christmas dinner by Yoko and Jess, and by several other friends at church. I'd declined them all. I didn't even find time to be close to them anymore, and when I wasn't working I wanted to be by myself. I was turning into a social hermit. And even though I had Henry Li's money in my desk drawer at home and my immediate financial problems were solved, something was missing and it wasn't just David.

I glanced up at the sky. Storm clouds had swallowed the thin slice of moon, and the sky seemed black and infinite, though empty. I needed to spend more time nourishing my spiritual life, but even that seemed like a dead end at the moment. The discontent roiled in around me like smoke. I had a nasty urge to lash out at something, even myself, just to destroy the surge of frustration that was welling up in me.

High up on Tantalus, the houses far below me, I drove slowly along the lava-rock wall that separated me from a sheer, lethal drop-off. Three cars containing lovers or tourists were parked alongside the wall; several dark figures stood gazing down at the amber and ice-blue city lights with their flickering cherry-red air traffic warning signals sprinkled atop the high-rises. Beyond the city lights, the dark sea spread out all the way to China. The occasional lights of tour ships and freighters blinked against the deep black fusing of sea and sky.

I drove past the rock wall and switched back again, to the far side of the hill. I was in dense, black bamboo forest. This was the far side of Tantalus, seldom used at night, not even by lovers. Several bodies had been discovered here in the past decade. The area had a sinister reputation that had my teeth on edge. I was watching carefully for the lime-green Mercedes sports car.

Suddenly car lights blinked on then off, cutting through the inky night. The Mercedes was backed off beside a clump of enormous bamboo trees. I reached back and unsnapped my holster, shrugged my shoulders to make sure I could easily reach my gun, then I cut my lights as I swerved in and parked.

I switched off my ignition and waited. As my eyes became accustomed to the darkness, I saw a silhouette behind the Mercedes' steering wheel.

I waited.

He waited too.

Then, finally, he rolled down his window and beckoned for me to join him in his car.

I reached up and turned off my overhead light so I wouldn't be spotlighted as I opened my car door. A nerve jumping in my cheek, my hand poised near the .38, I walked the short distance across the grass to the black silhouette of his car.

It startled me when the Mercedes' interior light came on as he reached across and opened the car door. For that instant, he was illuminated like a male mannequin in a nighttime shop window. His sea-green eyes held both curiosity and hostility; his longish hair was sun-streaked to near blonde. He was probably thirty-five or even forty, with strong, handsome features. He looked like one of the professional surfers from the North Shore, muscled and tanned to perfection.

I thought about the man who'd been watching my condo a few days ago. Marty had described him as a beach bum with wide shoulders. As I slid in and shut the door behind me, the light went out, leaving us in inky darkness.

He said, "I thought you'd look like a marine sergeant, from all I've heard about you."

I let it slide. I look good enough not to have to worry about it, and I learned a long time ago that it's impossible to get past all the negative stereotypes of being a female P.I. It used to drive me crazy. Now I analyze the source and try to make it work for me.

He pulled out a pack of cigarettes; a match flared in the darkness as he lit one. I rolled down my window. Better a midnight stalker leaping out of the forest than lung cancer.

There was an uncomfortable silence. Finally, he said, "I'm Johnny Tavares, DEA. I knew your husband for a short time about five years ago. We worked together on a heroin bust, from different ends. I'm out of the San Francisco field office."

I was astonished, but I made a fast recovery. I said, "Do you know Walt McClean, the San Francisco AC?"

He chuckled. "*Craig* McClean is the agent in charge of the San Francisco office. But don't bother calling him to check me out. 'Undercover' is supposed to mean undercover from everybody— especially ex-DEA people who roll over and sell out to the syndicate. If he knew I was talking to you, I'd be off the job and on a plane home tonight—without retirement."

"I haven't rolled over," I said tightly.

"Yeah? That's not what I heard."

"Heard from who?"

He studied me for a second then said, "Forget about it. Look, I want to tell you I'm real sorry about what happened to your husband. David was a really good cop."

I blinked hard. Maybe I wasn't going to need my gun after all.

A hint of moonlight had climbed over the edge of the hill. I could see the contours of his face, and even the expression in his eyes. He really was drop-dead gorgeous, but he looked troubled. He said, "What happened with David proves that you can't let your guard down ever. Which is why I'm here. I do not intend to let anything bad happen to me." He turned and fixed me with a heated glare. "So—what's your problem, anyway?"

"*My* problem?"

"Yeah, you. What keeps you in the middle of my business these days?"

I reined in my anger, and said quietly, "I'm working on a case. And what's *your* problem?"

His jaw flexed a few times. I'd hit a nerve. He said, "My problem is that I'm hamstrung by a bureaucracy that messes me up every time I make a move, and now I've got to watch out for you too."

I bit my tongue. Hard.

Which was evidently the right thing to do, because he stuck out his jaw and looked at me defensively. After a minute he realized he wasn't going to get a fight and the tension in his shoulders relaxed. He said, "You must have figured it out by now anyway."

"Figured out what?"

"That I'm curious about your new client."

I nodded. I wasn't going to ask which one. She who talks first loses.

"So." He paused, then took a long breath. "Here we are in paradise. The detective and the narc. Why did you leave the DEA, anyway?"

"To get married," I said. "They were cutting back the Honolulu field office, and they wanted to transfer me to L.A. I didn't want to live in L.A., and I did want to marry David. Period."

"People still say nice things about you."

"Thank them, if you can ever admit you talked to me."

"Yeah," he said. His jaw went tight again. "In fact, I'll mention how I was risking my life working a case with the local cops hip-deep in Chinese aliens, the dealers flooding the streets with China White, and all of a sudden I'm tripping over Little Miss Sunshine."

"Look, I don't know what's eating at you, but life is hard for everybody, so don't blame me."

A cloud that had been covering part of the moon slid past. I could see him better now. He pulled his lips back in a grimace that surprised me, but all he did was blow out a long stream of smoke through clenched teeth, in caricature of a melodrama villain.

He said, "I came to Hawaii from the Thailand end of the pipeline. I was at the top of the ladder before I ever hit this crummy island. Now? I'm about to pull in the top gun of the whole operation, when all of a sudden you're dead in my way."

"Heroin?"

"What else comes out of Thailand? Sometimes I think I've got to be crazy to even care what happens to the junkies who use that stuff."

I stayed silent. It wasn't the right time to start asking questions.

He shook his head and again stared at me, this time with curiosity. "So you're the one who found the Yuen kid's body?"

The shift in subject disoriented me for a second, then I caught up with him. "Yes."

"You get around."

"So they say."

"You heard he died of an overdose?"

"That's one theory."

"It bothers me when it happens to kids. Did you know they'd already started him working as a courier?"

"*Who* started him dealing?"

"The people I plan to bust."

"Who?"

He looked disgusted, then looked out into the forest. "Easy money," he mused. "Easy to make, easy to get dead making. Harder and harder to bust up the people making the money. We take down one supplier, another one pops up. We're sitting on a powder keg."

"So who's the big target?"

His head rotated toward me, and his face said he wasn't pleased. "Where's the information you were supposed to have for me?"

My sense of perversity got the better of me. "I lied. I just wanted to see if you look as unpleasant as you sounded on the phone."

"And?"

I was surprised that it hadn't even fazed him. "Look," I said, "the last thing in the world I'd ever want to do is screw up a drug investigation. But I don't even know what I'm doing wrong."

His eyes measured me. "Tell me a little bit about your client."

"You know better than that."

"Yeah, well . . . I know who your client is. That's no big deal. But do you?"

"That doesn't make much sense."

"Stick with what you're doing and it will make all the sense in the world. If you're alive to learn the lesson."

I was getting tired of his superior attitude and oblique insinuations, but I still hid my thoughts. I said, "I just need a thumbnail sketch of what you're doing so I'll know where not to be and who not to see."

He grinned then. "You're sharp, I'll give you that. But I'll ask the questions, you answer them. Let's start with your interest in Kimo Chang."

So that was it! He'd somehow stumbled into me while I was tailing Kimo. My sense of relief at knowing where he'd linked into me was instantly inundated by a flood of concern. If the DEA was watching Kimo Chang, the kid was indeed on the verge of getting into some serious trouble far beyond the impending arrest when Benny Frietas shut down his hukilau and nailed him for selling stolen goods. I shook my head.

But why was the DEA interested? Kimo certainly wasn't the top gun in any international drug ring. This could get complicated. Was Tavares after Paké, by way of Kimo? Could Paké actually have managed to become the top gun of an international syndicate, in addition to his local business? I thought about Paké's hooded eyes when he'd talked about his trip to Hong Kong. I didn't like this new slant on things.

"I'd like to see Kimo straightened out," I said. "So would certain members of his family, and that's the extent of my interest in him."

Tavares emitted a mirthless laugh. Then he slumped down and

folded his arms across his chest. "You think it's that easy? Man, you don't have any idea how bad things are getting in these islands. I'm already walking on ground glass barefooted, trying to keep my balance here. Now on top of that, I have to worry about you."

"You keep saying that. What on earth are you talking about?"

He sighed and slumped farther down. "I'm talking about the crucible. The trial by fire. What it's like out here on the edge, with everybody else selling out, even the people you have to rely on sometimes. It's all about money, nobody cares anymore—"

"I haven't sold out—"

But he didn't hear me. He was saying, "Sometimes I think I'll give it up, you know? Everywhere it's the same. Man, we used to think the Cosa Nostra was bad. At least you could figure out where the Italians were coming from. Now? You try to deal with the Chinese? Forget about it. You can't even figure out what they're saying when they finally decide to rat on each other, and the whole kit and caboodle would rather have their heads chopped off than rat out another Chinese anyway. 'Face,' they call it. They lose face if they talk to the cops. They think they're supposed to tolerate whatever comes their way, or fix it themselves."

"Hawaii's Chinese aren't like that," I said defensively.

"I'm talking about Hong Kong Chinese."

"You're investigating the Triads," I said, articulating my growing fear.

"Bingo. And by the way, you think you can get Kimo Chang straightened out, all I can say is good luck. That kid is too far gone for anybody's help."

"Why do you say that?"

"Keep going, you'll find out."

"What on earth does Kimo Chang have to do with the Triads?"

"Wrong question."

"You're beginning to get on my nerves. Can't you tell me anything?"

"I can tell you to butt out. I can tell you that your small-fry operations are about to wreck my investigation. I shouldn't have to tell you that if I can stop even a few of these subhuman pieces of slime from peddling their poison, I can keep hundreds—maybe thousands—of kids from turning into rotting, breathing corpses. I'm talking about kids who might still have a chance against the slime you're trying to protect." His voice had turned harsh, and his face was menacing as he turned to glare full at me. He said, "I'm telling you again. Whatever you're doing, stay out of my way. Don't jam me up!"

I felt a surprising surge of empathy for him. I remembered what it was like out there in the ice-zone where you're always one short step away from a violent death. More than one agent had succumbed to drugs or booze, just to shut off the night sweats and nightmares. It could get very cold out there indeed.

Tavares sensed my momentary weakness. He said, "So what's your real angle with Kimo Chang?"

I shook my head. "What I already told you, period."

He leaned back and eyed me with borderline paranoia. "You involved with Mr. Seven and those scumballs from the Shatin Lounge?"

That surprised me. "You mean that rat-hole bar down in Chinatown?"

"It may be a rat-hole, but there are some high-stakes games being played there these days."

"He's running games in the back?" That surprised me too.

He smiled mirthlessly. "Gambling is one of his enterprises, but it's not exactly the game I was talking about."

I had a sudden memory of walking past the ammonia and urine scented cavern of the Shatin Lounge; of glancing in to see the solitary man sitting on the barstool nearest the door—at the Shatin Lounge.

I remembered his startling blink and my sudden realization that this was a living, breathing being, locked inside the dark, cavernous room through the chains of drug or alcohol addiction, or both. I suppressed an involuntary shudder.

"I've never even been in the Shatin," I said. "What does that place have to do with all this?"

"Good," he said. "Stay far away from that action. We got an idea the new owner, Mr. Seven, might be bringing in the Triad's drugs."

"So the Triad *is* trying to move in here."

"No kidding." He rolled his eyes.

"Who's Mr. Seven?"

"The new kid on the block in Chinatown, as if you didn't know. I've picked that bloodless vulture out as my own personal target, so stay out of my way."

"It would be my pleasure."

"If you talk to him, tell him that I'm going to nail him."

"If I *talk* to him? I don't even know who he is."

"Yeah. Sure."

It bothered me that Tavares didn't believe me. I was nevertheless pleased that this Mr. Seven was the target, rather than Paké Chang: though on second thought Tavares wouldn't have told me if he was after Paké anyway—not if he knew Paké had hired me. But I still wasn't sure how much Tavares really knew, and how much he was guessing.

I had a sudden flash of insight. "This Mr. Seven has something to do with trafficking illegal aliens—as in the human cargo aboard the *Dragon Venture*? That's also Triad action, right?"

Tavares was silent.

"That is the connection, isn't it? And this Mr. Seven works for Paké Chang?"

He gave me a startled look. "You've got to be kidding me."

"Isn't Paké who you're really after?"

He studied me for a second, then grinned. "Close, but no cigar."

I figured it was time to take my own shot. I said, "Word has it that a renegade youth gang is moving into syndicate territory without paying dues and some heavy action is about to come down."

Tavares was quiet for a long time. I felt the tension press in on him like a steel vise. Abruptly he relaxed, flipped the butt of his cigarette out the window right past my nose, and said, "I don't really know what's happening. Something's messed up. But let me tell you this. I'm not going to let this small-fry local stuff screw up my operation."

I let the insult ride. "So this Mr. Seven—how long has he been around, anyway?"

He studied me quietly. He was suddenly steely and controlled. "You really don't know, do you?"

"I don't understand most of what you're talking about."

"Well stay out of it anyway."

"I would like to know who Mr. Seven is."

He sighed. "I guess I owe you that much. He's been here in Honolulu for a couple of years, has an import-export business and a couple of fishing trawlers. He keeps a low profile, locally. He opened up the joint in Chinatown a few months ago, has a manager who runs it. You seldom see Mr. Seven out and about; he lets his men do most of the work, but he's a heavy operator, no doubt about it."

"Where's he from?"

"San Francisco, same as me." He grinned. "And that's it. I've already told you too much."

"I won't jeopardize your investigation," I said.

He lit another cigarette and inhaled deeply. For a minute I thought he was going to tell me what was on his mind. But he hesitated, then said, "Forget about everything I've said."

"On my life, anything you tell me goes no further."

"If you don't quit mucking around in this, it could be your life."

"Are you threatening me?"

He turned to fully look at me, and his gaze was intense. "Look. Some heavy stuff is about to come down. Heavier than street gangs. I'm working solo with a task force based in Hong Kong. We're not even letting the local police in on this one, so let it alone."

"I can't stay out of it unless I know what 'it' is."

"Leave it. You're getting in my way, Alex. Move over, stay quiet. I don't want you to get hurt, but I'm not going to let you contaminate my investigation either, no matter what happens."

Contaminate? I wanted to smack him. Instead, I pasted a chagrined look on my face, and said, "I won't get in the way."

"You're already in the way, and now you're drilling me for information. Okay. You want to deal? You talk first. Tell me why you're hanging out with Paké Chang, and tell me the truth about why he hired you."

I felt a shock wave roll through me. So he did know I'd spent time with Paké Chang. They were watching him. I said, "How do you know that?"

"Word from a friend of a friend of Chang's."

That frosted me. Paké had made me promise on my life not to tell anyone I was working for him, and he was spreading it all over town? Testily, I said, "Tell your informant to tell Paké that he talks too much."

"Can't."

"Why not?"

He rotated his head slowly, to look full at me, and there was a look in his eyes that froze my blood. "Because my informant is dead," he said.

I felt all the fight go out of me. I thought of all the deaths in these past few weeks here in the islands. Car wrecks, drowning deaths, homicides. Who had his informant been? I thought about the young kid in the canal. No way. He hadn't been here long enough, and he hadn't been in the right place. He probably hadn't even been able to speak English.

"How did it happen?" I asked.

"You wouldn't believe it."

"Try me."

He shook his head and looked away.

I was quiet for a moment, both of us lost in our respective thoughts. Then suddenly he turned to look at me again, and said, "You sleeping with Benny Frietas?"

That stopped me short. "*What?*"

He laughed. "Forget it. Just something I heard, I should have known better."

"How are you involved with *him*?" This was getting thick and bewildering.

He shot me an odd look.

"Are you involved somehow in the hukilau?"

He studied me then said, "How do you know about the hukilau?"

"I stumbled onto the store."

"Yeah," he said, not believing me. "Well, it's your story, I guess you can tell it the way you want to hear it."

"Seriously. How do you know Benny Frietas?"

"I'm a narc. I know a lot of people in police work," he said.

I had a sudden, startling thought. "Are you investigating the police?"

"Not unless they get in my way."

We sparred a few more minutes, till we both realized we had all we were going to get out of each other. Then I said good night, climbed out of the Mercedes, and got into my Honda. Tavares had already cautioned me that he was going to leave first, putting some distance between our cars. He wanted to check the road on the way out. I waited while he sped away. He was around the bend before he switched on his lights to illuminate the dense fern and bamboo forest.

I was relaxed now. My eyes were adjusted to the darkness. I'd rolled my own car window down, wanting the fresh air. The night breeze was only slightly tainted by the scent of rotted foliage and mulch. I was relieved to be away from the evil-smelling cigarette smoke, away from the tension that had filled Tavares's car and our conversation.

In the sky, the half-moon slid behind a dark cloud. The chirrup of the insects was soothing.

I had learned a lot, but I didn't know how it all fit together. That's the way it goes sometimes. You gather a tiny bit here, some more there, and you hope that one day you'll wake up and see the whole picture.

For the moment it was enough to know that the DEA was watching Kimo Chang, that they were after Mr. Seven—who was probably a Triad front man—and that Tavares believed, like I did, that something big was about to go down.

Something from which he wanted me far, far removed.

Fat chance.

CHAPTER

12

L enni Apana was wearing a sky-blue silk blouse with a
flowing hemline, matching palazzo pants, gold jewelry,
including bracelets and rings, and dark shoes and bag—as usual
she was dressed to perfection, ready for the camera at any time.
She was also wearing big, round eyeglasses that made her almond
eyes look owlish. Her contacts had been giving her trouble, she
said.

She had been interviewing the organizers of the Narcissus
Festival that morning. The festival lasted for several weeks, beginning just before the Christmas holiday with various shows and
displays then continuing until the Chinese New Year in January.

We were sitting in the Rooster's Nest, near the HGTV studios.
Christmas wreaths hung on the walls, tiny colored lights were
strung here and there, and a small fake tree stood in one corner,
listing a bit. I was buying Lenni's lunch. I had phoned her that
morning and caught her in the newsroom before she left. "Lenni.
Let's talk about your suggestion that we share information."

She'd been happy to make time for me. "Lunch, one o'clock," she'd agreed.

Now I was preparing to chow down on some shoyu rice and pickled cabbage, while Lenni was enjoying tofu sushi. We were both waiting for the tea to brew inside a blue-lacquered teapot.

We'd been talking about Chinatown, about her special, about the Immigration and Naturalization Service and the *Dragon Venture's* human cargo, and the still-missing Chinese boy. There was a slight pause in the conversation as Lenni again checked the teapot then gracefully poured the tea into our small round cups. I picked up my teacup and took advantage of the lull. "What do you know about a bar owner in Chinatown named Mr. Seven?"

She started, sloshing her own tea, and shot me a look of pure astonishment.

"Did I say something wrong?" I picked up a napkin and handed it to her. She set the cup down and dabbed at her shirt.

"Why do you ask about Mr. Seven?" she said. Her eyes were guarded.

"His name recently came up—"

"Where?"

"In a casual conversation. I'd heard his name before, and I got curious. I didn't mean to upset you."

She looked suspicious.

"Lenni. What on earth is wrong?"

"Give me a minute, Alex. You caught me totally off guard. Let me think about how much of this I want to tell you."

I rearranged my chopsticks and picked up my napkin. The wood table, burnished to a high gleam, reflected the sunlight that filtered through the venetian blinds. Lenni tapped her fingertips on the table, lost in thought. Then she said, "Okay. I've decided. But you're sworn to secrecy on this, right?"

I raised my hand, made the Boy Scout sign, which my nephew had taught me, and grinned. "Absolutely."

"Remember when I told you we should try to find the missing Chinese kid?" A spark of excitement illuminated her eyes.

"You were right," I said, "but where would we start?"

She lowered her voice conspiratorially and leaned closer to me. "I already started. I have an informant in Chinatown, someone who volunteered his services and who's really at the heart of things. Believe me, Alex, I'm not totally content to do social events and ancestor interviews. I really am down there for a reason."

"I know."

She brushed me aside. "My informant says a new shipment of illegals is en route. Once here, they keep them in an old abandoned sugarcane warehouse out past Waipahu."

"When will they arrive?"

"He wasn't sure. Maybe a few days, maybe a few weeks."

"What happens once they get here?"

"They feed them into the system and on to the Mainland in small groups after they've been given false documents. Some go to factories in Manhattan, some to restaurants and hotels in San Francisco, all of them owned by the Triad. They're locked in basement apartments when they're not working, and beaten if they so much as talk to strangers—"

"*Who* feeds them into the system?"

"The smuggling network. I don't have the details totally figured out yet. Remember that I told you the Snakehead is right here in Chinatown—"

"Paké Chang's people?"

She looked surprised. "Why would you think that?"

"He's the crime lord of Chinatown, isn't he?"

"Well . . . yes . . . but things are changing. Paké is losing some ground—"

I felt a little zing of trepidation. "What's happening?"

"Simple. New people are trying to move in."

"Mr. Seven?"

She folded up like a hibiscus at nightfall. Her gaze darted around the room as if she were looking for a way to escape, then returned to fix on me. Her voice was low and angry. "Don't say that name so loud when you're with me."

"Okay, okay." Though nobody was close enough to hear us, I lowered my voice to a near whisper. "But you do think it's him."

"Maybe. Probably."

"You think he's the Triad's front man here?"

"He could be."

I felt my interest kindle. I could almost hear his evil hissing. I leaned forward, animated. "You said you had a lead into the whereabouts of the missing Chinese boy?"

"I've been told he's being held in an old abandoned plantation house."

"Who's your informant?"

"Can't say, but he's been around Chinatown for a good long while and he misses nothing."

"Someone in your mother's tong?"

"Really, Alex. Can't you just leave it alone?"

"Okay, okay. But why would the bad guys be holding the other kid?"

"I don't know. Maybe he saw something when his friend was killed."

"Then why wouldn't they kill him too, just to be safe? It's not as if these people had the first inkling of respect for human life."

"I don't know, Alex. I'm just feeling my way through this. There are still a lot of unanswered questions."

I thought about what she'd said. There were countless acres of old sugarcane and pineapple plantations in the Waipahu area. There were any number of old houses, abandoned sheds, and other buildings that had at one time or another been associated with the sugarcane industry, which had shut down its last mill a year or so ago. It could take a lifetime to find the right abandoned building, even assuming Lenni's information was correct. On the other hand, a persistent person might get lucky right away.

"Let's drive out and look for him," I said.

"Can't," she said around a bite of sushi. "I'm filming the contestants for the Narcissus pageant at two o'clock. My mother would kill me if I didn't show up."

"She's on the planning committee?"

"Always. She's a true social animal, in the middle of every cultural event."

"We'll go later then." I bit into my food. It was so-so. I took a small splinter of wood out of my mouth—the chopsticks were cheap—and put it in the ashtray. "How about tomorrow?"

"Well—maybe later today," she suddenly said. "I'll see if I can duck out early. Try me on my portable phone about three." She wrote down the number and slid the paper across the table.

I put the slip of paper in my pocket. "Good enough. Any lead on where the illegals get their documentation?"

She smiled mischievously and leaned in close again. "Have you ever heard of the Thirteen Fifty?"

"The what?"

"It's a very old scandal. About Manoa Chinese Cemetery, where my grandparents are buried."

"I've been up there. It's beautiful."

"Yes. It was founded in the middle 1800s. Do you know the story?"

"Probably not."

"You know the small knoll the cemetery sits on, in the middle of the valley?"

"Yes."

"In the 1800s a Chinese immigrant named Lum Ching and a friend of his hiked up into the valley, with a compass and mirror. For some obscure reason they wanted to survey the region. It was all lush country and jungle then. Not a house around for miles. And beautiful—you know what it's like up there—still beautiful, with all that lush greenery and the grass and the view that slopes off all the way to the sea."

"It is," I agreed. That part of the Manoa Valley was one of the loveliest parts of the island, though it was now largely developed. But the houses had wide, tree-sheltered lawns and the area was quiet and peaceful, with the Koolaus looming up just behind the cemetery: lush, steep, and green.

Lenni took a quick sip of her tea and said, "My grandfather used to tell me the story. Lum Ching determined through his scientific instruments that the knoll was the pulse of a watchful dragon that lived within the earth. He declared the area sacred ground and convinced the Chinese to buy it as a gathering place where they could take care of the dead. At that time most Chinese still wanted their bodies returned to China for burial with their ancestors. But gradually they came to think of Hawaii as their home and were mostly buried here."

"So what's the scandal?"

"There have always been illegal immigrants from Asia," she said, twirling the noodles in her bowl around her chopsticks. She kept doing that, then untwirling them, then twirling them again. Nervous energy. "Mostly the number of Chinese immigrants was so small that it didn't matter all that much until recently. Now the Triads have turned it into big business and are turning the illegals into their virtual slaves."

"America, the Golden Mountain," I said. "What a surprise when they get here."

"It's still a whole lot better than China," she said, with a hint of fire. "I went there to do my master's thesis for my journalism degree. You'd never believe what it's like. Most of the aborted fetuses are female. Women are treated like dogs. They're sold like livestock by their own parents, or forced to marry foul old men and slave all their lives for them, the state forces them to have abortions—well, don't get me started. My great-grandmother actually had her feet bound in order to make her more attractive to a potential husband. She was only five years old. Her parents tightly wrapped both feet with long strips of cloth. The bones gradually broke and the skin became infected. It was very painful. Her feet turned to stubs. Can you imagine? Never even being able to walk by yourself, just so you can be some twisted old man's precious possession?"

"I've read about it," I said. "They called the feet Golden Lotuses. They were supposedly a real status symbol—for the husbands."

"Ugh," she said. She looked into the distance and frowned.

She shook her head slightly, in disgust, then looked back at me and said, "Anyway, the U.S. Immigration Service impounded all of Manoa Cemetery's records in the 1950s. There was a major traffic in Hawaiian documents for illegal immigrants at that time. The people paid $1,350 each for the so-called proof of U.S. citizenship. That's why they called the cases Thirteen Fifties. Nobody could ever prove it, but the speculation was that the illegal immigrants were being provided with the birth certificates of the people buried in Manoa Cemetery. The cemetery's elders are still mad about the accusation; Immigration lost most of the records, and nothing was ever proved, but—"

"Are you saying that the current batch of illegals stop here long enough to be provided with birth certificates from dead Chinese Hawaiians?"

"Exactly."

"Who's doing the paperwork?"

"I'm not sure yet, but I suspect it might be this hip-shooter Taiwanese lawyer who has an office down on Smith Street. I'll let you know what I find out."

Finally she left the noodles wrapped around the chopsticks, lifted them into her mouth, and swallowed. I was glad to see the end of them.

"I'll definitely go with you to Waipahu," she suddenly said. "I'll skip the talent interviews." She smiled as if pleased by the thought of escaping.

I shrugged. "Maybe we should notify the police and let them conduct the search."

She looked alarmed. "No. If they start an all-out search, the smugglers might kill the kid, assuming he isn't already dead. They won't want him around to talk about what happened to him."

I thought about that. "Maybe we should wait till tomorrow," I said. I'd suddenly remembered Frietas's sting operation. I wanted to run by there and do some more comparing of his jade with Henry Li's missing artifacts, and try to find out what he knew about Tavares. "I have to drive up to the Waianae coast tomorrow morning anyway, I could meet you in Waipahu on the way back—"

"Why are you going to Waianae?"

"A job." It was my turn to be on the question end of the conversation.

She got that secretive, delighted look on her face again. This woman loved investigative reporting. "Something I should know about?"

"I'm just riding shotgun on a kid who's probably already leaped over the edge."

Lenni suddenly turned serious. "Who for?"

"Sorry, I can't say."

She shrugged it off. "That's okay; I understand." She finished her food, put her napkin beside her plate, and glanced at her watch.

I said, "By the way, what do you think of Paké Chang?"

She looked as if I'd slapped her, managed to recover, and said, "Why?"

"You're plugged into a wider information bank than I am, especially in Chinatown. What's the deal with him losing ground?"

"He's just getting a little pressure, that's all." She was very defensive and was watching me carefully.

"From who?" I heard a hard edge come into my voice.

"Others who want a cut of the action. What's your interest in him, anyway?" Her lips pursed in disapproval. She was sharp, she'd sensed something. Was she honing in on me?

I reversed directions. "I'm just tying up some loose ends I don't understand on another case. So, what's your evaluation?"

She gave me a measured look and said, "I don't know the first thing about what you're really doing, but if it involves Paké, count me out."

"I hadn't expected you to exhibit such media-evoked prejudice." I said it in a light tone of voice. I didn't want to offend her, just make her defensive and draw her out.

She gave me a long-suffering look. "I'm the media that evokes the prejudice," she said. "We present the news from the perspective of my professional bias."

Then, just in case I didn't believe her, she frowned in ferocious caricature.

I laughed. Sometimes I couldn't believe how much we thought and acted alike.

"Okay, okay," I said. "So Paké is bad news. But what about Mr. Seven? Do you think he'll improve the neighborhood?"

"He's already improved Upper Nuuanu," she said, with an exaggerated look of distaste on her face. "I hear he's just doubled the size of the swimming pool in the new estate he bought up there last year. Whatever he's doing, it looks like he's here to stay."

I leaned forward again, suddenly anxious. "Tell me about him, Lenni."

She hesitated only an instant, then sighed and said, "Real name, Phan Lo. He's Chiu Chow, and his family originated in Swatow Province. He's forty-eight years old, divorced. He lived in Saigon during the height of the war, and then moved straight to Chiang Mai, Thailand, where he stayed for a couple of years."

"Heroin," I said with certainty.

Since the fall of China and their old Shanghai stomping grounds, the Chiu Chow had worked their heroin pipelines wherever the traffic took them, though now the financing was mostly done in Hong Kong, the harvesting and processing of the opium was done in Thailand, and the distribution pipelines covered the world. During the war, Saigon had been the center of the action: a central transshipping area.

She said, "Mr. Seven moved to San Francisco after the war was over. Before that he was in Hong Kong."

I tried to fit that into what I knew about the drug trafficking pipelines. There were long-standing Triads in San Francisco—there had been since the days when Chinese labor had been used to build the railroads that helped build up the United States. The Bing Kung, the Hip Sing, the Hop Sing—all had San Francisco cells. Maybe a San Francisco branch of the Hong Kong syndicate was trying to break into Honolulu's action.

"Why do they call him Mr. Seven?" I asked. "Something to do with Chinese lucky numbers?"

"You know about Chinese numbers and their symbolism?" She looked surprised.

"A little bit. I know that all numbers have meanings: some have extremely good joss. I remember reading in the paper about a Hong Kong businessman who paid $336,000 for the only government-issued license plate with the single number six on it."

Lenni nodded. "Six symbolizes longevity, which is what he was really trying to buy, of course. But seven isn't exactly a lucky number, not in China. No, I suspect Mr. Seven is called that because he's a seventh son. Or maybe he played dice with the GIs in Saigon, and rolled a lot of sevens. Who knows?"

"Are you investigating him for your special?"

She deliberately ignored me, looked at her watch, then did a double take and looked again. She stood and tossed her napkin on the table. "Sorry, Alex, I'm running late. Don't forget to phone me at three. I'm going to use your call as an excuse to get away."

"Three it is, " I said. I wasn't looking forward to trying to find the holding pens for the illegal aliens, but I really did want to find that missing kid.

CHAPTER

13

fter lunch, I phoned Mi-Lin, gave her a preliminary
progress report—basically told her nothing—and then
listened to the veiled contempt in her voice as she told me Henry
Li was pressuring her to straighten things out with regard to the
upcoming exhibition and the missing jade.

"He's being beastly about everything," she said.

I knew that Henry Li could probably become downright glacial
when it came to money. He just had that ruthless look about him.

A sad, plaintive note crept into her melodious voice. "Please
help me get this straightened out. If I have to listen to him complain
for another day, I'm going to walk out. I can't do that. Everything
I own is tied up in this exhibit."

That surprised me. "You're partners?"

There was a long pause, then she said, "I have some money tied
up in it. But mostly I want to recover the jewelry. Oh, Alex, most
of it belonged to my mother. It was the only thing she left me; my
elder brothers got everything else—" She sounded like she was about
to cry.

I felt a sudden flood of sympathy, and I promised to do what I could to rush things along.

After I hung up, I vowed to pry away my interest in Chinatown and refocus on Mi-Lin Ming and Henry Li. Their check had cleared, and it was enough to tide me over the holidays and repay Paké his retainer besides. But it wasn't going to last forever. I really needed to refocus on money, so I wouldn't find myself in the same shape after the first of the year.

Next I phoned Benny Frietas at the grocery store. I asked him, sweetly, if any new jade had come in. He said no, but was I interested in looking at a couple of diamond rings? I asked him when he planned to actually arrest Kimo Chang and wrap up the sting. He said that was private information. I hung up. So much for him.

After lunch I drove up to the leafy region that spreads out slightly above the downtown high-rises, at the base of the Koolaus. It's called Makiki, and the area is largely inhabited by Hawaiian-born Chinese.

I wanted to see Auntie Elma Chang. I wanted to hear her version of the two Chinese boys' escape. Plus, I wanted to ask her some questions about Kimo.

The youth home surprised me. I'd expected something fairly ramshackle. Instead, I pulled to the curb beside a large, well-kept white frame house with an old-fashioned porch. The yard was well tended and filled with greenery, some of it decorated with Christmas lights. A new brown Ford van sat in the driveway, and there was a large, homemade wooden creche on the front lawn, with slightly peeling paint.

I parked at the curb and walked onto the porch. There was a small window in the door, and I could see through the sparkling glass into a vestibule and a room beyond filled with old, dark furniture. A decorated Christmas tree stood in one corner, though the lights weren't turned on.

I rang the bell. Two small white poodles yelped then danced into view. They were unclipped, and they sprang and yipped around the room like wind-up toys gone mad. Someone shouted at them, and they bounced through a doorway and out of sight.

A moment later the door in front of me swung open. The woman who stood there had come from the side of the room.

She was in her late sixties or early seventies, but was still spry. Her face was like a wrinkled-up fist. Her hair was short and gray-streaked. Her head came to my shoulders, and she was boyishly thin. She wore a spotless flowered house dress—the kind without a waistline—and white socks. Her legs were slightly bowed, the sign of a poorly nourished childhood. She looked up at me quizzically.

I stepped out of my own shoes—an Island custom when entering a house—and said, "Mrs. Chang?"

"I'm Auntie Elma, yes?"

Like so many older Hawaiian women, the honorary title "Auntie" had for all practical purposes become part of her name.

"I'm Alexis Albright," I said. "I'm working on an investigation that may have some connection with the Chinese boy's death. I understand he was staying here before he disappeared. May I—"

Her face crumpled and tears welled into her eyes.

"I'm sorry. Are you okay?"

"Eh." She managed to get a grip on herself. She stepped back. "Come, then." Her English had a combined pidgin lilt and the clipped cadence of a Chinese accent, like so many of the old-timers who had spoken mostly Chinese at home.

We were inside the vestibule. She stood looking at me, and she didn't offer me a chair.

"Forgive me for intruding, but I really need to ask some questions," I said. "You know, of course, that the Yuen boy overdosed on drugs?"

The tears in her eyes welled over and trickled down her cheeks. Angrily, she brushed them away. "That boy. He so sick, all the time." She stopped short and looked at me, suddenly suspicious.

I said, "Sick? How?"

She hesitated, then nodded. "I seen it before, they wan' get sick but they hide it good. I try tell those men he need one doctah, but they say to keep him here. They say all the people on that boat been eating bad food, if he gets too sick just take him to the hospital."

"You mean the men from Immigration?"

"Those ones. They no listen. I try help, but—"

"Was he still sick when he ran away?"

She grew suddenly wary. "No."

"What were his symptoms?"

"Chills, fever, bad stomach cramps."

Well. It could fit either the flu or a heroin withdrawal, take your pick. But if it was narcotics, why no track marks except the fresh one, the so-called hot-shot?

I wasn't sure just how long the journey had taken. More than a few days, and the traffickers could have them well hooked by the time they got here, if that's what they were up to. At any rate, the length of time for withdrawal would depend upon the intensity of the addiction, which would depend upon the strength of the doses and how long they'd had the kid using drugs.

I remembered the news footage of the illegals coming ashore beside the Coast Guard station. They'd seemed quiet, even morose, but I hadn't noticed anyone in real pain, no throwing up, no clutching of the stomach as a reaction to cramping. Certainly not the agony that would indicate withdrawal from heroin or opium.

I said, "Did he seem to be better before he ran away?"

She nodded and her eyes flooded with anguish. "If I had known—"

"You can't blame yourself for what happened."

Her eyes went wide with an emotion I couldn't fathom. She was rigidly silent for a moment, then she nodded slowly to herself. She seemed to have made a decision.

I said, "Mrs. Chang?"

"Eh. Come, then." She motioned for me to follow her. "Make house. I like cook." Which meant to make myself at home because she planned to do some cooking.

I followed her down a hallway and into a clean, old-fashioned kitchen. The window over the double-wide sink was open and screened. It framed a yellow oleander tree in a leafy backyard, backed by heavy green koa trees. The small trumpet-shaped flowers were the most fragrant in the islands, next to pikake. And in fact there was also a bank of white pikake flowers running along the hedge, their fragrance wafting on the breeze.

She went to the stove and stirred something in a large iron pot. A wonderful fragrance filled the room, making my mouth water.

"Monk's Food?" It was a traditional vegetarian dish for the Chinese New Year.

She turned, looking pleased, and nodded. "I try one new recipe. My boys get tired of plate lunch."

A large tray was on the counter. It held mushrooms, cut into bite-sized bits. Bamboo shoot, bean curd, rice, won bok cabbage, and black fungus were also arranged in neat sections. She scooped them all up in her gnarled hands and dropped them into the boiling pot, then picked up a wooden spoon, stirred, then tasted it. "More ginger and hoisin, yeah?" She looked at me and her dark eyes twinkled, then she added the flavorings. "You like eat?"

"Thank you, I just had lunch. Are any boys still staying here?"

"No more. Only those two."

"Do you live alone?" The idea of it sort of worried me, especially if she was trying to take care of young boys, who could be a handful.

She got a disgusted look on her face. "I got one social worker, help me. And one nephew, Kimo, he comes and goes. He plenty stubborn. I like break his head sometimes."

I thought I heard a rustling outside the opened window. I stopped, tilted my head to listen, then heard a shrill barking and the scampering of feet through shrubbery. I relaxed. Apparently Mrs. Chang had put the poodles outside and they were romping around the yard.

I leaned forward. "Kimo spent time with the two Chinese boys who disappeared?"

"Eh. Dat boy. He wan' be one big shot. Sometimes I like ask him—you got pukas in your head, o' what?"

"Mrs. Chang. I'm sorry to pry, but can you please tell me if Kimo had anything to do with the boys running away?"

She turned fully from the stove, the wooden spoon slightly raised like a weapon. She tilted her head and stared at me. Her eyes were challenging, slightly angry. I had suddenly become a potential enemy.

"I want to find the other boy," I explained. "The one who may still be alive. What was his name?"

"Ask da kine cops." The hostility was out in the open now.

"I can't."

"Why?"

"I'm a private investigator. They don't tell me much, and I don't like to let them know what I'm doing." Which was true, with the exception of Jess.

She looked at the floor. "Who would wan' hurt that little rascal anyway?"

"I'd like to find out."

"You think you find that other boy alive?"

"I'm praying that's how it will work out."

She looked surprised. "You pray foah real?"

"Often."

"Buddhist or Christian?"

"Christian," I said.

She smiled. "I go Makiki Baptist," she said. "Make my boys go with me. Eh. Your heart's good, okay. I tell you what you need, you try find the rascal."

As she talked, I began to get a feeling for the situation. "Those two boys were cousins," she said. "Fook Chows from Fujian Province. Good boys. No trouble. They work hard."

The now-dead boy had told her that his parents listened to a Snakehead. The man had been combing the countryside, looking for the most intelligent boys, he said. He promised that the boys would become rich American doctors if the parents would pay for their passage to the Golden Mountain. The Snakehead promised to get them into school, then let them pay him the rest of the passage after they'd graduated and become wealthy. To pay for the passage, the Snakehead had taken all their money and all they could borrow from family and friends.

"Dat boy they killed," said Elma Chang. "He knew they all pilau." This was a Hawaiian word which meant filthy, dirty, very bad indeed. "Dat other boy that ran away, he only fourteen. Mock Sing Druan was his name. He like listen to his cousin, and run off too."

"The two boys left at the same time?"

"They did."

She told me how Kimo had taken the two boys in hand. He'd spent much time with them, and at first she'd been pleased. But then she'd caught the three of them in the backyard smoking reefer and sniffing white powder.

"I don' wan' that steenk weed around my house," she said. "I call Peter. I say come and get your boy, he no mo' bettah than before. That Peter, he has his hands full with da kine poho."

I was seeing where Paké had picked up some of his expressions.

"I understand that Peter is Paké Chang's brother," I said, fishing, then instantly regretted it.

Her head snapped around so she was looking full at me, and her face closed up. "You no moah say that name in this house," she said.

"But—"

"He pilau too. He makes this family feel shame."

I hesitated, not sure what angle to use now. I wanted to know if Kimo had helped the boys leave here, but I didn't seem to know how to frame the question in a way that would evoke a response.

She scowled at me. "You go. I like take rest."

"I'm sorry if I've upset you."

"No hui-hui. Just go." She waited patiently but stiffly for me to stand and leave.

Before I stepped out the front door, I turned to her. A bad shot is better than no shot. I said, "Mrs. Chang, *did* Kimo help those two boys get away from here?"

"That Kimo pilau too," she said. "Just like Paké. He come back this time, I don' know if I let him in." She sighed. "Only thing is, I don' wan' see him put in jail."

"This is strictly between you and me," I said. "Do you think Kimo would know where the other boy is?"

She eyed me curiously. But then she said, "I don' know."

"All right, I understand. And thank you, Mrs. Chang. For helping. I know it's not always easy to do."

She grunted, as if disgusted by the whole affair, and started to shut the front door.

I had taken two slow steps toward my car when she reopened the door and said, "Try wait."

I turned. She looked around to make sure we were alone and said, "Kimo took those boys. He say he gon' take 'em around Honolulu and show them the ropes. That Kimo's brain wen' all chop suey from pakalolo. You find that other boy, Mock Sing. He good boy, I no like see him get hurt."

"Thank you, Mrs. Chang."

"You call me Auntie Elma."

"With pleasure," I said. "And I'll do my best to find Mock Sing."

自由

As I buckled my seatbelt, I noticed that my rearview mirror was slightly crooked. I readjusted it and caught a glimpse of movement at the side of the house. I turned quickly, to see Kimo Chang move into shadow.

Oh, no. Oh man.

What if he'd been listening at the window? I thought about the sound I'd heard, then about the questions I'd asked, and what Auntie Elma had said about him.

I thought about the violent side of his nature, and the pleasure he'd taken in the bloody fray on Waikiki. Halfway down the hill I made a U-turn and went back up. Sure enough, from my new vantage point I could see Kimo's red Firebird parked around the corner.

Would he hurt Auntie Elma? From what I'd seen of him so far, I wouldn't put it past him to work over an older woman.

I parked the car out of sight and quickly walked back down to her house, staying shielded as much as possible by trees and high hedges swollen with trumpet flowers. The neighborhood was quiet, almost deserted. Mostly retired people lived here.

I got close to the house and heard the dogs barking in the backyard, then voices shouting inside. I got closer still and heard Elma Chang yelling: "You don' tell me who I can have in my house!"

An enraged male voice shouted back. I couldn't make out the words.

But I could sure hear Auntie Elma. She yelled, "Then get out, you lolo! You wan' smoke that steenk weed, you don' come to my house again!" She was yelling at the top of her lungs.

There was a sound of something breaking. I remembered the look of evil gloating on Kimo's face as he worked over the kid in Waikiki. I wondered if Kimo had hit her. I was just getting ready to break in and make sure she was okay when the front door burst open and Kimo came charging out, slamming the screen door behind him so hard it should have come off the hinges.

I had ducked behind the neighbor's fence in time, and he didn't see me—thank God. I watched him through a gap between white pickets while he ran around the corner to the Firebird, climbed in, revved the motor, then screeched out and burned rubber down the hill toward the freeway.

I hesitated, wondering about Auntie Elma, but just then she came to the front door, shaking her fist toward the disappearing Firebird. She looked fine to me.

Only then did I drive away.

I had the feeling that everything was suddenly out of control. I had reached the bottom of the hill and was just about to turn toward the freeway, when the *slap-slap-slap* of a deflated tire hit my ears and I groaned. That was all I needed. I pulled to the curb, got out, and went back to check it. It was the right rear, and it was flatter than a snake's eyes.

Too flat, too fast. I leaned in closer and inspected it. A nail was sticking out of the side. Someone, probably Kimo, had driven the nail in with a hammer. In addition, the valve stem had been yanked out, so the air could escape even faster.

Oh, man.

That meant that Kimo Chang had almost certainly come home to find my car there, and had crept around to the kitchen window to listen and see what was up.

I replayed our conversation. Kimo had heard plenty.

I thought about his violent temper, about his sociopathic personality, about his viciousness that night on Waikiki. I wondered what he might do now that he knew I was probing into his questionable life.

I was going to have to watch myself more carefully now.

I stopped at a drive-in, dialed Lenni's digital beeper, and punched in the pay phone number at 3:25—a bit late because of the time it took to change the tire. I sat on a concrete stool, sucking on ice from a too-sweet Coke, waiting for her to return my call. When she didn't, I figured she was either on the road or had gone back to the newsroom, so I dropped another quarter into the pay phone and dialed HGTV.

Barry Leong, the audio man I'd met in the Chinese restaurant, answered the phone.

When I asked for Lenni, he said, "Sorry, Alex, she caught a fast-breaking story. Said she'd try to reach you when she got back."

"What's up?"

"Some kid got shot in Chinatown."

My first panicky thought was of Kimo. But he hadn't had time to get down there.

"Where'd it happen?"

"In front of the porno shop next door to the Shatin Lounge."
I felt a little rush of adrenaline.

"Thanks Barry, I appreciate it. If you hear from Lenni, tell her
I'm on my way."

自由

My face felt warm, my breath was shallow. My blood was
pumping too hard for me to be crawling along at twenty miles an
hour. They were doing road repairs on the freeway—not that
they'd bothered to post that fact in time to give you the choice of
another route. Yellow flares and lighted arrows had shut down
two Ewa-bound lanes of traffic; the two remaining lanes were so
gridlocked that I would have turned around and gone home—if I
could have turned around.

The traffic ground to a stop. The frustration was killing me. I
sat for five full minutes, drumming my fingernails on the wheel,
and was about ready to leap out of my skin by the time the bus in
front of me moved. The traffic in the left lane began to crawl
forward, and then I could barely touch the gas and start moving
again.

I finally reached Chinatown and parked in the same garage as
before. Three minutes later I was turning the corner near the
Shatin Lounge. The steady grind of the city gave way to the crackle
of two-way radios, people shouting, the sound of someone sobbing. The area was thick with foot patrolmen, three-wheelers,
blue-and-whites, and several of the bicycle cops that patrolled
Chinatown—every type of cop who had ever worked a beat
seemed to be congregated at this one crime scene.

An ambulance had wheeled into the curb and stopped at an
awkward angle, its red lights flashing. I could see two young
attendants with stricken expressions. They seemed strangely idle
and unsure of what to do, which told me that whoever had been
shot was probably already far beyond help.

Homicide hadn't arrived yet. A uniformed precinct sergeant
controlled the crime scene. Across the throng of people, I could
see Lenni standing near a small cluster of police. They were all

looking down at something. The crowd was thick with merchants, an occasional tourist, and street people in various stages of disrepair. This was a high-crime area, and I saw a couple of syringes discarded in the shadows near a dumpster as I passed the alley. There were empty Zip-loc bags there, and empty wine and beer bottles.

Even though I stood on tiptoe and craned my neck, I couldn't see what had Lenni's attention. But I could guess.

I stepped carefully past the other gawkers, elbowed through the crowd, then came up behind Lenni. Suddenly I saw the victim, sprawled facedown in a pool of his own blood. He was a young man, probably in his mid-teens, short black hair, dressed in a green T-shirt and dark denims. He seemed somehow familiar. I looked away, sickened and saddened. I tried to remember where I'd seen him.

Suddenly it came to me, and I looked back, astonished. Sure enough, it was the slender young Chinese man I'd seen struggling in Waikiki the first night I'd followed Kimo and his friend. I moved to a different angle and I could partially see his face. There was no doubt about it. This was the young man the haole kid had attacked that night in Waikiki.

Kimo again. He had a connection, no matter how distant, to this brutal death. Here was the common thread to everything that had been happening. I was sure of it. I suddenly wondered what had happened to the haole kid he'd dragged through the glass. Maybe I'd ask Jess about it later, let him solve that part of the puzzle for me. In the meantime, I wanted to know what was going on right here, this very minute.

My gaze landed on a thickset Chinese man in a red silk shirt who was surprisingly close by. He had a perfectly round face, a tiny button nose, and his bullet-shaped head was bald as a bean. A uniformed cop was talking to him, writing things down, while the Chinese man seemed to speak only an occasional chopped-off syllable. The expression on his blunt face was wooden, his eyes were reptilian and flat. I figured he was in his mid-fifties or so, and he was flashy. He didn't have that casual, Hawaiian-born look about him.

Something about my gaze or my movement caught his attention, and he turned slightly. His gaze flicked over me, his eyes kindling with sudden interest. I almost heard the little click as he blinked hard, filing away my appearance. I felt as if I'd been photographed. It spooked me, and I quickly stepped back into the crowd, averting my eyes. I looked again at the crime scene.

Lenni was conferring with her cameraman and hadn't seen me. I stepped closer and touched her arm, causing her to turn. She was shocked. "What on earth are you doing here?"

"Lenni," I said tensely. "The man in the red shirt. Do you know who he is?"

She turned to look. Her eyes were filled with dislike. "That's Mr. Seven's front man and bar manager, Zhing Qu. He's a Jook Kok."

"He's *what*?" I felt my heart drop to my knees.

"I said that he's a Jook Kok. Alex?"

A dark wind rushed past my face, making me giddy.

She was looking at me strangely. "Alex, are you okay? Your face went snow white."

I took a deep breath and regained my balance. "I'm okay, just tired. What's a Jook Kok, Lenni? I've been meaning to ask you." I tried to hide the anxiety I felt.

"You have to ask right now?" She looked at me strangely again.

"It's important, Lenni. What is it?"

She shook her head in exasperation. "Jook Kok is Cantonese for a Hong Kong-born Chinese. A Jook Sing is an American-born Chinese. Why? What's the point? I mean, couldn't this language lesson wait till they've at least scraped this poor kid off the pavement? For Pete's sake, I'm trying to work."

"Sorry, Lenni. My timing is pretty poor today. Look, there's no reason for me to hang around. Phone me later."

She nodded, but she was already preoccupied with the cameraman again, discussing the background shot he'd use to frame her while she did her crime scene intro.

自由

Driving home down Kalakaua Avenue, I felt disoriented. Waikiki's nighttime festival of hustlers and tourists was about to begin. I started to make a sharp right turn, toward my condo. Suddenly I spotted a lime-green Mercedes tooling down Kalakaua, a surfer-type at the wheel. I hit the brakes and slowed down, forcing him to pass me, one lane over. It was Tavares all right, though his head was turned toward the ocean as if he was enjoying the scenery, his left arm casually draped on the window ledge. I moved slowly into the lane behind him and started to follow, but he instantly spotted me in his rearview. He hung an abrupt right, cutting me off, then he hit the gas and was gone, speeding toward Kapiolani Park.

Excellent. Was this guy following me, or was it coincidence? And why did I need one more thing to worry about? I turned back and hung a left into the winding concrete driveway that led up to the eighth floor of my parking garage. I shoved my passcard into a slot on a ticket machine, the security gate lifted, and I was home.

Mail had piled up beneath the door slot. I picked it up, sifting through it. There were a few Christmas cards, a note from Troubles, some bills. I went into my bedroom and tossed them all on the dresser.

I was still agitated from the homicide and the surrounding furor, but it felt good to be home. At an angle through the doorway, I could see the Christmas tree standing silent and unlit: a sentinel to my unmerry Christmas. Only a few more days till the holiday. I would be glad to have it here and gone.

I ignored the tree and ripped off my jacket—I wanted a long, hot shower, something to scrub away the scent and feel of violent death. But as I passed the bedroom answering machine, I noticed that the green message light was blinking.

I touched the button and played my messages. Paké Chang had called twice. Both times he'd snarled, "Call me," then hung up.

The third call was from Mi-Lin. In her wind-chime voice, she asked me to phone, and to come for lunch tomorrow so she could talk to me.

I was just stepping out of the shower, wrapped in a towel, when the phone rang. I sat down, picked up the bedside receiver, and said, "Albright Investigations."

Paké said, "Where you been all day?"

I gritted my teeth. I hate that demanding tone of voice. I said, "Several places, actually, including a homicide scene in China-town."

There was a silence while he thought about that. Then he said, "Who got whacked?"

"When I left, the victim hadn't been identified yet."

"You see him?"

"I did."

"How old?"

I thought that was an odd question. I said, "Looked like a kid, in his mid to late teens."

"Local?"

"I don't think so. I think he was a Jook Kok."

There was a moment's silence. Then Paké said, "Dead for sure?"

"Yes."

"What time?"

"A couple of hours ago."

"How?"

"Shot."

I heard him let air out through his teeth. "Where exactly?"

What was this? Why was I bringing information on Chinatown crime to the crime lord who more-or-less ran Chinatown? I hesitated. Then I shrugged my shoulders. What was the difference? He'd hear it on the news anyway.

I said, "Do you mean where was he shot, or where was he when he was shot?"

"Both."

"I don't know where they shot him. But his body was lying on the sidewalk in front of the porno bookstore next to the Shatin Lounge."

"What you doing at the Shatin? Was Kimo there?"

"No." Why would he think Kimo was in the Shatin?

"You're supposed to be watching Kimo," he said, suddenly surly.

I sighed. "Look, Paké, I've had a long day. What exactly did you need?"

He surprised me by chuckling. "I need foah see you."

"You're welcome to come here."

"Nah. You come at 1 A.M. to the Calabash. Got that?"

I could here bar noises in the background.

"No problem," I said, "but—"

It was too late. He'd already hung up.

I glanced at my watch and was surprised to see that it was only ten till five. A long time before I could find out what Paké had on his mind. My brain was a turmoil of worry and bewilderment. I had to keep moving. I picked up a few things, washed and put away the dishes that had been accumulating in the dishwasher—in short, did anything physical that came to mind in order to vent my nervous energy.

I was concerned about this sudden swirl of death I kept stepping into. Why were they all teenaged Chinese kids? The killing today had brought back the memory of the young Chinese boy in the Ala Wai Canal. As I worked, I tried to add up the pieces of information I'd accumulated step-by-step, to see if anything made sense.

I mulled it all over till my mind was a whirlwind, then I shook it off with an effort, took a frosted glass of fresh-squeezed limeade out to the balcony, and sat down and propped up my feet on a chair. A gentle breeze stroked the island. The sky was soft blue and filled with fluffy clouds, the water pure aquamarine. I glanced at my watch. Only five-thirty. Still a lot of time to kill.

I kept trying to understand the drug angle. Were they really turning the illegals into junkies that would make a complacent and dependent army when they arrived here? That would be no surprise. Drug traffickers were by definition incapable of respecting human life. But if Dru Chun Yuen had been addicted to drugs, why no track marks?

Unless . . .

Oh, man.

I suddenly realized I'd been looking at things through the tunnel vision of my own cultural bias. Most Caucasians used hypodermic needles to inject heroin dissolved in water. But most Chinese smoked it! Of course. That was it.

China White, the king of narcotics, was the top-grade heroin, powdery, white in color, the drug of choice for American junkies since it was easily dissolved in water and easy to inject. Injecting gives the fastest, most intense high—and also carries the highest risk of overdose since it goes directly into the bloodstream.

When first processed, China White was as much as 99 percent pure, which meant there was a lot of profit margin in the pipelines. By the time it hit the streets, it had often been cut so many times that the purity was down to around 5 percent, which meant the volume had been increased by about twenty times. Snow falling all over the city, most of it milk sugar, but enough left to addict you for the rest of your life whether you smoked it, injected it, or sniffed it.

Chinese Brown Sugar was a less refined version of the same product. It was more granular or rocky, and not so easy to dissolve and inject. It was cheaper, easier to process. This was the drug of choice for the Chinese. They placed a few grains on a piece of tinfoil, heated it over a candle, then inhaled through a rolled-up dollar bill or other small tube. This was called "chasing the dragon," and it was equally deadly, though it took a bit longer to become addicted this way.

If track marks were the only criterion the medical examiner had used in determining that Dru Chun Yuen was not an addict, he'd been on the wrong track indeed.

How on earth had I missed such an obvious explanation? But on the other hand, did it really matter? I already knew with a growing certainty that the two kids had been involved in the drug world. Tavares had said they already had Dru Chun Yuen working as a courier. It didn't matter if they were using, dealing, or just hanging out with the big guys. Drugs had gotten one—maybe both—of them killed.

CHAPTER
15

I went into the kitchen, picked up the phone, and dialed Jess.
After three rings, he picked up the phone.

"Jess, it's me. Do you have a minute?"

"Hello, Alex. Merry Christmas. What's up?"

"Merry Christmas, Jess. Did you catch the call on the homicide in Chinatown?"

"I did. Why?"

"I was down there, but I didn't see you."

"Busy day, Alex, we were running a little late. What's up?"

"Did you ID the victim?"

"Tentatively. Why?"

"You're going to love this," I said.

I told him about recognizing the dead kid. I told him more about the rest of what I'd seen that night on Waikiki with regard to Kimo Chang's interference in the bloody melee.

Jess's voice turned sharp. "You're sure it was the same kid?"

"Positive. It was definitely the slender young Chinese man I saw in the knife fight, and Kimo definitely stepped in to stop him from getting hurt. I thought at first that he was local, but after seeing him again I'm not so sure."

"Why did you change your mind?"

"Oh, you know, the haircut, the way he carried himself, the indifferent expression on his face when he was alive."

"I tend to agree with you on that. We think he was from Hong Kong, by way of San Francisco. A member of a youth gang. We're running a check with the San Francisco P.D. on him right now."

Jess paused before adding, "You know anything else about the haole kid who came at him with the knife in Waikiki?"

"Only that he's probably carrying scars for life that will remind him not to start trouble. They took him away in an ambulance, but I doubt if they arrested him. Nobody stuck around to press charges and he definitely got the hard end of the fight."

"I guess I can start by looking at hospital records and see where it leads me," Jess said. The reluctance in his voice told me that he already had his hands full and wasn't looking forward to the extra work.

"You'll let me know what you find out?"

"As long as this stays strictly between us. Don't mention this connection to anyone else just now, Alex. There are things going on that you can't begin to understand, and unfortunately, I can't fill you in." I thought about that. I had a feeling that I was figuring out a great deal more than Jess suspected.

Sweetly, I said, "Deal, Jess. And by the way, is there anything new regarding Dru Chun Yuen's autopsy? I'm wondering specifically what they found with regard to the level of drugs in his body."

"Why?" I could almost see the frown on his face. I could certainly hear it in his voice.

I told him what I'd been thinking about Dru Chun Yuen's possible heroin habit. Maybe he'd been smoking heroin rather than shooting it, which would explain why there were no needle scars.

He said, "Good point. But why would it matter?"

"My first thought too. But don't you see? Maybe the same people who brought in the illegals are also bringing in drugs. They certainly would be if they were addicting people in transit. Maybe the boy learned something that could give them away and they killed him to shut him up."

"That's a lot of 'maybes'."

"Yes. But why else kill him?"

"Maybe he was going to talk to the feds about the Snakehead."

"But what would he know? I mean, he was in the ship's hold, certainly in no position to infiltrate the upper ranks. No, he stumbled into something else. I'm sure of it."

"Okay," Jess said reluctantly. "Let's say he did. What would it mean?"

I shrugged. "You've got me."

Wearily, he said, "I'm not getting anywhere on this case. I've been at it for over a week. Even with an interpreter I can't talk to the illegals at the Sand Island holding station. They clam up and won't say a word. It's beginning to look hopeless."

"Were any of them tested for drugs?"

"I don't think so. You'd have to ask INS about that."

"Are you going to check it out?"

"I could."

"Let me know," I said. I had a sudden rush of anxiety. "But don't pull in Kimo Chang right now for questioning about the kid who just got killed in Chinatown, okay? I want to check some things out first."

"No problem, Alex. I have plenty of other things to do just now."

I wondered how Paké would feel when he knew I'd gotten his nephew involved in a murder. It was bad enough that Freitas was going to nail Kimo for selling stolen goods, and I wasn't about to tell Paké about that.

Jess apparently picked up on my train of thought. "You still running errands for Paké Chang?"

"Really, Jess, it's not the way you think it is."

"Maybe not yet. It will be."

"I'm just finding it a little harder to cut loose than I thought."

"Watch out for him." Jess sounded uneasy. "I know he comes on like you're one of the family. But he's murdered more than one person in cold blood, and if you cross him . . . well, he has a short fuse."

There was no point in asking why Paké wasn't behind bars if they knew that about him. The front-door, backdoor policy of Honolulu's criminal justice system was common knowledge. Most of the habitual criminals in Chinatown considered a month or so in the slammer just part of the cost of doing business, and they almost never got more than that.

I had a sudden thought that I couldn't articulate. Maybe Dru Chun Yuen had learned something *Kimo* didn't want him to know. Now that was a possibility, considering all the things that Kimo was apparently into. After all, Paké had known where to find the body. But if Kimo had murdered the Yuen kid, Paké would surely have cleaned up after him, taken the body and buried it in quicklime, or taken it out to sea and dropped it into a few hundred fathoms of water. He certainly wouldn't have called me and suggested I go find the body and notify the cops. And he certainly wouldn't have linked me to Kimo and told me to watch him. No, that theory had enough holes for a school of whales to swim through.

"Alex? You still there?"

"Sorry, Jess, I got sidetracked for a minute. Look, I'm probably interrupting your dinner. I'll call back later."

I hung up. Suddenly I didn't want to share my thoughts. Not even with Jess.

I knew in that instant that I needed to refocus my attention on Kimo Chang, Honolulu's would-be one-man crime wave. If I could talk to him face-to-face, maybe he'd even tell me the truth. *Fat chance!*

But somehow a communication link had to be established. Because Kimo was our only possible witness to what had really happened to Dru Chun Yuen, the only possible link to Mock Sing's whereabouts.

I sighed, feeling overwhelmed. My mind was unraveling. But I couldn't quit hashing over the problems. What about another angle? It would help if I could just talk to Henry Li's chauffeur. But he was back in Hong Kong, discharged from his job, totally out of bounds.

I worried myself full circle, till I was thinking about Paké's midnight phone call again. I stared out at the waterfront. *They come across the water and even the sky doesn't know. They come like ghosts.*

Triads.

What else?

Moving across the sea as stealthy as whispers, moving into Honolulu, infiltrating the power centers, the financial centers, turning Honolulu into Asia's new heroin-financing hub, into the center of a cold-blooded organization devoted to a level of greed that would taint and corrupt everything it touched. The very concept made the pressure close in on me.

Was it really happening? Could that be what I'd stumbled into?

Johnny Tavares had as much as told me it was, that night up on Tantalus. Beginning at his home base in San Francisco, he'd tracked the network from Thailand to Hong Kong to San Francisco to Honolulu, where Mr. Seven was a key link, he'd said. Mr. Seven had come here from San Francisco, where the Hong Kong Triads had set up shop a century ago and now controlled the streets with a bloody iron fist. Was Mr. Seven a 14K? This was the biggest Hong Kong Triad, with branches in Japan, Taiwan, Macao, Europe, Southeast Asia, Vancouver, San Francisco, and New York City. This was also the most powerful Triad, and once they decided to move in, stopping them wouldn't be easy.

Or perhaps the Triad was the Wah Ching, long entrenched in California and ruled from Hong Kong. Or maybe it was San Francisco's Wo Hop To, or Bing Kung, or Hip Sing. I surprised myself by remembering them all. Whatever was happening had both a San Francisco and a Hong Kong connection, that much was certain.

I knew that a lot of Hong Kong money had been moving into

the Islands over the past couple of years. Several major commercial properties that had belonged to the Japanese were now Chinese-owned, and who knew if they were legitimate businessmen or criminals? But it seemed almost impossible that the Triads could literally infiltrate Honolulu's criminal community and begin to take hold at the street level here. It had never been done before. The thought made me cold with fear.

Once again I thought of the phrase, "Better the devil you know than the devil you don't." A lot of bad things happened here, but it could definitely get worse. At least we didn't have youth gangs engaged in regular shoot-outs so brutal that the news media labeled them "massacres." Here, there was some police control over the prostitution and gambling, at least enough to keep it relatively clean, all things considered. Underage girls weren't abducted and brought into brothels wholesale, as happened in Triad establishments. The high-stakes gambling rarely erupted into an execution. Violence happened from time to time, but with nowhere near the frequency as in the Triad-ruled Chinatowns of San Francisco, New York, and Vancouver. There, people tended to get gunned down or stabbed a dozen at a time.

No, give me a choice between the local syndicate and the Triads, and I'd have to side with Paké Chang every time. Not that I wouldn't like to see him out of business too. But he wasn't going to go out of business until people quit supporting his enterprises. Or until someone *put* him out of business, and when he went, it was going to create a very large and very dangerous vacuum.

I gazed out over the sea. The water was silver, streaked with a wine-red sunset. Soon it would be black, all the way to the rim of the world; all the way to China.

My thoughts darted here and there, but everything kept leading back to the same old question. Why on earth had the young boy been killed? What had he found out that made him so dangerous? Suddenly I was eager to talk with Paké. He had some answers, if I could only pry them out.

I glanced at my watch. Three minutes past six. Seven full hours till I could talk to Paké, but I was just in time to catch the six o'clock news.

Lenni had apparently edited her Chinatown footage in time to make the broadcast. I'd missed the lead-in and the advertisements, and she was already on-screen, tilting her regal head so the camera could catch her best angle, and she was rolling right into the action.

She said, "This afternoon in Chinatown, eighteen-year-old Shan Wo Loo died in an execution-style slaying, shot twice in the back of the head at close range by a .38 caliber semi-automatic. The HSP ran the boy's ID through the San Francisco police. They learned that the victim was an illegal alien from Hong Kong and was reportedly a member of the San Francisco Chinatown youth gang known as the Shadow Dragons. He was wanted for questioning in the deaths of nine of that city's Chinatown gamblers, who were found shot to death in a basement gambling den in October of this year. Shan Wo Loo has been missing since then, though a local informant states that he was dealing drugs in Waikiki."

Well. They'd done some fast work indeed.

She said, "Homicide detective Jess Seitaki believes this killing is linked to a new gang of youths who have been threatening merchants and other teens who frequent Chinatown."

Jess came on the screen, stern-faced and angry, while Lenni—on film—held the mike out for him to speak into.

He said, "We believe that Shan Wo Loo was a Red Pole in the San Francisco branch of the Shadow Dragons. The youth gang that's been growing in Honolulu's Chinatown also calls itself the Shadow Dragons. At this point, we're still hoping they're just emulating the San Francisco gang, but it's possible that the San Francisco gang is attempting to establish a foothold here."

Lenni on film, said, "And what does this mean to the long-time merchants in Honolulu's Chinatown?"

Jess scowled. "In a word, trouble. The Asian youth gangs in other U.S. cities specialize in extorting merchants in addition to their other illegal enterprises. We seem to be looking at a new era in Chinatown. If the increasing violence isn't stopped soon, the results will have repercussions throughout the Islands."

Lenni drew the mike to her own mouth. "Are you talking about the possible economic impact?"

Jess said grimly, "It will certainly hurt tourism in Chinatown. The merchants there are already feeling the bite, people are choosing not to shop there. The rest of the island is bound to feel the ripple effects. Right now, all we can hope to do is keep the lid on and find out who's behind this so we can stop it."

Lenni said, "We understand that a witness saw several teenage boys running from the crime scene."

Jess looked annoyed, but said evenly, "We are presently taking witness statements, and I'd like to withhold further comment until all the information is in."

Lenni came back on screen live. "If anyone has information about this crime, please phone—"

She gave the station's hot-line number.

"And now for the rest of the news—"

I clicked off the TV and opened up that part of my mind that contained my lessons from DEA-101.

Youth gangs were a primary tool of the Triads. In New York City, in San Francisco, in Vancouver, they handled all the hatchet work and street-level enforcement for the criminal tongs, which were actually Triad cells. These youths were unbelievably cruel and contemptuous of human life.

Occasionally a street gang member could even climb up through the ranks and into the upper hierarchy of the tong societies. With names like Ghost Shadows, White Eagles, Black Eagles, Flying Dragons, and other colorful titles, the street gangs developed junior criminal organizations of their own and created adult-sized mayhem. They were especially brutal and cold with their own people, extorting money and gunning down merchants who refused to pay, demanding subservience from all others in their territory. The criminal tong members were the only ones who were more powerful than these street gangs, and even here there was sometimes conflict.

Well. I was surprised by how much I remembered of my DEA training. I was also surprised that this was all starting to come together, in a crazy sort of way. I was going to figure it all out. I knew it. And it really was time I talked to Paké Chang.

CHAPTER

16

The Calabash was on the bottom floor of the Royal Seashell Hotel. It was one of the few Waikiki cocktail lounges that drew the locals as well as the tourists. Pua Kapakiha owned the bar, though I'd heard that Paké had bought it for her with syndicate money. He had his own bar in Chinatown, called the Lucky Lion. That was his headquarters. Apparently the higher-classed Calabash was where he did his private business.

At 1:00 on the dot, I walked through the doorway and into the faintly lit barroom. The tobacco smoke was thick. The room was decorated with huge carved tikis, thick vines and ferns, real baby palm trees, and tapa cloth. It had a jungle ambiance, with a tiny waterfall in one corner spilling into a rock basin. Overhead, old-fashioned tropical ceiling fans stirred the conditioned air. The bar itself was carved with Hawaiian petroglyphs and designs, and the booths were partly concealed by giant pothos plants and riotous flowers. I looked around, didn't see Paké, so I sat down on the end barstool nearest the door. There were only half a dozen customers sitting at the long bar, and all of them were at the far end.

Pua was tending bar. She was in her mid-forties, tall and slender. Her face had a seasoned look—she'd seen some action if she'd been with Paké all these years.

She moved fluidly from one customer to another, pouring beer from bottles into mugs, smiling and talking and generally tending to her business. A hard, knowing look came into her eyes as she approached me. "You the detective?" she said. She looked me up and down, and I could see she was wondering if I was competition.

"I'm Alex Albright," I said. "Your husband said for me to meet him here."

There. I'd just let her know right up front that Paké was her property, and it was fine by me.

Her blink was a silent acknowledgment of my message. She smiled as if she'd been caught at something, and I liked her instantly. "You want something while you wait?"

"Maybe a Seven-Up."

She brought me a tall, frosted glass garnished with tiny vanda orchids, then went into a back room. A second later she came back and gave me a slight nod, directing me down the hall toward the rest rooms.

By now I was thinking about Peter Lorre and all those Bogart movies, but I grabbed up my purse and my drink and headed down the hallway. The office door was slightly ajar. I stuck my nose through the opened door. Paké, sitting behind a cluttered desk, nodded.

"Ey, Alex," he said, motioning me in. "Make house." Which is pidgin for make yourself at home.

I could see now that he'd been chewing on a hamburger. He took another quick bite, then looked at me again. "Eh, like eat?"

His friendly attitude surprised me, after all his surly phone calls. I sat down, dropped my purse to the carpet beside me, held onto my Seven-Up, and said, "I've already had dinner, thanks, Paké. What's up?"

"You one working *wahine*, I nevah can catch you home. Say, what's that you got, one Seven-Up?"

"Yes."

"You want one whiskey? I get Pua to bring us back a little something . . ."

"No thanks. This is fine."

"Maybe you like one Puna bud mo' bettah?" A mischievous look came into his eyes.

"Thanks, no, I don't smoke pakalolo either." I sat on the edge of my chair and kept my face stoic, to let him see that his feigned camaraderie wasn't going to thaw me out.

He followed my lead, turning serious. He said, "Okay. So. I wan' know if you got anything to tell me about Kimo."

"I do."

"You been finding time to check him out, see what the little buggah is up to?"

"As a matter of fact, I've been wanting to talk to you about Kimo. I don't think I can handle him anymore."

His head snapped up and he glowered at me. "Why not?"

I told him about the incident on Waikiki where Kimo had sliced up the kid who'd been dealing bogus. When I'd finished, I said, "I don't understand that, Paké. I don't want to get into your business, but there is something really wrong with that scenario. Is Kimo addicted to drugs?"

Paké suddenly looked ashamed, then he quickly hid it behind a note of arrogance. "I don' hire you to worry about Kimo's dope."

"Which is another reason why I think I'd better bow out of this job."

"You made one deal."

"I did. But I can't keep my end of it. Too much is happening, and I believe that Kimo is on to me anyway."

I told him about my visit to Auntie Elma Chang, about Kimo's spying and the noise at Auntie Elma's kitchen window, about what I'd overheard with regard to Kimo's verbal abuse of his auntie, about my flat tire.

"Why you wan' see Auntie Elma?" He was looking at me with narrowed eyes. "You learn any more about that puka-head kid you found in the canal?"

"Not really, though I was asking questions."

I expected him to get mad, but he just got curious. "They can't find out yet who whacked 'im, eh?"

"Not yet. But whatever is happening with Kimo fits into it somehow. I wonder, too, about the boy who is still missing. I wanted to see if Auntie Elma could tell me anything about him."

"What did she say?"

"She said that Kimo had talked the kids into leaving with him, and she'd never seen them again."

Paké's face turned dark with rage.

"I gon' whack that little buggah."

"Beating on him won't help. If he's doing drugs, he needs professional help to get clean. If he's not, he needs professional help of another kind. He's violent. I honestly don't think I can do any more for you in that direction."

"He follow you?"

"No. At least, not that I know of."

Paké cursed. "I wan' take care of him. You see if I don't."

"Paké, I'll be honest with you. I can't remember when I've seen a kid who is so screwed up. If he doesn't get help, he's going to get in serious trouble sooner or later, and my bet would be on sooner."

Paké was looking at me incredulously. "Why you think I wan' you to check him out?"

"I don't have a clue, but whatever is happening is beyond me."

He nodded glumly and studied the floor.

I figured this was my chance.

"Paké, I want to know about the youth gangs. The ones in Chinatown. That kid today got shot by gang members. What's happening down there?"

"Who said?"

"I heard it on the news, like everybody else."

"You talk to the cops?"

I was silent.

He drew in a long breath, then his shoulders slumped and he said, "You know Phan Lo?"

"Mr. Seven, who owns the Shatin Lounge?"

"Yeah. He's one San Francisco paké. He wants to start one beef with me. I don' want trouble, I got enough, he can have one place or two in Chinatown, run a little game, what do I care? When I told Kimo I wouldn't turn him out, next thing I know Kimo is hanging out with Phan Lo—Mr. Seven."

I was astonished beyond words.

"Yeah," Paké said, hard-faced. "That buggah Kimo wan' help get rid of me because I won' help him. Next thing, he's hanging with these Chinese boys, street trash, I don' see them around before, then I hear he's become one Red Pole."

"What's that?"

"Red Pole is an enforcer. Chinese."

"For Mr. Seven?"

He tilted his heavy head and studied me for a moment. His eyes were dark as death. Finally, he said, "You don' tell your cop friends about this."

I sighed. "We've been through all this before." I opened up my purse. "Tell you the truth, Mr. Chang, once in a while I come across something I'm just not very good at, and I think this is it. Especially if you insist on keeping me in the dark about everything and lying to me when you do say something. I've brought your retainer back."

He held up his hand to stop me. For a second I saw a spark of rage in his eyes, but he quickly glossed it over and said, "What you want to know?"

My face almost twisted up in disbelief. This was the last reaction in the world I would have expected from him.

As if reading my mind, he smiled. "Kimo's one worthless little buggah, but I promise his mother I'd watch out for him. You take a look when you can, you keep the money, you tell me what you can find out, no huli-huli." Which meant no pressure. Well.

I said, "Some things are puzzling me."

He smiled, sphinxlike, leaned back in his chair, and said, "Ask."

"What's the deal with the illegals? Who's bringing them into the islands?"

He almost came up out of his chair, but caught himself and said, "Ask something else."

"Okay, I'll compromise. Tell you what: answer just one other question and I'll change the subject."

"Ask."

"Why did you phone that morning and tell me to watch out for the water?"

He looked at me with such sudden fury that I almost flinched. He said, "You sound like one of those poho news reporters now, like that nosy wahine you been hangin' round with."

I felt a look of astonishment on my face, and I couldn't force it away. I said, "I just want to know why you targeted me."

His eyes smoldered. "I didn't target you. They did."

"*Who* did?"

His anger deepened. "The Jook Koks."

"Wha—"

"I wan' help you out, I hear they set you up, I wan' fix it. I remember your old man; he one good cop."

"My husband? Yes, he was, but what on earth do you mean, 'help me'?"

At that very instant, the phone rang.

He swept up the receiver in his ham-hock hand. "Yeah?"

He listened intently—I could barely hear a deep voice crackling through the line, obviously excited, talking fast. Paké's face turned darker and darker with rage, till the expression sent shivers through me. Finally the voice fell silent. Paké dropped the receiver into the cradle, and suddenly I didn't matter anymore.

"I got to go," he said. "Business. I'll get back to you."

And without another word he picked up his jacket and walked out the door, leaving me sitting there alone.

But only for a second. Because Pua, evidently sent back by him on his way out, came in and said, "We're closing now."

"Right," I said. I was already standing up with my purse in my hand.

I found my own way out.

自由

That night, I had tormented dreams. I was warm, getting warmer, and suddenly I was roasting, melting. My eyes flew open, and I was in a crucible, a huge jadeite bowl atop a white-hot fire that was trapped in nothingness.

Gemstones tumbled into the jade crucible around me: glittering emeralds, ice-blue sapphires, blazing diamonds, fiery rubies, pristine pearls. They were being sifted, churned; they filled the bottom of the crucible like glistening gravel turned white-hot. They were like sand, and I was being heated and melted and purified by fire along with them.

I heard evil, hollow laugnter. Suddenly I saw Paké, Mi-Lin, Mr. Seven, and Henry Li peering over the giant, bowl-like rim. I knew they were taking turns stirring the blistering fire, fueling it, their faces tight with anger, their eyes black with hate. They kept churning the crucible's contents—me included, the motion nauseating me and making me giddy. They were stirring with a long red pole topped with a stylized red dragon. They occasionally dropped in one of Henry Li's stolen jade pieces: the shiny little black beast I'd seen on Frietas's shelf came first, the deer-dragon-unicorn called a Ch'i-lin; then came the bearded dog of Fo.

The jade and gems were melting. I was burning, and the pain was excruciating. Sweat was pouring from my body, and I had a thirst like nothing I'd ever felt before. The fires of hell were around me, devouring me. The gemstones were melting, the light in them turning into molten color; I was melting too then, seeping into a wide river, into seawater, the steam misting the world around me, swallowing me completely.

Suddenly a great, white dragon of smoke coiled up out of the steam and solidified, its face implacable, indifferent, a cold hatred brooding in its topaz eyes. The gems were visible again, beautiful and brilliant and shimmering—yet somehow evil, so very evil, as evil as the dragon and yet so beautiful and beguiling—

I awakened in terror. The room was cold but I was sweating.

I had to deliberately will my fear-frozen limbs to work as I stiffly sat up and turned on the bedside lamp. The terror stayed with me. Almost sleepwalking, dreading what might appear at any moment, I climbed out of bed.

I checked every room. Nothing. No reason for my horror except my own bizarre imagination. I went into the kitchen and gulped a glass of water, though in truth I was no longer thirsty.

But at least the fear had begun to subside.

The images of the dream were beginning to fade, and I considered how empty the condo seemed since Troubles had gone home. I focused on the unlit Christmas tree.

For some reason my thoughts shifted from Troubles to Tavares. Then I realized that the concept of a crucible came from his comment about being in the crucible, tried by fire, that night we'd been talking up on Tantalus. The words had burrowed into the dark recesses of my troubled thoughts to merge with other symbols of recent distressing events. Finally the images had exploded as the eerie nightmare.

I knew about the crucible. This was the melting pot, the testing place where the most severe lessons were learned. The fiery crucible forged the night sweats that undercover drug enforcement agents lived with, the knowledge of the evil that fueled the drug traffic, the knowledge of their own imminent deaths and the limits of their own abilities as they did silent battle with one of the most insidious evils in the world.

But I shouldn't be having night sweats. I wasn't out there in the midst of the evil. I was here, safe in my own home, a Christmas tree in front of me, my own familiar possessions surrounding me. For some reason, none of that comforted me. On an impulse, I stepped over and turned on the Christmas tree lights.

They glittered coldly, like the gems in the crucible. I looked at them again, trying to manufacture the warmth of the Christmas season.

Nothing happened. The lights remained beautiful, delicate, yet distant as the cold, brittle stars.

I remembered something. I'd read in a news magazine about a Chinese man who had been arrested for some small civil error in Beijing. He had been put into the Bamboo Gulag, China's inhuman prison camp. He'd worked there for eight years, almost working himself to death, making—of all things—Christmas tree lights. He said that many of the lights—and other Chinese goods—were manufactured behind the Gulag, through slave labor, and he'd been petitioning the people of the United States to stop purchasing such goods.

I turned off the lights. On my way back to the bedroom, I made an impulsive detour through my office, switched on a lamp, and rummaged through the stack of boxes in the corner that had held the Christmas decorations. I hadn't gotten around to storing them back in the closet yet. I picked up the box that had held the lights, and sure enough, there it was stamped right on the side. MADE IN CHINA.

Nothing was sacred. Nothing at all. The evil had leaked into every aspect of my existence.

Suddenly I felt an almost tangible pang of loneliness. I missed Troubles. I missed David. I yearned to go home for Christmas, to be with people who loved me, to be safe and warm in a normal world where the black, scabrous claws of the dragon had not yet dragged across the face of the world to spread their poison.

I felt a rush of resentment that I was alone. I felt rejected, abandoned. The feeling welled into a sense of total failure. If only I'd had the common sense to do something that would pay a decent livelihood—like my sister—I could be home right now, instead of alone here awakening to nightmares. I felt a sense of self-disgust that was totally new to me. When had I decided it was up to me to change the world, anyway? What business was this of mine?

I didn't like the way I felt. It was almost as if something was eating at me. I tried to pray, but even the heavens seemed empty. The loneliness and the feeling of self-disgust remained.

I went back to bed and lay there with the lights on, thinking about the dream for a very long time. Finally, feeling absolutely desolate, I fell into a dreamless sleep.

17

The phone awakened me at 9:30 A.M. "Alex?" It was Mi-Lin's melodious voice.

"Speaking."

"Are you busy?"

"Not really. I was planning to return your call, but I slept late."

"Well darling, Henry is in San Francisco on business, and he won't be back until late tonight. I'm alone in this huge house—except for the servants, of course—and I'm worrying myself silly about the upcoming jade exhibit. I don't know whether to call it off or change the exhibit lists, or simply escape to Switzerland and ski, and let Henry worry about it all."

"Switzerland sounds like the best bet to me."

She made that tinkling laugh that enchanted me. She always seemed so carefree. I felt a touch of self-annoyance. Why couldn't I be more like that?

She said, "If I go, I shall take you with me. Perhaps you can use your detective skills to discover some handsome, unattached men, and we'll have ourselves a holiday."

"When do we leave?"

"Ah, Alex. It would be wonderful, wouldn't it?" Her voice was filled with longing. "But Henry really couldn't handle the exhibit, he'd make a total mess of it all. Actually, I was wondering if you'd learned anything about our missing artifacts."

I considered telling her about Frietas's sting operation, but something stopped me. I said, "I'm still working on it."

"Well work, then, darling. Present Henry with a huge bill when he gets back. It's all his fault that this happened, and he deserves to pay for it."

I felt a little uncomfortable at that. I said, "Actually, I'm hoping to crack the case in another day or so."

"What a shame. The longer it takes to find our jade, the better I shall get to know you and the better friends we will become."

"That's very kind of you."

She laughed again, merrily. "Well, when you've done your wonderful work and gone on to other adventures, we shall miss you. All the same, I do hope you can get our jade and my jewelry back."

"I have a pretty good lead on where some of it is."

"Ah, Alex. You're a genius! What on earth have you done, to learn something so fast?"

I felt a rush of embarrassment mixed with pride. I had done a good job, better than she knew. But most of it had been pure, dumb luck. I said, "I need to do some more investigating before I hand you the report, but I think you'll be pleased."

"How excellent!" The pleasure in her voice seemed so sincere, her appreciation so complete, that I felt a surge of indebtedness. At least someone in the world appreciated me.

"Perhaps I can help you a bit more," she said. "I'm afraid I've been naughty and kept things from you, but Henry can be so horrible when he's crossed, and it was impossible to explain much with him listening to my every word, prepared to criticize. Could you come for dinner tonight, so we can have a heart-to-heart chat?"

I felt a tinge of resentment at having my time tampered with. Then I remembered my bills and Henry Li's very generous retainer, and suddenly I was annoyed with myself for not diving into the job and truly giving them their money's worth. It was just that all these things in Chinatown kept derailing me from my usual diligence—interesting things, but nevertheless it wasn't like me to ignore my responsibilities.

I said, "I'd be happy to come for dinner."

"That's wonderful, darling. Can you be here at eight?"

"Sounds fine."

"Is there anything special we can make for you? Our cook, Syn Siu, used to be a master chef at the Shi Ching in Hong Kong, and his dishes will break your heart."

"Just what you'd like to have. I'm not fussy."

"Well, ta-ta, then. See you this evening."

It was only 10 A.M. I had a lot of time to kill. All of a sudden I was ravenously hungry and the world looked promising again.

I dressed and went to the Sheraton's Ocean Terrace for their buffet breakfast. I bypassed the eggs and bacon, and stuck with the poppy seed muffins and fruit—papaya, mango, banana, and grapes. The room was decorated for Christmas—red wreaths everywhere, holly, pinecones, and other nontropical splendor. The terrace was open-air, and the sea spread out in front of the white railing, bright blue welded to a paler blue sky.

I drank too much coffee. When I got home, the caffeine high kicked in and I was so restless I couldn't sit still. But I wasn't getting anything accomplished either. I'd wanted to go for a swim and work some of the anxiety out, but the beaches were so crowded that I'd changed my mind.

I felt as if I was waiting for something to happen. But at the same time, I knew that nothing was going to happen unless I *made* it happen. I picked up the phone.

The news manager told me that Lenni was filming again in Chinatown and asked me if I needed the location. I said no, I'd call later. I wasn't in the mood to fight the downtown traffic, and Chinatown didn't seem very inviting when I remembered the pool of blood around the young shooting victim.

Next, I phoned Jess. When he answered, I said, "Morning. Did you get a chance to talk to anyone at the INS about the drug testing?"

"Not yet, Alex." He was irritable, as if he'd been up all night.

"Okay, sorry to bother you. Let me know when you do."

"The very minute. Say, what are you doing for Christmas? Yoko told me she'd asked you a month ago. Have you decided to grace us with your presence yet?"

I felt a little pang of resentment that I was alone for Christmas. Still, I said, "I guess not, Jess. I made other plans. I don't want to intrude on your family holiday, and several singles are volunteering their services at the River of Life Mission, to help feed the homeless their Christmas dinner."

"Virtuous," Jess said. "But a tough way to spend the day."

"Call it penance," I said. "I'll be a better person for it."

Though in truth it was really just a way to keep my mind off my own problems. And besides, the pastor's wife had more or less roped me into doing it.

I switched on the TV and watched CNN for a few minutes, catching the top of the news, then I phoned my mother's house in Colorado. Troubles answered. They were on their way to a church concert and ice-skating in the park. They were already running late, so I made it short.

Feeling unloved, put-upon, and rejected, I drove up to Kaimuki, to where Frietas was holding his hukilau. The store was tightly padlocked, though it was already noon. I stopped at a pay phone at the 7-Eleven store, called HSP, and asked to speak with Frietas. He wasn't available. As I climbed back into my Honda, I wondered if he'd wrapped up his case and I'd missed my opportunity to check out more incoming goods. I'd ask Jess later. The jade and jewelry would end up in the police evidence room—unless Frietas actually pilfered some. But he hadn't been serious. It would be safe till I got to it. In the meantime, I had other things to do.

I drove back of Diamond Head, cut down Kaimuki Avenue, hit Kapahulu, then hung a left on Ala Wai Boulevard. I drove past the place where I'd found the young kid's body. I still hadn't resumed my early morning jog. I wasn't ready to relive my grisly discovery. Plus, I was still uneasy about someone keeping an eye on me—even if it was Tavares. I was certain he was the man who'd been spotted by the security guard. He'd probably just been checking me out. But if that was true, how had Paké known about my morning jogs? Were Paké and Tavares acquainted? I shook off the thought. That line of thinking was futile.

As I turned toward home, I started thinking about Dru Chun Yuen. I parked my Honda in its customary stall, checked to make sure that Troubles's fire-engine red motorcycle was intact (it was). Still preoccupied, I walked through the poorly lit garage to the plate-glass door that opened into my hallway. I inserted my key in the lock and started to open the door.

I wasn't watching my periphery, and *whack!* Something hit me on the left of my head, I reeled and dropped to my knees, ears ringing, flesh tearing on the rough concrete, stabs of lightning zapping through my head from the blow.

I was stunned. I didn't know what was happening as I tried to stand up, my knees turning to rubber, and then I felt something kick me in the side, a brick foot inside black cloth kung fu shoes. I rolled, and I was looking up at Kimo Chang, into his gleeful, malevolent eyes. He cocked his head to one side and shook it slightly, poised like that for just a split instant, and then he lunged and raised his fist to hit me again. I rolled away from the blow just in time.

In the mad rush of violence I glimpsed his companions, two small-boned Chinese boys in their late teens, not local, dressed in black jeans, T-shirts, the same black cloth fighting shoes, knives in sheaths at their belts. Both boys had the look that comes to people who have been brutalized beyond feeling.

They hung back, watching impassively, while Kimo braced himself. Angry that I'd avoided his blow, he rushed in again to deliver a kick to my ribs. The blow glanced off as I moved again, but it hurt—a lot—and I cried out. He smiled cruelly.

I rolled to one side in time to blunt the next blow. I wanted to scream for help, but I couldn't get enough breath. Gaining momentum by bracing myself against the wall, I sprang to my feet, surprising Kimo for a second, but he was instantly on me again. He saw my slight skill in martial arts in my movements. He intensified his own attack because he had been bested by a woman. He'd have to save face with his friends.

I braced myself against the wall as he came in and swept my arms up in a karate block. Three years of tae kwon do training did the trick and his blow glanced off my crossed wrists. His eyes slitted in fury.

In that moment our eyes locked. Suddenly I knew. He was peering out from the depths of a long jagged tunnel that held him in an inescapable cage: the prison of an enraged, drug-deadened soul.

Processing that information at the speed of light, I knew why Kimo had been able to drag the haole kid through the glass that night. He hadn't even felt the pain—his own, or his victim's.

He had deadened his feelings by chasing the dragon. But the dragon had suddenly lashed about, to catch Kimo in its scaly, deadly claws. Now it was mauling him, toying with him. It would keep him for all eternity.

Kimo's eyes flooded with renewed hatred. He'd seen the shock in my eyes. He knew I'd seen the truth. He drew back and started to punch me again. I reeled backward, terrified but trying to defend myself. I wasn't going to win this one—especially when his two silent reptilian allies finally stepped in to help him. But if I was going to die—and I thought I was—then I was going to die fighting.

Kimo punched, I dodged, and in that frozen instant I heard a faraway "ping" as the parking garage elevator stopped and the door slid open.

A familiar voice shouted, "Hey! What are you doing—"

Kimo stopped in mid-motion, exchanged looks with the Chinese kids, and then they were racing down the spiral driveway that led to the street security gate—a gate that could be opened from the inside without a key.

I was sobbing, but didn't realize it until the daytime security manager was leaning over me—a wiry young man named Frank with a mop of flame-red hair and thick shoulders, a gun in his hand, hanging limp.

He said, "Miss Albright, are you okay? Oh, stay still, you're bleeding, these no-good kids today, wait, don't move, I'll call an ambulance—"

But I was on my feet, moving through the door now, my keys miraculously still gripped in my hand, and then I was running down the hallway to the window at the far end, looking down at the security gate. I saw them run out onto the street, and then they were hopping onto three snow-white motorcycles they'd left parked in the loading zone, three sleek, expensive Kawasakis. They yanked their matching helmets from behind the seats and put them on, making them faceless now, anonymous, and then the security guard was beside me.

Gently, as if talking to a madwoman, he said, "Miss Albright, they've hurt you, stay right there, I'll phone the police—"

"No police." I felt a cold, steely anger grip me. It actually overwhelmed my dizziness; suddenly my head was as clear as glacial ice. I said, "Someone else should handle this."

He stopped short, puzzled.

In a gentler tone of voice, I said, "I'm sorry, Frank. I appreciate your help. But I know one boy's uncle. He'll take care of it. If he doesn't, then we'll call the cops."

He argued a bit, a bewildered look on his face. But finally he seemed to agree that I was in my right mind in spite of the cut to my right temple and the bruises on the left of my face.

"You do what you got to, then you phone me," he said. "I'll drive you to the doctor."

I agreed, though I had no intention of calling him back upstairs once he left. He insisted upon helping me to my door, and hesitated as if he was going to come in. I deliberately blocked his way, assuring him I'd be okay. As soon as he was gone, I locked up behind him then dialed the phone number of the Calabash. The bartender got Pua on the phone.

When I told her it was an emergency, she told me where to find Paké. He was at his bar down in Chinatown. "Upstairs," she said. "You tell Keone at the bar to get him. I'll phone ahead and tell him it's okay."

"Thanks, Pua."

Fifteen minutes later I was downtown, parking in the wide alley behind the Lucky Lion. I could see rectangular windows cut on the second floor of the old wooden building. Shades were pulled, and they were heavily barred. That was where Paké ran his gambling games.

I went through the propped-open door. Though it was only two in the afternoon, an assortment of multiracial patrons sat at the bar, or hustled the pool table, or clicked their little white tiles and made their bids at mahjong tables in an adjacent room. There were rough-looking women who made the Chinatown area their home. A few prostitutes. Many Chinese of various ages, and seemingly from all walks of life. The tables held a few dissolute street people who'd somehow put together enough money for a few drinks, and other miscellaneous types.

Even here the Christmas season was in evidence: moldering red tinsel hung above the mirrored back bar, fake pine wreaths hung here and there on the wall. But there were even bigger posters announcing that the Chinese New Year was approaching, that this would be the Year of the Boar: indeed, a snarling, tusked boar in bright red and gray filled the bottom part of the posters. Bright red lanterns with tasseled bottoms hung from the water-stained ceiling; several posters with splashy, blood-red Chinese characters hung on the walls, proclaiming amusements or edicts that I didn't understand.

Keone, the barman, must have already told Paké I was on my way, because as soon as I came in he nodded to a thickset man in the back, who in turn made a signal to someone at the top of a stairwell. Paké appeared almost immediately, coming down the stairs, wearing a faded aloha shirt and Levis.

I'd taken time to wash the blood from my face and straighten my clothing, but the bruises were starting to show and some swelling was setting in. I felt a killer headache coming on.

As soon as Paké saw me, he seemed to know. He looked away, his jaw tightening, then he motioned for me to sit down.

We sat in a booth in the back, away from the patrons. The red plastic upholstery was faded and patched, the table was cheap gray formica, and there was a smell of disinfectant, urine, and stale beer in the air. The gambling money that passed through here certainly didn't stick.

Everything looked about a hundred years old, including a few of the older Chinese patrons who sat at the bar, and at a mahjong table in an adjacent room. This was a friendly neighborhood game. Upstairs was high-stakes. There, they'd be making book on sporting events—big here in the Islands. Paké almost certainly made a fortune on sports betting, with Hawaii's "juice" or house-cut running at a 6/5, or 20 percent. That meant if you bet ten dollars you'd win ten, but if you lost you'd owe twelve. That's a nice markup. And that didn't even count Paké's take on the fan-tan, poker, and other high-stakes games.

Paké said, "You wan' something to drink?"

"No."

He measured me, almost angrily, then he said flatly, "Kimo hurt you."

"Yes."

"Why?"

"I don't know. I guess because he saw me earlier, at Auntie Elma's."

"Where'd he nail you?"

"In my parking garage."

"How'd he know where to find you?"

"Good question. He must have followed me home that day."

He shifted uneasily and motioned for the barman. When the

man came over, Paké said, "Find Kimo. I wan' talk to him. And bring me one beer."

"I'm off the job," I said, when the barman left. "It's not that I can't handle a little rough stuff, but I need a good reason to pit myself against three teenage psychopaths. And anyway, I'm getting nowhere with this."

He stared at me, and then he looked away, his heavy face sagging in outrage.

The barman brought Paké a beer. Without looking at him, Paké said, "Kimo's still with the Jook Koks. You find him, you wan' look in that place above the porno bookstore, down by the Shatin Lounge. Bring him here to me, I wan' beef with him."

"If he don' come?" The barman had a scarred face and the build of a professional wrestler, but he was obviously worried. He was trying to keep his face impassive, but his eyes darted here and there, as if he knew serious trouble was coming and he wanted to spot it before it spotted him.

Paké looked down. His hands were balled into fists, his knuckles were white. "Do what you gotta do." He looked up again and his eyes were frightening.

After the barman walked away, I said, "I keep getting the feeling that something is about to explode and I've landed in the middle of the powder keg."

He looked into the distance. "I don' wan' one turf war, but the buggahs gon' push me." He suddenly looked old and tired.

"Who killed the Yuen kid, Paké?"

"You don' wan' know. Go home. This job is pau. Forget about it, keep the collah. You all bus' up, this pilikia gon' stop. It's not your kuleana anymore."

Translated, he'd just told me that the job was finished, or pau. I could keep the retainer he'd advanced me, I was all bus', or busted up, and the pilikia—trouble—was going to stop, because he was going to stop it.

He was wrong, though, when he said it wasn't my kuleana, or business. It had never been more my business.

I said, "How long has Kimo been strung out?"

Paké's eyes went cold. "They wen' strung him out?"

"He's a walking zombie. Surely you knew."

His eyes went flatter. "I knew Kimo all mess' up, I thought he wen' smoke."

"Come on, Paké, you've been around junkies all your life. How could you not know?"

He studied me. I had a sense that I'd insulted him.

He confirmed it. "You think I hurt my bruddah's kid?" He uttered an ugly word.

What was I supposed to say? That Kimo couldn't have used the heroin if Paké's people and others like them didn't bring it into the Islands? The direct approach didn't seem wise at the moment, so I stayed silent, and even kept the accusation out of my eyes.

He said, "I don' see Kimo or spend time with him for six months or more. He don' wan' nothing to do with me, after I tell him to stay in school, stay off the streets, get his head together, and stop playing the big shot. Then I see him down heah, messing around with those Shadow Dragons—"

"Is it as bad as the cops think?"

He fixed me with a stare that kept getting more hostile. "This one gang out of Hong Kong and San Francisco, illegals, junkies, a few come in, then more, now we got maybe two, three dozen of Mr. Seven's street enforcers, they wan' set up one street business, cock-a-roach everything."

He studied me closely, to see if I'd react to his admission that the gang wanted to cockroach, or steal, his business. Which was the same as admitting that his business was drugs and other illegal street action.

I kept my face stoic and nonjudgmental. "Kimo's one of them now?"

He was silent, thinking, and the hostility in his eyes matured into fermenting hatred.

He blasted me with it. "What do you wan' know anyway, you stupid haole? This Island wen' get all bus' up? You just get on one jet and fly home."

He stood and jerked his head toward the exit. "You like go

home already, forget about it, eh? I don' wan' see you washed up tomorrow morning in the Ala Wai Canal."

"Excuse me?"

"Eh. You not such a tough wahine after all, you wen' let Kimo whack you around." His face was twisted in contempt.

"Really."

I started to tell him that he wasn't so tough either, if he couldn't even control his own nephew. But I stayed silent. When the word *haole* is used in that contemptuous tone of voice, it is indeed a racial slur, though most of the time it simply means Caucasian. Like most people who are on the receiving end of racial slurs, I felt angry. But I let it slide. There was a pain in Paké's eyes that made me understand why he was lashing out.

I picked up my handbag and started to leave.

"Eh!"

I turned back to him.

"You wan' tell that one wahine to lay off? Tell her she's not big enough to pull it off. I don' wan' see her get hurt."

I thought he meant Lenni, of course. Who else was snooping around Chinatown? I said, "She's just doing her job."

He gave me an utterly contemptuous look. I chose to ignore it.

I said, "Good joss, Paké. I wish you hadn't dragged me into this, and I still don't really understand why you did."

He grunted.

"I hope you get things straightened out. I mean that sincerely. Because as bad as things are, I know they could get a lot worse."

His face was again as dark and impassive as a tiki carving, his eyes a black evil glitter. He said, "You wan' let that one she-dragon ride you, you *make* 'em worse. I try geeve you some sense, but you one thick-headed lolo."

I knew I was being insulted, but I didn't quite understand why. I wanted to ask him what he meant, but at the same time I wanted to get away from him before he made me mad and I said or did something stupid. I actually opened my mouth, but he tensed up. His posture said he was through with me.

As I walked out the front door and turned into the alley where

my car was parked, I saw two Chinese-Hawaiian men coming out
the back way, both of them dressed in black slacks, T-shirts, and
running shoes. They were what the locals call "Beef." In other
words, they were solid muscle, few brains, and big trouble. They
glanced my way, ignored me, then turned in the direction of the
Shatin Lounge.

I felt a quick twinge of sympathy for Kimo, but he had to be
stopped. When the men vanished around the corner, I felt my
shoulders slump with relief.

I went home, took a hot bath, then pulled on my robe. I still
had a couple of hours before my dinner date with Mi-Lin. I paced
the floor, thinking, for an hour or so. Then I sprawled across my
bed and fell asleep.

自由

When I awakened to go to Mi-Lin's for dinner, the swelling
had already started to recede—I'd managed to block most of
Kimo's blows after all. I brushed my hair to a sheen, carefully put
on my makeup to conceal the remaining bruises, and even did a
quick manicure on my nails, since several of them were broken.

As I looked in the mirror, I was impressed with the change in
my appearance. Maybe there was hope for me after all. I felt a
sudden wash of relief that I was moving into the upper crust, and
didn't have to go back down to the crime and grime of Chinatown.

My mother was right; there was no reason for me to be
spending time with such brutal people. I'd given eight years of my
life to the DEA, but that was different. I was accomplishing
something then. Now, I was just dabbling in the muck, and not
making much of a living doing it. I truly needed to rethink what
I was doing with my life.

I hoped I would never again get into such a financial bind. I
vowed never to take on scummy jobs like this one. I would start
picking my clients more wisely. In fact, I was going to see what I
could do about generally upgrading my life.

On an impulse, I opened the closet and moved shoes and boxes and debris out of the way until I could get into the small floor safe that David had installed at the far back of the opening.

I took out my snow jade ring. It was carefully stored in a black velvet box, then wrapped in tissue and bubble wrap. As I removed it from the box, the pavé rubies and diamonds shimmered and the snowy jade gleamed with the same pure beauty that had drawn me to the ring when it had been displayed in the window at Tiffany's.

I looked at it for a moment. I was surprised that the pain associated with it had receded to a dull ache.

I put it on my left hand and held it out to catch the light. It was indeed gorgeous. Suddenly I felt elegant and worldly and pampered—though I was of course doing the pampering, but at least someone was. It certainly beat being knocked around by teenage thugs and insulted by crime lords.

I felt proud of the ring. For once, I'd be able to display a symbol of worth that was in the same general ballpark as the expensive baubles of the lovely, worldly-wise Mi-Lin Ming. I wanted very much to emulate her sophistication and effortless elegance. I wanted to be free from the responsibility of trying to change the world.

The back side of Henry Li's mansion was built flush against the ocean, with only a seawall to hold back the water. The lanai rested on pilings set into the seabed, while potted palms and other huge tropical plants turned the area into a lush seaside jungle. Orchids banked one stone wall. Jade vines twined among them.

A storm was moving in from the south. The waves were up, and they made a soft and constant wash against the stone wall beside us. Along the edge of the sky, the clouds were catching the last rays of sunlight. Gold-rimmed and pale-blue, they were scudded along the rim of the sea by the rising trade winds.

Dinner was over, the remains of two salads and two excellent lobster tails sat in front of us. Mi-Lin was dressed in an elegant sand-colored silk cheongsam: that's the sleek, form-fitting, floor-length dress with a slit up one side. It was obviously expensive. It had embroidered silk branches and flowers sewn over the breast, in the same sand color. It brought out the gold flecks in her brown eyes and made them sparkle in the waning sunlight. Her jewelry consisted of a glittering ring and a one-strand necklace in matching canary-yellow diamonds. Flawless, priceless. Her hair was swept up to display matching earrings that were easily two carats apiece.

She'd exclaimed over and over about my ring. She wanted to buy it. She even offered to trade it for her own jewelry, which had to cost at least ten times what David had paid for my ring. I explained it was a gift.

She tilted an eyebrow. "Somebody cares very much for you."

"It was my late husband. He was killed three years ago."

"I'm sorry, Alex. We know the story, of course. You seem to have a lot of tragedy in your life. Like finding that young boy's body in the canal."

A sudden cold wind blew off the ocean. I shivered.

"Does it bother you to talk about it?"

"It bothers me that it happened."

"How did you find him? I know you told everyone you were just out jogging, but what really happened?

"What do you mean?"

"It was almost too much for coincidence, wouldn't you say?"

"Not really. I jog that same route almost every morning."

"But the boy wasn't drowned. He was thrown in after he was dead."

I'd heard the same thing on the news, so it didn't surprise me that Mi-Lin knew. "He'd been beaten while he was already dying of a drug overdose," I said. "It breaks my heart to think about it."

"Then we'll talk about something else, darling. But I am curious. If you learn anything, please share it with me."

The houseboy came in just then with a fresh pitcher of iced tea and a new shaker of martinis. Seeing that the wind was growing stronger, Mi-Lin asked him to shut the upstairs windows. When he left, we talked about Henry's business, the exhibit, and Hong Kong.

Then she raised her ever-present martini glass, and in a very British voice, said, "Cheers."

I hoisted my iced tea, clinked it against her glass, and said, "This really is a lovely house."

"Yes. Well, I still prefer Hong Kong, but the political uncertainty there makes it necessary for us to rethink our position with regard to our primary place of business."

"You've decided to move here permanently?"

"More or less. Though of course I'll still keep my place on the Peak—"

"In Hong Kong?"

Her laughter tinkled through the air. "Is there any other Peak in the world?"

I didn't reply. I knew that Hong Kong's Victoria Peak was considered to be the epitome of ostentatious wealth in Hong Kong—in fact, in all of Asia. But I'd only been to Hong Kong once, and then just through Kai Tak airport on my way to Thailand, where I'd lived in a wooden hut in the semijungle, near the hill tribes for a month while helping with a DEA intelligence analysis of the efficacy of the U.S. opium crop eradication program. Suddenly, thinking about the differences in our worlds, I felt ignorant and outclassed. The feeling surprised and puzzled me, and made me absolutely miserable.

I forged ahead in spite of it. "Are you and Henry—well—together?"

Mi-Lin set down her glass and laughed her wind-chime laugh. "Lovers? Is that what you mean? But darling, didn't you realize?"

"Excuse me?"

She laughed again, thoroughly amused. "How naive you are! And a detective too! My dear, I'm afraid I'm all wrong for our friend Henry Li."

It took me a second to realize what she meant, and then my heart sank. I didn't want to be disapproving or judgmental. On the other hand, I didn't want to be involved in a situation that violated my own sense of ethics, and if she meant what I thought she meant, Henry Li was living a lifestyle which I considered totally destructive.

She said, "In fact, that's what I wanted to talk to you about. Henry's appetites."

"I see." When in doubt, say nothing. Not until you know what you're talking about.

"Yes." She speared the green olive in her martini glass with two long, coral fingernails, nibbled on it, then said, "Henry's trunks were stolen. That part is true. But not quite the way he told you. And since my jewelry was in one of the trunks, I want you to know the truth so you'll have a better chance of recovering every last gem."

The English accent held icy overtones that made me feel mildly hostile toward her for an instant. I forced the feeling away. In fact, I even toyed with the thought that I was beginning to unfairly dislike her just because she was breathtakingly beautiful, elegant beyond belief, brilliantly intelligent, and most of all carefree. She made me wonder where I'd picked up so much emotional baggage. Was it my church background—some misplaced puritan ethic? What, after all, was wrong with enjoying life once in a while? Did I really have to spend every waking moment trying to save the world?

On an impulse, I said, "What's your secret?"

She seemed startled, then apprehensive. "Secret?"

"I don't mean to be forward. But you're so—I don't know, so merry. I know that's an old-fashioned word, but no other one seems to fit."

"Thank you, Alex, I do believe I've been paid a compliment."

"You have."

"I suppose it's my outlook on life."

"Something to do with your faith?""

She looked puzzled. Then she said, "I don't know that I actually have what you'd call a faith. I grew up Buddhist, that created my philosophy, but I don't think that explains all of it."

"What philosophy?"

"Frankly, I believe that we make our own rewards and punishments. We can choose to be happy or miserable; it's really up to us."

I suddenly wanted very much to quit worrying about my tomorrows and start enjoying my todays. I said, "Were you born in Hong Kong?"

"Of course not. Shanghai. My parents owned a furniture factory there. Mostly teakwood. We had a big lovely house and even a small shipping company. I was only ten years old when the Communists burst in and shot them to death. My three elder brothers and I escaped. We fled to Hong Kong that very night."

"You saw it happen?" I was aghast.

"I did. It was hard. I still have an occasional nightmare."

But she'd said she was only ten when it happened. That surprised me. She looked about thirty-five, maybe a very young forty. The Communists had taken over Shanghai in 1949, which meant she'd been born somewhere around 1939 if she was ten when it happened. If the dates were correct, she was approaching sixty. Impossible.

She smiled mysteriously, as if she guessed my thoughts.

She was twirling the stem of her glass. I felt for an instant like a bird being watched by a cat.

She said, "You're a Christian, aren't you?"

I said, "Most of the time." It was a weasel answer and I knew it, but for some reason I suddenly didn't want to pigeonhole myself as someone bound by rules and regulations, or culturally unsophisticated.

She nodded knowingly. "When I was a child in Shanghai, my amah—I suppose you would call her a nanny—was Christian. She'd been converted at the Baptist mission. She taught me the Bible and other things, and talked all the time about your Jesus. But I'm Chinese. Our ways are ancient, they far precede all the Jewish and Christian cultures. My mother fired her. She said the missionaries were insulting us, that it was all part of the colonial mentality."

I could have argued with her about the age of Judaism, but I didn't. I said, "Then you don't believe in Christianity?" I wasn't being judgmental, just curious about what made her tick.

She said, "I don't believe in an afterlife—at least not the way you do, Alex. I suppose I make my own way." She laughed, kicked off her shoes, and curled her legs under her. "I don't mind that you're Christian. Though I don't believe in forcing my beliefs on other people."

I was silent.

"Come now, I've been around missionaries, I understand. You Christians can't bear to have anyone think differently than you do." She laughed merrily again, teasing me. But there was something cunning in her eyes.

"That's not exactly true." But in my sinking heart, I knew it was. Christianity was an all-or-nothing proposition. It was mutually exclusive to every other religious faith, and you either believed it, or you were lost forever.

I didn't want to be lost forever. On the other hand, I didn't want to be narrow and sour and miserable, and in that moment I blamed my misery on my moral responsibilities, as dictated by my faith.

She said, "You see, darling, you Christians have to spend all your time worrying about whether this is right or wrong, about whether you're going to heaven or hell if you do any little thing. I just worry about whether or not something works the way I want it to, and sooner or later I always get my own way." She emitted that tinkling little laugh again.

"You think the secret is to live in the present."

"Of course. It's all we have. If you accept that fact, you can enjoy every single moment, no matter what else is going on."

She took a cool sip of her drink and said, "You're very unhappy."

"Yes. I guess I am."

"Why?"

"Truthfully? I don't know. It's totally unlike me."

"Maybe your time working for the drug enforcement people left you sad. It must be a very hard world out there."

"It is."

"You know we had you checked out. Our people don't miss anything."

I nodded. I suddenly wondered who her people were. If those people were so sharp, why did she need me?

She said, "Your time in drug enforcement was part of the reason we decided you were so perfect for us."

Abe had said the same thing. I wondered why it mattered.

She said, "I can't begin to imagine all the exciting things you know about the way things work in American law enforcement. What adventures you must have had. The whole thing gives me a delicious shiver."

"I can't talk about it. They more or less make you sign your life away."

"It must have been very dangerous."

"Not really. I was in Intelligence Analysis. I didn't do much actual work in the field."

"The people we talked to said you were very good indeed, Alex. It must have been fascinating. Did you travel?"

"Not much." I was uncomfortable, and wanted to get off this subject.

She said, "I always thought it would be exciting to be a policewoman. I never had a chance to do much with my life. Chinese women of my generation were taught to think differently. Until the past few years, my brother totally controlled my very existence."

"I thought you'd worked for Henry Li for a very long time."

"I have. He's my brother's friend. My brother got me this job. He's too sick now to interfere in my life anymore."

"What's wrong with him?"

A fleeting look of distaste curled her bottom lip. "They say his heart. I think it's melted into a lump of coal." She smiled again, dimpling this time, showing her pure white teeth.

"You're still young enough to do many things," I said. I was hoping she'd mention her age.

She graced me with a charming smile. "Yes, I am. And in spite of my brother, I'm doing very well at the moment—or I will be, if I can entice you to get back my jewels and Henry's jade."

"Yes." Time to get back to work. "You were telling me about Henry?"

She sighed and twisted the stem of her glass again, watching it move and catch the light. "I must tell you the full truth, Alex. How I have dreaded doing this."

"It always helps to know the truth."

"This truth isn't pretty."

"Truth seldom is."

She gave me a worldly, knowing smile, then laid it out for me.

Henry Li had been approached by a flirtatious teenage boy in the airport, who had seemed to be available. The security guard and chauffeur had been sent away for a half hour, since Henry believed he was about to engage in debauchery. A real winner, this Henry Li.

Disgusted, Mi-Lin had taken a cab home. But about three hours later, the chauffeur arrived, also in a cab. They had gone for coffee, leaving Henry and the boy in the limo, in an underground parking garage. When they'd gone back half an hour later? No limo. And no Henry Li. And no boy, and no trunks full of jade.

I was listening intently. This made a lot more sense than Li's tale about being robbed of two heavy trunks in broad daylight while his chauffeur and security guard were both on hand. But there were still some missing pieces.

Mi-Lin said, "Henry phoned us shortly thereafter from Sand Island Road, near the docks. I have never heard him so upset."

"What happened?"

As soon as the teenage boy had Li alone, two more boys appeared, jumped in the limo, and overpowered him. They drove off with him in the back of the limo, took him to Sand Island, beat him ruthlessly when he tried to get away, and robbed him of everything of value.

Well. That explained the fading shiner.

"Henry was furious, darling. In a near-lethal fit of rage. In fact he swore he was going to kill those three boys if he could find them. They made a complete fool of him."

Suddenly I disliked Henry Li very much indeed. But I was

already beyond my revulsion at his sexual degradation. My mind was racing. Three teenage boys, and he said he was going to kill them? This certainly put a different slant on things.

I thought anew about the dead boy floating in the Ala Wai Canal, and then I thought about two other boys peddling jade they'd looted from Henry Li's trunks. This was beginning to make more sense.

But had Henry Li killed Dru Chun Yuen? Somehow I didn't think so. That just didn't fit the rest of the pattern.

And why had the boys targeted Li? Because they had definitely targeted him, if they'd made the initial approach to him. Had they already known what was in the trunks? Or did they nail him just because he was in a limo?

Hardly. A man in a limo with a chauffeur, a woman, and a security guard wouldn't be everyone's favorite victim. No, there was still something more going on here.

What if Paké had asked Kimo to set Li up and rob him, and Kimo had taken the two Chinese illegals along? That seemed more likely.

I shook my head, more confused than ever. For every solution, ten new questions popped up.

Mi-Lin said, "You're frowning, Alex. What's wrong?"

I decided it was time.

I said, "I already know where some of your jewelry is."

I'd expected her to be delighted. But her face turned into ancient parchment, her eyes grew opaque, a new distance made her seem cold and aloof like a marble statue. "Where?"

Her reaction startled me. I drew my cards back close to my chest. "The police have it."

With a visible effort, she forced a smile to her face. "But, darling, that's wonderful! And the jade? Have they recovered any of that?" She was searching my eyes, trying to read my thoughts.

I said, "Some. Not all of it."

"They have the trunks?"

"Just some of the contents."

She grew more tense. "Which contents?"

I described the pieces I'd seen.

"Any papers? Invoices?"

"No."

I saw her relax. "How did they find our things? When will I get them back?"

Her delight was feigned. I watched her face carefully, trying to understand what was going on with her.

I said, "Right now it's all in police evidence, pending the arrests of the people who sold it to them."

She tensed up again. "How did the police get it?"

"It was a sting operation. I'll find out how soon they'll let you have it back."

"Can I at least see the items and make certain they're ours?"

"I'll find out."

"And there's no sign of the trunks?"

"Not yet."

"Can the police ask the thieves what they did with them?"

"They haven't arrested them yet, but I'll find out."

She made a helpless little face, and said, "You'll handle that for me?"

"I'll do what I can."

"But Alex, you really must learn more about where they put the trunks." Her eyes were searching mine again, searching, and suddenly I realized that there was another layer of deceit going on here.

I said, "I'll check things out tomorrow and see what I can do. In the meantime, I really can't tell you much more."

She quizzed me for a moment longer, mostly about who had taken the trunks and where they might be. I couldn't answer her questions. Finally, she looked at her Patek Philipe watch. "Oh, darling, I forgot. I *must* make a business call to Hong Kong. I'm afraid it will be a dreadfully long chat. Do you mind? I'll just have our boy show you out."

I was changing lanes, preparing to turn onto my street, when I spotted a lime-green Mercedes turning onto Kalakaua from the opposite direction.

Tavares! I hadn't seen him since he'd peeled out toward the park a few days ago, and I hadn't heard from him since the night on Tantalus when he'd warned me to stay away from just about everything on the island.

I squealed into a driveway, did a quick U-turn, then tailed him. Straight to Chinatown.

I swung into the alley and parked just as Tavares pulled to a stop in front of the Shatin Lounge and shut off his headlights. I leaned back, wondering what to do next.

Tavares climbed out of the Mercedes, illuminated by the streetlight. He was wearing white cotton slacks and a white knit shirt that made him look like something carved in marble by Michaelangelo. I mean, that man was gorgeous! Too bad he had such a surly disposition. Too bad he was a fed. No more narcs for me. I'd rather be alone for the rest of my life than have to go through that again.

Tavares nodded to the surly bouncer as he strode into the bar. After a few moments, the doorman went in after him. I had parked my car behind some trash Dumpsters, so there was room for another car to pass. It would be okay for a while.

I locked the door, clamped on my Club so nobody could steal it, then I stepped inside a small vestibule at the bar's seedy entrance and peeked in.

The bar was dark and packed with people. Tavares was at the far end, near the pool tables, talking with the thickset Chinese man with the perfectly round face and bald, bullet-shaped head. Zhing Qu. Mr. Seven's front man and bar manager. They were talking like old friends having a mild argument. The bouncer was standing back, arms crossed, keeping an eye on the room so they had privacy.

Their conversation grew hotter. Tavares looked mad. It was just possible that I could edge my way through the crowd and grab a corner table without being seen by him.

I was contemplating that very action when a wine-and-silver Rolls Royce sedan purred up to the curb behind me, directly in front of the entrance. I stepped back out of the doorway and leaned into the building, moving out of sight.

The Rolls had stopped under the streetlight, in front of Tavares's lime-green Mercedes. The black-clad driver stepped out and opened the back door. A small, slightly bowlegged Chinese man climbed out.

I'd never seen him before, but his proprietary air was enough to label him "the boss." I got a good look at him. He was facing me, but his attention was fully focused on the driver.

It was Mr. Seven. It had to be.

He wore a black tailored suit and white silk shirt. The huge gems in his several rings glittered in the neon and streetlight. But his most striking feature was his eyes. Even from where I stood, I could see them clearly.

They were large and protruding, giving him a toadlike look.

The lids drooped. I inched closer, still out of sight. Immense evil was etched into the soul that shined its malignant light through those eyes.

Both men walked into the bar. I stayed in the shadows, wary now. I could tell that the bar had gone quiet. Everybody was watchful, as if a giant snake had slithered into their midst. I stayed just outside, hidden, and waited.

I'd planned to follow Tavares around for a while just to get a handle on how he played the game. But now, when Mr. Seven and his driver came back out a few minutes later, I waited while they got into their Rolls and started the car, then—on a sudden impulse —I leaped into my car, revved it up, and tailed them instead.

Their wine-and-silver Rolls was easy to follow. They drove down Beretania then swung right and into the Nuuanu district. Up Nuuanu Boulevard we went, past ever-wider, foliage-shrouded yards, till finally the Rolls turned into Jasmine Lane, a dead end that winds between two Buddhist temples set back in leafy yards, then fingers out to service several huge walled estates sheltered at the back by the towering mountains.

I switched off my lights and followed from a distance, till I saw them drive through an opened gateway in a lava-rock wall. I pulled off into the weeds, gave them a minute, then grabbed my flashlight and got out.

A light rain fell. I moved carefully along the stone wall. I'd almost reached the gate when a stab of car lights stopped me cold. I pressed back into the damp wall, thankful now for the rain clouds that hid the moon, and for the mist that helped hide me.

A black airport limo purred past me and made a wide turn through the gate. As the lights brushed past, I thought for a second I was nailed. But the car continued on, past my line of vision. I heard the engine idle then die.

I heard voices. I strained to hear what they were saying, but I was too far away.

I shoved through the wet ferns and weeds then peered through the black iron bars in the gate. Lights flicked on in the downstairs dormer w ndows of a massive, rain-sheened stone house, three granite stories with turrets, and small attic windows. A monstrosity, with tall koa trees sheltering most of the lower windows and a row of ironwoods and Norfolk island pines demarcating the left side. Two men were standing beside the wine-and-silver Rolls. One was Mr. Seven. I assumed the other man was the chauffeur.

The airport limo had pulled to a stop beside them in the wide flagstone driveway. The driver climbed out and opened the back car door.

A slight man climbed out. The rain and the car blocked part of him, so I got only a fleeting glimpse of his full outline. The chauffeur stepped forward and unfurled an umbrella and held it over the slightly-built man's head, further obscuring him.

The three men walked up to the door, leaving the airport limo driver inside his car. The door opened, and a thin wedge of light illuminated the falling rain. The small man turned to motion toward the airport limo, indicating it should wait.

I felt a zing run through my veins, instantly warming me. It was Henry Li!

The men disappeared inside the house. My mind was reeling.

Water ran off the roof and dripped from the drain pipes above me, but I was oblivious. My mind was working at the speed of light as I tried to stitch this new connection together. Henry Li, Mr. Seven, the Hong Kong connection, the San Francisco connection, the missing jade, the Triads, the brutal youth gang that called itself the Shadow Dragons, Paké Chang and Kimo, the dead kid in the Ala Wai Canal and his missing cousin.

It all added up to—

Chaos.

Try though I might, I couldn't get a lucid picture that adequately put it all together. Unless . . .

Maybe Henry Li was the Dragonhead. The top gun of the Hong Kong Triad, to which the San Francisco faction paid obeisance. Maybe Henry Li was the man who called the shots for Mr. Seven and his cruel, teenage hatchet men.

I thought about the possibilities. Then I thought about Li's cold, ancient eyes, his foreboding intelligence and chilling, cold indifference. It would fit the picture. So would his elaborate jade business, which would allow for movement of people and goods, enormous financial deals that might easily hide heroin financing and shipments, payments for illegal aliens transported into life-long slavery, and other criminal income.

But one thing didn't quite fit. Unless I was totally off base, he simply didn't have the strength of will to occupy such a powerful position. The Dragonhead of a Triad controlled billions of dollars worth of illegal commerce, keeping an iron fist on networks that ran all the way around the world. A Dragonhead controlled all the little Snakeheads who did the dirty work; he fomented death and destruction, encouraged slavery in all its myriad forms. A Dragonhead had to be more cunning than his adversaries, and evil enough to control the brutes and killers who did the hands-on work.

That picture just didn't fit Henry Li. He might be evil enough, but he wasn't cunning enough. If Henry Li was so weak-willed that he could be conned by a teenage thug, he simply wasn't the right man.

But if not him, who?

I felt a sudden shiver as I thought about Mi-Lin. She'd told me her elder brother came from Shanghai. That he was cruel, and she hated to be with him. He lived in an elaborate house on Hong Kong's Victoria Peak and was rich beyond belief. She'd as much as said that he was old, in poor health, and oh, so evil.

Perhaps her brother was the missing link. Maybe Henry was just a stooge. So where did that put Mi-Lin? In the middle. Or maybe she'd just been born into something that she had no way of controlling. Maybe she was riding the dragon, just as the addicts were chasing the dragon. Everywhere I was looking now, the dragon had left its scaly clawprints, even on my own soul.

I felt a little lick of outrage at Mi-Lin, realizing that in a way I wanted to blame her for what was happening. I caught myself and felt ashamed and small. I was jealous of her, pure and simple. She had everything—beauty, grace, happiness in the face of catastrophe. So what if she had been born into a situation that was totally beyond her control? Maybe she wanted out.

I forced myself to wait a full five minutes, then I made my way through rubbery foliage and beneath dripping jacarandas. The chauffeur was sitting in the limo, the light on, reading as he waited. I climbed the iron fence, dropped easily to the earth, then edged around to the back of the house where a puddle of light now fell on the damp lawn. Moving an inch at a time, my feet occasionally squishing in the grass, I found a large bay window partially obscured by a low-riding tahinu tree, pulled myself up into a crook in the tree's umbrella-shaped trunk, then leaned forward.

I had a perfect angle of vision through the many-paned window. The three men sat inside a room with the trappings of an Asian study. I noted their identities again.

Mr. Seven. His flat-faced driver. And of course Henry Li, purveyor of jade objets d'art, my present employer, moral degenerate, and liar par excellence.

More pieces of the jagged puzzle were beginning to fall into place. And yet the little tableau brought up a flood of new questions. Why would an international jade dealer from Hong Kong be sharing this cozy study with Chinatown's would-be new crime lord on this rainy subtropical night? I thought I knew. These men weren't planning an art exhibit, not in any museum in the world. But the business they were discussing was certainly global in scope.

I watched them a bit longer, growing frustrated because I couldn't actually hear what they were saying. I became aware of the water running off my face, dripping off my nose, drenching me and chilling me through and through while my mind reeled with the possibilities of intrigue.

Finally, I'd seen enough to cast a whole new light on every event that had happened to me these past couple of weeks, ever since Paké Chang had first sent me out to find the young boy's body. I didn't know what it all meant yet, but I soon would. I knew I was getting close now.

I silently climbed down from the tree, tiptoed across the damp yard, than scaled the wall to get back out.

I moved down the road with my back to the high wall, my head down. The rain was falling so hard I felt like I was standing under a waterfall.

When I reached my car—interior light turned off so I wouldn't forget and spotlight myself—I climbed in with relief, grabbed a wad of tissues out of the box I kept there, and dried off my face and hair. I turned on the engine and started the heater before I began to slowly back down the lane, headlights out—and suddenly I froze, my foot slamming on the brakes, the engine dying.

I'd seen someone! Moving past Mr. Seven's stone gate, shoulders hunched furtively, a white face caught for just an instant in an incongruous glint of light.

Heart racing, I checked to make sure all my doors were locked, then I scanned the shrubbery, the dark shadows along the stone wall, the blackness of the thick trees.

Nothing.

I switched on my lights, hoping to catch someone lurking in the darkness.

Nobody. Nothing. I quickly switched them back off again.

But I had seen somebody.

I sat there waiting for the hackles on my neck to go down, and then I heard it. An engine turning over, then dying. The noise came from down the road behind me, so whoever had been here had certainly seen my car parked back from the road.

Quietly, as if someone was trying to make sure the spark caught with a minimum of noise, the engine growled again then caught. The noise came from behind me, near the Buddhist temple. Which meant that whoever had gone to the car—assuming it was the same person I'd glimpsed coming from Mr. Seven's house—had made it right past me while I was scanning the area. I felt frustrated. Was I dealing with a ghost?

No. No such thing as ghosts, Alex, in spite of this spooky night. The rain was streaking the windows now, making it impossible to see out until I turned my wipers on.

I saw it then. A flash of lime green, illuminated by a faint glint of light from the temple. It was the spooky Mr. Tavares. He had also followed Mr. Seven home. He'd been spying on any number of people who also interested me.

I started my car and made a swift U-turn, intent upon catching up with him and demanding some answers. But the vehicle had made it to the end of the dark, rainy lane.

By the time I was beside the temple, he was turning onto the street, going downtown. The lights switched on as soon as he entered traffic. By the time I got to the street, the taillights had blended into the spotty traffic and the rainy night, and my chance to confront him was long gone.

20

Morning came. At dawn, I swam in a chilly gray sea then showered, changed, and jogged up to the Diamond Head lighthouse and back. Later, I caught up on my paperwork, keying a report into the computer for Henry Li, doing my time sheets for him and Paké—I intended to be scrupulous when I returned the balance of Paké's retainer.

In the morning mail I found a Christmas card from a long-ago client whose runaway son I'd help find. I dug into my box of stray cards and prepared a return card. I'd received cards from a few others not on my Christmas list. I took care of that, too, and paid a few bills.

Lunch was a trip down to the Thai restaurant for some brown rice and summer rolls. I tidied up the condo and caught up on my laundry. That evening, I still felt the weight that had settled down over me. I wanted to stay in, sheltered from the cruel realities of the world. My mind was a turmoil.

I watched some TV, read my book on forensics, called my

family, then felt sorry for myself because they were having such a good time without me. All the while, in the back of my mind, I was trying to understand what I'd fallen into.

I went to sleep early. Surprisingly, I had a peaceful and restful night.

The next day was a busy one. Jess phoned. He told me the haole kid who'd been cut up in the street fight had gone back to the Mainland, terrified for his life. He'd been here only a few weeks, had run out of money, and was selling drugs to get a ticket home. He'd been a not-so-innocent victim who'd fallen in over his head and had the good sense to run.

Jess told me that it was common knowledge in the streets now: Kimo was working with a new group of people who were at direct odds with anything Paké did. The narcs who'd been asking around weren't getting much more than that out of people. The street dealers seemed to be more afraid of Kimo and his gang than of Paké these days. It looked ominous.

I said, "It looks like the beginning of a turf war."

"Amen," Jess said. "We've got a major problem on our hands."

"I think the Shadow Dragons' headquarters is above the porno bookstore near the Shatin Lounge."

"Near where the other Chinese kid got killed the other day?" Jess was surprised.

"Right upstairs."

"How would you know that?"

"That's where Kimo hangs out."

"I owe you one. We'll check it out, Alex. Thanks."

自由

At one-thirty the next morning, Lenni and I were sitting in the back section of the Coco Surf Restaurant on Nuuanu, beside the aquarium that separates the dining room from the bar.

Christmas wreaths hung on the paneled wall, and a miniature poinsettia plant decorated our table. The dark, quiet downtown streets were visible through the wide windows, the waitresses were doing their nighttime side work, a few people sat in the bar watching TV. An occasional car drove past on Vineyard, headed toward the freeway. Chinatown was unusually quiet, probably because of the upcoming holidays. All but one raw section had fallen sound asleep, complete with people huddled in doorways and alleys.

I'd been checking out the action, driving through the dark streets, looking for Kimo and the Shadow Dragons, or Mr. Seven's shiny Rolls or whatever else might come my way. I had watched the Lucky Lion for a while, then I drove to the next block and spied on the Shatin Lounge. Business was slow in both places. Nobody interesting showed up. Nothing seemed to be happening in the rooms over the porno bookstore, the windows there stayed dark.

On the way home I drove past the creche and other Christmas finery on display at Honolulu Hale. At the sight of the huge Christmas tree, I was filled with a sudden sense of emptiness.

The season was overwhelming me. I didn't want to be alone. I'd stopped and called Lenni from a pay phone near a 7-Eleven and asked her to meet me for coffee. The TV studio was only a few blocks from Nuuanu Avenue.

Lenni was ready to take a break, but she couldn't get away till one o'clock, which was why we were out and about so late.

Now we were talking about the peculiar swirl of events in which we were both entangled.

She told me about the latest on the forthcoming shipment of illegals. It had been postponed till right after the first of the year—something on the other end was holding it up. But it was coming. Thirty new slaves, fresh from China. She was still determined to find out where the illegals were kept while they were being moved through Hawaii, who was supplying their fake documents, and how they were shipped on to the Mainland.

"I'm close," she said, eyes shining. "If I can crack this, it's going to get me a Pulitzer prize."

"Or a trip to the bottom of Honolulu Harbor," I said dryly.

"I'm being careful. I have a lot of friends."

"Have you told Immigration?"

"Don't be crazy. Once they know, every reporter on the island will be out in force. Just like they did with the *Dragon Venture*. That hit the networks before I even got it on the air."

A sudden question whizzed into my mind. "Who tipped the INS on the *Dragon Venture*, anyway?"

She looked thoughtful. "Believe it or not, I've always suspected it was Paké Chang."

I was stunned. "You're kidding."

"No."

"Why him?"

"Who has more to lose if the Triads get a foothold here?"

I thought about that. Maybe she was right.

"Anyway," she said, "this story is mine. They're my people—who knows, some of them might even be related to me. I want hard, solid evidence. I want to know the exact score. As soon as I have it all put together I'll tip Immigration and let them do the cleanup, while I write the story and win the prize."

"It's too dangerous."

"And I suppose what you're doing isn't?"

"That's different. I'm not out in the open like you are."

She laughed. "You stick out like a sore thumb down here. Don't you even realize that?"

"Okay, okay, I'm not your average denizen of Chinatown."

"On the other hand, you have the blessing of Paké Chang. That will carry you a long way."

"I do?" That surprised me.

"I heard it a week ago. Paké put the word on the streets that if anybody messes with you, they'll have to mess with him."

It worried me. If Paké had told people to give me wide berth, then he'd drawn a lot of attention to me. It didn't matter if the attention was good or bad, people would be curious. Besides, he had probably put out the opposite word after he'd fired me.

She caught my attention again, when she started talking about the missing kid, Mock Sing Druan.

"Everyone thinks he's dead," Lenni said. "Otherwise, something would have turned up by now."

"Kimo Chang has the answer," I said. "But I don't think it would do a lot of good to ask him the question."

I was wondering if I should tell her about Kimo helping the boys escape. Would she be able to sit on it, or would it go into tomorrow night's news broadcast? I decided to find out, and was just starting to talk when I glanced to one side and my words stuck to my tongue.

Benny Frietas had just swaggered in the front door. He turned toward the bar. I breathed a prayer that he wouldn't see me. He paused for a second, then looked dead at me.

Rats! In my haste to meet Lenni, I'd forgotten that this restaurant was a favorite with cops, news reporters, and others who prowled the mean streets at night. I'd also left my Honda in plain view.

Frietas sauntered over to our booth, slid in beside me, and said, "So, what deep, dark secrets are you leaking to the press, Albright?"

Keeping my irritation under control, I minded my manners. "Lenni, this is HSP burglary detective Benny Frietas."

Benny gave her a wolfish grin, looking her up and down. She ignored him and went to work on her french fries.

Frietas turned to me. "So where you been keeping yourself? I thought you were going to come up and—you know." He rolled his eyes toward Lenni, as if to say he couldn't talk in front of her.

I said, "Look, Benny, we were just about to—"

"Looks like you're just getting ready to eat," Frietas said, eyeing the untouched sandwich on my plate.

Lenni busied herself gazing into the aquarium. I looked too. There were parrot fish, clownfish, wrasses, and a few featherdusters. A bunch of tiny strawberry crabs crawled around on the bottom, feeding off what they could find.

The waitress came up. Frietas said, "Hey, baby. You working nights now, huh? I'll have some coffee and a grilled cheese, and a plate of those french fries if you got one handy."

The woman gave him a long wink. "Sure thing." She moved

slowly back to the waitress's station, hips swaying. Her hair was streaked blonde and permed into Shirley Temple curls.

Frietas settled back, brushing against some of the dusty plastic plants as he put his arm on the back of the booth behind me. He caused a small dust storm.

Frietas might have been sitting beside me, even flirting with me, but he was trying to impress Lenni. Now, he turned to her. He said, "I watch you on TV."

"Thank you." She kept a chilly demeanor. Either she already knew his reputation or she had good radar.

"So what's going on here, anyway? Anything a cop should know about?" He stuck a toothpick in the corner of his mouth. It hung there like the last shred of a termite's meal.

Lenni gave him a disdainful glare, then gave me a puzzled look that telegraphed the message: What are we doing sitting here with this jerk? She gazed back into the fish tank.

"You know, Benny," I said, "one of these days your wife's going to catch onto how you live and she's going to nail you. You're going to lose the house, the car—it's not going to be pretty."

Frietas gave me a genuinely perplexed look. "Why should she care? I pay the bills. What she don't know won't hurt her."

I allowed myself a silent groan. You just don't break through that type of stupidity. I started to say more, but my lecture was interrupted by Goldilocks, who came back with Frietas's coffee. I waited till she was gone, decided I wasn't going to be able to insult him into leaving, then said, "So what's up with the case you're working? Anything new?"

He swallowed his coffee, watching Lenni out of the corner of his eye. He said, "You mean the hukilau? I guess we can talk in front of your friend here. Tomorrow's going to be my last day working the sting, maybe she'd like to come watch, get a scoop, go with us while we make the arrests." He looked like he'd just offered her a million bucks.

She said, "I work the anchor desk, but I can send the crime reporter to get the story."

He looked her over, seemed to decide she wasn't good enough for him anyway, then turned back to me. "Got those kids who sell me the jade coming in tomorrow with some more of the stuff. Been waiting for them to show up again, that's going to be my last buy. Then we take the videotapes in, put everything together, and turn all the evidence over to the prosecutor so he can start making cases."

"How long before you actually arrest them?"

"Probably another week before the prosecutor's office gets all the indictments drawn up. We're going to nail six kids in all." He shot a sideways glance at Lenni. "But that's off the record."

Lenni rolled her eyes heavenward.

I smiled, suddenly animated. I was going to be there tomorrow when the jade came in, you could count on it.

Frietas misinterpreted my joy. He leaned in close and whispered, "What you doing tonight?"

"We're both working. But I'm sure Lenni could find time to cover your last day at the store. It should be interesting."

Lenni caught my eye, and I telegraphed a silent message. Play ball. She frowned.

I said to her, "What do you think?"

She managed a weak smile for Frietas, and said to him, "On second thought I'd love to do the story. Stolen jade, you say?"

He looked at her again, the speculation back in his eyes. "The kids are coming right after I open up at eight. You come around about seven-thirty and I can get you backstage, into the operations room."

"That's not necessary. I'll pick up on the action from outside," Lenni said. "That way I can get some wide footage, and maybe later the HSP will let me have some clips from your videotape."

"Well—" That more or less put the wrench in any plans he might have had to put the moves on Lenni, but what could he say?

I shot Lenni a look of pure delight.

Lenni leveled a warning gaze at me: Don't start enjoying this too much.

I decided to bail her out. I turned to Frietas and said, "We'd better get some beauty sleep. I can't eat this sandwich now. Want it?"

He scooped it off my plate, pickle and all.

By then I was half-standing, making it impossible for him to keep from moving. He had to let me out of the booth. I told him good night. It was easy to be nice now—I was grateful for the information.

When Lenni and I got to the parking lot adjacent to the restaurant, she turned to me and wiped fake sweat from her brow. "You know, I never actually realized how tough your work could be. I shoot 'em and run, but you have to actually talk to them. How do you stand predators like that?"

"That's the easy part," I said. "The hard part is coming up."

"Meaning?"

"Meaning that we're parking my car in the lot across the street and we're taking your car to Makaha."

"What?"

"Apparently you didn't understand that conversation," I said. "So I'm going to fill you in. Let's climb into your car, we need to talk."

I told her most of what I'd been keeping back about Kimo Chang, about the jade, about Henry Li and the theft. When I was through she whistled, long and low.

I said, "If Kimo is bringing Frietas another delivery of jade in the morning, that means he's probably going to pick it up from its hiding place before then. Which means—"

"That we're going to stake out his house tonight." She smacked her forehead with the palm of her hand. "Oh, no."

"I think it will be worth it. My bet is that his parents are so straitlaced he'd never hide stolen goods at home. His Auntie Elma has kicked him out. He has to stash his goods somewhere else. Maybe he'll lead us to it."

"I have to finish my editing. I have to film again tomorrow."

"What time?"

She hesitated, then said, "Eleven."

"Plenty of time," I said. "You might even squeeze in a couple of hours' sleep by then. Come on. Let's get to work. It will keep our minds off our problems."

"But I don't have any problems."

"That's because you haven't been spending enough time with me lately. Come on."

CHAPTER

21

Lenni fell asleep while we were still driving the thirty or so miles to Makaha. When we got to the beach park she stayed that way. Which left me sitting behind the wheel of her new green Chevy Cavalier, watching the dark moon glide in and out of huge, inky clouds, watching the palms sway in the night breeze.

The pounders rolled in, their white crests catching moonlight. Across the highway, the houses were dark and silent. I rolled down my window and listened to the eternal crash of the waves against the rocks, smelled the ancient must of the sea.

I could have awakened Lenni to stand watch while I grabbed a nap. But the truth was, even after three hours sitting there—false dawn staining light into the sky behind the Waianae Range now—I was wide, wide awake. My adrenaline was pumping and my skin actually itched with anticipation. I was getting close to something. I wanted to reach out and make it happen, but some things you can't rush.

A lot of patterns began to fall into place as I sat there, sleepless, listening to the pounders crash into the jagged lava rocks. Then, at six-fifteen—me still wide awake though a little shell-shocked now—Kimo Chang's Firebird crawled slowly out of his street, no doubt reflecting the metabolism of its sleepy driver. I gave Kimo plenty of space, then I fell in.

As our car began to move, Lenni stirred, gave me a sleepy look, then blinked awake, stretched, and said, "What's up?"

"The sun, almost. Battle stations. Kimo Chang's on the move, and he's about to lead us to his stash."

"*That* would be a stroke of luck," Lenni said. "Turn on the headlights."

"Can't. He might see us."

"This is a brand new car, Alex."

"You can buy another one when you get your Pulitzer money. The traffic is too light. I need to keep the lights out until we merge into heavier traffic. Then I'll turn them on."

"What did I miss?"

"A lot of quiet, a lot of thinking. I'm beginning to get a handle on things."

"What?"

"Nothing I can really explain yet."

"Try."

"Not yet. I don't want to mislead you, just in case I'm wrong."

The Firebird took the Waipahu exit again. We parked at the end of the block behind a monster van and watched as Kimo pulled up in front of the wedding cake house. When the Chinese-Filipino kid came out, he looked sleepy, almost tripping as he climbed into the Firebird. He had two backpacks with him. Both seemed to be empty.

The Firebird quietly pulled away from the curb. They weren't planning to wake anybody up. I followed it past the residential area of Waipahu, then south toward Ewa Beach. The sun came up. The fact that they went that direction threw me a little and I almost missed a turn.

The ocean was to our left now, Diamond Head a small black bump on the horizon. This was West Oahu, dry country. Though it was barely daylight, the sky was turning hot blue. Virgin white clouds, lacy and diaphanous, lay like a mantilla in the sky. To our north, the Waianae Range lay with its heart open. The abandoned cane fields spread out on all sides of us.

The sleek red Firebird sped along the highway, toward the sparkling ocean. Lenni and I, both grumpy from a sleepless or near-sleepless night, were silent. I was getting hungry enough to consider stopping at a fast-food joint in the little town called Ewa Beach. Which meant I was really getting hungry.

Kimo saved me from all that by turning north at the Gas-N-Go, back toward the older sugar mill that had once fueled the economy around Ewa. I had been here before, but not often. There was a little shantytown of old plantation houses, nearly hidden in wide copses of trees and tall sugarcane, set back off the road.

Kimo drove in that direction. The Firebird was hidden from us most of the time by tall trees, brush, shoulder-high weeds, wild sugarcane, and thickly matted ferns. Weeded roads ran in every direction.

I lost them. I drove the Chevy through a gate into a field, stopped behind a shield of trees, turned off the ignition, then rolled down my window and listened. I heard the growl of the Firebird's engine, not far away. It stopped. I heard a car door slam. We climbed silently from the car, leaving the doors slightly ajar in case we had to beat feet back, then we moved into the tall cane.

We spotted them just as they entered a corrugated iron building adjacent to an abandoned shack. They were acting furtive, looking over their shoulders from time to time, though not so thoroughly that they'd have spotted even an amateur tail.

While they were inside we swatted at flies and I stewed about how many cane spiders—Hawaii's version of the tarantula—were crawling in the weeds around us.

Finally they came out, carrying two fat backpacks. They'd loaded up. We watched as they climbed into their car. Through a mutually understood nod, we agreed to let them go while we stayed to check out the padlocked shed.

Rats scurried as we broke though a window, the crash seeming to reverberate for miles. We waited. Nobody showed up. I used the handle of Lenni's large flashlight to push out the remaining glass, got a grip on the ledge, Lenni shoved me from behind, and I climbed through. Lenni came right behind me.

The light was milky, filtered through two dirty windows. There were two ratty cardboard boxes inside on an old wooden table. I opened a flap and looked. They were water-stained, nothing had been stored in them for a long time. The room held ancient packing straw, rusted-out equipment. Rats scurried as we opened two thin wooden doors to peer into cubicles that had once served as bathrooms. The place was empty. Nothing much to see really, though you could tell that people had been through here.

I'd decided to give up, when Lenni found it. A trapdoor behind a stack of mildewed straw.

"Help me," she said, trying to lift it.

It required a major effort to get it open, and once the door lifted, the stale smell made us step back, putting our hands over our faces.

A ladder descended down into a black pit.

"I'm not going down there," I said, through my fingers. I knew it would be full of rats, maybe even cane spiders.

"Give me the flashlight then."

I let her go first then followed, dreading every step. Inside the subterranean room, covering our noses against the stronger stench, she played the flashlight around, looking for the trunks. A smell of rotted food joined the other foul odors. I hoped it was only food.

I saw a heap of burlap bags in one corner. A wooden table in another. Along one wall, there were heaps of refuse. We walked over, and I kicked at the rubbish then jumped back as a rat ran out and disappeared into the blackness at the edges of the room. There were empty Spam cans, bean cans, remnants of other simple foods. Huge empty bags of rice. Empty plastic water bottles. Several blackened pots and pans, one half full of something burned beyond recognition. There was a kerosene burner. Discarded plastic eating utensils, and other debris, including tissues and some Chinese-language newspapers.

"People have stayed here, but not for a long time," Lenni said. "Probably a load of illegals from a few months ago."

"People have shot up here, too. Look at this." I pointed out a corner that held thick burlap padding. She shined the light fully on it. We saw a wooden box upon which were foil packets, empty balloons in a variety of faded colors. Dozens of used syringes, and a ball of twine that junkies used to tie off the arm and bring up the veins before the addicts shot up.

"I thought they smoked the heroin instead of injecting it."

"Maybe they smoke while they're on the high seas. Maybe the Snakeheads get more serious about making sure they're really addicted once they hit land."

"I guess that would make them more pliable and manageable," Lenni said.

"Maybe." I was getting a sinking, sick feeling. "Bring the flashlight. If the trunks are here they have to be under the gunnysacks."

Lenni kicked the bags around, not touching anything with her hands. I jumped back as a large cane spider scampered toward me. It darted behind another gunnysack, its long, hairy legs visible around the edge. I was torn between chasing and killing it, and keeping both eyes on the rotting burlap sacks to make sure worse things didn't lurk therein.

Suddenly she stubbed her toe. "Ouch!"

"What?"

"Something there."

I gingerly pulled back the bag she'd kicked. There was a wooden fruit crate, with sawdust and several new cardboard boxes inside. Empty. This was probably where the boys had been storing their stash. If the trunks had ever been here, they were long gone. But as I turned toward the ladder, Lenni following, the flashlight played across a small alcove that we'd missed. I said, "Lenni. There!"

She stepped to one side and peered into the opening, playing the light around. The small area held tattered burlap, arranged into two thin stacks that had obviously been used for beds. In a corner was a kerosene lamp. We saw food wrappers, bags, and leftovers from several fast-food restaurants, along with several unopened cans of food, a box of teabags, several pairs of discarded wooden chopsticks, and half a loaf of molded bread. I couldn't believe the squalor.

"The Chinese kids hid out here," she said. "Look, the food isn't all that old."

I was too depressed to talk. I wondered if this was the place where Dru Chun Yuen had died.

As we climbed back into Lenni's car, I thought about Dru Chun Yuen. At least we hadn't found Mock Sing's body here. But if Dru had died in the terrible black hole, why had his body been taken to the Ala Wai Canal, and who had moved it?

We drove silently back to Honolulu. I kept my face averted, looking out the window. I didn't want Lenni to see the tears in my eyes.

I missed Kimo Chang's delivery. When I arrived at the hukilau, Frietas was miffed that Lenni hadn't come along, but he showed me Kimo's latest deal. An additional dozen pieces of Henry Li's priceless jade, a sapphire and diamond pendant, and one pair of diamond earrings, white, one carat each, pear-cut solitaires. With these items, the better part of Mi-Lin's jewelry had been recovered, and almost all of Henry Li's jade.

At two o'clock that afternoon, I phoned Mi-Lin and told her I had recovered most of her stolen goods. Frietas wanted to move it to the evidence room at headquarters, so I asked her to come right away and identify it.

I met her up in Kaimuki at the saimin stand. I led her next door to Frietas's dilapidated grocery—he had shut the store down a scant hour before and was already packing up.

Mi-Lin was gorgeous, in a coco-brown pantsuit that brought out her pale gold complexion and her doe-brown eyes. Slender as a reed. She smelled of yellow roses, was as graceful as a gazelle, and she was wearing yellow topaz jewelry: a huge pendant, drop earrings, and a double stone that could have been used as collateral to remodel the store.

I had never seen Frietas totally speechless before. He led us around in a trance and couldn't take his eyes off her. It may have been the first time in his life that he met a woman he didn't try to hustle.

Mi-Lin was oblivious to his reaction. In her world, everyone acted this way. I felt a pang of jealousy again, not because she had Benny Frietas's attention—that was a blessing—but because she was so exquisite and yet so guileless. All the other truly beautiful women I'd known were so wrapped up in staying beautiful that they spoiled it. But not Mi-Lin. No strain, no attempt to impress anyone. It just happened effortlessly.

I felt ashamed for being so petty and small. I couldn't remember the last time I'd been jealous of someone. Maybe my older sister, when we were kids and she'd started dating. She'd looked glamorous and grown-up to me then, and I'd wanted to be that way too. But that feeling had been nothing compared to this deep, slicing stab of envy that I felt for Mi-Lin from time to time. I was usually happy with what God had given me. I had never met anyone I'd trade places with. Until Mi-Lin. I must admit, she brought out my insecurities. Which means she brought out the very worst in me.

Mi-Lin caressed the jade, the jewelry. She asked a thousand questions about the missing trunks, but we couldn't answer any of them. Finally she turned to me, starry-eyed. "Oh, Alex, you're a genius. What a wonderful job you've done. When can we take our treasures home?"

"It's evidence," Frietas said, coming to his senses a bit. "It has to go through the proper channels."

She turned her charm on him and told him about the jade exhibit. By the time we left, she had him promising to do everything but leap off the Aloha Tower to see that she got her jade back in time.

She climbed into her dark green Jag while I stood by the driver's window. Her eyes slitted up and suddenly she wasn't quite so beautiful anymore. "It was those dreadful boys who beat up Henry, wasn't it, Alex? Did you get their names?"

"I think I know who they are." It didn't cross my mind to lie. But when she asked for names, I said I wasn't at liberty to tell her until after they'd been arrested. I still hadn't mentioned that the dead kid was probably one of them.

She wheedled a bit, then said, "You don't trust me."

"It's not that—"

"Then why can't you tell me?" Her lip stuck out in a little-girl pout. Then she gave me a sudden toss of her head. "Oh, never mind. I'll just phone that nice detective inside and ask him. He'll have all their names."

I shrugged. If she got the names that way, it was her and Frietas's business, not mine.

"But Alex, darling. I'm still out a few small pieces of jewelry, and we haven't recovered the trunks, of course. We would especially like to have the trunks back. They were custom-made, and will be hard to replace. Do you have any idea where they might be?" Her mouth was drawn tight across her teeth.

"Maybe."

"Where?" Her eyes were suddenly frigid.

"So far it's just a guess. I need to check it out."

With a forced effort, she relaxed. "Then look for them, darling. If you find them before I go back to Hong Kong, I'll give you a wonderful bonus. Maybe something to match your white jade ring. Or maybe even those wonderful diamond pendant earrings."

I was astonished. According to the appraisal sheet, the earrings were valued at around $26,000. Quite a bonus. I said, "You're going to Hong Kong?"

"The day after Christmas. To select new pieces for the exhibit. Though perhaps I won't have to if we can get these back in time. Help me, Alex. You've done an amazing job, but we still have much to do."

"It will work out," I said.

And in that moment, in the glow of my one singular accomplishment, I truly believed it would.

Lenni disappeared that night.

She left the house at 8 P.M. to go to the studio for a night of editing. She never arrived.

At 10 P.M. the studio phoned her home. Lenni's mother had no idea where she'd gone. Calls were traded back and forth, and everyone started looking for her. At eleven-thirty, Lenni's mother phoned the HSP and said she feared her daughter had been kidnapped.

At midnight, Jess phoned me to see if I knew where she might be. "Benny Frietas says he saw you together in the wee morning hours yesterday. You know anything that might help?"

"Just that she was working on her Chinatown special. She thought she might have a lead on the missing kid. She may just be off on a story."

"She always tells the news manager where she's going to be. They have her on constant call."

"Maybe she didn't want him involved this time."

"Or maybe she's been hurt."

I already knew that. I just didn't want to accept it. I choked up. "What do you think, Jess?"

He sighed, weary. "There's so much going on in Chinatown right now that anything could have happened. If you think of anything that might help us find her, let me know."

"I will."

He hung up.

I drove down to the studio. They were in a turmoil, drinking coffee, several of them chain-smoking until the air in the studio had turned blue. Everyone had a theory. I learned nothing—they knew nothing. Not even what specific segment she'd been filming that day.

I phoned her mother then drove up and talked to her. She was gracious. The father was pacing the floor, and a neighbor had come to sit with them. Lenni had been helping her mother clean and get ready for Chinese New Year. They lived in a sprawling house in Makiki. Lenni had a small apartment with a separate entrance. She'd had dinner with them, then said good night before she went to do her editing. She liked to do it at night, when nobody bothered her.

I wanted to know who Lenni's informant was. I asked if anyone at the tong had been helping Lenni with information.

"Everyone," her mother said. But she couldn't think of anyone special.

I wheeled into a gas station, filled up my Honda, and phoned Jess. Nothing new. There was an APB out on Lenni's car. They were hoping she'd just gone off on a call and gotten stranded somewhere. But we all knew better.

By the next morning, everyone was frantic. Every cop on the Islands was looking for her. It was on all the news, and even CNN picked it up—I heard it when I first awakened after two tormented hours of sleep.

"Honolulu anchorwoman Lenni Apana is missing. An island-wide search is in full-throttle, but thus far the authorities have failed to locate her 1995 Chevy Cavalier or any information as to what may have happened—"

I wept.

I looked for her all day, cruising Chinatown, stopping every hour or so to phone either the HSP office, or the newsroom, or my answering machine. I stopped at the tong and asked questions and got some honest but worthless answers. They were all distraught. Nobody had seen her spending an inordinate amount of time with any particular person. Nobody had a clue as to what had happened to her.

I drove back out to Waipahu, to the abandoned warehouse. I even descended into the black pit all by myself. She wasn't there.

Nothing good happened all that day, nothing good happened all that night. Again, I managed a few tortured hours of sleep, awakening off and on with the realization that something was dreadfully wrong.

The next morning, Mi-Lin phoned, asking me about the trunks. I had nothing to report to her, so I cut her short. I went looking for Lenni again. Nothing.

Some forty-eight hours after Lenni's disappearance, I found out, through pure serendipity, what had happened to her.

I had decided to do something to keep my sanity that day, after exhausting every idea I had about where to find her. I did a few odds and ends, then around three that afternoon I phoned Auntie Elma to ask some more questions about the Chinese boys who'd run away from her house. I suppose I thought there might be some strange connection to Lenni's disappearance, and I was hoping, too, that she might have heard something from or about the missing boy, Mock Sing. Maybe, just maybe, Lenni had been pursuing her lead into that when she disappeared.

Auntie Elma invited me to come see her anytime, but she had no new information. During the course of our chat, she dropped the news that Kimo was coming by around four-thirty to pick up some things.

I decided to resume my surveillance of him. He'd been involved since the trouble began. He'd helped the kids escape from Auntie

Elma's house, and if anyone knew where Mock Sing Druan was hiding—or buried—Kimo was the likely choice.

There was also a remote chance I might learn something new about the missing trunks. It was worth another shot. If I waited a few more days, Kimo was going to be arrested and put behind bars, and he'd be talking through a lawyer and saying absolutely nothing. It was now or never.

I was parked in a neighbor's driveway, sheltered behind a bank of trees, when Kimo spun gravel into his aunt's driveway at 4:46 P.M. He left his red Firebird running, came out with a handful of clothes, tossed them angrily in the trunk, then sped back out again. I recognized the two Chinese kids riding with him: they were the Shadow Dragons who stood dispassionately by while he attacked me.

I had driven my battered Chevy van, the one I'd inherited from David. I was also wearing my .38, complete with shoulder holster and baggy T-shirt to hide the outline. If Kimo attacked me again, I was going to win this time, hands down.

I tailed him to Diamond Head Lighthouse, where he and the boys watched the evening windsurfers and killed a few joints as they stood in front of the Firebird and talked. The sun set while I watched them from a turnout down the road, where tourist cars and a tour bus camouflaged me.

Next they drove to Sandy's Beach, where they made what I was sure was a drug drop-off to some people in a gray van. By then it was getting too dark to see well. I followed them back to China-town. At 8:05 I watched from down the block as they piled out of the Firebird and went up a stairwell beside the Shatin Lounge. Lights came on in the windows above the porno bookstore. Kids came out of the shadows and alleys like cockroaches, scampering up the stairs, a dozen or so teenagers of various ages, most of them Chinese. But there were also several kids who obviously came from other Asian and Hawaiian backgrounds, including the Chinese-Filipino kid I'd seen with Kimo Chang the first day I'd followed them. The Shadow Dragons were having a meeting. And they were obviously recruiting Hawaiian kids, of various types, probably to act as drug couriers, enforcers, lookouts, and what-ever else their dirty business required.

I was about to call it a night. By then it was moving on toward nine o'clock—when Kimo and the Chinese-Filipino kid came back out.

The other kid climbed into the passenger side of Kimo's Fire-bird. Kimo drove, a worried look on his face. They went north, up H-2 Freeway, me behind them, expecting them to take the Waipahu exit toward the Chinese-Filipino kid's home, then Kimo would probably drive on to Makaha. Once they turned toward the Leeward Coast, I was going to peel off and go home. I wasn't in the mood to drive all the way to the North Shore just to see Kimo turn into his father's driveway and go to bed.

Instead of taking the cutoff they kept going north, past Pearl City, past Waipio, north toward the center of the island and the miles and miles of pineapple and cane fields. That piqued my interest again. Maybe I was going to discover where they'd stashed the trunks.

Still—I was tired, and it was getting harder to tail them. I had to stay well behind them. I'd slept a total of six hours in the past two days. It began raining, and the sloshing of the windshield wipers almost lulled me to sleep. I was ready to give up for the day.

A couple of cars passed me, waking me back up. Soldiers, on their way home to Schofield Barracks. Other than that, there were just Kimo's taillights ahead of me in the blackness and the white lines at the highway's center, all beneath black sky and falling rain.

The highway crested a small hill, my headlights mirroring the wet pavement as I crested it. I cut my lights, hit my brakes, and edged for the side of the road, slowing down just in time to see that Kimo had pulled off the road and stopped at a turnout on the bridge that crossed Kipapa Gulch.

I stopped too, dousing my lights, and climbed out of the van, braving the rain to see what the boys were up to.

They had climbed out and were standing at the guardrail,

looking down, Kimo gesturing toward the bottom of the gulch. I tried to follow his gesture, but the gulch was the size of a small, steep-sloped valley, and it was feathered full of dark trees and foliage.

The cold rain brought me wide awake. The boys climbed back into their car and made a fast U-turn then peeled out, tires screaming, coming up on me now. I jumped back in the van, watching them, wondering if they'd recognize the van from earlier in the day. I pulled my .38 out of my holster, put my hand down beside the gear shift, and waited as the lights came at me.

But they passed me, in animated conversation, not seeing the dark van against the black background and foliage. I sent up a prayer of thanks.

I waited until their car lights had vanished toward the glittering city skyline, thirty or more miles away. Then I pulled up onto the widened spot just before the bridge, making sure any oncoming traffic had plenty of room to pass. I climbed out of the van and locked the passenger door.

I walked onto the bridge and peered down into the dark treetops. Nothing. I took my heavy-duty flashlight out of the kit in the back and again tried to figure out what the boys had been looking at.

There! The light glinted off something metal. I swept the light back and forth, then I saw it again.

It looked like the chrome on a car, maybe even a bumper, down in the trees, just barely visible.

I took a rain slicker and first-aid kit out of the van, pulled on the slicker, then tucked the first-aid kit in my large shirt pocket. I walked to the edge of the bridge, where the wall of the gulch sheared downward.

It was fifty or so feet to the bottom, slick with mud all the way. All the same, descending into the gulch was the only way I was going to find out what was really down there.

Twice I slipped and fell. It was dark, cold. A sense of emptiness overwhelmed me. Finally I reached the bottom, rain dripping, running off the leaves, the thick brush drenching me with its dampness and tearing at me all at once, running into my eyes so I had to constantly wipe at them to be able to see at all.

I got lost in the heavy black foliage at the bottom. Something wet brushed across my face, and I swept my arm up and brought up my flashlight at the same time, expecting to see a giant centipede—no snakes here in Hawaii—but it was only a fuzzy tree vine, dripping water, hanging from a branch above me.

It was dark and eerie, not a speck of light except for my own wide flashlight beam, rain dripping all around me, the wet loam smelling like the soil from a freshly-turned grave. I hoped I was moving in the right direction.

I stepped through a thicket of shrubs and trees and stopped short. I saw a car. Or what was left of one. It had been burning, the smell of scorched rubber and metal was all through the air here. The trees and foliage around and above it had been burnt through, which was why it had been visible from above.

I played my flashlight over it. The car was black and charred in most places, the paint bubbled and burnt off, but it was far from burnt-out. The rain had probably put out the fire. From the smell, the fire had been recent.

I shined my light into a back window, but it was pitch-black. It took me a second to realize that the burning interior had sooted up the windows. With a growing sense of dread, I shined my light on the plates. They were completely charred. But I knew by then what kind of car this had been. A Chevy Cavalier. Black. But not Lenni's, surely not Lenni's—this was a tourist's rental. Someone had driven off the road and left it here. There was no way this burned-out coffin could be Lenni's car.

I shined my light on the ground, looking for someone or something that might have been flung from the car as it came over the edge. Nothing there. I heaved a sigh of relief. I walked around and examined the front. One full side of the windshield had been broken out from the fall. I shined my light inside—

My heart stopped.

Literally stopped.

THE JADE CRUCIBLE 235

I heard a hollow sob, then realized it had come from me.

There, on the front seat, propped up behind the melted wheel as if going on a dreadful journey, was a charred body. The face, the hair, nothing was recognizable as human.

I stepped back, moving like a wobbly marionette dangling on the strings of a horrible reality. I could smell the gasoline that someone had used to douse the body and the car, before setting it afire.

Fighting for sanity, I made myself think clearly about what had happened here. The car had been pushed over the side, someone had climbed down behind it, straightening the tree saplings and brush on its path of descent, at least enough to camouflage it from the road. They'd doused the body and car in gasoline before setting it afire. But the rain had put the fire out.

It wasn't Lenni, it was just a body. It could be anybody in there. Why was I crying? I could barely see. I felt quiet now, entombed by a feeling of dread. Death and night were everywhere. Only the faint light from my flashlight kept me linked to a faint remnant of life.

Moving with a grim determination, I turned away from the car, leaving the horror behind me. I forced myself not to look back into the darkness. It was harder to ascend than it had been to descend. I felt weak, drained. When I was halfway up, I slipped and fell, and I had to pull myself up.

Finally, at the top, I pulled off my muddy slicker and shoes and dropped them in the back of the van. It was all I could do to insert the key and turn the ignition on.

I started to cry again: small, whimpering sounds welling up from within me. I hated the sound I was making, hated the weakness in my knees and the way I was shivering.

Anger and rage and fear and grief all poured out of me. I kept asking God, *Why? Why Lenni? Why didn't You let me know so I could help her?*

The sky was silent, black; the rain fell harder.

Finally I forced myself to drive slowly, carefully, back toward the lights of Honolulu. I drove straight to Jess and Yoko's house.

Yoko made hot tea and wrapped a blanket around me, put a warm towel around my wet hair. I drew strength from their comfort and their love, and I talked for two hours. I told them everything I knew about Lenni and what she had been doing; and everything I knew about Kimo Chang.

Police from the Waianae substation busted Kimo at five that morning, at his father's house in Makaha. They couldn't hold him for murder because there was no evidence. The only thing I could swear to was that he and his friend had stopped on the bridge and looked down at the car.

Fortunately, an indictment for Kimo's arrest had already been drawn up as part of the forthcoming busts linked to Benny Frietas's hukilau. That would allow the state police to hold him for a while. With skilled questioning, Jess thought they could crack Kimo and make him talk about what had happened to Lenni. Jess said if Kimo didn't talk, maybe the Chinese-Filipino kid would. The police arrested him an hour after they picked up Kimo, also on a warrant for dealing stolen goods.

I waited at home with Yoko while all this happened. During that time, a crime investigator and an emergency squad were dispatched to Kipapa Gulch. HGTV's news director went with them. He had identified the partly melted watch on the corpse's wrist. I'd been so distraught I hadn't even noticed it. The watch had belonged to Lenni. It was her.

Finally, just after dawn, I went home. I'd asked Jess and the others not to reveal my name or talk about me finding her. They didn't. I was grateful for that. When the early news aired and the newspapers hit the stands that morning, the story said that a friend of Lenni's had discovered what at first appeared to be a car accident, only later did the HSP decide it was murder.

I phoned my pastor and talked to him. We prayed together, and that helped. I spent the morning at home, mostly staring out over the gray, dank sea, thinking about everything that had happened and wondering what I could have done differently. In the midst of the turmoil that surrounded me, I'd completely forgotten it was Christmas Eve. I phoned my mother's house, hungry for the warmth of family love. They'd all gone skiing for the day.

I wasn't hungry, but at two o'clock that afternoon I started getting a killer headache. I knew I needed to eat something or I was going to end up flat on my back in bed. I dressed in a dark blue jogging suit, something warm. An arctic front had arrived, delivering both rain and some unusually cold winds.

I ached for Lenni. I wanted to see her, talk to her, save her from the horror that had befallen her. I wanted to roll back time to three days ago and change the tape that had played out into her death. I phoned her parents to express my sympathy. They were both under a doctor's care. A neighbor answered the phone.

I was just going through my wallet to count my cash, wondering if I needed to stop at the bank machine before finding a restaurant where I could grab something decent to take out, when Mi-Lin Ming surprised me by ringing me from the lobby.

"There's something I'd like to discuss. May I come up and visit for a moment?"

"Of course." I didn't want to see anyone, but what else could I say?

I gave her directions, buzzed her into the elevator, then rushed around tidying up the office as best I could. I stopped to look in the mirror, expecting to see my eyes red-rimmed, my face a disaster. But my eyes were clear. I'd slept since I'd cried last—that is, since I'd actually shed tears. I was crying inside, and I couldn't quit. I actually looked as if nothing had happened. I felt guilty for that.

When Mi-Lin touched the doorbell, I opened the door, greeted her, then ushered her into my still-cluttered office.

"Excuse the debris," I said. "I've had a busy couple of weeks and things tend to stack up." I lifted a pile of directories, then motioned her into the client's chair.

She nodded slightly, sat down uneasily, then looked around. She was wearing a tailored Donna Karan dress, mid-calf, in a sleek gray rayon blend that showed off her model-trim figure. Gray eelskin shoes and bag, pale gray nylons. The gold necklace was understated and expensive, the tiny bracelets on her left hand matched. No rings today, just the elegant French manicure that left her fingernails long and perfectly shaped. Her jet-black hair was swept up and held with a gray jade comb, and her porcelain face was perfectly made up to enhance her singular beauty.

Mi-Lin seemed out of place in my office, like a diamond set in tin. She seemed out of place in my life today.

She obviously felt out of place, too, for she gracefully shifted positions, recrossed her long, perfectly shaped legs and glanced around, as if surprised to find herself in such common surroundings.

I saw her sculpted nostrils narrow in disapproval at the clutter around her.

Looking at the room through her eyes made me compare it to the opulent surroundings of Henry Li's mansion. Suddenly I wasn't sure I liked the room either.

Sunlight filtered through the draperies that covered the double-wide glass balcony doors. My large desk was a jumble of papers, books, and other debris that drifted up against the side of the computer and spilled across the keyboard. I hadn't done my billing for the month; an expense book and a disheveled array of receipts lay atop the far side of the desk. In one corner of the room lay the jumbled remnants of the boxes that were used to store my Christmas decorations. Troubles had left them out when he decorated the tree. I'd offered to put them away, but had never gotten around to it. The room was basically clean, though a little dust had settled atop the typewriter cover. But it was in a high state of disarray.

Mi-Lin sat rigidly across the desk from me, her back straight. She managed a smile, but it seemed tight at the edges.

Usually, I loved this small office. It had been inherited from David. Now, I noticed that the paint was chipped on the bottom of the latticed doors; I saw the slight discoloration on the base-board of the wall where the pipes had broken inside the wall and leaked through two years ago. I'd never gotten around to touching up the paint. It was as though I'd gone through a perceptual shift, from comfortable to self-critical. I glanced down at my baggy jogging suit. Suddenly I felt tacky.

Mi-Lin said, "Really, Alex. It's not that I mind the clutter. It's just that you surprise me."

I gave her a puzzled look.

"Please forgive me. I don't mean to seem condescending. But I don't understand why you place such limitations on yourself as to live like this."

Suddenly she sounded a lot like my mother, who was always uncomfortable with the way I lived whether or not my dwelling was spick-and-span. Mom was a happily married homebody who couldn't understand why anyone with a decent education and other options would choose to comb the mean streets of Honolulu in search of a livelihood; she couldn't understand why I didn't remarry and settle down and do something safe for a change.

Sometimes I didn't understand it myself, and especially today. But it always irritated me when others were critical of my lifestyle; I felt that same rush of outrage at Mi-Lin's words that I always felt when my mother went to work on me. Even more so. Mi-Lin was little more than a stranger to me. What business was it of hers, how I lived? And how dare she be critical right now?

Mi-Lin sensed my irritation. She looked chagrined. "Please

forgive me for being so outspoken. I know this place means a lot to you, that you bought it with your husband, but really, Alex—"

I stared hotly at her. How did she know I'd bought this place with David? More information gained when she'd had me checked out? And what did she really know about David, anyway? Or about any other part of my life for that matter?

Mi-Lin saw my darkening mood and laughed her merry little wind-chime laugh. "Alex, don't be angry with me. I just want to be friends. Can't we?" She gave me a pleading look, but there was a teasing merriment in her eyes.

I thawed a bit. "I'm sorry, Mi-Lin. I had a very bad night. I was tailing one of the boys who ripped off your jade, and he led me to the body of one of my best friends."

Her eyes went wide. "The news reporter, Lenni Apana?"

"Yes."

"Oh but Alex, I didn't realize you had anything to do with that. An actual murder. Aren't you afraid?"

"No. Just exhausted, grieving, miserable, and wishing she was still alive."

"I'm sorry, darling. I wish I could make it all go away." She blinked and said, "You say the boys who took Henry's trunks are involved?"

"I don't know what all they're involved in."

She leaned in close, her eyes kindling with excitement. "Tell me."

I drew back. "I can't. It's under investigation and I'm sworn to silence."

She smiled. "That's one thing I admire about you, Alex. You can keep a secret. Can you at least tell me if they might still have Henry's trunks?"

"I don't know, but I'm trying to find out."

"Okay. But enough of all that anyway. I came to ask you something."

"Of course."

"First, I want you to know I've been considering this ever since we first met, and I've decided you're the one. Especially after the splendid job you did recovering almost all of our stolen jade. I'm looking for a full-time assistant, Alex. You'd have a chance to travel, to learn an exciting new profession—"

"I don't think I'm interested."

"Oh, Alex. Think about what you're saying before you throw away such a golden opportunity. Darling, that girl was murdered because she was doing a story—they said as much on the morning news. The same thing could happen to you. You should get away from this depressing, violent life, and do something that befits your talents."

"I'm happy with what I do."

"I'm sure you are, but that's because you don't know how much better it could be. Don't say no. I could offer you as much as a hundred thousand a year, plus expenses. The jade business pays very well."

"A hundred thousand?" I was dumbfounded.

"Maybe even more. Why don't we talk about it?"

"I don't think I could ever work for anyone else again, even for that much money."

"You wouldn't be really working for me, just with me. But you have enough on your mind right now. You can decide later. Oh, Alex, I can't bear to see you so sad. I know!" She sat up straight like a delighted child. "Why don't you go with me to Hong Kong day after tomorrow, and see the city? In fact, why don't we just go right away?"

I deadpanned her. I couldn't imagine a stranger thing to do just now than pack up and fly to Hong Kong.

"Several things have happened, not here but in Hong Kong, nothing serious but—you know, it's always nice to have company rather than travel alone. Abe told me you're a highly qualified bodyguard."

"I've done a few jobs."

"Then I want to hire you to be my bodyguard during my trip to Hong Kong. There, you can't turn down an additional job."

"I thought you wanted me to find the two trunks."

"We'll be in Hong Kong only a few days, plus flying time.

Nothing much is going to happen tonight and tomorrow anyway. It's Christmas."

"I'm sorry, I can't go."

"All expenses would be paid of course, in addition to your regular fee."

"I have to be here tomorrow to work in the homeless shelter," I said. "I don't like to break my word."

"But why, Alex? Your family is all in Colorado—I know, we'll hire someone to work at the homeless shelter for you. Or I could make a donation of a thousand dollars to them, to help with their holiday meals."

I was having a hard time believing how badly she wanted me to go. "You'd really do that?"

She picked up her bag and took out her checkbook. "I'll do it right now."

She did, handing me the check, the payee line left blank. Then she said, "I can't bear the thought of going by myself. My brother depresses me. He's so old and vile. And Henry is being so difficult since his precious jade was stolen. You'd think I'd taken it myself. I need a friend, Alex. You look like you could use a friend too. Please come."

I thought about Lenni, and the pain welled up. I felt guilty for even thinking about taking a break from the Islands right now. But everything would pretty much grind to a halt over the next few days, even the police investigations. Lenni was already dead. I couldn't bring her back. Dru Chun Yuen was also dead, and that wasn't my fault. I hadn't even known the kid—why was I still grieving for him? To be sure, I wasn't any closer to finding Mock Sing Druan than I had been a week ago, but chances of my finding him within the next few days were thin to nonexistent anyway. There was really nothing happening that I couldn't put on hold for a few days.

Suddenly, I wanted very much to get away from all the chaos and confusion that had ruled my life since I'd discovered the boy's body in the Ala Wai Canal. I wanted to step out of my middle-class dwelling and past my dead-end problems and out of my responsibility-laden life. I wanted to be beautiful and glamorous and carefree and not feel the weight of Lenni's death draped across my shoulders. I wanted to blot out the sight of that dead, charred body.

She seemed to sense my capitulation. Warmly, she said, "I've already booked our flight on Royal China Air. Is your passport in order?"

"It's current, though I never use it," I admitted.

"Then you'll go. Is it okay if I change our reservations? Let's go tomorrow."

"I don't see why not." Truthfully, I had nothing better to do on Christmas Day, and it would be easy to get a flight out on the actual holiday when few people traveled.

"I hate Christmas anyway," she said. "It's the most miserable day of the year. If we fly tomorrow, we'll just get rid of the day altogether."

That puzzled me. She saw it and said, "We'll cross the international date line and the day will vanish." She laughed her tinkling laughter.

Mi-Lin was smiling as she stepped into the elevator. As the doors closed behind her, I stepped back into my office and looked around again.

I suddenly felt depressed. My life was going nowhere. The room that usually comforted me with its familiarity looked seedy, as compared to Henry Li's opulent house. I felt seedy too, compared to Mi-Lin.

Suddenly I was very glad I'd decided to go to Hong Kong.

I needed to learn to be a bit more selfish if I was ever going to truly succeed in life. I needed to quit dwelling on everything bad in the world and grab some of the good things for myself.

自由

Tavares phoned me a few hours later. "Merry Christmas Eve."

I glanced at the clock. It was almost 6 P.M., six hours till Christmas Day. I'd been packing. I said, "Merry Christmas to you too." I waited to see why he was really calling.

"I hear you're going to Hong Kong tomorrow."

I snapped to attention. "How on earth do you know that?"

"We picked it up on a phone bug."

"From who?"

"Don't worry about it. We don't have any listening devices planted around you."

I believed him. I'd checked my phone and condo several times over the past few weeks, just to make sure nobody had me under surveillance. Though I was thinking more in terms of Paké and whichever people in law enforcement might be linked to him.

Tavares said, "Look, I need to see you."

"You know where I am."

"I can't come there. I'm over at the Sheraton, sitting on one of the beach recliners by the pool. Come over and talk to me."

"About what?"

"About the people who killed Lenni Apana."

I felt an electric shock go through me. "Give me five minutes."

The sky was filled with hazy purple twilight; the sea held shimmers of lavender and gold. The hotel was a white, thirty-one-story crescent. The illuminated turquoise pool was separated from the beach and the darkening ocean by a small rock wall and a hedge. The lights above the pool area had come on. The deck chairs were at the edge of the light, facing the ocean, the shadows already swallowing them. A perfect place for a clandestine chat.

I didn't see Tavares as I approached, but I sat down on a deck chair anyway and turned so I could watch for him. He came out of the hotel a moment later. He'd been hidden, waiting for me. He was wearing white mid-thigh shorts and a white tennis shirt. Spiffy. His gold-brown hair had recently been trimmed, though it was still a bit too long for my taste. White sneakers, snow-white socks. The drug-dealer disguise traded in for the tennis-pro look.

"This *Mission: Impossible* stuff is beginning to get on my nerves," I said, as he sat down on the chair beside me.

"It beats the alternative," he said tightly.

"Which is?"

"Ask Lenni Apana."

I felt like he'd slapped me. Stiffly, I said, "What about her?"

"She found out where they were keeping the missing Chinese kid. They stopped her before she could get to him."

I sat straight up, shocked. Was there anything this man didn't know?

"Where is he?"

"Don't know. All we know is that Lenni had an informant who tipped her to where they were keeping the kid."

"Who's the informant?"

"That's the big question, isn't it?"

"How do you learn all this? Who do you have bugged?"

"Not you. I already told you that."

"Then who?"

He shifted positions, uncomfortable. "If I tell you, you owe me big time."

"Done."

"Where we learned about you going to Hong Kong is off limits. But Mr. Seven is our source for the information on Lenni. We got him on one phone call. He was in an uproar—he'd learned that she knew. Unfortunately, the person he was talking to cautioned him to watch his tongue and he shut up."

"Who was he talking to?"

"Can't say."

"The people who killed Lenni?"

"Nah, the people who did the actual murder are just throw-aways. He had the Shadow Dragons do the actual hit. Tell you the truth, we really don't know who he was talking to, but it wasn't any of the street kids."

I had the feeling he was lying about not knowing. But I wasn't going to get the truth out of him if he didn't want to tell me.

He said, "We know about the shipment of illegals that's supposed to arrive soon. But INS doesn't. We'd like to keep it that way for a while."

"Are they bringing in heroin at the same time? Is that your angle on this?"

He grinned. It made his face turn hard and cold. "They wanted to. They ran into some problems with the last shipment."

"The missing trunks?"

He leveled a long, angry look at me. "If you know that much, why are you still mucking around in all this?"

"Because I want to know the truth."

"You should get out of this mess. They've been using you as a pawn from the very beginning. How much have you told them, anyway?"

"Told who? About what?"

He gave me a disgusted look. "Ah, never mind."

I said, "Who's been using me? How?"

"Forget it. Look, Alex, this thing is going to explode any day now. You're sitting in the center of the powder keg."

"More intrigue," I said, suddenly irritated. "Why don't you just come out and tell me what's on your mind?"

"Okay, I will. I need a favor."

"From me?"

"Who else?"

"What do you want?"

"I need one piece of information before I can wrap up my end of all this—"

"Which is?"

"The banker's name."

"Huh?"

He was really wrapped tight. He said, "It's getting bloody out there. Lenni shouldn't have been killed. She was acting like a cowboy, and they nailed her, but it just shouldn't have happened."

I felt an ache in my heart.

"We're accelerating the time line of our investigation to make sure nobody else gets hurt. It'll shave off a few counts from the indictments, but we should be able to bust up the network anyway. Trouble is, we can't wrap things up until I find the one missing piece of the puzzle. It ties all the rest of it together."

"The banker?"

"Bingo. I'm *this close*, Alex." He held up his forefinger and thumb, pressed together. "Give me that one tiny piece of information, and I can wrap up the whole thing from Thailand to Hong Kong to the U.S. We thought we had them when the trunks came in, but no dice, everything went haywire, then next thing we know everyone on the island is in the middle of our business."

"Maybe because it's our business too."

"Not at the international level. You're just a little blip on the larger screen of life."

"Thanks a lot."

"It's pretty simple. We're trying to penetrate the financing. Once we have that, we have them. Period."

"You've lost me."

"Stay lost. That's as much as you need to know. Mi-Lin is going to see a banker day after tomorrow in Hong Kong. If you go to Hong Kong, she'll probably take you to the meeting with her. You can angle it so she takes you with her. Do it. That banker's our key to the whole thing. I need to know his name, and the name of the bank. I also need a photograph, in case he's not using his real name."

"And how am I supposed to snap his photograph without making him suspicious?"

Tavares reached into his pocket and brought out a fountain pen. "Use this."

He showed me how it worked. CIA high tech, he said, a pinpoint lens in one side beside the clip, a tiny mechanism inside that held the microfilm. All I had to do was snap the end, to make the writing mechanism pop out, and that would simultaneously snap the picture. He showed me how to aim the lens.

I took the pen and solemnly put it in my pocket.

His eyes glittered with anticipation. He had been hunting for a long time.

I said, "You're trying to bust the Snakehead?"

His grin frightened me. "Not the Snakehead, Alex. Not one Snakehead, not many. We're going for the hydra-headed monster that spawns the Snakeheads." He paused for dramatic effect then said, "I'm going to chop the head off the Dragon and let the rest of the organization bleed to death."

I felt ice cold. "Who's the Dragonhead?"

His gaze was steady, almost taunting.

"Mi-Lin's brother?"

His eyes slitted up.

"Henry Li?"

He deadpanned me.

"Not Mr. Seven," I said, going down the list. "He's not the Dragonhead. He's just another hired gun."

"Right."

"Then who?"

"Just worry about the banker, Alex. Get me the name of the banker, and we'll take down the people who killed Lenni and the Yuen kid. Come back with that name, and I can tell you the whole thing."

"How will I know which banker?"

"There's only one. And that's all you need to know. See you when you get back."

He got up, did a quick professional survey of his surroundings to make sure nobody threatening had entered his arena, then he strolled back into the hotel.

We flew out Christmas morning, on Royal China Air. Christmas Day was about to vanish.

It would be a sixteen-hour flight, actual time, with a short layover in Tokyo. Hong Kong was eighteen hours ahead of Honolulu, because of the international date line. When we touched down at Kai Tak Airport, the clock would have leaped forward by a full thirty-four hours, it would be the twenty-sixth, and the entire holiday would have been swallowed up by the vagaries of time.

The thought of it pleased me. The swirl of trouble in my life seemed to be caught up around the celebration of Christmas. I was eager for the holidays to end.

Mi-Lin had booked luxury class, on a reconfigured 747. I hadn't realized so much opulence could exist aboard an airliner.

I sank into a gray marshmallow-leather swivel seat, complete with private television set and phone. A wide console separated Mi-Lin and me and gave us plenty of room. The comfortable seats could be reclined into sleeping position; full-length curtains could be tugged around to provide privacy. The charcoal carpet was thick and deep enough to curl your toes into. The several bathrooms had leather upholstered, brass-studded banquettes and gray enamel sinks. On the forward deck there was a mirrored stand-up bar that provided not only cocktails, but also fresh juice and snacks.

By the time the plane took off I had been given the brief guided tour, then I relaxed, letting my mind drift back over the events of the past few days, while Mi-Lin gazed out through the draped window, a small frown knit into her eyebrows. As we gained altitude, the problems in Honolulu began to fade into the distance and the future seemed to be rushing toward me, golden and mysterious. Tavares's warnings seemed surreal and almost foolish in the glittering light of day. Only my grief for Lenni remained real, and even it was muted by the novelty of the flight.

The Islands had barely receded into the distance when a handsome young white-clad Chinese attendant appeared with a crystal vase of fresh flowers. Miniature poinsettias in red, white, and green, but they were the only indications of Christmas aboard the entire plane. The attendant opened the leather-padded console between us. It unfolded into a small table. He placed the flowers in a niche made for that purpose, bowing all the while, then served us flutes of champagne, warm roasted almonds, and fresh sugared lemon peel.

Mi-Lin sipped her champagne and seemed to relax then. She looked around cooly, like a mistress inspecting the house before a dinner party. Finally, she said, "Welcome to my world, Alex. You really should consider moving here."

At that moment, in spite of all I knew, I wondered if she were right. Though I am generally a teetotaler, I sipped my champagne too. It gave me a giddy sense of well-being.

The attendant arrived with soft, hot cloths to wipe the salt from our fingers. Through the window behind Mi-Lin, I could see massive banks of clouds floating in a pale blue sky. Suddenly I felt alive, eager to step into a new beginning.

I needed a fresh start, whether as Mi-Lin's assistant or without her. I needed to finally leave David's death and all the other deaths behind me. Ahead was a whole new world.

At the same time, I knew I was flying into the lair of the Dragon. But all the evil and poverty and misery existed beyond this carefully crafted flying cocoon, and it was easy to distance myself from it. I convinced myself that Mi-Lin was being used by Henry Li, perhaps by her brother. Once the bad guys were out of the picture, the rest of this might well remain. Maybe I should follow Mi-Lin's philosophy and think of myself first, and let the rest of the world take care of itself for a while.

I napped, then we chatted about lighthearted, almost girlish things like shopping and traveling and men. She asked me if I was sad to be traveling on Christmas Day. I told her it was actually a relief.

Mi-Lin seemed interested in everything I said, and she offered merciless insights into male-female relationships.

"Never get involved with a man you love more than he loves you. Always keep the upper hand. And always remember that they'll leave you someday. Get what you can while you can."

She told me she'd been married three times. One husband had been killed, the other two had been unfaithful. One of them had beaten her. Her brother had chosen them all, and always to his own business advantage. I saw how badly she'd been scarred by life. I liked her, I understood her. She had been born into her world, had been forced to seal herself off from pain. Maybe that was the wise thing to do.

Three hours out of Honolulu, the attendant arrived to spread a white linen cloth over our table. We had already made our selections from the menu, and soon he was serving us an elegant five-course meal of Asian delicacies. We talked some more while we ate. The dessert cart came and we chose delicate tiramisu. I declined the after-dinner coffee. Then the private movies came on, but there was nothing I wanted to watch. Mi-Lin said she wanted to arrive in Hong Kong fresh. She slept, almost instantly. I leaned back, relaxed, and thought about what I was doing, and finally I also slept.

We napped, chatted, ate again. In Tokyo, we got out of the plane for a half hour and tried to stretch our legs, but the terminal seemed packed with wall-to-wall people and we quickly went back to our seats.

Finally, I awakened to an attendant's clipped English voice, informing us that we were about to land at Kai Tak Airport. He informed us that Hong Kong's weather was overcast, with rain expected.

The plane began to descend. We dipped beneath the clouds. Mi-Lin pointed out the sights as I looked across her through the large window. A spreading expanse of sea-damp green rolled off toward the People's Republic of China, against a graying sky. Storm clouds stacked up behind the mountains. We banked, and I could see the smog-tinted maze of high-rises in Central's financial district, the junks and ships and floating barges in the harbors, the urban sprawl of Kowloon beneath us on the Mainland. I felt her come unpleasantly alive, almost like someone going into battle. I also felt a sudden awareness of a churning surge of life beneath me, a cauldron of people on that boiling, seagirt rock of Hong Kong Island. I felt the challenge and the excitement, and the sense of a centuries' old weight.

Hong Kong was still the heart of Asian commerce: it would remain so even after China took it over. Mainland China was booming; some said it would be the central economy of the next century. Hong Kong would remain its door to Western capitalism.

Many people who had planned to bail out of Hong Kong had changed their minds. Hong Kong meant money. It always had. The banking laws here were secretive, the society a mixture of racketeers and opium dealers and spies and corrupted public officials and every other ingredient for opulent intrigue. But everyone fed on the money. That was the heart and mind and soul of Hong Kong. China—huge and formidable—loomed always in the background, a seething cauldron holding one-sixth of all the people in the world.

The landing was smooth. A thin, cadaverous chauffeur with sad eyes met us at the bottom of the loading ramp and escorted us to a burnished gold Rolls Royce limo that made me catch my breath.

Mi-Lin smiled at my reaction. She was completely comfortable, completely used to such luxury. Within minutes, we were lost in the sleek interior, behind tinted windows, being whisked past the tumultuous crowds.

Mi-Lin was silent. She seemed to be growing more tense. We drove through a long tunnel beneath the harbor, then cut past Central and drove up the winding road to the top of Victoria Peak. The rain had settled in. Lights had come on against the growing gloom. I caught one breathtaking view of the city below me, a gossamer of streetlights and neon giving it life now. Then we swept past the overlook, the roadside grew thick with foliage, the rain clouds settled down around us, and suddenly we were stopping in front of an immense carved gate with two enormous stone lions—smiling, frowning—standing guard.

The chauffeur spoke into an intercom. It was a language different from the one I'd heard spoken in the airport and by the many Chinese passengers aboard the airplane. I asked Mi-Lin.

"Chiu-Chow," she said. "In the city, you will hear mostly Cantonese and English, but in our homes many of us still speak our own family dialects."

We drove up a driveway and stopped in front of the mansion, a large, Chinese-style with a ceramic tiled roof and curved eaves. I was somewhat disappointed. Mi-Lin had told me her brother was the head of a hong—a massive trading conglomerate. I had expected him to be very rich, especially if his business also included trafficking in heroin. I had heard so many stories about the opulent consumption of Hong Kong's super-rich that I had expected something dazzling. Some members of Hong Kong society sported a different colored Rolls Royce for every day of the week, complete with matching full-length mink coats for their wives and mistresses. Gold-leaf on their gates, gold-plated doorknobs, and even gold flushers on their toilets. Here, money was the sole measure of any man; those who had it usually flaunted it.

We moved past two young, hard-faced men dressed in black, with short ponytails and dead, flat faces. They eyed me suspiciously, then lowered their eyes and nodded politely to Mi-Lin. She measured them with contempt and didn't bother to nod back.

She explained they were security guards. "My brother has many expensive things."

Inside, the chauffeur took our luggage down a dark hallway and disappeared, leaving us standing in the large, gloomy foyer.

"My brother is usually with his crickets this time of day," Mi-Lin said.

"His what?"

"Crickets." She smiled at my puzzled look. "Many older Chinese men hold cricket fights during late summer. The rest of the year, my brother cultivates them and keeps them as pets. It's a very old custom. He will probably not join us for dinner. He seldom does. But we'll go see him after you've freshened up."

I was looking past Mi-Lin at a shrine in the back of the foyer. On a wide lacquered table stood a carved deity, a Buddhalike figure sitting cross-legged, wearing a flowing robe that left its arms bare. The white lacquered face was serene, a gold hairpiece framed the face and the hair was swept up into a black bowl-like object. To each side were life-sized sacred brass deer, and red-lacquered tables holding candles and joss sticks. Three tangerines were set before the idol, carefully stacked into a small pyramid, the stems intact. Also a round glass of water, and some lighted joss sticks that smelled like pine.

I said, "What's that?"

"An altar to Mo, the god of martial arts and war," said Mi-Lin, looking offhandedly at the altar. "He protects people from harm and he goes with them into battle."

I felt a little lick of fear. My DEA training had included a small segment on the Mo temples revered by the Hong Kong underworld. The temples could be found all over, including police stations, where police and mobsters were often one and the same.

"It's my brother's," Mi-Lin said contemptuously. "Ah, here's Mae Kuan." A tiny woman who might have been a hundred years old padded in on cloth shoes. Her shoulders were stooped from too much work, her jaws had collapsed when her teeth vanished. Mi-Lin said, "She'll take you to your room and see that you have everything you need." She spoke to the woman in rapid-fire Chinese, then turned and strode away. I followed the maid down the hallway.

My room was comfortable, if not elegant. Not a trace of Christmas anywhere. The furnishings were strange to me. Tall black cabinets with tiny drawers, filigreed metal handles, rich embroidered tapestries on the walls showing scenes of misty mountains and tiny peasant people working farmland. Tables with dark-red lacquered tops. Mae Kuan laid out a fresh towel and washcloth and opened the door to a bathroom with a sunken tub and exquisite gold and green tiles. It was passable, if not exactly spotless. It hadn't been used for a long time.

"You like see anything else, missee, I make good for you."

I thanked her and told her I was fine.

"I make see you come dinner in one hour," she said. I assumed that meant she'd let me know when dinner was about to be served.

When she left, I bathed, dressed in my robe, pulled some books from the shelf, and paged through them. They were on art, mostly jade, complete with large glossy pictures. The text was in Chinese.

I turned on the television and watched a brittle English-speaking newscaster talking about the Asian financial markets, then I switched channels and watched a Chinese opera for a while—the costumes and makeup were incredible, but the actors kept doing the same things over and over with exaggerated motions and facial expressions. It might have been okay if I'd known what they were saying.

There was a telephone. Reluctantly, I dialed Colorado, putting the charge on my phone card. I really didn't want to be reminded of Christmas, but I'd never hear the end of it if I didn't let them know I'd arrived safe and sound.

After a brief pause, Troubles came on the line. "Alex?"

"How's the holiday going? Did you get some nice gifts?"

"I liked the T-shirt you gave me. How's Hong Kong?"

"Truthfully? I'm bored to death."

"Why don't you go sight-seeing or something?"

"I'm more-or-less working. I have to follow the boss's agenda. The flight was nice though." I told him about it.

"Sounds like you've hit the big-time."

"Maybe. I'll bring you along next time, if I decide to make it a regular part of my life."

"Well hang in there, it's only for a few days."

I talked briefly to my parents, then my sister, who seemed to think that if I could fly to Hong Kong for Christmas I could certainly have come home. I paged through the news magazines I'd brought from Honolulu then napped for a while. I awakened wondering if they were going to serve dinner. Then I realized what had awakened me. I heard voices, far away in the house, shouting, filled with rage. Suddenly I was worried about Mi-Lin.

I dressed and went out into the hallway. Mi-Lin was coming down the corridor, dressed in the same green pantsuit she'd worn on the plane. When she saw me, the storm on her face turned into a smile.

I said, "Everything okay?"

She looked irritated. "You heard the shouting? I'm so sorry, Alex. Mae Kuan gets so slovenly when I'm gone, I can't believe how she's let the house go. I told her to hire some girls to help, but—" She shrugged helplessly.

I glanced around at the masses of dark wood, the intricate furniture, the many mirrors. It didn't seem that bad to me—excluding my bathroom—but then I'd only seen a few parts of it.

Besides, I'd heard a man's voice too.

"Come meet my brother," she said. "He's waiting."

We went into a large room packed with furniture and art works and books and other items. He was sitting in front of a fireplace, lit against the growing winter chill. As I went in, he turned, and my heart sank.

He was in a wheelchair that seemed to dwarf him. He was frail, and part of his face was paralyzed, probably from a stroke. Mi-Lin had said he had heart trouble, but I hadn't realized how old and sick he really was. Liver spots loomed large on his pale face and his hands quivered as he tugged at the brown lap robe that covered his stick-pin legs. If Mae Kuan seemed a hundred, this man was a hundred-and-fifty. He had a small, wispy beard, like someone out of an ancient Chinese painting. He resembled the crickets he liked to tend far more than the fire-breathing dragon I'd been expecting to meet.

Mi-Lin nodded respectfully to him as she introduced us.

He craned his neck toward me, blinked his rheumy eyes, and said a few words of greeting that I could barely understand. Then, in a creaking, almost inaudible voice, he said, "Would you like to see my pi?"

I thought at first he was totally senile. I looked at Mi-Lin for help.

"Come," she said. She took keys out of his pocket and unlocked a door, then pushed him into an adjacent room, me following, and suddenly we were in an actual museum. A sense of incredible wealth oozed from the dark teak walls. The displays were locked behind glass, the electronic security apparent to anyone who cared to look. The cases held art work from every era in Chinese history, and a number of things from the West as well. Awed, I followed Mi-Lin to a glass case at the far side of the treasure-filled room. She pointed. "That's the pi."

There, behind a thick plate of glass, was a six-inch round disk with a hole in the center, set upon a velvet-covered shelf. The green jade was exquisitely carved, but it certainly wasn't the most eye-catching piece in the room.

"My brother brought this piece from Shanghai," Mi-Lin said. "It is very special to him."

She explained that it was from the second millennium B.C., a ritual stone. At one time the owner had been offered fifteen Chinese cities for it but had refused to sell. The object was still priceless. I would have passed it up in a heartbeat. Suddenly I wondered if my future as an assistant jade appraiser would be so bright after all. How on earth did they decide what was priceless? Some pieces were obviously superior, but most of it all looked the same to me.

Dinner was uneventful, and her brother joined us after all, spoon-fed by Mae Kuan. If I was in the presence of a Dragonhead who ruled a brutal international Triad, there was certainly nothing to indicate as much. I was simply having dinner with a bored woman who looked out for a much older brother in the last years of his life. Not my idea of high intrigue; not even my idea of a good time.

I slept well that night, tired from the trip and the events that had preceded it. When I awakened, the rain was pouring, the house around me was quiet. I looked at my watch, 10 A.M. I jumped out of bed and checked my bag. The CIA ballpoint pen was still inside, still intact. Apparently nobody had gone through my things during my deep, dreamless sleep.

I showered and was suddenly ravenously hungry. I dressed in charcoal slacks and a gold and charcoal sweater. Mi-Lin had warned me it could get chilly here this time of year and she'd been right. There seemed to be no central heating in the house, no individual heater in my room. I pulled on socks and shoes, then on second thought I took the shoes back off and carried them. I was supposed to be in the lair of the dragon. Perhaps if I were quiet I might stumble onto something interesting—though I didn't think so.

I moved silently down the hall. Nobody seemed to be home. I found the dining room and paused before a sideboard that held family photographs. One was of two people—her elder brother and another younger man, who was certainly his brother. In another photograph, the two grown men stood beside a young girl, a very plain child with almost homely features. She faintly resembled Mi-Lin. Perhaps an older cousin or sister who hadn't been so fortunate as to be blessed with Mi-Lin's beauty? I picked up another framed picture of the girl again, this one taken at an older age. She was standing in front of a pond with ducks and water lilies, flat-faced, her eyes small, a slight stoop in her shoulders as if she was aware of her unfortunate appearance. She looked so much like Mi-Lin that the photo gave me an uncanny feeling, like I was looking at a negative of her. I scanned the room. There were no photographs of Mi-Lin anywhere. Odd.

I had still not encountered anyone; perhaps I wouldn't. Mi-Lin had said that her brother was incredibly cheap when it came to paying household help. There were security guards, of course, but only two full-time servants: Mae Kuan, who was too old to go anywhere else, and the cook, Wo Sin, who lived in a Wanchai tenement and worked here twelve hours a day, preparing her brother's special meals. A nurse also took care of her brother, but he didn't like Mi-Lin and made himself scarce when she was around.

I hesitated, then moved into a hallway paneled with dark teakwood walls—the whole house was dark and gloomy, with a feeling of ancient must. It was so silent I could hear water dripping from the outside rafters. There were several doors, and I chose the one to my right.

I opened it and froze in place, horrified.

I was face-to-face with a six-foot long hooded cobra. A scream welled up, and my knees begin to buckle. The snake flicked out its tongue and stared at me with flat, cold eyes. It took me an instant to realize that a man held the cobra, his left hand behind the snake's hood, the tail held to the floor by his foot. In his right hand, he held a long filet knife, and the entire snake was stretched taut, its head angled so it was gazing straight at me with full, poisonous rancor.

The cobra's eyes flicked back and forth, the tongue flicked out again. There were only a few short inches between the snake's fangs and the man's throat, should the creature whip around. I wanted to help the man, but fear held me back.

I stepped backward, cautiously, but the door had swung shut behind me and I hit a solid, immovable force. I reached back and tried to turn the handle. It had an automatic lock. I was trapped face-to-face with the silent, stretched-out horror in front of me.

The man with the snake seemed to be glaring at me now, eyes

wide, the snake still strung taut, its tongue licking out toward me. In a burst of terror I broke free and lunged for a doorway at the far side of the room, crashing through. The door swung shut behind me and I was in pitch blackness. I bounced off the wall at the far side, while things all around me cascaded to the floor. The room was tiny; I seemed to be in some kind of pantry. There was something rustling—I had a sudden uncanny sensation of something slithering, writhing, and I reached out blindly and found a light-switch, turned it on—and screamed and screamed. I couldn't stop; *I was in a room filled with writhing, crawling, terrifying snakes!* Snakes slithered around me, up the walls, across the floor. Large snakes, hooded cobras, silver-sheened serpents, the pit of horrors filled to the brim with snakes of every kind. I bit off another scream as I suddenly realized the snakes were caged in thinly latticed bamboo. Several cages had fallen from the shelves when I crashed into the wall, and the snakes' heads darted about; the cages barely contained them. I tried to push back out through the door, only to realize that it opened toward me and I'd have to step farther into the snakepit to make my exit.

I caught my breath and made the move, amazed that nothing dropped down from the rafters to throttle me, no fangs lunged into my legs, arms, or stocking-clad feet. I reeled into the kitchen, surprising the man with the knife. As I crashed into him, he dropped the cobra's head but still had his foot planted on its tail, and its hood furled out farther, it snapped around, trying to lay its fangs into the man's feet, but the man leaped atop the table and I froze again, afraid to move.

The cobra was enraged, whipping back and forth, coiling up, its head darting around looking for something to strike, but I stayed absolutely still, not even breathing, and it suddenly uncoiled and slithered across the floor and into an open trash bin, just as my knees buckled and I slid down the wall and sank to the floor. The Chinese man was yelling furiously as he leaped down from the table and gestured with the knife as if to stab me. I rolled away, came to my feet, and bolted out the kitchen door—straight into Mi-Lin. I barely managed to stop in time, or I would have knocked her flat.

She was wearing a filmy peach nightgown and robe, and when I had disengaged myself, she shot me a horrified look. "Alex! What's wrong?"

The man blasted through the door, knife still in his hand, arms flailing. He stopped, his eyes shooting fire, then he shouted at Mi-Lin in Chinese, gesticulating toward me, a look of unmistakable rage on his face.

I kept saying, "He had a snake!" as he yelled and postured and bared his teeth at me, overwhelming my feeble comments, until finally Mi-Lin shouted back at him and stepped over and slapped him hard across the face. He fell silent and glared at her with a look of such poisonous hatred that the cobra seemed to have come into him for a moment. He hissed something at her, then he disappeared back into the kitchen, a sulk on his face.

I was dumbfounded. Absolutely bewildered, shivering, speechless with amazement, and totally confused by what had just happened.

Mi-Lin snapped, "What were you doing in there?"

"Looking for something to eat." My voice was quivering. "The man has a room full of snakes. He was holding a cobra—"

Her face changed, and then she started to laugh, that tinkling little wind-chime laugh, and then she was laughing and laughing, taking me by the hand into the dining room—I really didn't want to sit down since the cobra was still loose. I kept watching the floorboards near the kitchen, expecting it to slither into the room at any moment.

Still laughing, she said, "Alex, darling. That was our cook. He's just preparing my brother's breakfast."

"Snakes? For breakfast?"

"Of course. It's snake season. Snake is a delicacy in Hong Kong. It's especially good shredded and cooked with chicken and cabbage." She smiled teasingly. "Perhaps we'll have some for lunch."

"He was going to butcher that cobra?" I was still incredulous.

"Either that or slice out its gall bladder for my brother's

morning snack." She saw the look on my face, and explained further. "Really, Alex, it's very common. I'm surprised you don't know."

"Yes, but *cobra*?"

"The gall bladder is supposed to rejuvenate old men and revive their appetites. My brother uses at least one a day. Sometimes he'll eat the snake meat, or sometimes the cook just takes a snake and drops it in alcohol live, to die then decompose. They call it snake wine. My brother drinks it to help him swallow his gall bladders, though sometimes he'll use a shot of cognac instead."

I shuddered. "No wonder he's in poor health."

She smiled, but this one was cold. "Quite the contrary. I truly believe he'd have been dead long ago if he hadn't followed his doctor's orders. Things are very different here, Alex. You really must adjust."

I was embarrassed by what had happened, but also squeam-
ish and worried about the cobra. It had slid in under the
floorboards, which meant that two of the guards had to crawl
around under the house with flashlights, looking for it. The cook
was looking too. They were all furious with me, though Mi-Lin
assured me that this wasn't the first time her brother's "medicine"
had escaped.

Fortunately, Mi-Lin decided to take me with her on her business rounds, to keep me out of trouble. I sent up a prayer of thanks
that I hadn't been left behind, which had apparently been her
earlier intent.

The chauffeur drove us down the Peak Road. Though the sky
was still gray and overcast, the visibility was better. A wide swath
of white high-rises filled the waterfront in the Central district
beneath us. I asked if there was a bank where I could exchange
some American cash for Hong Kong dollars. Mi-Lin pointed out
the Bank of China, the Hong Kong-Shanghai Bank, the Bank of

America tower, the Chartered Bank, and the Shanghai Bank of Asia. "The Bank of China belongs to the Chinese government," she explained. "We're going to the Shanghai Bank of Asia. I need to sign some papers there. Then I'll take you to the jade market in Kowloon, darling. You're going to love it. But you don't need to worry about money. How much do you need?" She opened her leather purse and pulled out a thick sheaf of variously colored bills. Hong Kong money.

"I'd rather use my own money for personal things."

"Nonsense, darling." She shoved several hundred dollar bills at me. "That's for pocket money. When we shop later, I'll put everything on my charge card. You can bill me for the trip when we get back to Honolulu."

The sea was smoky blue-gray now, with ships and freighters and sampans weaving in and out of scraps of fog. My embarrassment began to fade into that sense of super-alertness and excitement that comes with visiting a new place.

We cruised into the Central district, past sleek buildings and an occasional colonial-style government edifice, through the bustling financial district and straight to the Shanghai Bank of Asia. It was close to the waterfront, and as I rolled down my window I smelled smog and freshly gutted fish. The chauffeur tooled up the curb and pulled into a loading zone in front of the huge marble-faced building. He opened the rear door for Mi-Lin, but when I started to climb out my door, Mi-Lin held up a delicate hand to stop me.

"Oh, no, darling, just wait here. I won't be a minute."

"I'd really like to stretch my legs."

She shot me a demanding look. "Wait here," she ordered. "You'd just slow me down."

I waited. The chauffeur was watching me in the rearview mirror, a passive look on his face. How was I going to use my CIA camera-ballpoint pen to photograph the banker if I wasn't even allowed into the bank?

After a couple of tense minutes, I was about to fly apart. The bank building was huge. I had no idea where Mi-Lin had gone, but I decided to find out. If the chauffeur was going to stop me, he'd have to do so by force. I turned the door handle, watching him out of the corner of my eye. He tensed up as I cracked the door; he jumped out just as I opened it. I was bracing for a tussle when I glanced up, saw Mi-Lin coming, and quickly slid back in and shut the door. She was floating down the white marble steps in front of the bank's large plate-glass doors. The chauffeur had seen her too; he'd just been climbing out to open her car door.

Mi-Lin slid in and said, "Sorry, darling. But I really did want to hurry. You can stretch your legs at the jade market. I think you'll have a good time."

We drove out of Central and through the cross-harbor tunnel, to emerge beside the long, low railroad station in Kowloon. We drove north, toward the city's plush hotels. We came to the Yaumatei district and were close to the waterfront again. I could see the teeming mass of people living aboard junks and barges and anything else seaworthy, covering the inner part of the harbor. A sense of alienation descended over me. Honolulu's Chinatown began to seem like a comfortable slice of home compared to this exotic place.

Planes zoomed overhead. I'd read somewhere that a plane lifted off every couple of minutes from the nearby Kai Tak Airport. Up the block I could see a welter of street stalls and shops with people milling everywhere. Motorbikes and taxis zoomed past us. An occasional rickshaw and people on foot scurried by, all of them teeming and churning and hurrying somewhere. We cruised in air-conditioned comfort past a staggering variety of small shops and markets, almost stacked one atop the other. On Canton Road, we passed upscale gold shops and other less cluttered businesses. At the end of the road we came to the open-air jade market.

Mi-Lin glanced at her watch. "It closes at noon, darling. We don't have much time. But at least you'll see how it works."

One part of me seemed to keep rushing me forward, telling me there was a future here, money and travel and all the things I'd ever wanted. At the same time, alarms were going off all over the place in another part of my mind. I watched closely, cautiously, wanting to learn everything I could for a variety of reasons that were confusing even to me. I wanted Tavares to be wrong. Mi-Lin couldn't be involved in all the destruction caused by the heroin traffic. She was an expert in jade; her affiliation with the evil people was a pure accident of birth. She wanted out too. I could see it in the various things she said and did. I would learn the truth and help set her free. With her knowledge and my ambition, we could still make quite a team.

Mi-Lin handed a thick wedge of cash to one thin, cadaverous Chinese man, who immediately carried several cardboard boxes to the limo. He and the chauffeur began to load them. I wasn't worried. The top guns never handle the drugs. If I was going to learn anything here, it wouldn't be the actual route of the heroin.

Mi-Lin was enjoying herself. She explained that the whole market was a massive gamble, that the jade rocks arrived unbroken, the jade buried in their centers. The merchants bid on the rocks and took what they found inside. Sometimes something exquisite, sometimes nothing at all.

We watched two older, hard-eyed merchants as they bid on the jade rocks. The signals were mysteriously hidden beneath towels that covered their hands. I wasn't quite sure how the dealers and the merchants actually communicated the bids. I asked Mi-Lin, and she laughed.

"It's a mystery to me too," she said, "but somehow they manage. Most of this business is conducted according to reputation. Henry Li's is so valuable to him that he'd lie forever to protect it. The auctioneers consider the person, his background, his reputation. The buyers consider the reputation of the auctioneer, the place where the jade rock was found—if the dealer will tell—and then they both factor in their respective astrological situation according to their signs. And of course, the merchants learn to read the rocks."

"This is what Henry Li does?"

"Not at all. His mistress runs his Hong Kong business. She handles the buying at this level—"

"Mistress?" That surprised me, after what she'd told me about his twisted appetites.

She realized her mistake, lost a beat, then said off-handedly, "He has a variety of interests. Come on, they're going to break open some newly purchased rocks. Let's see what's inside."

After we'd climbed back into the luxurious backseat of the limo, she began to talk freely. "You went to Burma once, when you visited Thailand for American drug enforcement?"

The scope of her information surprised me, but I hid my reaction. "Just inside the border, though you can't tell where it stops and starts up there—it's all jungle. We were in Thai military Jeeps, visiting the hill tribes. I almost died from the heat."

"Henry has a deal with the top jade rock supplier in that region," Mi-Lin said, then darted a quick, inquisitive glance at me. She wanted to see my reaction.

I nodded agreeably. "That would cut down on the overhead."

"He gets all his really precious jade from that area. We still buy a few things at the market, but not much. Would you like to see what we just bought?"

"I would."

The chauffeur had left one small cardboard box inside the compartment. She picked it up, ripped it open, then took out a small wooden chest. The red felt interior glittered with treasure.

Jewelry. Ruby rings, diamond earrings, gold bangles and chains. Emeralds, blue and golden topaz, pearl strands and brooches, all of it heartbreakingly beautiful.

She held it out to me. "Pick something. Several things, if you wish. We have more boxes in back."

Instinctively, I started to reach out, then I drew back my hand. "It's hot," I said.

She laughed that wind-chime laugh. "But of course it is, darling. Surely you didn't think I paid good money for all my lovely things. Our little boys in the streets get these baubles from hotels and other places where the people are so wealthy they scarcely miss them. Our man at the jade market will pay them. Go ahead, it will never be traced. Take whatever you want. Or maybe you'd rather wait till it's all been melted down and reset, as I do. Then you're even safe enough to have it insured."

"I'll think about it," I said. I felt a ripple of panic. I was in over my head here. I said, "You were telling me about Henry Li's jade business." I was surprised by how steady my voice sounded.

She laughed again. "Yes. That is, after all, the point." She shut the chest, tossing it carelessly to the floor. Then she flicked an imperial hand, and the chauffeur closed the window that separated him from our compartment.

She said, "The Burmese government nationalized the mining industry twenty years ago. It's illegal to sell jade privately, and most government stock goes to private auctions and dealers at very high prices."

Why was she telling me this? Suddenly I didn't want to hear any more.

I said, "Mi-Lin, I don't think I'll be accepting your offer, so maybe you'd like to keep the rest of this confidential."

"Oh, but you will join us. I'm sure of it. And you'll need to understand."

I was literally sick at my stomach from what I was hearing. It was tearing apart every nerve in my body, but I didn't dare let it show.

"The jade gets from Burma to Thailand by boat, mule caravan, people on foot, in small airplanes, and vehicles of various kinds. It's taxed by the different rebel groups who rule the regions it travels through. You're familiar with them?"

I was. She was talking about the armies of the opium lords in the Golden Triangle, Asia's major source of heroin. My DEA training kicked in and I remembered hearing about the jade that was smuggled along with the opium caravans. I really hadn't put two and two together. No reason to connect the effortlessly elegant Mi-Lin Ming with the brutal, bloodthirsty opium lords of the Golden Triangle.

Jade and opium. The two most lucrative, bloodiest businesses in Asia. Not bad money, if Mi-Lin's people had a lock on both at the same time. But why was she telling me this?

"There is a General Kwai Li Liang who controls an army of mountain people and longtime Chinese renegades along the Thai border in the Shan State. Do you know his name?"

I did. The DEA had been after him and his Shan Army for two decades. He was the key trafficker in the region, responsible for exporting tons and countless tons of opium gum, morphine base, and even processed heroin. I nodded.

"He is my uncle, though younger than my brother. He is from a second wife." She hung her head, as if in shame. "He has changed his name. There is bad blood in this family. My own brother is the worst of them all. And there is also another uncle, Wa Shan Liang, who takes care of the business from Chiang Mai and Bangkok."

I felt a shiver run down my spine. I was sitting square in the dragon's belly, and it was about to begin digesting me. Already I was floating in the evil acids of secret information. There was no turning back from here.

I said, "I don't think you want to be telling me this."

"Oh, but why not, darling? Half the police in Hong Kong know it. Even American drug enforcers. Most of them grow fat and rich off my family's business skills. We pay off hundreds of cops and soldiers and government people—from Burma to Thailand to Hong Kong to San Francisco—everywhere it's always the same. How on earth do you think we survive?" She shot me a pitying look, as if I was being foolish to even question her judgment.

"Ours is a risky business," she said. "But it's getting even worse. Have you ever heard of the Tai Hwin, the Big Circle?"

I had, but I couldn't register where.

"It's the Triad from the Chinese mainland," she said bitterly. "The Chinese government's secret agency that will take over Hong Kong's underworld and make it a tool of Mainland China. The rulers in Beijing try to say the Tai Hwin is ruled by people outside their control, but the control comes directly from them."

I was dumbstruck. Incredulous.

"Make no mistake about it, China is positioned to swallow all of Asia," she said. "Even us. Especially us. My family had a long

THE JADE CRUCIBLE 271

history of fighting the Communists, and they remember well. My brother is cruel, but not as cruel as some. That's why we must move our business out of Hong Kong before the Communists move in. Others may be able to compromise, but not us."

Suddenly I was thinking about Honolulu. About the very dead Dru Chun Yuen, about Henry Li, about his hard, ancient eyes and his elegant mansion, his reputation, and the theft of his jade.

I was also thinking about Paké Chang, syndicate boss and keeper of the keys to the drug markets in Chinatown and Waikiki. *They come across the sea*, he'd said, *without letting even the sky know. They're invisible like ghosts.* He'd known from the beginning, he'd tried his best to warn me—

"We need someone special in Honolulu, someone who understands how the U.S. government works, who can tell us how to operate in a way that we don't—as you say—make waves. The incident with the stolen trunks shows how different your city is from ours. Here, we have full police protection, and anyone who dared steal from us would already be dead. But that taught us a good lesson. We need someone who understands the culture and our business as well. Your experience would be invaluable to my family, Alex. And so I am making this offer to you."

She handed it to me like a one-two punch. It was the standard lead or gold approach. I could either join them and get rich, or pick lead out of some or all of my family. "We have information that certain people would like to harm your nephew," she said. "I understand you're especially fond of him."

I thought about my family. Colorado was only a short plane ride away.

"Why me?" I said. I was still astonished. When I'd worked for the DEA the possibility of something like this happening was always real, but *now*?

"Because you aren't a fool. I believe you're wise enough to see the inevitability of all this, and you'll use it to your advantage."

She might have been chatting about selling rice, so casually did she make her offer. In fact, she opened her purse, took out a gold compact, and began reapplying dark red lipstick. She smeared her lips together, to even out the freshly applied paint, then sprayed just a hint of expensive perfume behind each of her shell-like ears. She actually smiled at me.

"And you love your family," she said. "You won't let anything happen to them. That's another reason we chose you. So long as you're part of our family, we'll take care of them too. Your nephew wants to go on to medical school. We'll see that he gets the very best education. We have money, Alex. We can buy anything we want." She tilted her head and studied me, and I saw the cold indifference flash into her eyes. "Even you."

I wanted to bash her beautiful face in, but I held back my anger. That was one quick way to end up as fish food in the bottom of Hong Kong Harbor.

I said, "You obviously checked me out thoroughly before you targeted me. What about my faith? Didn't you realize that there would be too much conflict for me to accept your offer?"

She smiled again, and this time it chilled me. "At first I thought that might be a problem," she said. "But after meeting you, I saw that you weren't all that spiritual anyway. You have a great deal of common sense, Alex. We've been watching you closely. You quit going to church about the time we got you interested in our affairs. We considered that a very good sign indeed."

We had pulled up in front of the Parkway Hotel, on Waterbury Road. "We can work this out later," she said. "I'm sure things will be fine. Right now it's time for lunch. We're meeting someone special."

This was the top-of-the-line hotel. Mi-Lin led me into a colonial dining room, alongside a waterfront garden. A man was waiting for us. He stood as we entered, and the maitre d' led us to his table.

The man was rotund, almost jolly looking. Chinese of course, about four foot eleven, wearing a tailored charcoal gray suit with wide chalk stripes, a black silk shirt, and a diamond stickpin that would have choked a hippo. He was a slightly younger, much fatter and marginally healthier version of Mi-Lin's eldest brother. I recognized him from the photographs in Mi-Lin's house.

Mi-Lin nodded respectfully to him as she introduced us, just as she had to her brother. With these male elders in her family, she showed all the traditional Chinese obeisance.

"This is my honored uncle, Wa Shan Liang," she said.

I kept my face expressionless as I acknowledged the introduction. I was surprised I could talk. In an instant my entire world had changed. I had been totally wrong about Mi-Lin, about everything.

I'd let myself be lured here in pursuit of personal and financial freedom—and it had been easy to lure me, at that. I had fallen into the same trap as the other stupid people who had been lured by the dream of an easier life. The dragon had merely smirked, flicked its sharp claws, and now it had me pinned tight.

The uncle said a few polite words in English, though I could barely understand him. Then he ordered our meals—without consulting us—and turned to Mi-Lin. His eyes snapped evil lightning, though he kept his voice low and steady. At first, he spoke with the lilting, clicking tones I had come to know as Cantonese. But Mi-Lin replied in Chiu Chow, and he quickly fell into that dialect.

I had been abandoned, though I sat beside them. They spoke sharp words to one another, as if blaming each other for something. Then they fell quiet, shooting each other murderous looks as tea was served. I took the opportunity to excuse myself and go the bathroom.

I dug my CIA pen from the depths of my handbag, then I opened the hidden compartment and turned my built-in tape recorder back on. I'd had it running all the time Mi-Lin talked to me in the limo. On the way back to the table, I picked up several postcards from the stack beside the concierge's desk. When I returned, Mi-Lin and her uncle were still arguing, snakes spitting at each other, both furious. I still got the sense they were each blaming the other for something.

I took out my CIA pen, made sure the pinpoint lens was aimed correctly, poised it over the first postcard, then touched the tip to extend the ballpoint. In my mind, I could hear the click as the photo was snapped. I turned it to another angle and did the same again. Maybe I hadn't gotten the banker, but at least I was going to get something.

I'd put my handbag near me, the pinhole mike set to capture the entire conversation. They continued to hiss at each other in Chiu Chow until the entrees were served. Then the uncle got up, opened an expensive ostrich leather briefcase, rudely handed Mi-Lin a fat manila envelope, and strode out. I didn't miss the fact that four lean and hungry Chinese men who had been seated at two separate tables—angled to watch the door—also got up and left, two just ahead of him, the others just behind.

So—had I just seen the Dragonhead?

Maybe.

I was looking down at my salad, innocence pasted on my face. Mi-Lin interrupted my act.

"Alex."

I looked up.

She was looking at me, but her mind wasn't focused on me. She said, "I'm sorry. Business problems. He's a banker, you know, in Bangkok. I seldom have to see him. I'm sorry you were here to have to endure his evil temper."

I toyed with my London broil. It wasn't what I'd have ordered for myself.

Mi-Lin suddenly pushed her own plate away. "I'm not hungry either," she said. "Besides, we have problems in Honolulu. That's why he was so angry. I truly hope you don't mind if we fly back tonight." She picked up the manila envelope and put it in her large leather bag, then pulled the bag tightly under her arm. "I need to get these papers to Henry right away."

When we got back to the house on the Peak, the cobra had been found. It was being prepared for her brother's dinner, Mi-Lin said.

Our bags were already packed. Mi-Lin had made a quick call from the car phone, asking Mae Kuan to pack them. She'd also phoned the airline and easily got us on luxury class. Not many travelers could afford to fly that way. I prayed all the way to Kai Tak airport. *Please God, I know I blew it. Please keep my family safe, please just let me get home and forgive me for my stupidity.* When we finally climbed aboard the plane, I was vastly relieved.

Mi-Lin was quietly pensive during the trip. She didn't mention her offer of employment again, and I had the feeling she considered it accepted.

We were about three hours out from Honolulu when I suddenly awakened. My hand instantly went to my bag, to the pen with its microfilm and the hidden audio recorder. Both were still there. I sent up another silent prayer of thanks.

Mi-Lin was still sound asleep, her face turned away. She had the manila envelope tucked beside her, on the inside of the seat, so anyone who touched it would awaken her. I wanted to check out what was in it, but she had guarded it carefully ever since the uncle handed it to her. She shifted, and I decided to take a chance. Carefully, I lifted the envelope. She had already broken the seal to look inside. I turned my back to her and opened the clasp, holding the envelope so I could see down inside. I carefully lifted out a financial certificate, a bond of some kind, most of the lettering in Chinese. There was small print in English beneath the Chinese characters. It said, "Pay to the bearer of this bond the full sum of seven million dollars, Hong Kong, upon presentation of this document. Certified by the Shanghai Bank of Asia, Bangkok." The exchange rate was seven to one, which meant I was holding a cool million dollars, payable to whoever held the bond.

A cold stone settled near my heart. There were five of the bonds. Five million dollars. Mi-Lin shifted as I started to look at the next one, and she moaned softly. I quickly returned the bond to the envelope and put the manila envelope back in place. But she merely nestled down into another position, this one covering over the place where the envelope was stashed, and in that instant, looking at her closely, I saw the rest of the lie.

Her hair had come loose, and during her restless sleep she'd pulled it straight back and up from her ears. Suddenly I saw the scars. Thin white lines behind her ears. I gently touched her hairline. Small ridges. I took another serious look at her perfectly sculpted face. It had been sculpted, all right. No wonder it was so perfect. Her whole face—maybe even her body—had been created by a plastic surgeon. In that instant, I knew she was the same person whose photograph I'd seen in the cabinet in the house on the Peak, the homely little sister. What personal demons had caused her to so completely change herself?

自由

Mi-Lin's hard-faced chauffeur picked us up at Honolulu International. She was clutching the envelope; she had been from the time she awakened. He and Mi-Lin exchanged a few clipped words in Chiu Chow, then both fell ominously silent. He sped through Honolulu, then they dropped me off in front of my building, abruptly setting my bag on the sidewalk. Mi-Lin said she'd be in touch, and they sped away.

I dragged my suitcase up the elevator and into my condo. It seemed like I'd been gone for a year. The Christmas tree was still the focal point of my living room, though it was looking a little dried out. I put water in the holder then wondered why I didn't just throw the thing out, decorations and all. It made me feel guilty.

I checked my answering machine. There were many calls, but only two I wanted to return immediately: Johnny Tavares and Jess Seitaki.

Tavares hadn't left a number and I didn't know where to reach him. As for Jess, he'd be forced to share any information with the rest of his team. Tavares said he was working solo; I didn't want to jeopardize him.

I thought about phoning the local DEA office to try to find Tavares. But if I got the local office involved I'd be starting a territorial war that might well blow the whole case sky-high. Tavares had been out there on the razor's edge for a very long time. This was his information.

I knew now what he meant about tracking the network all the way from San Francisco to Thailand to Hong Kong and back. For Mi-Lin's people, Honolulu was just a very small part of a very big plan.

I watered my plants. Then, hungry, I checked the fridge. I'd cleaned it before leaving, but found a frozen pot pie in the freezer. I popped it into the microwave and went into the bedroom to unpack my suitcase.

An odd smell wafted up as I opened the clasps. I thought maybe something had been mildewed. But my clothing was neatly folded, professionally packed as if done by a valet. On the top was a black velvet box. Puzzled, I opened it, to see a glittering pink diamond pendant with matching earrings. Pink diamonds were the most expensive kind. About a hundred thousand a carat, retail. I stepped over to the mirror and held the pendant against my neck. I was wearing a beige, doe-skin sweater with chocolate-brown slacks. A perfect backdrop for the glittering pale-pink stone. The diamond was exquisite. I sighed. I wondered who it really belonged to. I couldn't have kept it even if it wasn't hot. It was payment for services I could never perform.

Placing the stone and earrings back in the velvet box, I then put it on the bed beside my suitcase. I started to lift out my clothing, the whole stack at once. As I ran my hand in under the pile, I touched something damp. I jerked out my hand and saw a brownish-red stain. Drying blood? I lifted the stack of clothing by the edges, carefully, everything at once. I shrank back and dropped everything on the floor. At the bottom of the suitcase was a cobra's head, severed maybe six inches deep into the body, the fangs sharp inside the drawn-back mouth, the hood flaccid, the eyes flat and empty and seemingly staring at me.

I went weak. I couldn't take my eyes off the hideous object. I sank back into a chair as my knees collapsed.

The symbols of my own stupidity lay there in front of me. The hideous, evil snakehead and the glittering, seductive gems. Lead and gold. I had sent out the signals that I was for sale. Now, it was going to be very hard to take those signals back.

Using an old pair of salad tongs, I picked up the cobra's head and dropped it in a large black trash bag. Unsure of what to do with it, I wrapped it carefully, over and over again, then took it out onto my balcony and stashed it behind my tangerine bougainvillea plant.

Snakes are illegal in Hawaii. Even the zoo is allowed to bring in only one sex of each variety because snakes aren't native to the environment; any species would wreak havoc on the birds and other native species. But this one had arrived dead. I had no obligation to turn it in. But I still wasn't sure what to do with it.

I was trembling, trying to figure out what to do to get free from the trap. Just then the phone rang, and I grabbed it like it was a lifeline. It was Jess.

He said, "I've been trying to phone you. We arrested the boys who killed Dru Chun Yuen."

I stopped short.

"You there?"

"Yes." I let him explain.

Kimo Chang was in a drug rehab hospital. He was coming off the worst of his heroin withdrawal, and he was talking. The truth was, he had indeed decided to outshine his crime-lord uncle by upstaging him at his own game. He'd been working the streets himself, selling pakalolo, pharmaceutical pills, and anything else he could get his hands on. He was going to make his money one way or another. Mr. Seven's Shadow Dragons had spotted him and took him to Zhing Qu, who offered to teach him the ropes about operating at the street level. They'd offered him a steady supply of heroin and legal protection. Zhing Qu had promised to make him a big man in the world of crime. Kimo had accepted, but immediately found himself in over his head.

Mr. Seven had set him up as the chief courier, the man to carry kilo-weight drug deliveries to the small army of boys who were spreading out to deal in the streets. Kimo in turn had used the two Chinese illegals as couriers, to actually carry the kilo-weight bags of drugs.

Dru Chun Yuen had wanted to be a doctor, not a drug dealer; he'd threatened Kimo that he was going to go to the authorities if Kimo didn't leave him alone. Kimo told Mr. Seven, who sent two enforcers, Red Poles, to deal with the two boys after Kimo lured them out of Auntie Elma Chang's house. Kimo left about the time the real violence started. He didn't know exactly how the boy had died or what had happened to Mock Sing, but he did know who had been working them over.

"Kimo identified the two Red Poles from surveillance photos we've been taking of the two dozen or so new faces in Chinatown. We have the Red Poles in custody, and we're looking for others involved in the incident. We've also got eyewitnesses who say that these two are the same ones who killed that other kid in front of the Shatin Lounge. He got it because he refused to work for them."

"And Lenni? Any word on who actually killed her?"

"Kimo doesn't seem to know anything about that end of it," Jess said. "But we'll get them. It's got to be part of the same crowd."

"Did he say what they did with the trunks that held the stuff they were dealing up at Benny Frietas's hukilau?"

"They borrowed a speedboat from a dock in Kaneohe Bay, emptied the trunks of anything that looked sellable, then took them out to sea and dropped them. Now, what's been happening with you? We missed you Christmas Day."

I considered telling him everything. But the more he knew, the more obligated he'd be to share that information with his colleagues.

It was a tough call, but I said, "I missed you too, Jess. And thanks for letting me know."

I was worried about Mi-Lin, about what she might be doing. I phoned her and sweetly thanked her for the diamond jewelry. I wanted her off guard, and she did sound puzzled by the cheery note in my voice. I got the feeling that she was under a tremendous amount of stress, that I'd become a side issue with her.

I phoned my mother to let her know I was back in Honolulu. I ached, I wanted so badly to tell her and the others to be careful, that there was evil in this world they couldn't begin to fathom, that I might have inadvertently delivered some of it to their very doorstep. But my mother would never understand. I felt confused, didn't know which direction to turn. I finally went for a quick swim in front of the Sheraton, hoping that somehow Tavares would be around and might see me.

Of course he wasn't there. In fact, I didn't hear from him till about three o'clock two days later, on the morning of the twenty-ninth. He phoned and awakened me out of yet another troubled sleep. He'd just returned from San Francisco.

We met up on Tantalus again, at 4 A.M. The area seemed even more sinister than before, with the silver hula moon fully hidden by dark clouds, the smell of dampness all around us from the night rains. When I'd joined Tavares in the lime-green drug dealer's car, I got right to the point.

"You told me they'd targeted me. You were right."

"I'm always right," he said dryly. "It helps, of course, to hear their conversations."

He looked at me and grinned, and suddenly I felt safer again.

He said, "They wanted someone who knew the DEA's operations, but they didn't want to approach an active agent or analyst. Besides, you had a reputation for being the best, and also for being disillusioned with the system. Who else would they target but you?"

"I've been pretty stupid," I said, feeling better for admitting it.

"Hey, it happens to us all. That's how the Snakeheads lure in the peasants in China, how the drug dealers get the kids to work for them in the streets, that's how the politicians and crooked cops and feds get sucked in. Everybody wants to believe the lie. It's all a big scam—they promise you a key to the big dream. Anyway, they studied you well before they came at you. I'm surprised they didn't wrap you up better than they did."

I wasn't pleased that he lumped me in with all the other suckers in the world, but I knew I had it coming. I opened my bag and handed him the pen. "Here's a little something to make up for it," I said. "Merry Christmas."

He took it eagerly, a kidlike grin on his face that edged out some of the hard worry lines. I hoped the film turned out.

"Now—where's mine?"

He was puzzled. "I'm sorry—"

"The information, Tavares. You said if I did you the favor, you'd tell me the rest of what's going on."

He was reluctant, but a deal is a deal and he finally told me part of it. During a routine electronic surveillance of an importer in San Francisco, he and fellow agents learned about a major heroin shipment. Tavares set up a cover. He disguised himself as a major buyer with East Coast connections. He followed the heroin trail to Bangkok, where he found three metric tons of China White stockpiled in a temperature-controlled, state-of-the-art warehouse outside the city, waiting to be transshipped to the U.S. via Hawaii. The shipment was supposed to come in on the *Dragon Venture*, along with the human cargo. But the seller—a bloodthirsty broker for one of the opium lords in the Golden Triangle—had refused to release the shipment because the money hadn't been deposited in his recently opened Honolulu bank account.

"A secret compartment in Henry Li's trunks held about five million dollars in bearer bonds, payable when the heroin was delivered," Tavares said. "When the trunks were stolen at the airport, the bonds disappeared along with them."

I was excited. "So *that's* what they were really after."

"Bingo. The jade and jewelry were only a cover. Mi-Lin and Henry Li are the money couriers for the big-time shipments. We've been watching electronic wire transfers pretty closely. We shut down one major operation in Bangkok not too long ago. They're doing business by hand again, until they get a new financial network set up."

"But how did Kimo Chang and his allies know about the trunks?"

"Paké was supposed to be in on the heroin deal. He flew to Hong Kong to help set it up, but when he found out that the Triad intended to take over his action and make him second-in-command, he balked. He phoned Kimo and told him to snatch the trunks, to screw the deal up and let them know he wasn't going to play. Kimo did."

I felt my eyes shooting fire, but it was for Paké, not Tavares. I said, "You had Paké's phone tapped?"

He laughed. "At the Lucky Lion and the Calabash, as well as his home in Kalihi. *They come across the sea,*" Tavares said in a raspy voice that mimicked Paké Chang's. "*They come without letting even the sky know. Watch out, they're invisible like ghosts.*"

I was embarrassed. I said, "What is that mumbo jumbo, anyway?"

His eyebrows arched. "You don't know?"

"No."

"It's part of the ancient Triad credo. One of their official thirty-six strategies to infiltrate and destroy the rest of the world, though that bit about the ghosts was Paké's own personal touch."

"What on earth—?"

"The first strategy is to cross the ocean without letting the sky know and to cheat all the people around. In other words, absolute secrecy and absolute treachery. Paké had obviously heard that bit. Second strategy is: if an ally is attacked by an enemy, they vow to attack the enemy's country to save the ally. In other words, they don't stop with an eye for an eye; they go for the whole body—the whole country, for that matter. Number three, they vow to kill a person with someone else's knife and to eliminate their victims without getting personally involved."

"Deception again," I said. "Deception is honorable, murder is honorable—"

"You got it."

"But Paké outsmarted them?"

"More or less. They thought they had Kimo slam-dunked; they'd already roped him in before Paké's little trip to Hong Kong. But Kimo's a punk; he has no loyalty to anyone. He was working both ends, thinking he'd end up some kind of boss."

"What about Paké? Why did he come to me?"

"That's the one redeeming thing he did. He knew they'd targeted you. He sincerely wanted to help you out. Of course, he couldn't resist trying to use you a little in the bargain. That's in his nature."

"So he knew when the Druen kid was killed, and moved the body to help drag me in?"

"That's what I figure, though he never said anything about it on the tapes."

"I can't believe how stupid I've been."

Tavares was shaking his head from side to side. "It wasn't just you. Man, these guys have deception down to a fine art. They've been doing it for centuries. I kept wanting to tell you, but I was afraid they'd compromise you after all."

"When the boys set Li up for the theft, were any of them pretending to be male prostitutes?"

"What are you talking about?"

"Mi-Lin told me—"

"Mi-Lin is the biggest liar of them all."

I thought for a second about everything she'd done, everything she'd said. I had to agree. But that was an especially evil lie to tell about Henry Li. How she must hate him.

I said, "Do you know what happened to the trunks and the bearer bonds?"

"I hear they're in the bottom of the ocean. Mr. Seven, Henry Li, and Mi-Lin have been doing one mad scramble to replace the money and get this shipment delivered."

"That's why Mi-Lin went to Hong Kong," I said, suddenly beginning to understand the whole big picture. "To get more money or bonds or whatever. I saw them. The banker in the photographs brought them to her. Seven million-dollar certificates, in Hong Kong dollars."

His eyes snapped with excitement. He was back in the middle of the hunt. He said, "That's what I was hoping for, praying for! Man oh man, don't tell me we've done it!" He held up the pen and looked at it lovingly. "If we have his photograph we can take him down from that end and bust up the entire network, from the small-fry in the streets to the Dragonhead himself."

I felt a zing of adrenaline. "Who's the Dragonhead? Not Mi-Lin's brother."

He gave me a superior smile. "You'll see when we make the arrests. Anyway, this thing is getting ready to blow sky-high. When it hits, they may come at you. You need to lay low, stay out of it, keep yourself safe."

"It's a little late for that advice. Anyway, I have a bonus gift for you." I reached back in my bag and brought out the tape I'd recorded, part of it Mi-Lin's offer to me during the limo ride, the rest her conversation in Chiu Chow with the uncle from Bangkok.

When I told Tavares what it was, a new look of respect came into his eyes. He took the tape and carefully placed it inside his jacket, in the same pocket that held the pen. Then he turned to me, reached out, put both hands on my shoulders, and leaned over to kiss me, tenderly, right square on the lips. I let him. I'd forgotten what it was like to feel that tenderness, the sweetness of something pure passing between two people, a communication far beyond words. There was passion in the kiss, but also respect and the promise that something more could grow from it, something decent and wonderful and clean.

Abruptly, he pulled away and said, "I'm sorry." He turned and stared out the window. "You'd better go now. I've got work to do."

I knew he was going to phone D.C. and play the tape into a scrambled phone, linking into the DEA language lab where they could instantly translate the obscure Chinese dialect and feed the words back to him. I knew this was no time to be fogging up his mind with a potential romance. Especially since I had no intention of getting involved. All the same, it was suddenly a starry night.

I told him good night. When I got home later, I thought about that kiss. It was a nice feeling. But as I drifted off to sleep, the memory faded into the immensity of the rest of what he'd told me. New arrangements had been made for payment of the three metric tons of heroin. Honolulu's streets would soon be buried in China White. The shipment was coming in with the next cargo of illegals—slaves—the ones Lenni had known about.

She may in fact have been killed because of that knowledge.

The Triads might still get a solid lock on Honolulu unless we all managed to nail the shipment of illegals and put this thing to rest.

By 10 A.M. the next day, the hot blue sky had been blanketed over by a solid pewter sheet of rain clouds. The growing humidity made people restless and irritable. It made me depressed. When the first gust of rain came at 4:05 P.M., it bled off just enough of the atmospheric pressure to take the edge off people's moods.

I knew it was vital that I act as if nothing at all had changed. I phoned Mi-Lin, just to keep up appearances, and suggested we have lunch. It was easy to pretend I had succumbed to greed, self-indulgence, and corruption. I'd come so close, I knew exactly what it felt like.

Mi-Lin snapped that she was busy. She sounded strange. I felt a pang of outrage at the way she had been manipulating me, but I was careful not to let her know. She said she would be busy for a few days, that she would phone when she needed me. She was cold, imperious. She no longer had to charm me; I was bought and paid for now. The next couple of days passed slowly.

Then suddenly, it was New Year's Eve. I went to our church's holiday vigil and saw Jess there, but his beeper went off and he left after a short time, before I got to talk to him. On the New Year's holiday, I rested, prayed, tried to understand just how I could have been so stupid. I didn't hear from Mi-Lin, and I didn't try to contact her, Tavares didn't call.

Two days after New Year's Eve, I stood by Lenni's grave at Manoa Cemetery, the fine rain falling, the same rain that had followed me back from Hong Kong and settled in over the Islands to stay. The autopsy had taken an inordinately long time. Some relatives had been unable to travel for a week or so, further delaying the funeral. I was sorry that her parents had waited so long to bury her cremated ashes. My grief for her was beginning to fade until I stood beside her grave. Then I wept again as if she'd just been killed. It was a sad way to begin a new year.

For the next few days, things in Chinatown were slow. It was always like that right after holidays. People were getting ready for Chinese New Year, but the activity was subdued. On January fourth, I drove through the area a few times. The Shatin Lounge and Paké's Lucky Lion were coexisting; they both seemed busy all the time. I saw a few drug deals in the daytime streets, but no Shadow Dragons. Jess had told me they were laying low after the arrests of the "big brothers" that Kimo had given up.

Chinese New Year came on January fifth. I drove through the area again that day, thinking about Lenni, about her mother and father, and all the Chinese people who had come and gone through this world within a world. Chinese characters were splashed in blood-red on banners throughout the area, welcoming the holiday. Food stalls were set up near the marketplace. A note of festivity was in the air, and throngs of people shopped and ate and chatted with one another. By night, when the true festivities began, the area would be a tangled mass of people, shoving and clogging the streets, filling the sidewalks and alleys to watch the many lion dances scattered every block or so throughout the area.

The popping of firecrackers met my ears as I drove past the Shatin Lounge, and I thought for an instant it was gunfire. I kept expecting something to happen, but nothing did. Only a few more isolated firecrackers, people jumping the gun against the evening's chaotic, deafening revelry.

I skipped the festivities. By midnight, I was once again sound asleep—until a familiar voice awakened me with a phone call.

"This Alex?"

"Paké? What on earth?"

"I wan' tell you one thing," he said. His voice was tight from stress. "That one wahine. The reporter, Lenni, the one they wen' whack out."

"Yes?" I sat up, wide awake.

"You been asking, you wan' know who was her snitch?"

I didn't say a word. In fact, I held my breath.

"I wan' let you know it was me. I was telling her what's what," he said. "You come to the Lucky Lion. I wen' shut down the bar, I'm upstairs, knock on the door, I wan' talk to you—" I heard something crash. Someone cursed, and it sounded like the phone had been dropped.

"Paké? What happened? Paké, are you there?"

I heard someone grunt, then the sound of firecrackers, distant— but suddenly I knew it wasn't firecrackers, the sound was too massive. I had heard four quick gunshots.

Dear Father, I prayed. *Don't let this be what I think it is.* But as I shouted Paké's name into the phone, someone hung it up.

I dialed 911, trying to stay calm. They promised to get someone to the Lucky Lion right away. I phoned Information and asked for the number to the Lucky Lion Lounge. The operator gave it to me. I punched in the number, twice, messing it up the first time, too anxious to slow down and get it right. I let it ring and ring, praying that Paké would answer. He didn't.

I threw on my clothes and raced out the door. Five minutes later I was on the freeway, speeding down the Vineyard off-ramp. Five minutes beyond that I was pulling into the periphery of Chinatown, where the clogged-up traffic stopped me short.

All available space was filled with vehicles of every type, surrounding the roped-off area of central Chinatown. The two parking garages were both filled, cars were double-parked in places, and the alley was filled bumper-to-bumper with vehicles. Even from this distance, the din of firecrackers and cymbals was deafening. I hadn't even seen the frenzied throngs of people and the lion dancers yet. I backed up, turned around again—and got lucky—a car was just peeling away from the curb. I swung in, put on my Club, and took off at a dead run.

I arrived breathless. The street in front was brimming with people. The firecracker smoke was so thick I choked on it, the noise was deafening; the accompanying cymbals and drums and gongs and shouting made my head reel. I stopped short when I turned the corner and saw the blinking neon sign of a stylized Chinese lion. Paké's bar. The front part of the building was already roped off, but several police cruisers had somehow managed to drive up onto the sidewalk. My heart sank and my knees went weak. An ambulance was parked in front of the cruisers. It had gotten here fast, no doubt from nearby Queen's Hospital.

I felt weak. I was whispering Paké Chang's name over and over again, still praying that he'd be okay.

I pressed through in time to see them bring him out on a stretcher. His head was bloody, his eyes were open. I felt a sob well up in my throat. In the background, the din of the cymbals and the barrage of the firecrackers continued, the noise growing louder and louder, the chaos swallowing and drowning me. The people celebrated their history and their future—but not their present, not if they had realized the truth. In this dark moment, a very old evil was invading Chinatown.

I moved into the crowd, along a curb already brimming with red paper firecracker skins. I watched as they put the sheet-clad body into the back of the ambulance. Then, almost blindly, I rounded a corner and stopped at the edge of a multiethnic crowd of people, all of them watching a lion dance, most with their hands over their ears against the immediate thunder of the firecrackers that were being lit in long red strands in a circle around the prancing lion. The smoke was choking me, the huge papier-mâché lion was coiling toward me, the body red and white and green, the golden fringed mane tangled and old and wispy in places, the eyes glowing yellow from a light within. The nine-foot-long beast danced toward me, writhing and twisting to the rhythm beneath the red-lettered banners flying from second-story windows. The crowd swarmed around it, the drummers and cymbalists marched right behind it. Just outside the ring of firecrackers, a small throng of young men lit first one long red strand then another, the thunder endless, while black-clad boys made a circle a few feet out from the lion so the inhabitants of the costume could move and make the lion coil and dart, feinting toward the nearest people as if to attack them. The people roared with glee; some were drunk, some were merely enjoying their heritage as the lion bore down toward me.

My heart ached for Paké. I was dazed, but I turned back to move out of the way. That's when I saw them. Four boys, clad in black slacks, black T-shirts, and black cloth fighting shoes with rubber soles were coming at me. I recognized two of them as the same boys who had been with Kimo Chang when he'd attacked me. The evil, gigantic monster that lived within the earth was loose; demons really could take on human form. The evil was ready to rampage through these people's homes and lives. The noise and light and the color red were not going to drive it away.

An immense pressure seemed to crush me from all directions. I felt like I was about to fly apart. The lion bore down from one side. People were shouting for me to get out of the way, but as I turned around I saw the four Shadow Dragons moving in, from the four corners of the earth now, their eyes vacant. They might as well have been four well-oiled machines moving toward me, for all the human compassion I would find there. The people were shouting louder now. I felt someone shove me out of the lion's way and I stumbled up against the curb, then I turned, trying to make a break for it, but the throng of people was too thick. There was nowhere to go.

Too late, I leaped to one side. Two of them came at me like striking cobras, punching and kicking at me. I reeled away, frantically trying to find help. I was shouting, screaming, but nobody could hear me over the clang of the cymbals and the fury of the firecrackers. I hit the alley at a dead run, two of them right behind me, two others closing in. I found a back door and tried the knob. It was locked. They were gaining on me. I managed to dodge the first blow, and then they were on me, tackling me, dragging me to my knees, the pavement tearing at my forearms. One of them pinned me down, and I could see metal flashing—*a knife?* I screamed again and rolled, feeling a knee land in my back, a kick in my side, and then the metal flashed again and I realized it was the metal band on the nun-chuks, a weapon used in ancient Asian warfare, a death as swift and sure as a bullet would bring. The wood flew at me with the speed of light, I dodged, then I felt a sudden crushing weight. I couldn't breathe, and the world turned black as the cymbals and drums and firecrackers in the diminishing distance ushered me into silent oblivion.

自由

I awakened in the pitch dark, my cheek against something dank and cold. My legs were cramped from staying in one position too long. I tried to move, but my hands and feet had been bound and my mouth was covered with something sticky that pulled hard, hurting, when I tried to open my mouth. Duct tape. Thank God it covered only my mouth. At least I could breath. I thrashed around, feeling what I could. I was chained to the wall, like a wild animal.

I was in a small enclosure, maybe four feet by four feet. Every part of my body ached. The smell of stale sweat and a hint of urine, decayed food, and other odors indicated that someone else had been here, someone who had stayed a long time, maybe even died here. I shuddered and forced that thought out of my mind. I prayed again. *Please God, don't let them win. If it's Your time to take me home, at least do it in a way so the evil can't win. Make my death count for something. Please, God . . .*

I heard voices, somewhere far away. A cry of pain. A door slammed somewhere. Another door opened. Lights came on in the next room and light leaked through a crack at the side of the door.

I realized I was in a small closet. I waited. Time passed slowly, and then I heard movement again. Someone spoke. I recognized the dialect as Chiu Chow Chinese. With a sudden deep-seated irony, I remembered my earlier arrogance. I'd thought it could never happen to me, that only a certain type of person fell into the vortex of enslavement.

Now, nobody even knew where I was. Even I didn't know. I wondered if I would die here, alone, and then I thought about Lenni. The tears that filled my eyes were not for me.

They kept me there for two days, with no food and only a dirty bowl of water. Someone reached in and threw a blanket over my head before they shoved in the bowl, so I wouldn't see their faces.

From time to time, I heard a strange mixture of screams and laughter. I wondered if someone was being tortured nearby. During the silent times, I tried to figure out where I was, and I envisioned Tavares, Jess, someone coming to my rescue, the cavalry arriving just in the nick of time. Another myth, another fantasy.

I cried, until I realized that crying would dehydrate me. Then I felt my tears dry up. Soon, I was dead inside. I slept. I awakened to the sound of more voices, all of them talking in Chinese. When I slept, I had nightmares. Masses of people huddled in darkness and filth, people being whipped into a frenzy for failing to work hard enough, young Chinese girls being herded onto ships and locked in a hold. I dreamed about my Christmas tree and awakened in a cold sweat, and instantly worried about dehydration again. I prayed and prayed.

That night, they dragged me out, into pitch blackness again. I started screaming as they bound my eyes. Someone struck me on the face and I shut up. I was too weak to fight back. I felt someone circling, padding around me like a jungle cat. I had the sense that the lights had come on. Someone else came into the room.

I heard other voices now, people talking softly to one another in Chinese. Someone grabbed me by the legs and started dragging me. I felt my head bump against something, the pain was intense. I started to black out but forced myself to stay conscious. I felt myself dumped, expected to hit the ground as dead weight, hands and feet still chained and bound, but instead I fell into something scooped out and metal. A wheelbarrow. I whimpered, someone punched me in the stomach, and I fell silent again.

I was dumped once again, into some sort of vehicle. I didn't realize what it was until we started moving.

It had been raining. I heard the sounds of traffic and a clap of thunder. After a while we stopped, and I could hear the roar of the sea. Still bound, my eyes blindfolded, I felt hands grasp me and haul me out. Someone pulled the binding from my eyes and looked at me, but I couldn't see. Slowly, I regained some vision. We were beside the ocean, at a pier. I recognized the old boat harbor. I heard a trunk lid slam, and after a moment my eyes adjusted for the new and lesser darkness. I recognized a form leaning over a boat tied up to a dock. It was Zhing Qu, Mr. Seven's henchman. He must have sensed me watching him, for he looked up sharply, his eyes ablaze with hatred.

He spoke and I felt two people move in behind me and lift me up, made a running start, and then I was heaved off the pier, expecting to hit water, but instead I felt the painful jar of wood. I had been unceremoniously dumped in the bottom of the boat, fishing gaffs and an anchor slamming into me and shooting anguish through a body that I thought was beyond feeling any more pain.

CHAPTER

29

We were in a powerboat. I heard the outboards rev up, felt the pelt of rain on my face. When the engines were running and we pulled away from the pier, I managed to lift myself onto my elbows and see above the transom. Zhing Qu was standing on the bridge, and someone else was steering. He and a short man clad in a pea jacket and watch cap turned and strode back to us. They were speaking English. I lay still and listened.

"I want them all," Zhung Qu said. His accent was scarcely discernible.

"We couldn't find the others," the other man said. I didn't recognize the voice, but the man was certainly American. "There's too much heat on the streets," the man said. "Besides, who's going to believe those little runts? You think they're going to talk about any of this? Every one of them is wanted for something by the SFPD, and if the INS nails them, they're going to get shipped back to China. They ain't going to rat you out."

"I want them on the freighter. The Shadow Dragons who

wouldn't fly back to San Francisco, the new shipment of illegals, all of them are going down. Immigration knows about the shipment—they're looking for the trawler right now. It's good joss that we hadn't yet unloaded the illegals. But I want the others, too, loaded onto the trawler before you set the charges."

I felt my heart stop in my chest. They were going to put us on a ship, and then blast and sink it. I struggled silently, trying to get free from my bonds. They were tight, professionally tied. I didn't have a prayer of a chance.

The man was saying, "You said you needed a couple of old tubs sunk for the insurance money. That's what you said. Now all of a sudden I'm a blasted slaver, helping you kill thirty or more of those skinny little grunts."

"If you want any money, you'll find those other boys and bring them out to the ship. I don't leave problems running around."

"Look, Zhing, I've done everything you said. I herded the little creeps over here, I made sure they had false IDs and everything else to take over this territory and run your dope. You've paid me well, but I can't spend the money doing life in prison. I'm going to finish out this end of the job, then count me out, forget about me, you never even knew me. I'm going back to San Francisco."

I was listening to yet another person who had been hired to do a job and got in over his head.

He said, "I have the nitro compounds all ready to go. All I have to do is set the charges. I'll put them outside the hull, so the blasts will be swallowed by the water. Anyway, if someone hears something, they'll just think it's more thunder."

I had indeed been hearing the thunder in the distance, moving closer. In the brief instant before being dumped, I'd seen a flash of sheet lightning illuminate the horizon to the shade of a black light.

There were several others with me on the boat. Steady rain pelted the heavy tarp that had been thrown over us. Water dripped around the edges, cold and wet. Panic overwhelmed me as I tried to get free from the ropes.

One person shifted as sheet lightning illuminated the sky. In that instant I saw two young Chinese boys, teenagers, illegals by the look of them, both slight and sallow and thin, under the tarp with me. One looked so much like the photos the INS had provided Jess of the living Dru Chun Yuen that I instantly knew it was his cousin, Mock Sing. I had finally found him.

The men's voices receded into the distance. As soon as they were far enough away, I whispered, "Mock Sing?"

He sat straight up, his face frozen in fear. There were bruises on his jaw and his thin shirt was ripped in a dozen places. I managed to roll around so I could see him better.

I whispered it again, "Mock Sing?"

His head shot around and he looked at me in horror. He whispered something in Chinese to his companion, who motioned for me to be quiet.

I tried to shift into a more comfortable position. The cold and dampness were causing my arms and legs to cramp painfully. The sea roared around us, and the driven rain fell harder. I managed to edge up and hang my chin on the side of the low boat. We were racing through black waves, foam flying off the icy sea. The smell of diesel fuel was strong. We were in endless, mysterious blackness. The storm was growing stronger. And then I saw the freighter, a huge black hulk on the horizon. We were coming up on it fast.

"Bring her around," a voice called. "We're cutting too near the stern."

I ducked back under the tarp and worked furiously, still trying to get free. I had a claustrophobic sensation that almost drove me mad. I had never even imagined how it might feel to be bound like this.

Someone threw down a rotting seine net and heaved us up in a ship's winch, then dangled us across the freighter's deck and dropped us into the hold. The net was broken free when we were still about six feet above the black hole. We fell the last distance, all of us crying out as we hit the bottom. We were in a black, slimy hole, and I could tell from the ancient slime, the smell of blood, and the stench of long-dead fish that we were in the hold of an old fishing trawler.

I heard something scraping the wood beside me and thought it might be rats. But in that instant a wide-beamed flashlight played over the interior, and the scene will stay with me all my life. There were maybe thirty Chinese in the hold, all of them bound hand and foot, huddled, seated, or lying on their sides. Some were emaciated, some I suspected were already dead. I wondered if the people were drugged, or just so sick and starved that they couldn't move. I glanced around. The young boys who had been transported with me were behind me. The one I thought was Mock Sing was almost touching my back.

In that instant, they shut the hatch. The blackness was complete. I wondered how long it would take them to set the charges that would blast through the hull and sink the ship. How many more moments would I have on this earth? Again, I prayed. *Please, Father, forgive me for my stupidity. Forgive me for not believing what You said about the evil in this world. Please help me get out of this. Let me be free again, let me know the safety of freedom, let me never again be so stupid as to even dabble in evil, let me never forget to thank You for the gift of being free. Lord, please help us all . . .*

Freedom. I needed to get my hands free. If I could only do that, I might still have a chance. But they were bound tightly behind me, there was no hope—

I felt something touch me from behind, something damp. I recoiled, lifted my arms, felt a face bent down to nearly touch my hands. What on earth?

I stayed motionless. Then I felt the gnawing. I said, "Mock Sing? Is that you?"

The boy said something in rapid Chinese, then set to chewing again. He was trying to gnaw through my ropes. The thought was a nice one, but unlikely. I pulled away, contorting myself into a new position. My body ached and weakness swept over me.

I wondered if there was anything sharp in the hold. Suddenly I remembered a glint I'd seen beneath a work table when the flashlight played across the room. I contorted myself around and inched in that direction. I rolled onto my stomach, in and under the table, and felt around, using my face as the touchpoint. I heard something ringing, like a hammer pounding against metal. What were they doing up there?

I touched something metallic. I moved my cheek around over it. It felt like a fishing gaff, probably something old and rusted-out. I managed to contort myself so it was pinned beneath my arm, then I inched back to my original position. I turned and dropped it behind me, near a body I hoped was Mock Sing. It was. He talked again, in rapid-fire Chinese, then I felt something tearing at the rope, and I knew he was using the sharp tip of the gaff to try to cut through it. His hands were also tied behind him. It wasn't going to be easy for him to get me free. It probably wasn't even possible. Then I felt something else touch me. Another body, this one cold, clammy, someone obviously sick. I moved to get the weight off me. The person said something, in Cantonese, that sounded insulting. While Mock Sing continued to saw at the rope, I stayed completely still. The only thing I could do was pray.

Suddenly, the rope gave way and my hands were free. I almost cried out, but realized that the sound might carry. I massaged them furiously, making the blood flow again, then turned and hugged Mock Sing. It was work to untie my legs, but I managed. Then with some effort, I used the fishing gaff to hack through Mock Sing's ropes and those of his friend. There were three of us now. We couldn't even communicate, but at least we had help. I stretched my muscles and tried to think. We had been working furiously for at least half an hour. That would give them plenty of time to set the charges. Any minute now, the entire ship could go up in a blaze of nitroglycerine.

I could hear something through the hold. An engine. The powerboat had started up—the villains were leaving. They would surely have allowed themselves time to get away from the ship before it blew, but that wouldn't mean much. We had only minutes to get free.

Suddenly the ship rolled. It started to go logy. I knew now what the ringing sound had been. They'd chopped through the wood, through the metallic inner wall. They were going to start sinking the ship even before the charges went off, making sure we went down.

In a sudden frenzy, I scrambled over and tried to reach the hatch. It was probably four feet above my head. I felt around in the darkness and actually found a ladder. I lifted it, muscles aching, and leaned it up against the wall near the hatch, feeling my way in the darkness. I prayed that they hadn't nailed the hatch shut or put something over it.

They hadn't. The wood was light, rotted and old. I pushed through and onto the deck, into a deluge of rain. The waves were black and monstrous, almost swamping the ship. There was a faint glaze of light on the horizon, the rain-misted glitter of Honolulu. We were well out at sea, in deep water. Once this ship went down, chances were it would never be found again.

I heard water rushing into the hold beneath me. Propping the hatch open, I gestured for Mock Sing and his friend to start helping the others up and out. There were thirty people, but I wasn't going to leave anyone to die in that stinking, slimy grave. I ran frantically around the deck till I'd found a long coil of rope. The boys used it to tie around the waists of some of the weakest ones, or the ones whose ropes were too hard to unbind. We worked feverishly until we had them all on deck. I kept expecting the first blast to explode the world around me.

With a final effort, we had the last one free, on deck, the sheet lightning helping us by illuminating the sky from time to time. The thunder was closer, crashing in the sky, and each time it sounded I nearly leaped out of my skin, thinking it was the first charge going off.

I still don't know if the old rubber inflatable lifeboat was on the ship when we got there, or if an angel set it down. Whichever way, I was grateful. We shoved it over the side and helped the people into it. I was the last one on the ship. I started over the side—and had almost made it when the world ignited around me. A gust of hot wind, a deafening thunder, a geyser of seawater rushed up around my face. I was flying, sailing in the air, then another charge went off, then another, and the ship was blowing up around me. The boards beneath me had blown free and now I was diving into the water, descending through the currents set up by the blast, debris crashing down around me, timbers and metal and other dangerous wreckage, and I dived, deeper and deeper, trying to get away from the objects that seemed to be hurled at me by some giant, invisible hand.

I was lost in black liquid, being lulled to sleep. The enormity of the evil had finally conquered me and I was ready to fold up, to let the water take me, just take me—

I felt hands gripping me. A sudden strength, a rush of motion, someone beneath me kicking out in strong strokes, and suddenly my face broke the surface and I was gasping at the air, but I could kick for myself now. I was swimming again, and I turned and saw the small, almost childlike head of the boy who had dived in to save me. *Mock Sing.*

We were both lost in the water now. I didn't know if the lifeboat had been blown free from the ship or had blown up with it, but the ship was sinking, a huge, tilted mass in front of us, great eddies swirling out around it, the debris still churning dangerously in the whirlpools, a plank or shard of metal occasionally going down. We bobbed in the black water, trying to stay free of the danger zone. I couldn't see any sign of the inflatable.

Then I saw boat lights coming toward us. I grasped at a plank that had drifted close to me and managed to catch hold. Mock Sing grabbed onto the other end.

The boat came closer, got caught in the eddies from the ship for a moment, then revved its engines and backed free. I prayed they wouldn't see us. I prayed the currents wouldn't suck us down. The waves still crashed around us, almost drowning us when they hit. My body ached even more. I was trembling so hard I could barely hang onto the plank. I was swallowing seawater, almost completely spent. Only a few more minutes and my hands would let go of the plank and dump me back into the hungry, crashing sea.

The boat moved in closer. I suddenly realized it was larger than Mr. Seven's powerboat. I peered through the drenching rain, and in that instant another flash of sheet lightning illuminated a Coast Guard cutter. There were men at the rail, and in that blessed instant, someone shined a light out over the dark water, and I heard a voice over a bullhorn. "Is anybody there?"

The wind took my shouts and hurled them back at me, but the cutter kept moving closer, playing the light across the water, and just as I was about to completely collapse, I heard a familiar voice saying, "Alex! Alex! We see you. Hang on just a minute longer, I'm on the way."

I felt strong hands lift me. I looked up and saw Tavares, sopping wet, pulling me into a dinghy. I managed to mumble, "Mock Sing? Did you get Mock Sing?"

"The Chinese boy who was with you? We have him. We spotted an inflatable too, full of people, just outside the periphery of the ship. Hush. Save your strength. You're going to be okay."

He carried me to a sheltered, lighted area of the deck. My wet clothes seemed to weigh a ton. I was shivering, icy cold. I chattered, "It was Zhing Qu, he tried to kill them all—"

"Shhh. Stop, Alex, we know. We busted them when they came back to shore—that little crook with him spilled everything. How on earth else would we have known where you were?"

I pointed a finger toward heaven and looked upward through the rain.

I have some semi-good news for you," Tavares said as he wrapped me in a blanket and settled me into the passenger seat of his Mercedes. "The doctors at Queen's Hospital found two gunshot wounds at the base of Paké's skull and two in the chest. But he's still alive. In fact, he stabilized enough to go into surgery yesterday and they got the bullets out, but frankly nobody is giving him very good odds."

"At least he's still alive," I said, shivering. Tavares put his arm around me and held me close for a moment. It was the sort of comforting gesture you'd give to a frightened child. I felt suddenly secure and warm, until he took his arm away. Then I began to shiver again.

He climbed in behind the wheel, switched on the heater, and turned to me. He said the police had received my 911 call regarding the attack on Paké, and some people had seen the Shadow Dragons kidnap me in Chinatown—though they hadn't realized what was happening till later, when they saw on the news that Paké had been shot and someone else had apparently been kidnapped from the vicinity of the bar. One man then came forward to say he'd seen the black-clad boys come out of the bar, hide, then later saw them throwing someone into a van. The police had found my car parked beside the bar and they'd figured it out.

They'd been trying to find me, but no luck. Tavares had of course picked up on the call and joined the search. He was actually apologetic for not riding to the rescue sooner, no hint of blaming me, nothing but genuine concern in his eyes. He wanted to take me to the hospital for a checkup. I said I'd be fine.

Tavares's handheld police scanner radio was tuned to the Coast Guard frequency. They were bringing all the Chinese into port. Two who had been in fairly good shape had verified that all were rescued. Some would go to the hospital, some to the INS shelter. Immigration agents had been aboard the cutter and they were taking charge of the illegals.

Tavares explained that he had linked up with INS and the Coast Guard to check out the tip that a shipload of illegals was due to arrive. When I'd vanished, Tavares had known the two events were linked. They'd started an all-out search for me. Thank God.

"We were watching Mr. Seven, watching Zhing Qu, watching the ports. We knew the ship was out there somewhere," Tavares said. "I didn't tell anyone about the heroin that was supposed to come along with the illegals. I still don't want to clutter up my own private terrain."

"What if it was on the ship?"

"No way they'd sink a ship with three tons of heroin aboard. They got it off two days ago, when the ship first came in. Too bad I didn't know it then. The pipeline is getting hot. They decided the money to be made from this boatload of illegals wasn't worth the risk; they already had the heroin."

"So they were dumping the evidence," I said.

"Exactly. And you. But not the heroin." He suddenly shot me a warning look.

"I understand. I won't say a word."

"Okay. Back to how we found you. The problem was, we lost

track of Zhing Qu for a while. Then I spotted his car parked in the Aloha Tower lot. A security guard had seen him take off with some people in a gray Chevy van. We spotted the van beside the docks, parked behind some Dumpsters. Mr. Seven's powerboat was gone. We wanted to send choppers to search first thing in the morning, if the weather cleared enough for them to see. I finally convinced them to send a Coast Guard cutter out tonight for a general search, even though it was a very long shot. But just then we saw their lights—they had returned to port and we nailed them."

The hired gun spilled his guts immediately. He wasn't about to take the fall for Zhing Qu.

He'd told Tavares and the Coast Guard about our sinking ship, and fingered Zhing Qu as the man who set it all up. Other DEA agents had taken the bar manager into custody. There was mounting evidence that he was the man who had ordered the murder of Dru Chun Yuen and the young Chinese boy killed in front of his bar, and had of course ordered the sinking of the shipload of illegals and me. Zhing Qu wouldn't be given bail.

"We could put him away for life just for this," Tavares said, "but he's still only a small-fry. I want the rest of them. And I want to make an airtight case."

Tavares said that my tape recordings and photos had turned out fine. "We have the last piece of evidence we need to start making arrests at the high end of the operation," he said proudly. "Agents are assembling in Bangkok, Hong Kong, and San Francisco. They're going to take down the entire cartel."

Tavares was worried that the press would pick up on the incident and spread the word before he could wind up the larger operation. "Got to kick you out, Albright, as soon as I get you to your car," he said. He still had a lot of fast work to do.

I tried to talk my way into the middle of things, but finally had to admit that I was in no condition to try to help. He dropped me at the HPD impound lot, where my car had ended up. I paid an eighty-dollar tow fee—borrowed from Tavares—and got it out. I had an extra set of keys in a magnetic box under the fender. I told Tavares good-bye and drove home.

I took a hot shower, made some steaming carob tea, and took it onto my corner balcony. I wrapped myself in a sea-green blanket, relishing the warmth, and turned toward the Koolaus, to watch the golden sun come up. My grief dissolved into a sense of majesty at the beauty of the approaching day. Suddenly I felt the scope of my personal freedom, the wonders around me, the bounty God had given to me, which I had simply stopped appreciating. I wept.

After a while, the tears dried up and a resolve began to fill me. This wasn't over yet. Not by a long shot. Lenni's murderer and Paké's assailant were still out there. It didn't matter that the boys who had actually committed the evil were behind bars. There were others back in the shadows, those who had created the evil. We still hadn't taken down the Dragonhead.

I didn't want to interfere with Tavares's work. Nothing can ruin an investigation quicker than information too soon revealed.

At the same time, I felt driven to action. I forced myself to settle back and think about what I wanted to do.

Like most criminal organizations, the Triads were compartmentalized. Apparently, the Shadow Dragons had been getting their drugs and working orders through Kimo Chang, who had been the sole conduit for Zhing Qu. Zhing Qu would in turn be the solitary link to the criminal side of Mr. Seven, and Mr. Seven was apparently linked directly to Henry Li, who was either the Dragonhead or the Dragonhead's second in command. At each level of the cellular structure, there was absolute secrecy, which meant that Mr. Seven might have given the orders to kill Paké, to abduct me, to sink the illegal's ship and destroy the evidence of a shipment of illegal aliens. Or Zing Qu might have taken it upon himself. It was even possible that the whole thing had happened without the approval of the Dragonhead or any others at the very top of the violent pinnacle. A slim possibility.

There were a dozen or more messages on my answering machine, and I finally listened to them. They were from Jess, Tavares, the police department, my mother—who had apparently not been notified, thank God again. No word from Mi-Lin. Maybe she'd known I wasn't home.

At nine, I finally decided to phone her. I wondered how much she knew of what had happened to me. But most of all I wondered if she knew what had happened to the heroin.

Had Mr. Seven, Zhing Qu, and their thugs gotten her approval to kill me? Or had they taken it upon themselves to do whatever was necessary to cover their tracks?

She answered the phone. "Alex, darling! I've been trying to reach you. Where on earth have you been?"

"Tied up," I said.

"Well, come and see me. We're having some problems right now, but maybe you could drop by a little after two?" Her voice sounded strange.

"I'd be delighted," I said.

At two-thirty that afternoon, I wheeled my car into the opulently landscaped driveway of Henry Li's estate. Within seconds, the trees had hidden the driveway from the street. I drove through the dark filigreed thickets, turned the corner, and at last came to the house. I parked beside Mi-Lin's Jag, at the curb by the front walkway. Henry Li's black Mercedes sedan sat in the opened garage. There were no other cars in sight.

Crimson-flowered trees flanked the entryway.

I checked once again to make sure I had my holster unsnapped, my gun ready if I needed it. Then I rang the bell.

I heard footsteps inside, but they were immediately drowned by the lapping of waves into the seawall at the right side of the house.

I hit the doorbell again, waited for a few moments, then went around to the side of the house where the doorway entered into the staff's quarters. I rapped at that door. No answer.

I walked across well-tended grass, past profuse flower beds flaming orange, golden, and red. A tall hedge separated the front lawn from a thin path of sand and the sea. I pulled it apart, making a space barely wide enough to squeeze through, so I could climb past the seawall and onto the balcony where we'd had lobster the other day. The hedge sprang back in place behind me.

The water had eroded the land away so there was perhaps a four foot drop to the sea. To my left, the seawall began, a cobblestone hodgepodge in black and gray rock that widened to perform its double duty of holding up the house with its extended patio jutting out above the water, and holding back the sea.

It was low tide. I could see straight down into the water. This was all coral reef, with great, skeletal knobs of fauna-coated coral alternating with shadowy depths. Flickers of movement caught my eye: small schools of fish were flitting away from my shadow where it fell, dark blue, into the translucent turquoise water. To my left, the whitecaps rolled in across the water, dissolving into one to two foot rushes of froth where they hit the seawall. The setting was serene, but there was an eeriness in the silence, a feeling of doom in the air.

I thought about wading to the dozen or so carved stone steps that led from the water up to the lanai. From here, I could see the tops of the tallest plants. Another look at the sharp, chunky coral I'd have to wade across made me change my mind.

Turning carefully, I worked my way back through the hedge and walked back to the front door. I rang again. No answer.

The house was strangely empty. The cars were still in the driveway.

I had just started to walk back past the flower garden and through the redwood fence that separated the grounds from the patio and the pool, when I heard the door open behind me.

"Hello?"

It was Mi-Lin's tinkling voice.

I turned. "Hello! I had just about decided that no one was home. I was getting worried about you."

Mi-Lin stood inside the doorway. I could see only her outline.

"Oh," she said, "Alex. Hello, come in." She sounded strange.

"Where is everybody? Are you okay?"

"I've dismissed the staff. I'll be leaving for Hong Kong this evening. I was just doing some packing."

I frowned, surprised.

"Come in, Alex. This has all been rather hard on you, hasn't it?"

I had an uncanny sense that I'd stepped into another dimension where I didn't understand anything that was going on.

I watched her closely. She had a somewhat vacant look on her face that further bewildered me.

When most criminals are caught in the act, there is usually a trapped and furtive quality about them. But Mi-Lin seemed preoccupied rather than furtive, disinterested rather than evasive. There was no sign of flight or fight in the way she stood, shadowed in the doorway—not even so much as a nervous tremor in her voice. She casually lifted one sleek hand and used it to wipe back a wisp of hair that was coming loose from her ivory combs. A smear appeared across her temple and across her forehead, a smear of bright red where her hand had grazed her face.

I swallowed hard but kept my face unreadable.

She was oblivious to the blood. Yet it had to be damp. Surely she could feel it. Was she bleeding? No, she didn't seem to be.

"Alex, what's wrong? You look so worried." She smiled at me reassuringly.

I looked at the blood on her hand. There was a lot of it, on the palm. She followed my gaze and looked too, then let it fall back to her side as if it was something alien that had somehow become attached to her wrist.

This was one of the few times in my life that I had absolutely no idea of what to do.

Mi-Lin solved my problem for me. "Come in," she said. "I need to get back to my work."

I hesitated, then followed her inside.

She beckoned me into a room at the far side of the house, closest to the seawall. As she turned to enter, I saw a large smear of blood on her gray silk slacks. And yet she moved regally, holding herself erect, completely composed, unaware of the carnage.

A sense of unreality settled over me.

She led me through the house and to a rec room, where a door opened onto a white-tiled patio beside a large swimming pool. I could see only a corner of the water.

But I could smell it now. Drying blood.

I wanted to flee, and then I wanted to lunge past her and see what ghastly, grave-bound thing lay beyond that newly opened doorway. But something kept my feet fixed to the floor.

Mi-Lin turned and gave me a fleeting smile. I tensed up as she stepped toward me, but all she did was put her hands on my shoulders and blink two tears from the corners of her haunted, vacant eyes. They ran down her cheeks and she made no attempt to stop them. "You must help me, Alex. I have no other friend in the world."

My sense of unreality grew stronger. I hadn't begun to fathom what was happening here, but a sense of something primeval and raw and deadly filled the room. I sensed the evil, but my conscious mind didn't process it as something that emanated from Mi-Lin, in spite of her bloodstained pants and her blood-soaked hand.

"They tried to hurt me," she said, and her voice had turned into a pitiful child's whimper.

I stepped back from her. She was too close, oppressive.

Her face crumpled as if I'd hurt her feelings and her shoulders sagged. Again, she gazed innocently into my eyes.

I shook my head, as if recovering from a blow. I said, "Who tried to hurt you, Mi-Lin?"

"My brother. All those terrible people he hired. You have to help me. I can't lift them."

Mi-Lin's forward motion had moved me a few feet backward. Suddenly I looked up, following her gaze. I stared in horror at the turquoise blue of the water in the swimming pool. It was slowly turning wine red.

I tried to move past her.

She stepped in front of me. "They made me. I had to stop them, they wanted to kill me."

I tried to move past her, but she grabbed onto my arm, dragging me backward. "Please, Alex, I'm all alone, everyone has left me. You must help me. I have to hide them. I can't move them. Please."

An aura of icy evil had filled the room. The contradiction of the blood and her gaunt, ancient-seeming face and the childish voice and the childlike posture was eerie, uncanny.

I said, "Did someone attack you?"

"Yes."

"When?"

"Last night. I was asleep and they came."

"Who?"

"All of them. It's because of my brother. When he got sick, it was different, then I could run things, people had to listen to what I told them to do. But I didn't know yet—"

"Know what?"

"That—that they would all want to kill me."

"What happened?"

"Last night. They were going to shoot me and I fought back. I got the gun. I didn't know what to do," she said helplessly. "They came here to hurt me."

I saw him then. Mr. Seven.

He lay part in, part out of the pool. A stain of red flowing from him to stain the water. He had fallen at the shallow edge of the pool, on the steps, his head and one shoulder beneath the water.

I stepped forward and touched his temple. The body was still warm, he had died much more recently than last night.

"Mi-Lin, this man hasn't been dead an hour. Where's Henry?"

"Gone, darling. He always leaves when there's trouble. I have to take care of everything." She looked at me with wide, wide eyes, then suddenly she laughed, that tinkling, merry laugh that had enchanted me, but there was a harshness in it now and it quickly moved into the range of hysteria.

It was then that I finally realized that this woman had been turned into a plastic shell encasing a century of cumulative evil; she had been driven totally, completely insane.

I could see it then. The enormity of the lie. The dragon had tried to lure me in. Once the evil got into you and took hold, it sapped your soul, left you with nothing but a flat, black, painful void. This was the final and ultimate consequence of lust and greed and a life devoid of love. This was where the deception and self-gratification at any cost would lead you. This was what the battle was against, the dehumanization of humanity. Mi-Lin had been a part of a process that had destroyed so very many people.

But you can't destroy another human being without destroying some vital part of yourself. Now, inch by inch, grain by grain, the dehumanizing process had taken its awful, inevitable toll.

She looked at me in a new way now. There was something twisting and writhing in those eyes. Something serpentine and blacker than death and locked behind a wall of ice, a wall that was rapidly melting—

This battle wasn't being fought on the secular plane. It was a confrontation with the pure dehumanizing evil that wanted to enslave the entire human race. The evil was almost tangible; it chilled me through to the marrow of my bones and trivialized every attempt at comprehension.

"Mi-Lin." I spoke in a soft, steady voice, trying to jar her into some vestige of sanity. "Where is Henry?"

She laughed again, this time one small snort of mirth. "He actually thought I'd take him back to Hong Kong with me," she said. "The fool. The stupid little fool." She led me toward the seawall, then pointed.

Here, the wall rose only about a foot above the grass, just high enough to demarcate the sea. I looked down into the water. There lay the body of Henry Li. I turned away in revulsion.

"Mi-Lin," I said, "I'm going to have to use your phone."

"Why, darling?"

"You've killed people. I have to take you in."

"But, darling, they were going to kill me!"

"Perhaps. And perhaps you can't tell the truth anymore."

"It's true! They were afraid I'd tell the authorities what they've been doing. They came last night—"

I was tired now. I took my .38 out from the shoulder holster and held it on her.

She looked at me in disbelief.

As I picked up the phone and dialed HSP, she said, "You're a fool. My brother will have me out by morning. And he'll have your head on a platter by noon."

I didn't want to talk anymore. I knew now who the Dragonhead was. The brains belonged to her eldest brother, the golden claws to her uncle in Bangkok. But Mi-Lin Ming was the fangs, the lethal part. I held my gun steadily on her and waited for it all to end.

Thank God the police came quickly. I didn't take my eyes off her for a second, even as they led her away. I was afraid that somehow, some way, she'd still manage to lunge at me and strike.

CHAPTER

31

Mi-Lin was in maximum security, booked on two counts of first degree murder. They didn't need her testimony against the others in the Triad; they already had enough to put them all away for life. She'd do some very hard time unless her attorney could get her off on an insanity plea.

The feds seized the jade and all the stolen jewelry, the Black Point house, the Shatin Lounge. With other respective police agencies they seized the house on the Peak, Henry Li's jade business, and all the Triad's assets from Bangkok to Hong Kong to Honolulu to San Francisco and beyond. What hadn't been stolen outright had been bought with drug money. Tavares phoned to say good-bye; he was leaving for Bangkok to oversee the asset seizures there and help prepare that end of the case for prosecution. I tried not to feel bad about seeing him go. I had known it had to happen, but still I felt depressed.

Two days later, on the following Friday, I put a Christmas CD into my player then went in and opened my Christmas presents.

Troubles had given me an elegant wool muffler and cap in beige-and-red Highland plaid. "For when you finally come home to ski," his note said.

Yoko and Jess had given me a wonderful book on inner healing by one of my favorite Christian writers. Inside, Yoko had penned two Bible verses: John 8:32 and John 8:36.

I thought carefully about those verses. Before Mi-Lin, I wouldn't have appreciated them. Now, they had a special meaning to me.

I had planned to take down the tree as soon as I opened my gifts. It was long past time to discard it.

But as I sat there on the floor, looking up at it, it suddenly seemed revitalized. I hadn't watered it for some time, but it was still a deep, rich green. I stroked my hand across the needles. Not one fell off, and the scent of fresh pine filled the air.

Strange.

I got up, walked backward, and sure enough, the tree looked as fresh as the day Troubles had brought it home. I went back over and plugged in the lights. They glowed in blue, green, gold, and red, evoking the wonders of a season to honor the birth of Jesus Christ.

Suddenly I knew what I wanted to do. I checked my bank balance. I'd almost used up all the money from Henry Li's retainer. I'd offered to give it to the feds, but they declined on the basis that it had been a fee for services rendered, and I had indeed provided those services. They'd been pleased just to get the pink diamonds.

Henry Li's trunk and the waterlogged, worthless bearer bonds had been retrieved from the spot where Kimo and friends had dumped them in Kaneohe Bay. I had earned Henry Li's retainer, but like I said, the money was almost gone. I reached in my wallet and pulled out my MasterCard. I hadn't put anything on it since David's death, but maybe it was time.

I phoned Yoko and Jess, Pastor Mike and his wife, and a few other friends from church. Then I phoned a caterer and ordered a large baked turkey with stuffing, cranberry sauce, sparkling punch, and all the other Christmas treats. Pumpkin pie, custard, even a cake.

I phoned Merry Maids and got someone to come over that afternoon to help me clean for my Christmas party that night. I wanted the place to sparkle. And then, I went shopping for gifts for everyone. I even picked one up for Paké Chang, who was still in the hospital, making a slow recovery. I had his delivered: a copy of the book on inner healing that Yoko had given to me, complete with the same verses written inside:

> *"And you shall know the truth, and the truth shall make you free. . . . Therefore if the Son makes you free, you shall be free indeed"* (John 8:32, 36).

I also added one final, personal note:

> *Paké:*
> *There are many kinds of bondage, but only one kind of freedom. I'll be praying for you to find it.*
> *Best always and thanks for the help,*
> *Alex*

ABOUT THE AUTHOR

Janice Miller (a.k.a. J.M.T. Miller) is an accomplished writer of several books. She has published books in both the Christian and general markets, nonfiction and fiction.

The Jade Crucible is the second in the Alex Albright, Private Investigator series. The first book is entitled *The Plum Blossoms*.